CODE 13

OTHER BOOKS BY DON BROWN

• • •

THE NAVY JAG SERIES
Detained

THE PACIFIC RIM SERIES
Thunder in the Morning Calm
Fire of the Raging Dragon
Storming the Black Ice

THE NAVY JUSTICE SERIES
Treason
Hostage
Defiance

The Black Sea Affair
The Malacca Conspiracy

CODE 13

The Navy JAG Series

BOOK 2

DON BROWN

 ZONDERVAN®

ZONDERVAN

Code 13
Copyright © 2016 by Don Brown

This title is also available as a Zondervan ebook.
Visit www.zondervan.com/ebooks.

Requests for information should be addressed to:
Zondervan, *3900 Sparks Dr. SE, Grand Rapids, Michigan 49546*

Library of Congress Cataloging-in-Publication Data
Names: Brown, Don, 1960- author.
Title: Code 13 / Don Brown.
Other titles: Code thirteen
Description: Nashville : Zondervan, [2016] | Series: The Navy JAG series
Identifiers: LCCN 2015041908 | ISBN 9780310338079 (softcover)
Subjects: LCSH: United States. Army. Judge Advocate General's Corps--Fiction.
| Murder--Investigation--Fiction. | GSAFD: Suspense fiction. | Christian
fiction.
Classification: LCC PS3602.R6947 C63 2016 | DDC 813/.6--dc23 LC record available at
http://lccn.loc.gov/2015041908

Printed in the United States of America

16 17 18 19 20 RRD 23 22 21 20 19 18 17 16 15 14 13 12 11 10 9 8 7 6 5 4 3 2 1

This novel is dedicated to my mother, Alva Rose Hardison Brown (December 9, 1937–December 12, 2015), who, like her mother, Marina Roberson Hardison, became one of the sweetest ladies on the planet, and who instilled within me my love of classical music.

CHAPTER 1

. . .

The Pacific breeze whipped off the bay, gusting in from her left. The wind, brushing against her ears, blended in with the glorious sounds of the great gray fleet in port.

Under warm sunshine and magnificent blue skies, bells chimed, seagulls squawked. Smiling sailors turned their heads as she passed by, some grunting catcalls her way as her light-blonde hair bounced off her tanned shoulders and blew in the breeze.

Sporting navy blue shorts and a light-blue T-shirt that matched the color of her eyes, she jogged past Pier 2 on the final leg of her sprint. Two quick gongs sounded from the loudspeaker on the ship moored at the pier.

These were the sights and sounds of late spring along the naval waterfront in San Diego, known as America's City. And on a day like today, who could argue with that description?

"USS *Cape St. George* arriving."

Two more gongs meant the commanding officer of the cruiser USS *Cape St. George* had crossed over the catwalk and boarded his ship. The smells and sounds of the fleet produced within her an intoxicating high.

Lieutenant Commander Caroline McCormick, Judge Advocate General's Corps, United States Navy, jogged onto Senn Street. Just two days ago, she had been on board the *Cape St. George*, along with a team of two JAG officers and three legalmen, hosted by the captain himself.

Her team of Navy lawyers and paralegals had worked into the evening to finish preparing wills and powers of attorney for every member of the crew, who were all preparing for next week's deployment across the Pacific, through the Malacca Straits, and from there to the Andaman Sea, the Indian Ocean, and finally, the Arabian Sea.

In grateful appreciation, Captain Paul M. Kriete had offered to buy her a drink at the officers' club.

She'd almost accepted.

Problem was, she was still hung up on another officer. Or was she?

Lieutenant Commander P.J. MacDonald had transferred to the Pentagon, to the Navy JAG's prestigious and mysterious Code 13, a selective billet offered only to a small handful of JAG officers.

Soon they would be shipping her out, too, for her orders were about to expire at the Regional Legal Service Office.

But where?

Japan? Guam? Afghanistan?

Last week the detailer had suggested Italy—Sigonella, to be precise. She longed for a change of scenery. Perhaps a foreign port might provide a nice change of pace.

Whenever the detailer mentioned a more exotic duty station like Sigonella, or Japan, or even London, he always weaved the conversation back to an aircraft carrier. And one aircraft carrier in particular kept coming up.

"You know, USS *George Washington* needs a senior judge advocate," he would say. "You would be the perfect match. There're five thousand sailors on board. You'd be the principal lawyer for them all. Plus, you'd be the senior legal advisor for the captain of the ship. If you do well there, punch your ticket on your sea tour, that billet will line you up for deep selection to commander. Perhaps even captain."

After teasing her with exotic jobs at exciting ports of call, the detailer kept pushing her to a two-year sea billet. Detailers, the officers in charge of assigning officers to their next duty station, were the used-car salesmen of the Navy. The detailer's job was to fill jobs. Period. The detailer could simply cut her orders to her next duty station, and that would be that. But jockeying for plum assignments was common-place in the Navy, and it was better to make the officer receiving the orders believe he or she had "volunteered" for the billet.

In the give-and-take of the Navy detailer world, the fact was that some commands wanted to handpick certain officers to fill billets, and often the detailer's job was to serve as schmoozer-in-chief, keeping the commands happy while keeping the officers receiving orders happy, too, if possible. But that wasn't always possible.

Many commands called detailers, saying, "I want Lieutenant So-and-So," or, "I want Commander So-and-So to fill this billet." The detailers tried to accommodate those requests.

Commanders in Sigonella, Japan, and London had probably called the detailers already and requested some officer other than Caroline as their first choice, and that was okay. It was nothing against her. It was just that most commanders had their favorites.

The detailer had tried persuading her to volunteer for the USS *George Washington*. But she hadn't yet complied with that, because frankly, her first choice was London, where she hoped to become staff judge advocate for CINCUSNAVEUR—the acronym for Commander in Chief, United States Naval Forces Europe.

She had heard through the grapevine that Commander Torp Kinsley was the top choice of CINCUSNAVEUR. But she had also heard that Vice Admiral Brewer was pushing the detailer to order Kinsley to Washington to Code 13, the most selective billet in the JAG Corps, where he would work alongside P.J.

Be still, my soul.

Deep down, Caroline hoped Kinsley would be unable to say no to the lure of Code 13 and that London would fall into her lap. She had stalled in volunteering for the *George Washington* for this reason.

Still, despite the detailers' used-car salesmen reputation, she knew the *George Washington* would be a great career move for her, because sea duty, and especially carrier duty, was an absolute prerequisite for the selection board for captain.

Plus, there was a political push to get women into sea billets, another reason the detailer kept throwing the USS *George Washington* into the mix. Not only that, but her first cousin, Commander Gunner McCormick, was the senior intelligence officer attached to the *George Washington*.

Gunner had grown up in Tidewater, Virginia. Caroline had grown up in Raleigh, North Carolina. And all the McCormick cousins had spent memorable Christmases and Thanksgivings together.

Gunner was scheduled to rotate off the *Washington* within the next six months. So their time together on the carrier, if that happened, would be short. But it would be nice to spend some time with Gunner, if only for a few months.

So going to sea at this point in her career wouldn't be the worst thing. Still, she could almost hear the sounds of Britain calling— Scottish bagpipes, the long, deep gongs of Big Ben booming down Whitehall and off the banks of the Thames, the precise clicking and flash of the changing of the guard at Buckingham Palace.

Why not hold out for her first choice? Life only gives you one shot.

Even so, she would miss this place, and she was lucky to be completing her second tour at the 32nd Street Naval Station.

At the end of the day, only God—and the detailer—knew where she would wind up next.

But this she did know: the U.S. Navy was hard on relationships.

When P.J. left for Washington, she thought about resigning her commission to follow him there. But he hadn't insisted. At least not to the degree she had hoped he would. A couple of bland suggestions that maybe she could "get out and move to DC" didn't give her the incentive she needed to resign her commission and forfeit her naval career.

Now he was on the East Coast and she was on the West Coast. Still, she hadn't been able to shake him, nor could she forget what they had together.

In fact, her lingering memories of P.J., and her still-powerful feelings from their romantic whirlwind that had lasted for a year, were what had kept her from accepting the invitation for drinks from the handsome, steel-chinned, charismatic skipper of the *Cape St. George.*

Her flame for P.J. still burned in her soul. Until that flame smoldered into smokeless ashes, she couldn't look another direction, no matter how attractive another direction might appear.

Her girlfriends had encouraged her to get out, to get her mind off P.J., to turn her heart to a place of new beginnings. "Caroline, you're crazy," her best friend in San Diego and fellow JAG officer, Lieutenant Ginger Cepeda, had told her last night at dinner at the North Island Officers' Club. "Captain Kriete is a hunk. If you're not going to have a drink with him, put in a good word for me," she said, half teasing and half serious.

"I'd be an accessory to fraternization, Ginger," Caroline had told her younger comrade with a smile. "Your ranks are too far apart. You'll have to wait till he retires as a captain and you're promoted to at least lieutenant commander. And if he makes admiral, and he probably will, then it's hopeless for the two of you."

"Technicalities, technicalities." Ginger smiled, sipping a glass of pinot noir that was nearly as red as her hair. "Okay, I'll have to put in for deep selection to close the gap within two ranks. But seriously, Caroline, I support you no matter what."

Caroline smiled at the thought of Ginger's words. At thirty-one, Caroline was three years older than Ginger, but Ginger had been her best friend ever since she had been in the Navy. The thought of leaving Ginger was nearly as painful as the memory of P.J. getting ordered to Washington.

Ginger meant well. She almost talked her into accepting the captain's invitation. But of course, even if she did accept the invitation, he, too, would be gone within several days, commanding his powerful cruiser on a voyage to the far side of the world.

What was the point?

The Navy was a jealous mistress—but strangely, in a way she could not understand, a jealous mistress she had grown to love.

Anyway, nothing cleared her head more than a run along the naval station waterfront.

Caroline leveled out her run, picking up the pace for the final stretch of two hundred yards, straight up Penn Street. With the sparkling waters of the San Diego waterfront to her left, she jogged north toward downtown San Diego, toward the northwest corner of the naval station. As the cool, refreshing breeze swept in from the bay, she fixed her eyes on the USS *Cowpens*, an Aegis cruiser identical to the *Cape St. George*, which was moored at Pier 1.

Just across the street from Pier 1 and the *Cowpens*, two flagpoles, one bearing the American flag, the other the blue-and-gold flag of the United States Navy, stood in front of the one-story, yellow stucco building known as Building 73, housing the Navy's Regional Legal Service Office.

The wind whipped into the flags, bringing them from gentle fluttering to full-fledged flapping. The sight of the flags energized her, igniting her quick-paced run into a full-on sprint.

Caroline kept her eyes on the flagpoles and pushed harder. Faster.

When she broke past the imaginary finish line she had drawn in her mind from the American flag on the right side of the street to the bow of the *Cowpens* moored at Pier 1 to her left, she decelerated from a furious sprint to a galloping stride, then to a slower jog, and finally to a stop, prompting her to bend over and grab her knees.

All the decelerating, from her furious sprint to now gasping for air, had taken place over a few seconds. She should have taken it easier, slowed more, jogged a couple of minutes after the sprint.

But she was running short on time. She needed to be across the bay by 1330 to meet with a group of sailors on the USS *Ronald Reagan*, the supercarrier that would soon be deploying to the Indian Ocean, leading the battle group with the *Cape St. George*.

She needed to get into the building quick, take a shower, then drive across Coronado Bridge, all within the next forty-five minutes.

Too much work.

Not enough time.

The life of a naval officer preparing the fleet for deployment.

"Commander McCormick."

Caroline looked up toward Building 73. Legalman Master Chief

Richard Cisco was walking across the grass toward her. "What's up, Master Chief?"

Cisco was the command master chief and the highest-ranking enlisted person at the RLSO, which, as a practical matter, made him the third-most-respected member of the command, behind the captain and the executive officer. "Skipper wants to see you, ma'am."

She looked up, her hands still grabbing her knees, and squinted at the tall, graying officer.

Great.

Another sidetrack before heading to North Island for her meeting.

"Great. What time?"

"Now, ma'am."

"Now?" She stood up, allowing her pulse to slow a bit. "I'm not even in uniform."

"Skipper knows you're p-teeing, ma'am." *P-teeing* was military jargon for physical training. "But he says he wants you to report immediately. Says it can't wait."

What could this be about?

Whatever, it couldn't be good.

"Okay, Master Chief. Tell the skipper I'm on my way."

"Aye-aye, ma'am." Cisco saluted, then did an about-face and walked back into the building.

Caroline checked her watch.

12:30 p.m.

This would be a tight squeeze. But if she were late getting to the *Reagan*, she would just have to be late. The orders of her own commanding officer took precedence.

She gathered herself for a second, then walked across the luscious green grass to the shell-and-concrete walkway leading to the quarterdeck of the RLSO.

Just as she stepped onto the first step leading to the outside entrance, a swishing sound arose from all over the front lawn. The lawn sprinkler system sprayed her ankles and calves with a round of cool water drops.

Fantastic. Now I'm sweating and dripping from the knees down.

She ascended the four concrete steps, opened the front double doors, and stepped into the command quarterdeck, past the U.S. flag on the left and the U.S. Navy flag on the right.

"Afternoon, Commander," the duty officer said from behind his desk just to her left.

"Good afternoon, Ensign."

Leaving a trail of water drops along the deck, she turned left and walked down the passageway toward the command offices.

A moment later, she entered the suite with a sign reading Commanding Officer.

The captain's secretary, Becky Carney, a sweet, gray-haired San Diego native, looked up and smiled. "Good afternoon, Commander McCormick."

"Good afternoon, Ms. Carney," Caroline said. "Sorry for my appearance, but the master chief said the skipper wanted to see me now."

"Yes, they're waiting for you now, Commander. The captain said for you to go on in."

"Thank you." Caroline stepped to the doorway of the captain's office and knocked three times.

"Come in."

She stepped in and came to attention. After seven years in the Navy, this marked the first time she had ever come to attention in running shorts and a T-shirt.

"Lieutenant Commander McCormick reporting as ordered, sir."

Captain Rudy, wearing a service khaki uniform, rocked back in his large chair behind his desk. Commander Al Reynolds, who was the XO, and Cisco stood behind him.

Rudy, a stocky, ruddy-faced officer from Texas, looked at her, put his hands behind his head, and smiled. "Glad to see you could make it, Commander."

"My apologies, Captain. Just got in from a run before I have to head over to the *Reagan* to do some will preparation."

"Don't worry about it. And stand at ease."

"Thank you, sir."

"Master Chief, the commander looks like she could use a towel."

"Already got it taken care of, Skipper."

Cisco handed her a white towel, which she hadn't noticed he was holding until now. She took it, wiped her face, and draped it around her neck.

"Like some water?"

Why this constant grin from the captain?

"Thank you, sir."

"Master Chief?"

"Aye, Skipper."

Cisco poured ice water from a pitcher sitting on the captain's desk and handed it to her.

"Thanks, Master Chief."

The cool water provided instant relief as the captain uncrossed his arms. "So I guess you're wondering what's so important that I pulled you in here before you could take a shower."

"My only thought is service to my country, service to the Navy, and service to my command, Captain."

Rudy's belly laugh broke the tension. He poured himself a cup of water. "You know the reason I have you in command services doing wills and powers of attorney and not in court, Commander?"

"I'm afraid to ask, sir." She allowed herself a smile.

"It's because you're a terrible liar."

She tried to suppress her giggling but ended up bursting into loud laughter. "Sorry, Captain. You're right."

"Anyway, if you want to know the real reason I hauled you in off your run, look over your shoulder."

She turned around and felt her heart leap. "Gunner!"

The slender naval officer with the three gold stripes of a Navy commander on the sleeves of his service dress blue jacket smiled and opened his arms in a give-me-a-hug gesture.

"How's my favorite cousin?" he asked.

Caroline started to hug him. "Wait. I'm sweaty. I'll mess up your dress blues."

"Who cares?" He pulled her to him in a big, affectionate bear hug, and she noticed he wore the same cologne P.J. used to wear.

She smiled and kissed him on the cheek.

"Oh, I'm sorry." She turned back around. "Captain, this is my cousin, Commander Gunner McCormick."

"Yes, I know who Commander McCormick is," Rudy said. "Everybody knows Commander McCormick. Not everybody makes international headlines for hauling prisoners out of North Korea. There is a method to the Navy's madness, you know."

"Yes, of course." She looked back at her favorite cousin. "What are you doing here, Gunner?"

"Skipper asked me to drop by." Gunner nodded at Captain Rudy. "He thought you might need a little extra help with some things."

"Extra help? I . . ." She looked at Gunner, then at Captain Rudy. "I'm afraid I don't understand."

Rudy took the lead. "This has been in the works for several days, Caroline, but it was just finalized this morning. I knew Commander McCormick was in town for a symposium on the Law of the Sea over at the Justice School detachment. So I called him and asked him to come help me break the news. He's on a tight schedule and has to be back at the symposium by 1330. That's why I had to call you straight off your run."

She tried processing that. "Wait a minute. You're in town?" She looked at her somewhat-famous cousin. "And you didn't call me?"

"Last-second thing," Gunner said. "They flew me in off the carrier. We're doing ops off the coast a few miles west of Point Loma. I was going to call you, but the captain called me first."

"Wait a minute." She looked back at Rudy. "Sir, did you say you brought Gunner here to help break some news to me?"

"You're a quick study, Commander," Rudy said.

She turned to Gunner. "Is everything okay? Please tell me nobody's died."

That brought laughter from everybody in the office except Caroline. The good-for-the-soul belly laughter brought instant relief, but also more confusion. "I give up. So what's this news Gunner is supposed to help break to me, sir?"

"The detailer called," Rudy said.

"The detailer?" She knew what that meant. "PSC orders?"

"Yep." Rudy nodded. "It's permanent change of station time, Commander."

"London?" Maybe this was her lucky day.

Captain Rudy shook his head. "Washington."

The air swooshed out of her internal tires. She looked at her cousin. "Well, I've wanted to go to sea too. And at least I'll get to spend some time with Gunner."

"What?" Gunner grinned and raised an eyebrow.

"Don't you have six months left on your orders with the *George Washington*?" she asked. "I mean, I know we'd both be on board for only a short stint, but it would be like a reunion of sorts."

Gunner looked at Captain Rudy. "She's thinking about the ship, sir."

"I know." Rudy grinned. He looked at Caroline. "I'm not talking about the USS *George Washington*. I'm talking about Washington, DC."

The captain pronounced the word *Washington* in a funny Texas accent that sounded like "Wershington." A quirk in the captain's dialect.

"You mean they're sending me to DC, sir?"

"That's right, Commander. Congratulations. This should be an excellent career move for you."

"But wait a minute." She scratched her head. "The detailer has talked about London, Sigonella, Japan, and the USS *George Washington*. I haven't heard him say a word about DC. This is the first time I've heard of it."

"You've been in the Navy long enough to know that every day is a new first time for everything, Commander," Rudy said.

"May I ask where in Washington?"

The captain paused, then exchanged a glance with Reynolds, then Cisco, then Gunner. Then he looked squarely at Caroline, smiling like a possessive daddy bear and proud papa all wrapped into one. He crossed his arms and sat up high in his chair for the announcement. "You're going to the Pentagon, Caroline. You're going to Code 13."

The announcement froze the passage of time and everything around her. The shock had come from left field, like an unexpected left hook from a Golden Gloves prizefighter. She looked out the windows of the captain's office, out at Pier 1 where the USS *Cowpens* was moored.

Sailors walked up and down the catwalk between the pier and the ship, exchanging salutes. Two U.S. Marines carried a plywood box up the catwalk and onto the deck of the ship, disappearing behind the quarterdeck.

Had she heard that right?

"Code 13? Did you say Code 13, sir?"

"That's what I said, Commander."

"I don't . . . wait . . . I'm confused. I thought the officers at Code 13 were hand-selected by the admiral himself."

"They are."

"And I thought officers considered for Code 13 had to be approved for top-secret clearance before they could even be considered."

"They do. You've been cleared."

"But, Captain, I barely know Admiral Brewer. Why would he hand-select me for Code 13?"

"Maybe you don't know Admiral Brewer well. But people who know you do know the admiral well. Put it this way. A few things shook out and a few things fell out. Next thing you know, the admiral wants Lieutenant Commander Caroline McCormick at Code 13. What the admiral wants, the admiral gets."

She looked over at Gunner, who stood beside her with his arms folded, grinning. His grin was matched by grins on the faces of all the men.

"I don't know what to say." She lost her thoughts. "May I ask who recommended me to Admiral Brewer?"

Rudy smiled. "If you think about it hard enough, I have a feeling you might be able to figure it out."

Her mind was in a fog. How could this be happening?

The lightbulb went on. *P.J.!*

And her heart quickened. In the midst of the shocking news, her mind had gone into a fog about the fact that somehow, not only had she been ordered to the JAG's most prestigious duty station, but she had been given orders that would reunite her with the only guy in her life whom, if he had proposed, she would have married.

She had to get ahold of herself. "Was it Lieutenant Commander MacDonald, sir?"

Rudy smiled. "That's a good guess, Caroline. But no, it wasn't P.J. MacDonald. But I can't say anything else about it right now because..." Rudy scratched his chin. "Put it this way ... there's some information concerning the officer who made the recommendation that cannot yet be released."

"I understand, sir." Caroline tried to hide the disappointment in her voice and tried changing the subject. "Uh, Captain, when does the admiral want me to report to the Pentagon?"

The grin disappeared. Rudy's face turned more serious. "That's the other reason I called you in here on short notice. They want you in Washington and reporting by the end of the week."

"End of the week?"

"Afraid so. Dominoes are dropping fast. That's one of the reasons your cousin Gunner is here. He's going to help you pack and get moved out. Sorry about the short notice, but that's life in the Navy. You know how it is."

Her mind spun faster than a dryer on high-speed cycle. So little time. So many good-byes to say. She was already starting to miss San Diego and Ginger. What would it be like to be at Code 13? And why had she been selected, seemingly out of the blue?

She never imagined she would be considered for such a position. She thought her relationship with P.J. had ended. How hard it had been to surrender the hope of them being together forever.

And now this?

Was she wrong?

Was fate about to perform another incredible feat of one-upsmanship? To send her world into an unpredictable whirlwind?

"You okay, Commander?"

"Yes, sir. Sorry, Captain. I was just thinking."

"Well, there's one other thing I need before you ship out."

"Yes, sir. Anything, sir."

"I got a call from the skipper of the USS *Cape St. George.*"

That got her attention. "Captain Kriete?"

"That's right. Seems he's pleased with your work aboard his ship."

"Oh. Well. Thank you, sir. It was a team effort."

"You're too modest, Caroline. Anyway"—Rudy scratched his chin—"it seems the captain has invited me, you, and Commander Reynolds on board his ship for dinner tomorrow night in the wardroom."

"Excuse me?"

"It seems the officers and crew want to express their appreciation to the command, and to you, for the hard work in getting their estate plans done prior to their sailing. Dinner will be in dress whites. Meet me and Commander Reynolds here tomorrow evening at 1800. We'll walk over to the ship."

It seemed that Captain Paul Kriete would have his way, even if he had to go through official channels. Wow. She couldn't help but admire that.

"Commander? That gonna be a problem?"

"Oh, no, sir. I'll meet you and Commander Reynolds tomorrow at 1800, then be prepared to execute orders for transfer to Washington after that."

"Excellent. Well, as I recall, you've got an appointment on board the *Reagan.*" He checked his watch. "Seems to me you'd better go hit the shower, throw on your uniform, and get moving. I don't need any calls from the skipper of the *Reagan* about my star lawyer being late."

"Aye-aye, sir."

CHAPTER 2

...

WARDROOM
USS *CAPE ST. GEORGE*
PIER 2
32ND STREET NAVAL STATION
SAN DIEGO, CALIFORNIA
FRIDAY EVENING

Despite great progress made in the expansion of opportunities for women, the United States Navy remained, and forever would remain, primarily an armed service run by men.

Caroline, unlike some of her more militant female friends who remained quite vociferous in the cause of feminism, never objected to the lopsided gender makeup favoring the opposite sex. Likewise, tonight, in the officer's wardroom of the guided-missile cruiser USS *Cape St. George*, she did not object either.

One man alone, trim and well fitted in the choker whites of a naval officer's uniform, could stop most women dead in their tracks. But tonight she was the only female officer in the wardroom of more than twenty-five men, authentic naval officers, with even the least of them proving to be handsomer than the studliest actor Hollywood had to offer.

Caroline sat in the third position on the right side of the elongated table, to the right of her own executive officer, Commander Al Reynolds. Just to the left of Commander Reynolds, at the end of the table but not at the head of it, sat her commanding officer, Captain Al Rudy.

These three seats occupied by her, Reynolds, and Rudy had been reserved for the ship's guests of honor, and all had been positioned to the immediate right of the ship's commanding officer, who oversaw the meal proceedings from the table's head.

Caroline knew why they had been invited here: The swoon-producing hunk of a man bearing the four gold stripes of a Navy captain on his black shoulder boards had invited her out, and she had declined the invitation. And the joint invitation to her commanding officer ensured she would have to tag along.

Slick.

Of course, declining that original invitation to spend one-on-one time with the captain had gone against every natural inclination in her body, and he had no doubt sensed that she'd been tempted to accept before declining.

Why should she have declined?

After all, she and P.J. were done. Weren't they?

Or were they?

Then came her orders, not only transferring her to DC, but transferring her directly to P.J.'s command!

Now what?

It would have been easier if they'd transferred her to London, like she had hoped. Had she received orders to London, or to any other duty station in the world other than Washington, she would have accepted Captain Paul Kriete's invitation faster than your head could spin—if he had asked again, that is, rather than planning this dinner.

That was how badly she'd wanted to accept.

But these orders . . . the thought of reuniting with P.J. . . . .

Besides, when he had asked her for that drink, Captain Kriete was preparing to sail with his crew across the Pacific, all the way to the Indian Ocean. So what would have been the point anyway?

Maybe all these crisscrossing orders and ships' movements were God's way of telling her this rock-solid hunk of a naval officer was forbidden fruit. Moreover, maybe they were God's way of telling her that she and P.J. were destined to be together.

In fact, she felt somewhat satisfied with herself. By turning down Captain Adonis again, assuming he thought for a minute that this latest ploy would work, she was bravely going with the hope of another chance with P.J.

Of course, the glances and nods thrown her way from the head of the table, the quick, furtive looks, the irresistible dimpled smile, the shining, pearly white teeth against his chiseled, tanned face and dark, wavy hair—all were more than enough to make her weak-kneed.

There!

He did it again before turning his conversation to Captain Rudy.

The tension was so thick in the wardroom that it would take a laser to cut through it. And that oh-so-hot atmosphere was even hotter because only the two of them knew.

Those sly glances. Those heart-melting smiles. Maybe he didn't intend to ask her out again. Maybe this was his revenge, his way of torturing her for turning him down.

If only P.J. knew how she had sacrificed for him.

On the bulkhead, the ship's clock showed a sweeping second hand racing toward the top of the hour.

Caroline saw Captain Kriete glance up at the clock, and as the second hand swept past twelve, he rose from his chair.

Soon she would be transferred across the country to her new duty station at the Pentagon, at the mysterious Code 13. But for the time being, her mind was anywhere but at her next duty station. His presence, as he stood looming over the end of the table with the gold pin of command on his white uniform jacket, was larger than life.

When he lifted his spoon and rapped it three times against his water glass, he proved more commanding than the fiercest judge she had ever faced with the loudest gavel slammed against the largest courtroom bench.

And then he spoke.

"Gentlemen." He glanced at her furtively. "Commander McCormick. I have an announcement." Three more dings on the glass.

Silverware stopped clanging. Water glasses and wineglasses found their places on the table. Enlisted mess stewards, wearing white dinner jackets and black slacks and holding silver trays as they moved back and forth between the wardroom and the galley, stopped dead in their tracks.

A weighty silence ensued, except for the hum of the ship's power system.

"As you know"—he paused, stealing a glance at her as all remained silent—"this ship is about to sail to the far corners of the earth. Tonight, as we prepare to get under way, we have in our presence our most honored guests, Captain Rudy, Commander Reynolds, and Lieutenant Commander McCormick, all from the Regional Legal Service Office here in San Diego. They have been invited here tonight because of the work of an outstanding naval officer, whose competence, professionalism, charm, and wit have helped us get our affairs in order on the eve of our debarkation.

"Gentlemen, let us raise our glasses in a salute to Lieutenant Commander Caroline McCormick, Judge Advocate General's Corps, United States Navy!"

All eyes turned to Caroline.

"Hear, hear!"

"I'll drink to that!"

"By all means."

Ding-ding. Ding-ding. The captain tapped his glass with his spoon again, practically hypnotizing her with his eyes. His men went silent under the authority of his command, waiting with bated breath as he prepared to speak again.

"I have another announcement. Last year I was honored to serve as your commanding officer as the *Cape St. George* deployed to the Western Pacific, and from there through the Malacca Straits into the Andaman Sea, then the Indian Ocean, and then the Arabian Sea. Each of you performed superbly on that mission, and to serve as your commanding officer in the War on Terror has been the highest honor of my life.

"As you know"—another quick glance into her eyes—"in less than forty-eight hours, this great warship will once again be under way to support the USS *Ronald Reagan* battle group. Commander McCormick and her staff have performed superbly in helping us get our affairs together so we are ready to sail. I am supremely confident that each of you"—he paused to eye his men—"will perform superbly once again, just as you did last year.

"However"—yet another glance in her direction—"there is something you should know." He waited a few seconds. "I will not be going with you on this voyage."

Had she heard that right? She glanced around the table. Stunned looks covered the faces of the officers around the dinner mess, their mouths open, eyebrows raised, and eyes darting back and forth in confusion.

"I know this is a shock to many of you," Kriete continued. "Frankly, it's a shock to me too. But as many of you know, the Navy is a jealous mistress. We are here today, gone tomorrow. Our duty as officers is to obey the lawful orders of our superiors, to be ready to move anywhere in the world on a moment's notice, and beyond that, to fulfill the ultimate duty of the officer's oath, which is to defend the Constitution against all enemies, foreign and domestic."

Not a word in response.

"Now I am pleased to announce that my good friend and colleague, and your executive officer"—he stepped to his left and put his hand on the shoulder of the ship's XO—"Commander Bill Turner, will serve as the ship's acting commanding officer on your voyage to Japan. And I'm pleased to announce that Lieutenant Commander Fred Carber"—Kriete smiled at the officer sitting to Commander Turner's left, directly across the table from Commander Reynolds—"has been promoted to interim executive officer."

Carber's eyes widened, a look of disbelief on his handsome face. "I . . . I don't know what to say, sir."

"What you say, Commander, is that it is my pleasure to assume whatever duties I am ordered to assume to accommodate the needs of the Navy and to defend the United States of America."

"Thank you, sir." Carber broke into a grin, accepting a handshake from Commander Turner, the ship's new commanding officer.

"Now then," Kriete said, "I am sure you all have questions. And it's my pleasure to answer all your questions so you aren't sailing into the dark. But before I do, I'd like to ask you to stand as I propose a toast to your new commanding officer and your new executive officer."

The stewards swarmed the table, refilling wineglasses.

Caroline stood up, stunned, uncertain of what to think. Was this Paul Kriete's unspoken motive for inviting her tonight? Because he was going to announce he was leaving his warship? He was as full of surprises as he was astonishingly handsome.

The indomitable captain spoke again. "The USS *Cape St. George* was named for the Battle of Cape St. George in the Pacific in 1943, which was the last engagement of surface ships in the Solomon Islands campaign. Under the command of the great Admiral Arleigh Burke, the American victory proved decisive, sinking three Japanese ships, marking the end of the Tokyo Express, ending Japanese resistance in the Solomon Islands.

"When you sail to the west, gentlemen, remember the battle for which this great ship was named. Be brave, decisive, and victorious. And do so under the banner of your new CO, Commander Turner, and your new XO, Lieutenant Commander Carber, for whom I propose these toasts."

"Hear, hear!"

"Hear, hear!"

Caroline smiled, nodded at Turner and Carber, raised her glass, then sipped her pinot noir.

Her eyes caught Paul's. Again.

Their little game of mutual catch-a-glance was driving her batty. The furtive looks between them were brief and hopefully unnoticeable to everyone except each other. But what the glances lacked in time, they made up in power.

"These two men are good men. I have supreme confidence that under their leadership, the *Cape St. George* will sail to even greater heights than ever before." He looked at Commander Turner and smiled, then continued.

"Now, we've spoken of this ship's great history, of the battle for which it was named, of the great victory achieved by the U.S. Navy over Japan in that battle. Therefore, I find it ironic that your first stop, forty-five days from now, will be in Japan, at U.S. Fleet Activities in Sasebo.

"When you arrive in Sasebo, I'll be waiting for you there. But not to reassume command of the ship. I've been called to other things. Instead, I'll be on hand, along with Admiral Clarke, for the formal change-of-command ceremony, promoting Commander Turner from interim commanding officer to permanent commanding officer. It will be a glorious day." He surveyed the room with a smile. "Any questions?"

Hands rose. Kriete nodded. "Lieutenant Mitchell."

"Sir, if it's okay to ask, how recently did you learn of the news?"

"Of course it's okay to ask, Harold. As a matter of fact, I caught wind of this as a possibility a couple of days ago, and just learned that the orders had been finalized this morning at 0800 hours local time. Commander Turner got let in on the secret so he could take a couple of hours to think about the notion of commanding a warship. Now, poor Lieutenant Commander Carber over here"—he nodded at the new XO—"I'm afraid he found out about his new job at the same time all of you found out." Kriete looked at Carber and grinned devilishly, as if he'd played a sneaky trick on his best childhood friend. "Surprise, surprise, XO!"

That brought a round of laughter.

"Other questions."

More hands rose. Kriete pointed at an officer sitting across from Caroline.

"Lieutenant Rouse."

"Sir, are you at liberty to say where they're sending you?"

"Yes, I am at liberty. Before assuming command of the *Cape St. George*, I completed a dual master's at the Naval War College in counterintelligence and counterterrorism, specializing in domestic littoral regions. And that relates to my next assignment.

"As you know, because of the curvature of the earth, the United States is always under threat from maritime terrorism. Our radar doesn't go beyond seven miles, and it's a big ocean out there. An enemy vessel with a hydrogen bomb on board could slip over the horizon undetected and sail into a large civilian port—New York, San Francisco, Los Angeles—and we wouldn't have much reaction time.

"Once that ship is within seven miles of the coast, depending on where it's coming in, it would be hard to get aircraft or other vessels in place quickly enough to stop it. So the Navy has come up with a solution. It's called Operation Blue Jay. Some of you may have heard of it. But the plan is to deploy thousands of drones, up and down both coasts and along the Gulf of Mexico, to be on station twenty-four hours a day to guard against terrorism and drug infiltration.

"The Navy has been awarded the contract, subject to final approval by JAG and final approval by Congress." He looked her way, flashing a quick smile. "Which we don't see as a problem. Just a formality, you know."

He followed the smile with a quick wink, making her weak in the knees. Captain Paul Kriete should be illegal. At least, it should be illegal to turn him loose in the presence of a single woman. Thank goodness she could think about P.J. The prospect of reuniting with P.J. excited her.

"Anyway, I've been selected to be the officer in charge of the project. So while you gentlemen are sailing to the west, I'll be headed east. To Washington." He looked at her again. "To the Pentagon, where I am honored to become commander of the very first littoral drone fleet in U.S. Navy history, the brand-new U.S. Navy Drone Force."

Another glance in her direction. An impish smile as he reveled in the applause and adoration of his men, which set her heart into such a loud pound-a-thon that she could barely hear their applause. She felt herself growing angry. So that was what this was about. He called her here to drop a bomb on her. He was going to Washington too. From the head of the table, more clings and dings on water glasses. This time Commander Turner took the stage.

"Gentlemen, gentlemen." Like Kriete, most naval officers, at least the largest single block of naval officers, were southerners. But Turner spoke with an accent that sounded Bostonian. "Your attention, please."

Ding-ding. "I think I can speak for Lieutenant Commander Carber in saying that we are honored and humbled to step into what will be a great leadership vacuum to replace a great man."

"Hear, hear!"

"Hear, hear!"

Caroline smiled plastically and nodded. Why the sudden urge to get up and walk out? Perhaps because all the adulation these officers had for their captain made him that much more irresistible? When she wished he were resistible? Perhaps she worried about the dynamic of going to Washington, of going to the Pentagon and facing both Paul Kriete and P.J. in the same building. A Washington-spiced love triangle was the last thing she needed right now. For now, she had to sit tight and resist Kriete internally. A hard task, but hopefully doable.

"Every officer strives for command." Turner's voice cracked. He looked reverently at Paul as if grasping for words. "But, Skipper, no one strives to take command in this way." He put his hand on Paul's broad shoulder. "I shall work hard to fill your shoes, sir." His voice cracked again. "Which will be next to impossible to fill, but I will do my best."

"You will do a great job, XO." Kriete stood, shook Turner's hand, and patted him on the back.

More applause.

The XO spoke again. "Gentlemen"—he, like Turner, apparently forgot that not all officers in the wardroom were gentlemen—"I want us to fully grasp what has happened here." He looked at Paul, then at his officers. "What's happened to our captain is not a relief from command but rather a major-league promotion as the initial commander of what will become one of the most powerful commands in the U.S. Navy—the U.S. Navy Drone Force." Applause. "And the captain didn't tell you this, because he's too modest. And he hasn't asked me to announce this, because again, he is a leader of men and he would never blow his own horn.

"But I will take a little liberty as your new commanding officer to announce that our skipper, Captain Paul M. Kriete, has been nominated by President Surber, subject to confirmation by the senate, to the rank of rear admiral!"

More applause. More "Hear, hear!"

"And, Captain." Turner spoke again. "I am happy for you." He wiped his eyes. "But I want you to know that no matter how many stars they wind up pinning on your collars, sir, you will always be my skipper. And you know what an affectionate term that is in the U.S. Navy."

The two men embraced in a big bear hug. The officers stood, and from the right corner of the table came, "For he's a jolly good fellow . . ."

Others joined in. "For he's a jolly good fellow."

Now the entire wardroom.

"For he's a jolly good fellow, which nobody can deny. Which nobody can deny! Which nobody can deny! For he's a jolly good fellow, which nobody can deny!"

As the singing died down, Catherine heard, "To our captain!"

"Hear, hear! To our captain and our skipper."

Glasses were raised in the air. Alcohol flowed.

Caroline sipped her red wine, then took another sip. As the wine lightened her head, his eyes found hers again.

Somehow she knew he had gotten his way. He would always get his way.

CHAPTER 3

• • •

The Pentagon, the nerve center for the most powerful military machine ever assembled in the history of civilized mankind, had been built in the middle of World War II, of Indiana limestone, on what amounted to swampland by the banks of the Potomac River.

In addition to its five equidistant sides, making it the most recognizable building in the world, especially from the air, the massive building had five "rings" and five "levels." The rings were associated with the order of prestige and rank. The most prestigious, the outer E-Ring, housed the Secretary of Defense and many four-star flag and general officers.

Just inside the E-Ring, separated by several feet of open-air space, was the D-Ring, which housed a lot of three-star officers. The C-Ring housed two-star officers. Inside the C-Ring was the B-Ring, and inside that, the A-Ring.

Each of the Pentagon's rings had its own exterior walls, and with the exception of the E-Ring, the exterior views outside the windows of each ring were only the exterior walls of the ring just inside of it or outside of it. Not much of a view. Only the E-Ring windows, which

25

overlooked the Potomac, Arlington Cemetery, or the snaking turns of the Shirley Highway, allowed anyone to see outside the entire building.

All the rings were connected by interior covered walkways radiating inward, from the E-Ring all the way to the A-Ring. The five inner walls of the A-Ring surrounded the open-air courtyard known as Ground Zero, so named because it was the bull's-eye target of Soviet intercontinental ballistic missiles during the Cold War and then of savage Arab terrorists during the War on Terror.

Ground Zero featured an outdoor food court, the Center Courtyard Café, where Pentagon employees would congregate for lunch during nice weather in the spring and fall, but which could be an open-air oven or a cold wasteland at other times.

Part of the mystique of the Navy JAG Corps' elite Code 13 was its location at the Pentagon, giving its officers easy access to the Judge Advocate General, the Secretary of the Navy, and even the Secretary of Defense.

But what remained unsaid, indeed unknown to the rest of the Navy JAG Corps, which looked upon the mysterious Code 13 officers as the super elite, was that the work spaces assigned to the crème-de-la-crème were among the dumpiest in the Navy.

Yes, they were the most powerful, the most influential, the brightest of the Navy JAG Corps, but their work environment sure didn't show it.

The problem was that they were in the Pentagon, which, for the midgrade officer on a military career path, was the plumiest of assignments. But the Pentagon was also home to more high-ranking brass than any other place on the planet. And a lieutenant commander, or even a captain or a commander at the Pentagon, would always take a backseat to the officer wearing stars on his collar.

Lieutenant Commander P.J. MacDonald, JAGC, United States Navy, had, before coming to Washington, been accustomed to receiving salutes, to having subordinates come to attention for him, and to sometimes having the waters parted for him, all because he wore a gold oak leaf on his collar.

All the attention had been kind of nice. Rank had its advantages. No problems waiting in line.

But he left all that behind in San Diego, a major working naval base, where something like 90 percent of all naval personnel ranked below him.

But P.J. MacDonald would never forget the day he first arrived at the Pentagon. He had parked his car way out in the hinterlands of the parking lot, walked across the asphalt for what seemed like a mile, passed what seemed to be about ten thousand cars. But when he arrived at the sidewalk by the entrance of the building, he witnessed a sight he would never forget.

A tall U.S. Air Force officer stood in the bus line, holding his briefcase, waiting for a public bus to Northern Virginia.

At first P.J. didn't think about it.

But as he walked past the officer, he realized his mind was now registering a delayed reaction.

Wait a minute. Had he seen that right?

Surely that had to be the silver oak leaf of a lieutenant colonel on the officer's epaulette. Why else would he be standing in the bus line?

P.J. stopped, turned around, and took another look at the officer.

His mind had told him it had to be an oak leaf, because an officer wearing a star would never be holding his own briefcase at a military installation. But the oak leaf, on second glance, really was a single silver star!

And when P.J. realized he was witnessing a one-star brigadier general standing in the bus line at the Pentagon, holding his own briefcase, waiting for a bus, reality hit him.

On any other military installation in America, any one-star flag or general officer, whether a brigadier general in the Air Force, Army, or Marines, or a rear admiral, out in the open would be the recipient of spit polish and brass, ruffles and flourishes. A star on an officer's collar, even a single star, usually meant the sounding of military band trumpets, a red-carpet rollout, and fanfare. Even without the trumpet call, when a general or an admiral entered the building, everyone jumped to strict attention, not breathing until the "at ease" command was given.

In the fleet, a general or admiral would have an entourage surrounding him wherever he went. Usually a junior aide would carry a flag officer's bags and take care of menial matters, while a senior aide took care of correspondence and more substantive matters. Then there would be an enlisted man serving as the admiral's driver, for the flag or general officer always had his own personal staff car, complete with flapping blue-and-white flags on the hood above the headlamps, depicting the number of stars on the officer's collar.

When a general or admiral's car pulled into a military installation, others, not part of the official entourage, would swarm around, trying to get face time with the high-ranking officer and to ingratiate themselves with the seat of military power.

Against this backdrop, and understanding the awe and reverence for a star on the collar out in the "real" military, P.J. found himself immobilized.

An Air Force one-star.

Standing in the bus line.

Carrying his own briefcase.

P.J. watched as the general stepped onto the bus and disappeared among all the other passengers. Then he thought about the gold oak leaf on his own collar, signifying a full three ranks below the general, and remembered the words of those around him when news broke of his assignment to the Pentagon.

"You'll be making coffee for the admiral. You'll be getting the admiral his toilet paper and taking him his lunch."

Well, it hadn't been that bad. Officers at Code 13 did, in fact, handle some of the most top-secret military matters confronting the Navy.

But in terms of the space where he had to work, it was that bad.

They put Code 13 down in the basement of the D-Ring, four decks below the office of the Judge Advocate General, Vice Admiral Zack Brewer.

Most people didn't even know the Pentagon had a basement, but for the Pentagon insiders, if anything resembled a dungeon in the building, this was it.

The sight of all kinds of creatures crawling about on the unpainted cement floors in the huge underground corridors circumventing the D-Ring of the Pentagon had a certain symbolic relevance. Midlevel officers, like Navy lieutenant commanders or Marine Corp majors or Army captains, all wielded about as much power in this great citadel as the rodents creeping about on the bottom floor. The midlevel and junior officers here were accustomed to the classic "low man on the totem pole" treatment.

Incandescent lights hanging from the ceiling cast a dim glow in the basement corridor. One could see, but there was always a bit of an adjustment period stepping out of the brightly lit office spaces into the large, darker corridor.

P.J. had walked down the corridor and up the steps to the main deck, then stepped out into the courtyard for a few minutes, trying to clear his head. After enjoying five minutes of sunshine and taking in the breeze, he finished his bottled water and headed back into the building.

He was on his way back to the Code 13 spaces when a huge gray rat crawled right in front of him, so close to his feet that he almost kicked it.

Like a schoolkid traversing a crosswalk, the rat took its time, undaunted by the presence of a human, as if it had legal, proprietary rights to the basement and could file an injunction if anything got in its way.

They were arrogant creatures, these river rats of the Pentagon basement, bold and fearless of the humans intruding on their spaces.

P.J. watched the huge rodent as it crossed from the left bulkhead to the right bulkhead, then squeezed its fat body into a small hole, its six-inch tail still protruding out onto the floor.

As ugly as these creatures were, somehow they proved mesmerizing, and something always made P.J. want to stop and watch. Maybe it was because he was one of the few people in the world who got to witness one of the Pentagon's best-kept secrets.

Rats in the basement.

One would have thought the airplane that exploded into the building on September 11, 2001, would have incinerated them all. But after the blast, it seemed that the cockroaches and rodents not only survived but actually thrived.

P.J. waited until the rat's black tail disappeared into the hole in the plastered wall, then walked up the concrete passageway to the next bend in the Pentagon.

No more than fifty feet beyond the rat, a simple blue-and-white sign over a door along the left interior corridor proclaimed "Navy JAG Code 13—Administrative Law."

Time to get back to work.

He punched in the security code, waited as the locking mechanism hummed and electronically unlocked the steel door, then stepped into the spartan work space.

Under bright fluorescent lighting and with a blue Astroturf-like carpet on the floor, the JAG officers of Code 13 shared adjoining workstation-cubicles in a largely open room. Only the division commander occupied an enclosed office.

Altogether, twenty-one JAG officers composed the JAG Corps' most elite operations: five officers in each of the four subdivisions, plus one Navy captain, Captain David C. Guy, also a JAG officer, who served as the division commander.

Many of them would be deep selected by the next officers' promotion board, meaning they would be promoted to the next rank at least one year before their peers. All of them were virtually guaranteed to make captain. At least one of them, probably, would one day become Judge Advocate General of the Navy.

Because of their elite status, they were often referred to by other JAG officers in an under-the-breath manner with several half-envious, half-sarcastic nicknames.

"The Chosen Twenty-One."

"The Lucky Thirteeners."

"The Bright Boys of the Basement"—a rather sexist moniker, because not all of them were male.

Together, these twenty-one JAG officers made up the legal brain trust of the entire United States Navy, whose bases and ships were scattered to the four corners of the earth.

P.J. had been assigned to Section 133, which handled legislation, regulations, and Freedom of Information Act requests.

"Welcome back, Commander," said the cute, new, redheaded lieutenant in the Ethics Division. "How was your walk?"

"Not bad. Only saw one in the passageway on the way back."

"Gross. I don't want to hear about it."

"Well, I think we're safe in here. But if you need an escort in the passageway, I'm your knight in shining armor."

"My hero." Lieutenant Victoria Fladager smiled, beaming those magnetic green eyes at him, a delightful split-second distraction before returning to his dilemma.

P.J. turned away from her, sat at his sparse cubicle, leaned back in his chair, and held the written directive he'd received that morning up against the fluorescent light.

How had he gotten into this?

The Secretary of the Navy and Captain Guy wanted his legal opinion, and no matter what opinion he rendered, it could potentially end his career.

After rubbing his eyes, he started reading it again:

From: SECNAV
To: Lieutenant Commander P.J. MacDonald, JAGC, USN (133.3)
Via 133
13
001
01
Classification: Top Secret
Subj: Request for Legal Opinion—Project Blue Jay

1. Project Blue Jay is a project proposed by Commander, U.S. Naval Air Forces, which, if congressionally approved, will begin a massive drone surveillance program of the coastal regions of the United States, including all of the U.S. East Coast, all of the U.S. West Coast, all of the U.S. Gulf of Mexico coastal regions, and the coastlines of Alaska and Hawaii.

2. While the basic political elements of the project have been

disseminated to the public, the specific details, for which we are requesting a legal opinion, remain top secret.

3. Included also within the top-secret elements of the project are so-called surveillance areas, coastal regions within 100 miles of the seacoast of all the United States, within the area of the so-called Fourth Amendment–Free Zone, otherwise known as the Constitution-Free Zone.

4. The plan for joint implementation with the Department of Homeland Security remains top secret at this point, as the public has only been aware of a potential "Navy Drone" contract. However, your legal opinion is sought as to the constitutional and statutory permissiveness of joint implementation of this program with the Department of Homeland Security, including commentary on the following issues:

a) The Constitution-Free Zone, in which the federal government has claimed Fourth Amendment exclusion, includes the following:

- Currently, two-thirds of the United States' population lives within this Constitution-Free (or Constitution-Lite) Zone. That's 197.4 million people who live within 100 miles of the U.S. land and coastal borders.
- Additionally, nine of the top ten largest metropolitan areas as determined by the 2010 census fall within the Constitution-Free Zone. (The only exception is #9, Dallas–Fort Worth.)
- Some states lie completely within the zone: Connecticut, Delaware, Florida, Hawaii, Maine, Massachusetts, Michigan, New Hampshire, New Jersey, New York, Rhode Island, and Vermont.

b) The Secretary of Defense has selected the U.S. Navy as the armed service to enforce Project Blue Jay, later to be renamed Operation Blue Jay, under which over 100,000 drones would be manufactured and placed into service by the defense contractor, AirFlite, for monitoring against terrorist activities in the Constitution-Free Zone.

c) Under the proposed arrangement, the U.S. Navy shall serve in charge of operational command of Project Blue Jay.

d) However, an interagency agreement has been reached between the U.S. Navy and the Department of Homeland Security and is incorporated into the proposed legislation, whereby DHS will assume subordinate command and control of all U.S. Navy drones operating over U.S. soil and, in particular, operating over the aforesaid 100-mile Constitution-Free Zone.

e) The U.S. Navy, however, will operate drones over domestic and international waters, conducting surveillance and interception of ships and aircrafts that may be hostile to the United States.

f) The contract is expected to draw political opposition from various Tea Party groups and civil liberties groups, such as the ACLU, which has already opposed the establishment of the Constitution-Free Zone as set forth above.

g) Legal authority for the Constitution-Free Zone is established at § 287 (a) (3) of the Immigration and Nationality Act, 66 Stat. 233, 8 USC § 1357 (a) (3), which provides for warrantless searches of automobiles and other conveyances "within a reasonable distance from any external boundary of the United States," as authorized by regulations promulgated by the Attorney General. The Attorney General's regulation, 8 CFR § 287.1, defines "reasonable distance" as "within 100 air miles from any external boundary of the United States."

5. You have been requested to generate a legal opinion, if legally defensible, for the Secretary of the Navy, to be forwarded to the Secretary of Defense, to deal with the anticipated objections from various Tea Party groups and civil liberties groups, like the ACLU, that will claim that the Fourth Amendment and

the constitutional doctrine of *posse comitatus* would prevent implementation of Project Blue Jay.

6. In particular, you are to focus upon the legality of the proposed joint-cooperative agreement between the Navy and DHS, and whether overall Navy command and control over the project violates *posse comitatus* at times when DHS is operating Navy drones over domestic U.S. soil.

7. Note that the DOD has selected the Navy over the Air Force because of its coastal emphasis, as it was felt that anticipated arguments would have greater effect against the Air Force and Army than the U.S. Navy.

8. The public purpose of Operation Blue Jay will be to prevent the infiltration of terror groups into the United States by intercepting such groups attempting to enter through coastal regions, and to track terror activity occurring within the coastal border areas of the United States and, in particular, the Constitution-Free Zone.

9. Please note that your opinion may serve as the legal basis for final approval of the contract to AirFlite, pending clearance of legal issues addressed herein, and further pending congressional approval.

10. In your analysis, bear in mind that approval of this contract is of utmost importance to the Department of the Navy.

11. With these considerations, you are directed to have a legal position paper prepared to deliver to CDR Pete Fagan, JAGC, USN, SJA to SECNAV, no later than 72 hours from the date-time stamp of this directive.

> Respectfully,
> Hon. H. Lawrence Anderson
> Secretary

"Great," P.J. mumbled to himself. He put the memo back into the envelope and laid it on his desk.

SECNAV's ordering me to come up with a legal position to justify awarding a contract of who-knows-how-many billions to a big-time defense contractor, and they want me to find legal justification for it, whether or not there is any legal justification.

P.J. crossed his arms and thought. He didn't like the sound, smell, or feel of this.

"Are you okay?" He felt Victoria's hand on his shoulder and whiffed the aroma of her pleasant perfume.

He whirled around in his chair, picked up the envelope, and handed it to her. "Take a look at this."

She removed the document from the envelope and stood there reading it. While she did, his thoughts turned to her, not as a fellow officer but as a woman.

He hadn't been interested in anyone since Caroline. But Victoria?

Lieutenant Victoria Fladager was proof-positive of the dangers of mixed-gender work environments in the military. He didn't want to relinquish the idea of being with Caroline again someday. He wasn't ready for an interest in anyone else. Not now, anyway. At least that's what he told himself.

But deep down he felt himself beginning to develop an interest in Victoria. And he didn't want to develop an interest.

He'd never dated a redhead. But the senior lieutenant standing by his cubicle, in her summer dress white uniform skirt, with her shoulder-length hair up in a bun, had become a distraction he did not need.

Why did she have to possess the delectable combination of an irresistible personality, a brilliant mind, red-hot looks to match her red hair, and a top-secret clearance?

Watching her stand there, flipping the pages of the document that had him so torn up, invoked a sense of delectable guilt.

Sure, he nearly asked Caroline to marry him. But it wasn't meant to be. So why the guilt about this attraction? After all, Caroline wasn't here. She remained in San Diego, for the time being, and would probably be ordered overseas. What was the point?

"Wow." Victoria's eyes widened. "Looks like a huge contract depends on your opinion." She handed the memo back to him. "What are you going to do?"

"What do you think I should do?"

She smiled.

Those dimples.

"Well, it's not like you've been ordered to reach one conclusion or the other. Right?"

"Is that the way you read it?"

She moved closer to his chair. "May I see it again?"

"Sure."

She perused the document, more quickly this time. "Well, the directive says you're requested to provide a legal opinion, if legally defensible."

"So you think the phrase 'legally defensible' gives me some leeway?"

"Looks that way to me. Don't you think?"

"Sure. The directive pays lip service to the phrase 'if legally defensible,' but then it's got this not-so-cryptic suggestion that makes it seem like the Secretary wants a rubber-stamp legal review."

"And they want this in seventy-two hours?"

"Can you believe it?" The knots returned to his stomach. He felt a strange sense of comfort that Victoria was there. For some reason, she was like a calming influence in the midst of a brewing storm. "Hey, what are you doing tonight?"

Why did I just ask that?

"Why?" Her face lit with a tantalizing smile, sending his heart into an embarrassing thump-fest. "What did you have in mind?"

"You want to meet for a glass of wine? Maybe we could talk about this a bit more."

"I'd love to." She kept smiling. "You want to meet somewhere?"

"Sure. How about Old Town Alexandria? There's a little wine bar called the Grape and Bean. Do you know it?"

"Oh yes. Isn't that the one over on Royal Street? Rosemont?"

"That's it. It's private. We can chat without anyone overhearing."

"Can't wait." She had not stopped smiling. "I'd better get back to work."

Victoria stepped back to her workstation. Probably a good thing.

He needed to start on this legal opinion, but he couldn't get beyond his knotted stomach. His deadline was looming, though, and like a giant tsunami, it came closer by the second. Why did he have a premonition that something awful was about to happen? Something about the money. That was it. P.J. had come to the realization that billions may be riding on his decision, and no doubt some people in powerful places were going to be extremely angry—angry with him especially, if his identity were ever revealed as the author of the legal opinion that cut against them.

He hit the space bar, taking the computer out of sleep mode, and began typing.

From: LCDR P.J. MacDonald, JAGC, USN (133.3)
To: SECNAV
Via: 133
13

"How's it going, P.J.?"

P.J. turned his head.

Commander Bob Prohaska, his immediate boss, stood over his shoulder. Hopefully Prohaska hadn't overheard his conversation with Victoria, either about the top-secret assignment he had received or about the date he had just set up.

Actually, if Prohaska had overheard their talk about the top-secret AirFlite project, that was no biggie. All the officers in Code 13 were cleared for top-secret projects and collaborated on the legal issues they had been assigned.

But the date he couldn't believe he'd just gotten himself into? The last thing he needed was gossip of a burgeoning office romance. Not good in an environment like this. He turned his chair around.

"I'm fine, sir. I was . . . uh . . . reviewing the assignment on Project Blue Jay."

"You mean the AirFlite project?"

"Yes, sir. Internally code named Blue Jay."

Prohaska chuckled. "Interesting code name. Most military operational code names take on a more menacing title, like Operation Desert

Storm, Operation Urgent Fury, Operation Overlord. But Operation Blue Jay doesn't fit any of that."

"That struck me too, sir. Do you think there's a reason for it?"

"Sure I do." Prohaska took a sip of his coffee.

"Do you mind if I ask what it is, sir?"

The commander set the coffee cup down on P.J.'s desk. "Blue Jay is a benign-sounding name to distract attention from the project. Sounds more like a requisition order for a Navy Ornithology Department than a massive plan to flood the coastal regions of the United States with light-blue drones in the skies."

A massive plan to flood the coastal regions of the United States with light-blue drones in the skies.

Prohaska's last sentence made P.J. want to puke at the notion that his legal opinion could become a component of making that happen.

"What do you think, sir? Are they expecting me to write this with a predetermined conclusion already in mind?"

Prohaska sipped his coffee again before answering. "Did you read the memo thoroughly?"

"Yes, sir."

"Well, I think you'll find your answer there."

P.J. hesitated. "I was afraid you might say that, sir."

Prohaska grinned, giving him a look that said, *We both know billions are riding on this project and SECNAV needs rubber-stamp legal approval.*

But instead, Prohaska chose words more politically correct. "You'll do an excellent job. Captain Guy, Admiral Brewer, SECNAV . . . they've all got confidence in you. It's an honor to be selected for this assignment. Your opinion could lay the groundwork for a fundamental change in how we fight terrorism in this country."

Yeah, P.J. thought. *A fundamental change in more government terror by giving the government more spying power over its citizens.*

Prohaska started walking away but then stopped and turned around. "I almost forgot to mention something." A raised eyebrow. "Did you serve in San Diego with an officer named Lieutenant Commander Caroline McCormick?"

P.J.'s heart shifted into overdrive at the mention of her name. What kind of psychological torture were these people playing?

"Yes, sir. Commander McCormick and I served together in San Diego."

"Well, guess what?"

"What, sir?" He opened another bottle of water from his desk drawer and took a sip.

"We just got the word. Lieutenant Commander McCormick has received orders to Code 13."

P.J. almost choked. He set the Aquafina bottle on his desk. "Commander McCormick's coming here?"

"Yep. Admiral Brewer made the selection based on a handful of recommendations he asked for. He's getting more involved in handpicking selectees for Code 13. Apparently she made quite the impression during a project she directed aboard USS *Cape St. George*. Word filtered up the chain, and somebody from SURFPAC called Vice Admiral Brewer to compliment her, and one thing led to another."

"Wow." P.J. fought speechlessness. "What division?"

"Don't worry." Prohaska chuckled, as if he already knew about P.J.'s yearlong relationship with Caroline. Of course he knew. The JAG Corps was a small community. Everybody knew. He was sure even Victoria knew, for that matter, although she had never said anything about it. At least not yet.

Prohaska continued, "She's going to be assigned to personnel, section 131, doing legal opinion letters for SECNAV on officer personnel matters."

"Okay. Uh . . ." He struggled for words. "When's she reporting aboard?"

"They're fast-tracking it. She's replacing Lieutenant Commander Rummel, who is being fast-tracked to Pearl Harbor to become XO of the trial command out there."

"This week, huh?"

"Maybe even in a couple of days." Prohaska grinned again. "Just thought you'd want to know."

"Thank you, sir."

"My pleasure." Still grinning, Prohaska nodded, turned, and walked away.

P.J. turned his chair around and stared at his computer, waiting for his mind to unfreeze.

CHAPTER 4

• • •

Richardson Wellington DeKlerk, resting his slender six-foot-one-inch frame in the plush red-leather chair behind his huge mahogany desk, sipped brandy and looked over the slow-rolling, blue-green waters of the Savannah River.

He got up, checked the mirror to make sure his salt-and-pepper hair was properly in place, and decided that his suntan would need a bit more work by next week. He sipped another spot of brandy and then stepped out of the air-conditioned confines of his office onto the balcony, enjoying the sound of a couple of seagulls' high-pitched cries and the fresh, warm, southern breeze blowing off the river that caressed his face.

He liked it out there, because down to his left the colonial-style buildings of Savannah's historic waterfront came into view, hosting a buzz of modern activity and swarming with tourists, including lovers and honeymooners. He took another sip of his brandy, set his glass on a small outdoor table, picked up his binoculars, and commenced people-watching.

Through his binoculars, sometimes he would discover delectable creatures of the opposite sex milling about down on the waterfront, their hair and blouses flapping in the inland Georgia sea breeze, which sometimes had the effect of halting his horizontal sweep of the area.

On rare occasions, if his visual target appeared unaccompanied, loitering about with no gentleman companion, absorbing the ambience of the waterfront in a way that signified she didn't appear to be in a hurry, Richardson had been known to take his lunch hour on the spot and head down to the waterfront, hoping for the appearance of a happenstance encounter to ignite conversation.

Sometimes he had been successful in achieving the "happenstance" encounters. At least all the southern belles he happened to bump into thought they were happenstance.

On one occasion, he wound up accompanying the attractive wandering damsel around Savannah all weekend. Her name was Leslie, a ravishing blonde from Charleston who looked splendid in the assortment of yellow, blue, and white sundresses she wore. Their weekend proved to be fabulous. Almost too fabulous, in fact.

He smiled as he thought of her. For a lesser man with not so much on his plate, she would have been the ultimate catch. But for a man with tremendous demands upon his time, making decisions in business that could mean billions in profits and change the landscape of the country, maintaining any kind of committed relationship simply wasn't feasible.

Even if their weekend had been three days sprinkled with the unexpected magic of a fairy tale, Richardson could not thrive in a fairy tale, where all was bliss and giddiness and harmony—even if his fairytale mate, the smashing Charlestonian Leslie Grimes, could have given Christie Brinkley a run for her money even at her mouthwatering best.

Leslie had tried contacting him on numerous occasions after their weekend, but he hadn't responded. The temptation to respond had been enticing, but his business-oriented brain had sifted the pros and cons like a preprogrammed computer, determining that the type of discipline needed to accomplish his goals left little room for play.

In the end, he had no time for feelings, no time for ambiguous nuances, and no time for relearning woman-speak, where one had to understand that what they say is not what they mean.

Despite strong temptations, he just didn't have enough time for all that.

He'd been through it all before, leading up to his nasty divorce after twenty-three years of marriage.

Never again.

Still, he enjoyed people-watching through his binoculars from his balcony off the CEO offices at AirFlite headquarters, preferably with a glass of brandy.

He always thought he might see Leslie down by the waterfront again someday. If he did, he wasn't sure what he'd do. And today he saw nothing else worthy of freezing the sweep of his binoculars. Only a sea of humanity milling about, stepping into waterfront shops, moving in and out of restaurants, holding hands along the dockside, all hoping to discover and become enraptured in that mystic, romantic aura of Savannah, made so famous in southern lore and history, and captured by great works of literature like *Midnight in the Garden of Good and Evil*.

Savannah, he concluded—in part because it reminded him of his native South Africa in that it had its own history of apartheid, which southerners called "segregation"—had become the perfect spot for both his personal repatriation and the repatriation of his great international business empire. AirFlite was once a South African hot-air balloon company, focusing on small commercial dirigibles designed for aerial photography marketed to residential and commercial real estate companies. But Richardson was among the first to understand the explosive potential of the drone industry. He knew that to make a fortune as a dronesman, one would need to juxtapose one's surfboard on the first large wave crashing onto the beach. For beyond that, the beach would become overcrowded, with the waves receding into the sea.

Although he loved the peaceful waves of the Indian and Atlantic Oceans lapping upon the gorgeous beaches of his native South Africa, he understood that the financial waves for the drone industry would be found rolling in toward the military-industrial complex in the United States.

As a naturally astute businessman, he purposed to position himself to be in the right place at the right time. If that meant moving AirFlite to America, by golly he would do just that. In fact, he had done just that.

He would let nothing and no one stand in the way of what he would accomplish.

The intercom buzzer rang from the phone on his desk.

He picked up his glass and stepped off the balcony, back into the office. "Yes, Ivana?"

"Sir, Mr. Patterson is here for your meeting." His secretary, Ivana Jirotova-Martin, had a heavy Eastern European accent.

"Send him in." The empty glass went onto the coffee table.

"Yes, sir."

The office door swung open, with Ivana escorting the six-foot-six former Georgia offensive lineman into the plush offices of the CEO. The man, now in his late fifties, wore a gray, personally fitted Tom James suit, complete with a personally tailored white shirt and a Georgia-red bulldog tie.

Jack Patterson's hair over the years may have turned nearly as gray as his suit, but still a rock of a man, Jack was the type of chap one would want in one's corner in a fisticuffs brawl in a dark alley.

"Jack!" Richardson said. "How 'bout dem Dawgs?"

Patterson laughed. "Sorry, Richardson. I appreciate the sentiment, but I'll never get used to a man with a British accent trying to speak southern redneck."

"South African accent," Richardson quipped.

"South African. British. Australian. It's all the same."

"Jack, you're impossible." Richardson extended his hand to Patterson. "That will be all, Ivana."

"Yes, sir."

"Have a seat, Jack."

Patterson took a seat on the leather sofa in front of the desk. "Care for a drink, Jack?" Richardson picked up his own glass.

Patterson shook his head. "CEOs of Fortune 500 companies can drink on the job. Law firms that work for those CEOs can't afford to."

"Now, Jack Patterson." A sip of brandy. "Is that your way of angling for a raise of your rates from eight hundred bucks to a thousand an hour?"

"Hold that thought. I'll be back to see you when this drone contract is finalized."

"Ah. I never forget why we've retained you as general counsel. You always know how to zero right in on what the CEO wants to talk about."

"You mean my raise to a thousand bucks an hour? Or do you mean the new secretary? Or do you mean the drone contract?" Patterson grinned.

"Jack. My man. You help us get this contract shepherded through, and we'll make sure your firm gets the kind of bonus that makes you forget you even joked about a grand an hour."

"You know, Richardson," Patterson said, still grinning, "you never let me forget why you're my favorite client."

Richardson stood. He couldn't sit for long. He walked toward the balcony and looked out. "To answer your question, we just hired Ivana's American husband as one of our aeronautical engineers who will be working on the Blue Jay project. Nice guy. Name's Harold Martin. Typical engineer. Kind of a boring guy, really. We're hoping to keep him employed. That is, if you get this contract through the military's red tape." He turned around. "Ivana? She's icing on the cake."

"Nice icing. Just keep your hands to yourself, Richardson. I don't need you getting deposed in a domestic case between Ivana and Mr. Ivana, and our divorce lawyers are as expensive as I am." Patterson checked his watch, something he would do occasionally whenever Richardson initiated a discussion of legal fees, as if to subtly remind Richardson that AirFlite was still on the clock. "Not that you can't afford the legal bills."

"Well, that's plenty of incentive to behave myself, the prospect of being double-billed by the high-priced, silky-stocking, old-line Savannah firm of Patterson & Landry." He laughed, then stared down at his empty brandy glass. "Now then. Down to business. Where do we stand on Blue Jay?"

"Here's the deal." Patterson eyed him, speaking in a southern drawl with a tinge of Savannah aristocracy, making one-syllable words like *deal* sound like two syllables, something like "dee-yul."

"The contract is sitting on the desk of the Secretary of Defense for the United States of America, waiting for the Secretary's signature. The money's already been approved by Congress for the Navy's discretionary budget, so that's not a problem, contingent on the Navy's legal review process."

"What's that mean? Contingent on the Navy's legal review process."

"Good question, Richardson. You mind if I take you up on that drink offer after all?"

"No problem." Richardson picked up his phone. A sultry-sounding Ivana came over the intercom. "Yes, sir?"

"Bring me another brandy, Ivana. Prepare one for Mr. Patterson too."

"With pleasure, sir."

He hung up. "So, Jack, we were talking about the Navy's legal review process."

"Yes. Bureaucratic stuff. They have to conduct an internal legal review to be able to justify that what they're doing under the contract complies with domestic law, since they could get into all kinds of legal trouble if they don't comply with the law."

A knock on the door. "Come in."

"Your brandies, gentlemen."

"Thank you, Ivana. Put them down on the coffee table."

"My pleasure."

Richardson waited as his Anna Kournikova look-alike of a secretary set the drinks on the table, gave them each a flirtatious smile, then turned, walked out the door, and closed it.

"Now, what's this about, Jack?" He picked up his glass and handed Patterson his. "Some sort of legal stuff the Navy has to do? I thought the Navy operated under the rules of war or something. And how long is all this going to take? We've been gearing up for this production and have hired tons of people in anticipation of this contract. Like her husband, for example." He nodded to the door through which Ivana had just exited. "We can't afford any delays. We've got billions on the line here. So whatever this legal mumbo jumbo is, I need you to cut through it."

"Patience, my dear Richardson. The Navy and, in fact, all the armed forces have different rules, regulations, and laws they must comply with when they operate inside the United States as opposed to operating at sea."

"What kind of rules? We're talking about flying a bunch of drones through the sky. It's not like they're going to sail an aircraft carrier up the Savannah River. That should be simple enough."

Patterson leaned back on the sofa. "Well, they've got to get over something called *posse comitatus* first."

"*Posse* what?"

"*Posse comitatus.*" He took a sip of his drink, then loosened his tie. "A federal law passed after the Civil War, signed by President Rutherford B. Hayes. It prohibits the military from being used for law enforcement inside the borders of the United States. It originally just applied to the Army.

"But they later amended it to include the Navy. So they're waiting on this legal opinion from some Navy lawyer at the Pentagon, saying that the proposed use of the drones complies with the law. That's part of the contingency they need to make this happen to get the funding cut loose."

Richardson steepled his fingers together and thought. "Let me see if I can get this straight. We have an opportunity to begin a production project that will make AirFlite one of the top three defense contractors in the world, will pump millions into the Georgia economy when the production lines start rolling for these Blue Jay drones, and will pump billions in profits into the corporate treasury, and all that is being hung up by some penny-ante legal opinion from some low-level, no-name Navy lawyer in the Pentagon?"

"I'm sure it's just a formality, Richardson. I'm sure the Navy wants this project as bad as we do. I hear an internal war broke out at the Pentagon over whether the Navy or the Air Force would control

Operation Blue Jay. The Secretary of Defense decided on the Navy because of the argument that the Navy should be in control of the coastal areas."

"Yes, I know all about that," Richardson said, "which is why I want us to pitch the Air Force for the interior continental United States drone project after we get this one rolling. But all that's beside the point. It's already been three weeks since we sent our final revision to the contract to Washington. This is taking way too long, Jack."

"I'm sure it's going to work itself out. Our firm has handled government contracts for years. We've delivered on projects at the Savannah River Plant, at Fort Benning, and at the Kings Bay Naval Station. We're the best in the business, remember? That's why you hired us." He emptied his glass and set it down. "Patience, Richardson, patience. These things take time."

"I know your record. But this is taking too long. I've never been one to sit around and leave matters to chance."

"What are you going to do?"

"Watch me." He picked up the phone. "Ivana?"

"Yes, sir."

"I want you to get Senator Talmadge's Washington office on the line. Tell them I want to speak with him—now!"

"Yes, sir."

"You're making a mistake, Richardson."

"We'll see about that."

CHAPTER 5

• • •

In the world of politics in the great state of Georgia during the late twentieth and early twenty-first centuries, only a handful of surnames commanded instant recognition, instant attention, and, in some cases, instant respect.

Any Georgian who knew anything about politics could rattle off the names: Nunn. Carter. Chambliss. Cobb. Lewis.

Anyone who bore names such as these, even if they were not first generation, could always turn heads by the slightest hint of a dalliance into the political world in the Peach State.

One such iconic surname, capable of such political head-turning, even in the early twenty-first century, was Talmadge.

The original bearer of the name had been the late, powerful senator and governor Herman Talmadge, who served as the seventieth governor of Georgia from 1947 to 1955, then went on to serve in the United States Senate from 1957 to 1981.

But Herman Talmadge, whose daddy was the longtime governor of Georgia before the son began his long career of governor and

49

senator, remained too powerful and too ingrained in the consciousness of state politics to yield way to the negative aspects of the iconic senator's career, like his censure and his segregationist past.

None of this was lost on former state senator Robert O. "Bobby" Talmadge, who understood that campaigning with the last name Talmadge in Georgia was like campaigning as a Kennedy in Massachusetts or any of the liberal northeastern states.

Of course, the dirty little secret was that Bobby Talmadge was not related to the long-standing father-son political dynasty that cast a looming shadow over the landscape of the Peach State for the better part of a half century.

When, as a Georgia state senator representing Atlanta's ultra-wealthy, upscale Buckhead district, Bobby learned through the political grapevine that Georgia's long-standing senior U.S. Senator, Mack Coble, was stepping down, he hired a private political pollster to gauge his chances.

The results of the poll confirmed Bobby's hunch. His last name would provide a big leg up on his opponents in the primary, even without a real blood tie to the legendary Georgia dynasty. So he jumped into the race, and his campaign team crafted a theme subtly suggesting a connection without actually saying there was. They purchased billboards all over the state proclaiming:

TALMADGE
HISTORY, TRADITION, COURAGE, CONVICTION

No, Bobby Talmadge was no political dummy. If someone asked if he was related to the epochal Talmadge dynasty, he would answer truthfully, "We're not directly related, as far as I know."

But most people didn't ask. Most assumed. Low-information voters were easily manipulated. And he capitalized on the name all the way to the U.S. Senate.

To confuse the matter even more, Bobby had ordered his staff to hang on the walls of his office the portraits of several former U.S. senators from Georgia, both Democrat and Republican: Sam Nunn. Mack

Mattingly. Paul Coverdell. Zell Miller. Saxby Chambliss. Johnny Isakson . . . and, of course, Herman Talmadge.

Above the collection of portraits, he had his staff place a plaque in gold, engraved in black, titled "The Great Peach State—The Wall of Bipartisanship."

Bobby's portrait hung right beside that of his famous predecessor with the same last name for the benefit of those Georgia school groups, civic groups, and Chamber of Commerce types who came up for office tours. They would return to the Peach State and vote, and persuade others to vote.

Every potential vote had to be accounted for. No stones uncovered.

Hopefully, by the end of this first term, he wouldn't have to piggyback on the Talmadge name of the past, but instead would achieve reelection based on his own accomplishments.

He sat in his Washington office, his leather cowboy boots propped on his desk, going round and round on the phone with a young political reporter from the *Atlanta Constitution* who undoubtedly, given the young pup's liberal political bias, champed at the bit for some out-of-context quote to benefit the Democrats in next year's election.

Clearly an environmental wacko, the reporter opposed all forms of energy exploration, and not just worthwhile projects like the Keystone Pipeline or projects on Alaska's North Slope, but those of more immediate relevance. Like Exxon's request for federal approval to begin drilling off the Georgia coastline.

The proposal had generated fiery opinions from all corners. Bobby, who favored the project along with anything else that brought jobs to Georgia, measured his words to avoid any foot-in-mouth slipups that could be blown out of proportion.

"Yes, Johnny. Of course we must be environmentally sensitive. But we also need jobs in Savannah and along the Georgia coast. And if those rigs don't get built off the Georgia coast, Exxon will move them a few miles to the north, off the South Carolina coast, where their senators are lobbying for the project. If there's a spill, it could float down to our beaches anyway, and Savannah wouldn't have gotten the same economic benefit that Beaufort or Charleston would have gotten . . . Yeah . . . yeah . . . of course I respect their opinions.

"But I've also got to respect the Georgians who are still unemployed down on our coast from the last recession. They need jobs for their families to put food on the table . . . No . . . Yes, of course I remember the BP disaster off Louisiana . . . What do I think of it? Well, I think it's a rare occurrence for one thing, and we've got a ton of improved safety measures . . . Right . . . right . . ." He shook his head. "But, Johnny . . . with respect, you're missing the point . . ."

The cub reporter railed on and on. Was there a question in there somewhere? This kid should resign his job as a political reporter and just go ahead and seek the Democrat nomination for something or other.

Bobby checked his watch. *Atlanta Constitution* or not, he needed to cut this off.

"Hey, Johnny, I've got a meeting coming up with the Augusta Chamber of Commerce. I'm gonna have to—"

No luck.

His office door opened. Tommy Mandela, Bobby's wily chief of staff and an Emory law grad who never practiced anything except politics, stood there, decked out in his blue pinstripe suit. Mandela may have coincidentally borne the same last name as the great South African Nobel Prize winner, but in ethnicity, in political philosophy, and in shrewd cunning, he was opposite in every way. Bobby read Mandela's lips. "I need to see you."

"Johnny, hang on a second." Bobby punched the Hold button on his phone. "Find somebody else to talk to this guy."

"They all want you, boss."

"Tell me about it. Whatcha got, Tommy?"

"Sir, I'm sorry to interrupt, but Richardson DeKlerk's on the phone from AirFlite."

"DeKlerk? What's he want?"

"To talk about the drone project, sir."

"I'll be right with him." He punched the Talk button, reengaging the energetic reporter, mockingly known around Georgia political circles as Little Johnny White. "Johnny, I apologize, but something's come up. I'm gonna let you talk to my secretary, and she'll set a time for us to finish this. That okay?"

Without waiting for Little Johnny to respond, Bobby punched the line for his secretary. "Maryanne, pick up on two. Schedule a time for me to finish this interview. Find a way to tell him diplomatically that he's got ten minutes to wrap this up."

"Yes, sir."

"What line is Richardson DeKlerk on?"

"Mr. DeKlerk is on three, sir."

"Thanks." He punched line three. "Richardson. How ya doing this afternoon?"

"As well as can be expected." The business magnate spoke in his trademark South African accent. "How about you?"

"Doing fine. Hey, listen. You're on speaker so I can jot down some notes. That okay?"

"Bobby, I don't care if I'm on a bullhorn, as long as you do what we need you to do."

Bobby chuckled. "You always drive a hard bargain." He looked up as Tommy Mandela walked back into the office and DeKlerk kept talking.

"That's why I'm a multimillionaire, soon a billionaire, if we get this drone project through the worthless bureaucrats up in DC whose sole job is to single-handedly wreck the American economy. You know," DeKlerk added before Bobby could squeeze in a word, "if this project goes through, it won't be a bad thing for the Georgia Political Victory Fund."

Tommy grimaced.

"Now, Richardson, we'll do everything we can to help. But the GPVF is an independent political action committee. I've got nothing to do with them."

Bobby heard laughing from the other end of the phone. "You're hilarious, Senator. I've got my lawyer, Jack Patterson, with me, and he's in stitches at the notion that the Fund isn't your political ace in the hole. Heck, they even send the glossy flyers here to my office, reminding all dutiful Georgians of what a fabulous job-creating record you've built for the Peach State. You know we gave a hundred thousand to the Fund when you were first elected."

"Well, we're grateful for what they do," Bobby said.

"I know. I know. These political action committees that allow unlimited contributions to support candidates that are technically— quote—'independent from the candidates.' I'd give you a big wink if you were here in Savannah, Bobby. Anyway, there's more coming to the Fund if this drone deal goes through."

Bobby's mouth salivated. DeKlerk touched on all the hot buttons before even making whatever request he had. The Georgia Political Victory Fund was pro-Talmadge, had spent hundreds of thousands already on public relations maintenance during the off years to keep the senator's image positive, and would spend millions on attack ads against his opponent as the election approached. AirFlite could bank- roll a huge portion of GPVF's budget.

But Bobby had to be careful. He knew the right things to say. *They're separate. We have nothing to do with them. We can't control what they put out or who they support or what they say.*

But the party line was repeated with a nod and a wink, because everybody knew how this worked.

"Look, Richardson. You're a good friend. I appreciate your sup- port. But I've got nothing to do with the political action committees. The Supreme Court in the *Citizens United* case said corporations could make political contributions. And these super PACs were authorized under that case and can spend whatever they want, but must remain independent of candidates. That's the law, and I happen to agree with it. Otherwise we're suppressing people's First Amendment rights, and the federal government has no right to suppress the First Amendment.

"The Georgia Political Victory Fund is one of these super PACs, operating under the law, and I'm not connected with them in any way." Bobby glanced over at Tommy, who nodded his head and gave him a wink and a thumbs-up. "Now, how may I help you today, my friend?"

"Look, Bobby," DeKlerk said, "I appreciate your help so far on our little drone project down here in Savannah. But there's an unacceptable holdup that my lawyer has just informed me about."

"Hmm," Bobby mused. "What kind of a holdup?"

"Jack tells me the entire project is dependent on some nameless, midlevel Navy lawyer holed up somewhere in the bowels of the Pentagon, who is supposed to be writing some sort of legal opinion declaring the whole thing legal under some sort of posse— What did you call it, Jack?"

A pause. Mumbling in the background. Sounded like Patterson's voice doing the mumbling.

"Ah yes," DeKlerk said. "Some sort of *posse comitatus* nonsense or something like that."

"Oh yes," Bobby said. "That means the military can't perform police functions in the U.S."

"I've never heard of it. And I don't care about it. I've got billions riding on this project. My future depends on it, and frankly, so does yours." DeKlerk paused for a second. "Still there, Bobby?"

"Still here, Richardson."

"Anyway, my patience is running thin. Look. A number of us who sent you to the senate sent you there to cut through this ridiculous baloney-of-an-excuse red tape that has made the American governmental bureaucracy so bloated that, frankly, the whole thing should be burned to the ground so we can start over. I need you to get on the phone and call the Secretary of Defense and cut through all the BS and get this done."

"I understand."

"Well then, if you understand, then understand this: I want this contract signed, sealed, and delivered no later than one week from today. And if you don't deliver, Senator, then I'm sure our mutual friend, Joe Don Mack over at GPVF, might have an interest in knowing that. After all, the GPVF is interested in finding candidates who oppose big government and who can cut through red tape and make things happen. Are we clear on this?"

Silence.

Bobby looked at Mandela, who sat in the chair across the desk with a raised eyebrow.

"Richardson, I share your frustration. The bureaucracy needs to be reined in so we can pave the way for job creation, like AirFlite is trying to do in Savannah. And I'm behind you."

"With respect, Senator," DeKlerk said, sharpening his tone, "we need more than you sharing our frustration. We need action." He paused. "Now!"

Another pause.

"Tell you what, Richardson. I'll make a few calls and see what I can do."

"Excellent. I thought you would see it my way. Call me as soon as you hear something. One week. You have one week."

The line went dead.

Bobby looked at his chief of staff. "Tommy, if I didn't know any better, I'd say we just got threatened."

"You know, Senator, if I didn't know any better, I'd say you're right, sir."

Bobby turned in his chair and folded his arms. "We've got to stay in good with GPVF."

"No doubt, sir."

"DeKlerk's got a lot of sway with Joe Don Mack."

"When you give millions to an organization, you're going to have sway like that, Senator. You know the ole saying better than I do. Money's the lifeblood of politics."

"Right. And Joe Don Mack's gonna follow the money. And if I don't deliver here, they could throw a primary challenger at me, and the Democrats become the least of my worries."

"Right, boss. These super PACs are kingmakers. And incumbents are sometimes most vulnerable in the primaries, when you have a lower number coming out with an ideological purpose."

"No kidding. Anyway, we've got to figure out a way to get the Navy moving on this. I can't afford to lose that fund. Any suggestions, Tommy?"

"Let me think."

"Maybe I should call the Secretary of Defense."

A wry expression crossed Tommy's face. "Nah. Doesn't feel right."

"How come?"

"It might be more effective to call Roberson Fowler and see if he'll make the call. That way you get the long-standing chairman of the Armed Services Committee involved, and you've got plausible deniability. Fowler carries the kind of weight Jesse Helms and Ted Kennedy used to carry, even though they were from opposite ends of the political spectrum. He's more powerful at the Pentagon than any Secretary of Defense will ever be."

Bobby felt the lightbulb come on. "Tommy, you're a genius. On all fronts."

Mandela chuckled. "That's why you pay me the big bucks, sir."

Bobby picked up the telephone. "Maryanne, get Senator Fowler's office on the phone. See if you can arrange a time for me to speak with him. Tell them it's a hot topic and I need to chat with the senator ASAP."

"Yes, sir, Senator."

CHAPTER 6

• • •

Phillip D'Agostino kicked back behind his desk in his simple-looking offices in the concrete building down the street from Yankee Stadium, puffed on a Macanudo, and grew angrier by the word as he stared at the lower right corner of the front page of today's *New York Times*.

The madder he got, the faster he alternated between sucking on and blowing out the cigar. His wife had given him hell about oversmoking for years, but the smoking had kept him from overeating, which was a problem for many Italian men who ate too much pasta. Liquor wasn't the problem. It was the pasta. So unlike Big Sal and other godfathers whose bellies had grown rotund over the years, the smoking had kept Phil's waistline down to his fighting-weight, thirty-six-inch waist, and other than the fact that his black hair was starting to turn gray, the smoking definitely had its benefits.

But one vice the smoking did not cure was that red-hot Italian temper.

And it certainly wasn't stopping his blood from boiling at the moment. And the harder he blew out the stogie, the angrier he got and the more smoke-filled the president's offices of the New York Concrete & Seafood Company became.

Finally, after about the fiftieth blow, Phil had enough and ground the cigar into the ashtray.

"Vinnie! Get in here!"

"On my way, boss."

Phil slammed down the *Times* on the wooden desk, and the air from the sweeping newspaper caught the cigar ashes on the porcelain plate he'd used as a makeshift ashtray. This produced a dusting of gray ashes across the desk and onto the floor, just as his thirty-nine-year-old, right-hand man rushed into Phil's office from the office next door.

"What's going on, boss?" Vinnie Torrenzano stood in front of Phil's desk.

Phil looked up at the disgusting excuse of a creature, standing there in a white dress shirt, sleeves rolled up, suspenders holding up his pants, who had ascended to "right-hand man" status only because he had married Phil's oldest daughter. Otherwise Vinnie should have been cut to pieces and thrown to the rats in the sewers of the Bronx. Actually, the Bronx sewers would have been too good for Vinnie. Harlem would have been a better fit.

It had been nineteen years now since Phil had walked into his house, back early from a business trip to Miami, to catch the rat with his daughter, Maria—in Phil's own bed!

Phil remembered Maria's bloodcurdling screams as he proceeded to beat the little piece of garbage into a living pulp. When he'd finished the first round, Vinnie was lying on the floor with blood oozing from his mouth, and Phil ignored Maria as she tugged on his arm, sobbing and pleading, "Stop, Papa! That's enough!" He called in "the boys" to pick up the wretched scumbag by the collar, haul him out to an alley-way in Harlem, and give him another working over.

Later that night, the boys brought him back to the scene of his premarital sin, where, with his face looking like a purple cantaloupe, Phil proceeded to inform the scumbag, "Look, punk. If you're going to defile my daughter, you're going to marry her."

There was no negotiation on that point.

The next day the family called in Father Joe, the family priest.

Nineteen years later, Vinnie Torrenzano remained dutifully in the role of right-hand man, alive and well only because Phil loved Maria more than he hated Vinnie for what he had done to her.

"Have you seen this garbage, Vinnie?"

"Seen what?"

"There!" He pointed at the *Times* sitting on his desk. "It's in the paper! Look at that front-page article in the lower right."

The son-in-law scumbag picked up the paper. His eyes widened as he started to read. "'U.S. Navy Drone Contract Pending for Coastal Areas of U.S.'" He looked at Phil. "This the one you mean?"

"Yes. That's the one I mean. What do you think I meant?"

"Hang on, boss." Vinnie's lips started moving, at first silently, as he began reading the article. A second later his vocal cords morphed into synchronization with his lips.

"'The U.S. Navy is awaiting approval of a massive military contract that will make it the largest operator of domestic drones in the world and, if approved, would award AirFlite Corp the largest defense contract in history.

"'The plan, the *Times* has learned, would call for the construction of 100,000 Light Maneuverable Unmanned Aircraft Drones, referred to as LMUA drones, over the course of the next five years. Finalization of the contract awaits legal review by the Navy JAG.

"'AirFlite, a South African company that has its international headquarters in Savannah, Georgia, has been awarded the contract, pending legal approval, based upon its ability to manufacture the relatively low-cost but highly maneuverable, mission-ready LMUAs at a revolutionary low cost of $10,000 per aircraft.

"'The LMUAs are smaller and less expensive than the military's original Predator Drones, which ran upward of $4 million per unit.

"'AirFlite CEO Richardson DeKlerk told the *Times* that advanced technology and cost-efficient computer systems allow his company to provide the aircraft to the Navy for "pennies on the dollar in comparison to the original cost of the first-generation drone aircraft. It was a matter of time before technological improvement allowed us to build these drones cheaper than the cost of the average car."

"'According to one Pentagon official, who asked not to be identified, the drones will provide surveillance within the coastal areas of the United States, which includes the areas just inland from the coast, and will contain a dual capability of stopping and preventing terror attacks against the homeland. The drones will share vital information with the U.S. Coast Guard and U.S. Drug Enforcement Administration about illegal drug smuggling into the country.'"

Vinnie looked down at Phil, his eyes peering over his reading glasses. "That ain't good, boss. All them drones could make it difficult on our maritime fleet bringing the stuff in from Colombia."

"No kiddin' it ain't good. You know, I underestimate you sometimes, Vinnie."

Vinnie laid the paper down on Phil's desk. "Man. We're gonna have to go up on our prices."

"What do you mean 'go up on our prices'?"

The buffoon's eyes sparkled as if he'd just discovered the Pythagorean theorem or something. "You know what I mean, boss. I'm talking increased prices for tip money to keep our operation going. You know, like we do with TSA and DEA and border patrol. Simple, boss. We just raise the price on the streets and we're good to go. Seems simple enough. Like a value-added tax or somethin'."

"On second thought, I take it back about underestimating you."

"What do ya mean, boss? We've got all kinds of federal agents on the take. Won't be the first time the government's come up with a dumb idea. Won't be the last."

"Sit down, Vinnie."

"Sure, boss."

"Look, Einstein," Phil said as his bug-eyed protégé put his skinny backside in the wooden chair on the other side of the desk. "I know we got all kinds of feds on the take."

"Not just feds." Vinnie smirked. "State and local cops too. That's my baby, ya know."

"Yeah, yeah, I know. Your job is coordinating payments to make sure law enforcement stays on the take. I hate to compliment you, but you ain't done such a bad job of it.

"But, Vinnie." Phil stopped to strike up a cigarette, which he switched to because he suddenly needed a stronger nicotine kick than the cigars would give him, then inhaled a quick, satisfying drag. "We ain't talkin' about the FBI or the TSA here. We're talkin' about the U.S. military. And there ain't no way we can bribe the U.S. military. You can't even get to 'em, let alone bribe 'em. The military, they're a different breed. They ain't like these federal bureaucrats or these federal agents. You can't get to 'em."

Phil narrowed his eyes and sucked more nicotine into his lungs. "The military, I'm tellin' ya, Vinnie. I tried once with an Army colonel years ago. They're the only ones who still believe in this God-and-country and Constitution stuff. Sometimes they get out of the military, and occasionally you might get to one who became disillusioned or something like that. But when they wear that uniform, most of 'em believe in God-and-country, and you can't turn their heads. No matter how much money you wave at 'em."

A confused look crossed Vinnie's face. "You're saying it's too expensive to get some officers on the take?"

"What I'm saying is they can't be bought. And even if we could buy off some naval officer here or there, there are too many of 'em. It won't work. Like I said, they're a different breed."

"Ya got a cigarette, boss?"

"Here." Phil pulled out a Marlboro and rolled it across the desk.

"Got a light?"

"Here." He slid the lighter across the desk. "Make sure I get it back."

Vinnie struck the lighter, lit the cigarette, squinted his eyes as he took a drag, then formed his lips in an O and released smoke from his mouth and nose. He slid the lighter back across the desk. "Thanks. So how we gonna stay in business if this thing goes through?"

"Well, it's simple. We gotta make sure this contract never gets off the ground."

"How are we gonna do that, boss? Are we gonna go to war against the whole U.S. Navy?"

Phil crunched the butt of the cigarette into the porcelain plate. "That's exactly what we're gonna do. But we've got to be careful here. We've gotta work smart. We gotta call in every chip that's owed us. Political and otherwise."

Vinnie pulled off his reading glasses and set them down on the desk. The bewildered look on his face reminded Phil that while Vinnie could take orders, he would never be a mastermind in this organization. "What do you have in mind, boss?"

"Two things. First we call in our political contacts. We made some pretty big contributions to Chuckie Rodino's U.S. Senate campaign. He owes his seat to us, and I intend to remind him of that."

"You gonna call Chuckie Rodino, boss?"

"You're dang straight. And I'll remind him if he wants to get re-elected, it's time to scratch the family's back. I'll tell him he needs to oppose this contract on privacy grounds and that the money needs to be spent on welfare for his constituents here in the Bronx who need to stay in their places."

"You think he'll listen?"

Phil slammed his fist on his desk. "I guarantee he'll listen. We've had Chuckie Rodino on the take since he was an assistant district attorney in Brooklyn. We've bought every seat the little weasel has occupied. He'll listen, or it will get nasty."

"Remind me never to cross you up, boss."

"You already crossed me up. Remember?"

"Never again, boss. I promise. That was years ago. You know you got my loyalty, boss. You know I'll do anything for you and the family."

Phil stared at the weasel for a second. Yes, it was easy to hate him. But at the same time, it was hard to hate him. The weasel was right about one thing. His loyalty to the family had been unwavering since their initial disagreement.

"Yeah, I know you're loyal, Vinnie. I appreciate that about you. Plus, ever since you defiled my daughter, you've been good to her."

"And I always will be. But what's the second thing we're gonna do about this?"

Vinnie always changed the subject whenever Phil brought up Maria and the butt-whooping the family had administered to him all those years ago.

"Go back and read the first part of the article again," Phil said. "The part about the Navy JAG or something like that."

Vinnie picked up the *Times* and took a moment. "Okay. I think I see what you mean. You mean the part that says finalization of the contract is awaiting legal review by the Navy JAG?"

"That's it. And that's where you come in."

"What do you want me to do, boss? I know nothin' about the Navy JAG."

"I don't know nothin' about the Navy JAG either, Vinnie, other than I'd like to meet up with that hot-looking babe who used to play Major What's-Her-Name on the TV show."

"No kidding, boss."

"Watch it, Vinnie. You ever mistreat my daughter and I'll—"

"Sorry, boss. Major What's-Her-Name can't hold a candle to Maria. And I'll never mistreat Maria. Anyways, you were about to say what you wanted me to do to stop this."

"Yeah, right. Okay, listen. I want you to go down to Washington. I want you to be my eyes and ears and go figure out the Navy JAG thing. Now, while we might not be able to stop the whole Navy from flying all these drones around up in the air, there's a weak link in every chain. So maybe while I work the political angle, you can nip this in the bud before it starts.

"So I want you to go down to Washington. People talk in DC. Now, you might not have any luck getting the military to spill the beans, but the civilian bureaucrats who work for the government? Not a problem."

A sparkle lit Vinnie's eyes. "You mean, like, even though I might not be able to get nothin' out of the military, I might be able to pay off civilians that work at the Pentagon and stuff like that to get information?"

"You're all over it today, Vinnie." Phil struck his third cigarette.

"These civilian bureaucrats in the government, if you throw money at 'em, they'll sing like a canary and give you whatever you want. Most of 'em want to make a quick buck for as little work as possible. The more you offer, the more they'll sing. So I want you to go down there and snoop around, and ask questions of these bureaucrats and find out who in the Navy JAG is in charge of this contract. Then I want you to do whatever it takes to stop it. Talk to whoever you need to talk to. Spend whatever you need to spend. Just stop this contract dead in its tracks before it gets off the ground."

"This is an important thing, ain't it, boss?"

"As important a project as you've ever been involved with. Remember, if this project goes through, we're gonna have thousands of these drones flying around. Even if we got to a few of 'em, there's too many of 'em. They'll kill our business. In fact, they'll close down our whole export business, if you know what I mean."

Vinnie's eyes widened. "Boss, did you tell the old man about this? The old man's going to kill somebody over this."

By the "old man," Vinnie meant the legendary godfather of the family, Phil's uncle, Sal D'Agostino. Uncle Sal had been baby brother to Phil's father, Frankie "Scarface" D'Agostino, and held Frankie in his arms as he died, bleeding from gunshot wounds from an enforcement situation when another "business enterprise" began meddling in territorial connections important to D'Agostino's seafood operations. That was thirty years ago.

Big Sal, being next in line after Phil's father, ascended to the head of the family business. But he never had sons. Phil's cousins Mimi and Marguerita had married good men the family could work with, but only a D'Agostino would ever run New York Concrete & Seafood Company.

That's the way it always had been. That's the way it always would be. So when Big Sal had a heart attack requiring a quadruple bypass ten years ago, he'd passed operational control to his nephew, Phil. Still, even in his retirement, sipping liquor on the beaches in Miami and buying margaritas for hot pinups half his age, Big Sal carried a big stick in the family.

Phil preferred keeping Sal in Florida half the year, where there was no state income tax, and keeping Sal's big Italian nose, wild nasal hairs and all, out of the operations of the business. But Sal's big-bellied shadow loomed all the way up the Eastern Seaboard, as evidenced in Vinnie's question.

"Look, let me worry about Big Sal. Sal's no dummy. He'll figure it out. But when the time comes to brief him on our battle plan, I'll take care of it. Don't worry about Big Sal or nothin' else. Just go down to Washington and figure out the JAG stuff and kill this contract before it starts. You do your part, Vinnie."

"Will do, boss. You can count on it."

CHAPTER 7

...

THE GRAPE + BEAN ROSEMONT
118 SOUTH ROYAL STREET
OLD TOWN
ALEXANDRIA, VIRGINIA
MONDAY EVENING

Sitting on the outdoor patio of the popular neighborhood bar, the Grape + Bean, P.J. checked his watch and took another swig of beer. A cool evening breeze rolled in from the direction of the Potomac, which, combined with the subtle, levitating effects of the cool, full-bodied Heineken, soothed and buffered, at least slightly, the anxious feeling that had haunted him all day.

The anxiety had twisted his stomach since that morning, but the knots had become almost unbearable as the day went on. The feeling reminded him of the saying in the Bible: *"If it is possible, may this cup be taken from me."*

Right now someone would have to pry the cup, or rather the mug, of the rich Dutch beer out of his hand.

Victoria wasn't yet late, but she wasn't early either. Of course, if she didn't show at all, he wouldn't mind that much. He wasn't sure he wanted to jump into anything this soon after Caroline. He and Caroline had been apart now for over three months, ever since he reported for duty in Washington. And they had decided to end it even several weeks before he left San Diego, knowing that a long-distance relationship would be difficult for them both.

On the other hand, if Victoria didn't show at all, he would be disappointed. Even though he wasn't quite ready for this, he couldn't deny the mutual chemistry.

She felt it too. Of that he was sure.

But why did it have to be this soon? Really, he had no time for this. But still, he needed to talk to someone. For all the time he had spent in San Diego, Caroline had been his confidante. In fact, now that he thought about it, that's how their relationship got started. All those conversations, at La Jolla Cove, at Marietta Park, in Olde Town, at Balboa Park, all those times they spent together as friends before their relationship turned romantic, those times when he could share with her about anything.

The next swig of beer emptied his glass, and the slight buzz to his head calmed his nerves. But he hadn't drunk enough yet to forget that it was stupid for him to be drinking much at all under the circumstances.

Control.

He had to maintain discipline. And beyond one beer, alcohol and chemistry with the opposite sex offered a combustible combination.

The good news?

The place closed in an hour. Not a long time to do much damage. He had planned the back-end timing sort of as protection against his impetuous decision to ask her out. Besides, they both had to be back at work at the Pentagon in the morning.

But he needed someone to talk to concerning this whole drone contract scenario. She was one of a small handful of people who would be authorized, because of her position at Code 13, to even know about it.

Why had he taken this job?

Yes, Code 13 was a solid rocket booster if he wanted a high-level career in the Navy. Only a handful of JAG officers would ever rub shoulders with the Secretary of the Navy.

On the other hand, life would have been simpler if he'd taken that assignment to teach military law at the Naval Academy. If he'd gone to the Academy, or gone to a carrier, it was doubtful he would have been assigned a project that would cause him to lose sleep. He was sure he'd go to bed tonight sweating bullets.

"Good evening, sailor." Her velvety-smooth words coincided with a soft hand touching his left shoulder and an unexpected fluttering in his chest cavity. He stood, catching another whiff of her perfume, which proved more dizzying than the buzz from his Heineken. Her figure in civilian attire, in this case a nicely cut little black dress that accentuated her reddish hair and green eyes, achieved an instantaneous *wow* factor. She also wore heels just high enough for a glamorous, statuesque form. Her appearance caused him to lose temporary command of his ability to concentrate.

Focus, P.J.!

He rose from his chair. "It's good to see you. You look great tonight."

Her smile had a shy yet pleasant nervousness about it, as if she was pleased he had noticed how sensational she looked but didn't wish to fully signal how much it pleased her that he had noticed. Already the electricity was amped to high voltage.

"Thank you. You look nice yourself."

"Me?" He glanced down at himself in a solid black T-shirt and denims. "I just threw on a pair of jeans. Anyway—" He caught himself in an awkward moment. "Please have a seat." He reached out and pulled out her chair, then slipped it under her as she sat. "Could I order you something to drink?"

"A glass of wine would be fine. Pinot noir, please." Another smile. This was becoming a showstopping distraction.

"Waitress?"

"Yes, sir?"

"A glass of your best pinot noir, please."

"Yes, sir."

"On second thought, make that two."

"Right away, sir."

• • •

"This wine is fabulous." Her eyes danced with an exquisite sparkle as she smiled at him from across the table.

You're the one who looks fabulous, he thought about saying in response. Indeed, he would have said just that were it not for the fact that in a few days he would be facing the most awkward of situations he could imagine, working in the Pentagon, at Code 13, with the woman he had almost proposed to alongside this incredible new officer whom he suddenly found irresistibly attractive, against every impulse not to find her so desirable.

"Yes, it's smooth," he said. "They have some excellent selections here."

"Yes, they do." She kept her eyes on him as if she knew he had become entranced. "This is a great place to get away. Maybe we could try it again sometime?"

He hesitated. "Maybe so."

"That would be nice." Victoria's hand found his forearm, enough contact for an electric jolt, then teasingly broke contact. "So, do you want to talk about it?"

"You sure you want to hear?"

"That's why I'm here. To give you my ear, to give you my attention, and to be a sounding board. Right?"

"You're kind."

"That's part of my duty, as far as I'm concerned. To help a fellow officer in need."

He ignored that comment. "What part would you like to hear first?"

"Well . . ." She brushed a lock of hair from her forehead. "Why don't you tell me what's bothering you most?"

"That's a loaded question."

"I've got all night if you need it, P.J." She touched his forearm again. Her touch lingered a bit longer this time.

He took a sip of wine.

She withdrew her hand but compensated with another smile.

He looked around to make sure no one was in earshot. Two tables over, a young couple was enraptured with each other. Across the way to their left, three middle-aged women swigged their wine, engaged in blissful, cackling gossip.

No one was paying attention.

"Well, you know I've been assigned to write this legal opinion on the drone project."

"Of course, P.J. Everyone at Code 13 knows about it by now. It's an honor that you were selected. It demonstrates their confidence in you."

"Yeah, right. I'd rather they take their honor and confidence in this case and shovel it on somebody else."

"I don't follow."

He looked around again. He had to be careful about discussing this in public.

"Let me ask you something, Victoria. Have you ever heard of something called the Constitution-Free Zone?"

She gave him a questioning look. "Constitution-Free Zone? Are you talking about something in Russia or China or something like that?"

He sat back in his chair. "I think I need another beer."

"Suit yourself."

He raised his hand to summon their waitress. "Bud Light, please. You want anything, Victoria?"

"No, I'm good."

"Just one then."

"Yes, sir."

He waited until the waitress had stepped out of earshot. "See, that's what I thought too. At first. But in researching the *posse comitatus* angle of this brief that I'm writing—that's the part about how you can't use the military for domestic police activities."

"Right. Right. I got that part."

"Your beer, sir."

"Thanks . . ." He looked at the waitress's name tag. "Marilyn. Put it right there, please."

"Yes, sir."

He took a sip, waiting for the college-aged-looking waitress to walk away again.

"Of course you know *posse comitatus*. You're a JAG officer. What was I thinking?"

"No problem. So you found something when you were researching?"

"Did I find anything in my research." A swig of beer. "Let me ask you this. Did you know the executive branch of the federal government takes the position that the Fourth Amendment doesn't apply within one hundred miles of all the coastal and border areas of the United States?"

"What? What are you talking about?"

"What I'm saying is the feds claim they can stop anybody within a hundred miles of the border even without probable cause. They can search within a hundred miles of the border even without probable cause. They claim the Fourth Amendment does not apply within a hundred miles of the border and they don't need a search warrant."

"Are you serious?"

"I'm dead serious."

"How long has this been in effect?"

"It started back around 2008, with Homeland Security claiming the warrantless searches could extend a hundred miles inland. That includes most of the population of the United States."

"Wait a minute. You're saying they claim they can just stop somebody's car for no reason? Or search an American citizen for no reason? Or go into someone's house without a search warrant?"

"That's exactly what I'm saying. The feds are saying they don't need a warrant. They can search in the name of national security. I'm not just talking at the borders or at the coast. I'm talking inland. The heck with a warrant."

Victoria rolled her eyes upward as if she was thinking. "I don't understand this. If this is true, then how come I've never heard about it? I've never heard anybody talking about it."

"Hey, don't feel bad about it. I hadn't heard about it either until I started researching for this project."

"Well, I don't get it," she said. "If all this is true, then why hasn't the press reported on it?"

"The press has reported on it in spots, but indirectly."

"What do you mean, P.J.?"

"Do you remember back during the Boston Marathon bombing in 2013?"

"Sure. It was awful. There was a huge manhunt for the terrorists. Who could forget it?"

"Well, what do you remember about the manhunt?"

She looked quizzical. "I remember that it lasted several days, was pretty extensive. Seems like they killed one of the terrorists and found the other one hiding in a boat in somebody's backyard. Later convicted him for murder."

"You've got a good memory. What else do you remember about the manhunt?"

"Let's see. I remember that these terrorists were Muslim Chechens, from Russia."

"So you remember how they found the Muslim Chechens?"

"Seems like they found them in some residential neighborhood in Boston."

He took another swig of beer. "Found them in a residential neighborhood. That's an understatement."

"What are you getting at, P.J.?" A sip of her wine.

"What I mean is this. That for four days after these bombs went off—that killed five people, by the way—the Boston cops and federal troops got into this storm-trooper gear and drove around the streets of Watertown in military-style armored vehicles, ordering people out of their homes without authority, kicking down doors, entering homes without warrants. The Boston cops and the feds acted like the Gestapo, invading people's homes, violating their property rights, and ordering citizens around like a bunch of little Nazis."

"What?" A stunned look on her face. "Are you serious?"

"Dead serious."

"How many homes did they invade without a warrant?"

"Dozens. These jackboots rolled up in front of these old, middle-class frame houses in these black armored personnel carriers. Platoons of them moved up and down the streets. Police officers and FBI agents. All dressed like military Gestapo storm troopers, complete with black uniforms, black boots, and black helmets that made them look as intimidating as Darth Vader.

"They acted like big he-men, turning the neighborhood streets of Boston into what looked like an occupation zone from a World War II movie. They strapped M-16 military assault rifles around their shoulders and marched down the streets with their bullhorns, ordering people to come out of their houses."

"I can't believe it. You mean they did this without a warrant or without a court order?"

"Believe it. You can see it all over YouTube. It's all over the internet. All this was recorded by residents watching it in disbelief, even though the mainstream press decided to protect these illegal activities by not reporting on them. These jackboots stormed off the streets, rushed onto the sidewalk, stomped their way up the front porches of these houses, and banged on the doors.

"They banged on the doors three times and ordered people out of their homes. If the family opened the door, they pointed their rifles at them and ordered them to put their hands over their heads, then ordered them down to the street. If no one answered, they gathered around in a semicircle and aimed their rifles at the door while one of the jackboots kicked it down.

"Then they'd bring their rifles down into an aim position and crouch down like they were expecting incoming mortar rounds from the Russians. Then when they were all crouched down, they entered these people's homes, covering each other's backs like they were the SEALs hunting for bin Laden or something.

"It's like if you give them a gun and a badge and a Gestapo uniform, they start acting like the Gestapo." A sip of water. "I mean, these people in those houses had done nothing wrong. These were their homes. They were just minding their own business, and all of a sudden, these storm troopers showed up with armored personnel carriers and bullhorns and started banging their doors down."

A puzzled look crossed Victoria's pretty face. "I don't remember seeing anything at all about this on the news."

"Of course not. But it happened right in neighborhoods, family neighborhoods, in Watertown, Massachusetts. Google the Boston Marathon manhunt."

"I don't know what to say. I can't . . ." She seemed to be in thought. "Why wouldn't the press make more of an issue of this?"

"Because they don't care!" He caught himself. Had to restrain the anger growing within him. "Just like they've covered up the indefinite retention periods under the National Defense Authorization Act, like they've covered up federal agencies like the EPA and the IRS just grabbing people's properties or taking money from bank accounts without any notice, let alone them not getting a judge or jury."

"This is an outrage," she said. "I don't understand why the media doesn't give this type of thing more publicity, why they wouldn't care."

"Because the mainstream media is in bed with the government! The press is part of the cover-up. I'm not making this up! I've discovered all this as part of my research for this project!" He paused. "Sorry. I didn't mean to raise my voice."

"It's okay." She reached over and took his hand.

"All the mainstream press is owned by big, wealthy conglomerates with a financial interest in preserving the status quo. It's not about being a watchdog against government tyranny, which was the whole idea behind freedom of the press. Now the mainstream press has become part of the problem. They hid the fact that cops were busting into people's houses without warrants in New Orleans too."

"In New Orleans?"

He looked at her. A look of shock washed over her face. "Yes, in New Orleans. Right after Hurricane Katrina. They busted into the houses of little old ladies who had been stranded by the storm, stole privately owned guns without permission, never paid for them, and in many cases those guns were the only protection some of these elderly ladies had against looters."

Victoria shook her head. "Unbelievable."

"Unbelievable is right. Of course, all that happened before the federal government got so bold as to declare this hundred-mile"—he made mocking quotation signs with his fingers—"'Constitution-Free Zone.' Hurricane Katrina emboldened them. By the time Boston rolled around, I guess they'd been so emboldened by what they got away with in New Orleans that they took the position that the Constitution didn't apply because Boston is within one hundred miles of the coast."

"Hang on a second, P.J."

Victoria withdrew her hand, and he hoped she wouldn't withdraw it for long. *Focus, P.J.!*

"When was Katrina, again?" she asked.

"Hurricane Katrina hit New Orleans in 2005, during the second term of George W. Bush's administration."

"Okay. And Boston was 2013. Right?"

"Right."

"So you're telling me that sometime between 2005 and 2013, the executive branch came up with this secret policy of some sort, a Constitution-Free Zone, where they can do about anything they want as long as it's within one hundred miles of the coast or the national border?"

Her leg brushed his under the table, which once again momentarily distracted him. "That's exactly what I'm telling you. I'm also saying that even though the mainstream press refused to report on it, this policy change was not so secret if anybody was paying attention."

She looked at him curiously. "So where did you find all this?"

"Would you like to order anything else?" P.J. looked up. The waitress had returned. "Give us a few more minutes, please."

"Yes, sir."

He waited again until she had stepped away, then looked across the table at Victoria, her red hair mirroring a subtle sheen under the subdued lights. "Actually, I learned about this so-called Constitution-Free Zone from a source I'm not always that fond of."

"Let me guess. The Communist Party?" A coy smile.

He discovered that her smile, nicely timed, had a soothing effect on him. "You know the right things to say to get me calmed down, don't you?"

"I try. We don't want you having a stroke prematurely." She touched his hand again. "Seriously, though, how did you find out about this Constitution-Free Zone?" Her tone had turned solemn.

"Okay," he said. "I learned about it through the ACLU."

"You serious?"

"Dead serious. The ACLU, to its credit, is the only group aware of this or that even cares. They've been reporting on it since 2008. Nobody else has even noticed."

"You know," Victoria said, "even though they're off mark on a lot of stuff, like church-state issues, the ACLU does a lot of good in a lot of areas."

"Yes, they do. And exposing this policy is one of the good things they do."

A raised eyebrow. "Okay, why does the ACLU say the government claims they can search within a hundred miles of the border with no warrant?"

"They claim this because it's in a federal regulation. I've seen the regulation. The ACLU is right. It's a regulation published by Homeland Security at 8 CFR section 287.2. Basically it's a claim that they can stop-and-search whenever they have what is called a reasonable suspicion, anytime they want, as long as they're within a hundred miles of the coast or the border. They claim they don't need a warrant."

"That sounds unconstitutional."

"Of course it's unconstitutional," he thundered. "There's this thing called the Fourth Amendment that is totally contrary to this regulation, and there's this little thing called a search warrant that the Fourth Amendment requires be issued before a search can take place. But that's not stopping the feds. They do what they want to do and nobody's stopping them."

"Hang on." She pulled her smartphone out of her purse. The dim glow of the screen reflected on her face. Half a minute later, her eyes widened. "Wow. I see what you're talking about with Katrina. These pictures are showing exactly what you described. It's like a Gestapo army with soldiers in black Gestapo helmets with black armored vehicles and machine guns walking down these deserted residential streets."

"Keep looking. Google some of the pictures of these guys kicking down people's doors."

She modified her search. A moment later, another look of astonishment.

"And this is the tip of the iceberg," P.J. said. "The federal government, and especially Homeland Security and the EPA and IRS, are going hog wild."

"What do you mean when you say they're going hog wild?"

He leaned over the table, bringing his face within a few inches of hers, and lowered his voice. "Have you been keeping up with these gargantuan ammunition purchases by the Department of Homeland Security and the IRS?"

Another confused look on her pretty face. "What are you talking about?"

"Get this. During the Obama administration, the Department of Homeland Security put in orders for 1.6 billion rounds of hollow-point bullets."

"Did you say *billion?*"

"Yes, I said billion. Not million. *Billion.*"

"And did you say *hollow point?*"

"Yes, I said hollow point. The most lethal type of ammo you can imagine."

"Whoa. That sounds like a ton of ammo for a federal agency that isn't even military."

"That's a mild way of putting it. At the height of the Iraq War, the U.S. Army fired less than six million rounds per month. So that's less than seventy-two million rounds per year. Put it this way. Homeland Security bought more ammunition than the military uses in a war. In fact, that's enough ammunition to sustain the U.S. Army in a hot war for twenty years!"

"I don't understand." She paused. "Why would Homeland Security need all that ammo?"

"Bingo. You just asked the billion-dollar question. You know there are only three hundred million Americans. Who are they going to shoot?"

"Wait a minute. Where did you get this information? You didn't get this from one of those right-wing conspiracy sites, did you?"

P.J. chuckled. "Not unless you call *Forbes* magazine one of those conspiracy sites. *Forbes* reported on this on May 11, 2013. The *Denver Post* reported on it on February 15 of 2013. Fox News reported on it. But again, most of the mainstream media ignored it."

Victoria checked her cell phone again. "I see the *Forbes* article. This is scary. I mean, again, why do these agencies need all this ammo?"

"I'm sorry to have to be right. And you're right. It's scary. And the public has no clue."

"I'll say."

Her green eyes danced in the dim light, displaying an enticing mixture of curiosity, fear, excitement, and admiration. A moment passed.

"And you discovered this during your research on the drone project?"

"Yes. Every bit of it. I'd heard rumblings of some of this stuff, but I didn't believe it. Or maybe I didn't want to believe our government is turning the Fourth Amendment on its head. And it's not just Homeland Security. It's the Bureau of Land Management, the IRS, the EPA. And it's not just the feds. State and local cops are just as bad. I ran across this article in the *New York Times* from June 2014 about war gear flowing to police departments. They're all arming themselves to the teeth. The *Times* article talked about even small police departments going crazy buying armored personnel carriers, M-16 rifles, grenade launchers, silencers. You name it. You start researching, and one thing leads to another."

"This is mind-boggling." Victoria looked at him, her leg brushing against his knee again. "But again, why, P.J.? Why are they buying all this ammo?"

"You've again asked the right question, Victoria. I can't prove this, but to me there's only one explanation." He looked into her face. "To be prepared for martial law."

"Martial law?"

"Yep. In the event of an economic collapse. Americans already own so many guns personally, because of the Second Amendment, that these government agencies, in my opinion, feel like they need even more guns and bullets than Americans own. That's the only explanation. In theory, these agencies would have enough ammo to take on the U.S. Army."

"You think a collapse is coming?"

"How can it not?" He started to touch her hand but refrained. "With the national debt load exploding every day, it's not a matter of *if* it's going to collapse, but *when*. The law of mathematics will catch up with us."

She didn't respond at first but nodded her head and lowered her gaze out at the street before asking, "Okay. Another question."

"Fire away."

"I'm concerned too. But what does all this have to do with your legal opinion to the Secretary on the Navy's drone project?"

"Don't you see it?"

"I think I do, but tell me," she said.

"Look. Here's the problem. The manufacturer has already built a couple hundred of them. They've loaned them out to the Navy just to whet the command's appetite. But they're going to build so many of these drones that they'll be like a swarm of locusts in the skies. Part of the problem is that they aren't just going to be flying out over water. The bigger part of the problem is that they'll be flying over land. Over cities, towns, interstate highways, the countryside, you name it."

"That's a spooky thought."

"No kidding. You'll see them all the time. They'll be flying below the cloud cover in a lot of cases. And because of what the federal government claims is a 'Constitution-Free Zone,' these drones will be flying up to one hundred miles inland."

Victoria sat there a second, looking stunned. "So the game plan is for these drones to fly over domestic U.S. soil?"

"Absolutely. I've seen the plans. That's why they want the clearance on the *posse comitatus* angle."

"Well, there's something I don't quite understand. Since these drones are flying over domestic soil, why isn't the proposed contract with Homeland Security? Why not just a smaller contract with the Navy, then sell the drones to a domestic federal law enforcement agency?"

P.J. nodded his head. "That's a great question. And the answer is because of political ramifications."

"What political ramifications?"

"It's easier to sell the contract to Congress if it's sold to the Navy than to Homeland Security. Why? Because it's getting sold primarily on the need to combat maritime terrorism. The domestic surveillance part isn't emphasized as the main part of the contract. That's a second-ary part, on paper."

"By maritime terrorism, do you mean they say they need the drones to stop terrorists slipping into country by boat?"

"Well, that's part of it. But the threat posed by maritime terrorism is even more dangerous than that. Did you ever read that novel *The Black Sea Affair*?"

"Oh, yes. I read it in Justice School because it was written by that ex–Navy JAG officer. Somebody Brown. I can't remember his first name."

"That's right. The guy was in the JAG Corps back in the '90s. But do you remember what the book was about?"

"I'm pretty sure it was about this Russian freighter that got loose on the high seas, and these Islamic Chechens were building a hydrogen bomb in it. And the American president sends a Los Angeles–class submarine to go hunt it down."

P.J. nodded. "That's right. Brown's novel calls attention to this dangerous issue of maritime terrorism. See, most Americans aren't aware of it. It's almost impossible to keep track of a ship on the high seas unless you have another ship following it constantly, or unless that ship activates its GPS transmitter. So it could sail right into New York or San Francisco harbors with an atomic bomb on board, detonate the bomb, and no one would know what's coming."

"Now that's a nightmare scenario," Victoria said.

"Of course it is. That's what Brown addressed in the book. The problem is that radar can't see way out in the ocean. In fact, radar can only shoot out about seven miles. In Brown's book, nobody could find the Russian freighter on the high seas, and everybody worried that it was headed to London or New York Harbor. So they went looking for it to try to sink it."

"Yes. I remember that. It was a pretty tension-filled scenario."

"That's right. It was also a realistic scenario. And even though the public as a whole isn't aware of it, Congress has been discussing this disastrous scenario for years." He took a swig of beer. "For years, neither the Navy nor the Coast Guard could do anything to defend against it. Until now."

Her eyes lit up. "So this drone contract—"

"Exactly. With the sheer numbers of drones that would be manufactured under this contract, the Navy can send a swarm of drones hundreds of miles out over the ocean, in flight patterns parallel to the coastline, and vastly increase our visual coverage of the seas."

"Ah. So therefore, the drone project expands coverage of coastal waters to better fight against the possibility of maritime terrorism, because it enables the Navy to see many more ships approaching the American coastline."

P.J. nodded. "Precisely. The Navy can physically see more ships approaching the U.S. coast from miles out because of cameras on the drones, plus these drones also have radar in the nose cone. With these little drones buzzing out there over the ocean 24/7, we can extend effective radar coverage to fourteen, twenty-one, twenty-eight, thirty-five miles, even more. So this is what makes the contract so politically attractive—the notion, finally, of protecting the coasts against some unknown ship sailing into Boston or New York with a hydrogen bomb. In fact, that makes the contract very attractive for lawmakers." P.J. looked into her eyes. "But there's a catch." He paused again.

"There always is. I'm listening." She touched his hand. "Tell me about it."

"The catch is that when Homeland Security caught wind of this potential contract, they decided they wanted in on the action. So at first they floated proposals for their own contract. But both the administration and the Congressional Budget Office axed the idea, on the grounds that two major government contracts of this magnitude would be too expensive and unmanageable.

"But the Secretary of Homeland Security, Bob Bradshaw, wouldn't take no for an answer. So he pressed some of his buddies in the senate to draft language that would require, as a stipulation for funding, that the Navy would fly the drones over this so-called Constitution-Free Zone and secretly share the data with Homeland Security. In fact, there's language in the legislation that will allow for real-time camera feeds and data feeds from the Navy to Homeland Security headquarters when the drones are in flight over U.S. soil.

"So, yes, this project is technically a U.S. Navy command. For drones patrolling the coastline and flying over open waters, the Navy will be running the show without interference from Homeland Security. But for flights over this Constitution-Free Zone, everything gets shared between the Navy and Homeland Security. They're talking about setting up a joint ops center with Navy drone pilot-controllers and intelligence centers, but the intelligence centers would be manned by Homeland Security officers, and they would have authority to direct overland surveillance."

The wind whipped up again, and Victoria brushed back a strand of auburn hair from her forehead. "I think I get it. They sell the contract politically as a Navy project, with half really for DHS, so it's an easier political sell."

"Bingo. You've got it. That's why they want the *posse comitatus* opinion. Because these Navy drones are going to be used for domestic police actions. In fact, I think it will primarily become a DHS operation before it's over with. They're going to finish off whatever's left of the Fourth Amendment."

He stopped and gazed at her, and she did not break eye contact.

"So what are you going to do?" She spoke softly.

"I don't know. That's why my stomach is twisted in knots. I mean, in theory, they're asking me for an independent legal opinion. But billions of dollars are riding on this contract. There's no doubt in my mind they want a rubber-stamp opinion saying all is well from a legal standpoint and there would be no violations of *posse comitatus*. But it's not just *posse comitatus* I'm worried about. I'm more worried about the Fourth Amendment."

"Excuse me. Would you all like anything else?"

The waitress was standing over P.J.'s shoulder. Hopefully she hadn't overheard their conversation. Even if she had, she wouldn't understand it. "No thanks, Marilyn. You can bring the check."

"I have it right here for you, sir."

"Thank you."

He glanced at the bill and waited until Marilyn walked back into the bar.

"She's ready to close out," Victoria said.

"Yes, it's closing time." He checked his watch, then extracted sixty dollars from his wallet, put the money in the check holder, and slid it to the middle of the table. "So what do you think I should do?"

"Can I ask a question?" A soft smile.

"Sure."

"Do you remember our oath as officers?"

"Yes."

"What do you remember about it?"

"That we took an oath to defend the Constitution against all enemies, foreign and domestic."

"Then let your oath be your guiding star. That's my advice for you."

Her words had a soothing effect, even if his stomach was still knotted. "I like that." He felt himself smile. He checked his watch again. "It's late. We'd better go. May I walk you to your car?"

"I'd love that."

He stood and got her chair for her, gently touching her back and guiding her off the patio.

"Thank you, sir." Marilyn grinned when she looked at her nice-sized tip.

"My pleasure." He nodded at Marilyn, then led Victoria out onto the sidewalk.

The streetlights revealed the outlines of a few cars still parked alongside the bar. But since it was a weeknight, the street had mostly cleared.

"Where are you parked?" P.J. asked.

"I'm the blue Volvo. Right across the street, just past the park."

They turned left, walking on the sidewalk along the street, past the causeway park. The moon was three-quarters full, casting a dim white glow along the sidewalk to supplement the streetlights at the corner of every block down Royal Street.

"Nice car."

"Thanks." The Volvo beeped and flashed when she pressed the automatic unlock. "It's brand new. I treated myself when I got my orders here. I figured you've got to drive around Washington in style."

A cool breeze wafted in from the river. He stepped to the driver's door and opened it for her.

She looked into his face and smiled, her hand on his arm.

Time froze.

A starry magic descended on the moment, intertwined with a strand of awkwardness.

"P.J., I had a great time. Thank you for the evening."

"It's been my pleasure. Let's do it again."

"I'd like that." She started to get into the car, then stopped and turned to him. "Look, I know this is a tough time for you. But I also know you'll make the right decision. And no matter what you decide, I want you to remember one thing."

"What's that?"

"No matter what, I'm here for you, P.J."

She pulled his face to hers. When their lips touched, the awkwardness yielded to the magic. She drew herself close to him, and the starry canopy above seemed to surround them in the moment.

At some point, at a moment that came all too soon, their lips separated. She turned and, with a continuous smile crossing her face, got into the driver's seat.

She closed the door, rolled down the window, and started the engine as her headlights lit the street.

"Bye." She smiled at him, blew him a kiss, and drove away.

He watched the Volvo's taillights disappear out of view as the car hung a left from Royal Street onto King Street. Then he turned and walked back into another gust of cool breeze.

He pulled out his keys to unlock his black Audi, which was parked by the pub.

His phone sounded in his pocket. A text message.

He smiled. She missed him already! He'd give her a hard time tomorrow about texting and driving. He reached into his pocket for his cell phone.

The smile on his face vanished when he read the text.

Hey, you! It's me! I'll be at the Pentagon Wednesday visiting with ADM Brewer and getting ready for my new duty station.
Wanna go for a run? Like the good ole days? 1300? ☺
I can swing by Code 13, then we can go down to the Pentagon gym, change, and you can show me all the sights in Washington.
Can't wait!
XO, Caroline

Great. He did not immediately respond. Now what?

He got into the Audi, cranked the engine, and drove off into the night.

• • •

WEST SPRINGFIELD APARTMENTS
BURLING WOOD DRIVE
WEST SPRINGFIELD, VIRGINIA
LIEUTENANT VICTORIA FLADAGER'S APARTMENT

With a smile helplessly plastered on her face, Victoria walked up the concrete stairway to the second deck, inserted the master key, and turned it clockwise.

Even with the BAH allowance, the extra pay she got for housing based on the high cost of living in the Washington area wasn't enough for a junior officer to purchase real estate. Military housing, which was scarce, got snapped up so quickly that most naval officers resigned themselves to living in local housing.

So she had rented a modest but functionally adequate apartment in West Springfield, some thirteen miles from the Pentagon, and had tightened her budget to adjust to Washington living.

The lack of affordable housing was one reason she decided to treat herself to the new Volvo. Just because her apartment wasn't five-star didn't mean she couldn't splurge a bit on a car.

At the moment, however, financial budgeting was the last thing on Victoria's mind.

He had pulled her against his muscular, six-foot body, and as she ran her hand through his short brown hair, he'd closed his blue eyes, and she closed hers.

His cologne. His kiss.

Wow.

Perhaps she'd been a bit aggressive by initiating the kiss. But still . . . wow.

Regardless of who initiated it, he certainly cooperated. Oh, did he ever cooperate!

Victoria locked the door behind her and plopped down on the brown leather sofa in the living room, a smile still plastered on her face, her heart bubbling like a quart of festive champagne.

There was only one problem.

She had already heard the rumors. The Navy JAG Corps was a small community, and officers in the JAG Corps talked. It was odd that he had never mentioned her. Even tonight, with his mind on the drone project, she thought he might have mentioned her. But no, it was like she was the taboo subject, the elephant in the room.

Of course, from what Victoria had heard, Lieutenant Commander Caroline McCormick was anything but an elephant. More like a sleek tigress—fit, trim, and beautiful.

According to the rumor mill, they had been serious, to the point of marriage, even—or so the gossips said. In this case, Victoria's Justice School classmate Lieutenant Christie Perry, who was stationed in San Diego, had been her principal source of intelligence.

Victoria had done her homework by putting in several calls to Christie after she'd gotten to Code 13 and noticed the solid, muscular eye-candy minding his own business sitting over in the Legislation and FOIA section, serving as a guaranteed distraction to any woman's eyes that might wander in his direction.

"Oh my gosh!" Christie had said. "Vickie, I should have warned you when you got your orders to Code 13 from Norfolk. Like, every single female JAG officer was in love with this guy. I mean, P.J. MacDonald could pass for a young Cary Grant. But he and Caroline McCormick were such a hot item that nobody had a chance. Then when they broke up, everybody lined up."

"Do you know why they broke up?" Victoria had asked.

"Who knows? He must have done it. No woman in her right mind would drop that guy. I heard it was because he got orders back east and they didn't want a long-distance relationship."

Great.

They broke up because they didn't think they could maintain a long-distance relationship. And now, in a matter of days, they would be in the same city again.

How blissfully convenient.

Of course, what could she say? She had used the same "long-distance relationship" line when she broke up with Mark a month ago. She'd felt guilty about it. After all, was Norfolk to Washington really that long a distance? Come on. The 195 miles that separated her from Mark hardly mirrored a cross-continent move, like the real long-distance relationship between P.J. and Lieutenant Commander Lover Girl, which unfortunately was about to be long distance no longer.

The three-and-a-half-hour drive separating Norfolk and Washington wouldn't have doused the sizzle between them if there had been a sizzle to begin with.

Mark could figure out that her "long-distance relationship" excuse was bogus. He was a smart guy. But even though the split-up was hard, he never argued about her excuse. He was too much of a gentleman.

If Mark was guilty of anything, it was being too polite, clean, handsome, and considerate. It was sort of nice to have someone get the door for her, to send her flowers, to remember not only her birthday but also her parents' birthdays. In fact, Mark Romanov was the kind of guy who would be on every mother's approved list. That was part of the problem. He had no flaws.

Plus, he worked as a CPA for a "Big Eight" accounting firm in Virginia Beach before joining the Naval Criminal Investigative Service as an investigator with a focus on fraud.

That, too, was part of the problem.

She wanted another naval officer. Not an auditor. Not even an auditor who worked as an investigator for NCIS. The TV show *NCIS* had never matched the excitement of the *JAG* television series. And like so many millions of young women, she had secretly fallen in love with Commander Harmon Rabb.

A little nasty streak in a man. That turned her on. Not the angel Gabriel.

Still, after she arrived in Washington for her change of duty station, she found herself thinking of Mark—missing him, in fact, from time to time—until the day she reported to Code 13 and laid her eyes on Lieutenant Commander P.J. MacDonald. Victoria knew instantly, in that moment when their eyes first met, that she had met her own Commander Harm!

But now, Lieutenant Commander Lover Girl was about to burst back onto the scene.

In fact, Captain Guy had mentioned that McCormick might be visiting the Pentagon as soon as tomorrow. Not to formally report for duty yet, but just to meet the officers at JAG and at Code 13.

The idea of having to call Caroline McCormick "ma'am" had already gotten under Victoria's skin, and she hadn't even met the witch yet.

She needed another glass of wine.

No, that would be dumb. She'd wake up at three in the morning with a dry mouth and would feel like a worthless wreck tomorrow. She wanted to look her best tomorrow. Especially if Lieutenant Commander Lover Girl decided to show. Scratch the wine idea.

She got up off the sofa, walked across the room, and sat down at her desk. She decided to check her email.

Let's see . . . junk . . . junk . . . delete . . . Oh, there's one from Christie. She clicked on the email to open it.

Hi, Vickie . . . just a heads-up. I found out she will be at the Pentagon Wednesday. Don't worry. She can't compete with you. ☺

Love ya.

Christie

Oh great. Tell me something I don't know, Christie.
She went back to her email list.
Spam. Spam. Her eyes narrowed. *What's this?*

From: Aconcernedfriend@idbecareful.net
Subj: What you did tonight

I'd be careful dot net? What's that? She clicked open the email.

Lieutenant Fladager,
You were being watched tonight. I saw your display outside the Grape + Bean. Word to the wise. I wouldn't let it happen again.
A concerned friend

What the . . . ? Ice-cold shivers descended from the back of her head all the way down her spine.

What kind of creepy nut job would do something like this? Somebody was watching them. What to do? Call the cops?

No. That accomplished nothing. All they would do was take a report, but the local cops didn't have the resources to track this down.

Maybe she should call P.J.

But what could he do? Maybe she would talk to him about it later.

Her heart started to race. *The door. Did I lock the door?*

She got up and jogged back to the door. *Oh my gosh, I forgot to dead-bolt it.*

She dead-bolted the front door, then walked to her bedroom.

Her heart pounded. Her forehead felt clammy, and her hands seemed sweaty. Maybe she should call 911. But they would just send the local cops out, who would take a police report, leave, and solve nothing.

Maybe she should go to a hotel for the night.

But what if someone was already out there? Waiting for her the minute she stepped out of the apartment? But who could she call?

Then it hit her.

Yet every bit of her internal instinct screamed, *No! Don't make the call.* They'd already ended it. What if he took it the wrong way?

But competing against her instinct, her thumping heart screamed, *Call! Call now! He'll know what to do!*

His number had stayed on her speed dial. She had vowed to erase it. And now she was glad she didn't.

She closed her eyes and punched the number.

One ring.

Two rings.

"Hi, baby, what's going on?"

His greeting made her queasy. She cut to the point. "Mark, I think I'm in trouble."

"What are you talking about?"

"I think somebody just threatened me."

"What are you talking about? Who?"

"Well, I just got home a few minutes ago and opened this email, and there was this weird message that sounded like a threat."

"What did it say?"

"It was creepy. It was like somebody was watching me the whole night. The email was just creepy."

"Was there a direct threat?"

"No. Not exactly."

"Can you forward the email to me?"

She hesitated. "Sure. Hang on. Let me get my laptop."

"Take your time."

She picked up her laptop, went to the email, and clicked the *forward* option. She hit the *M* key and Mark's email address popped up. She held her breath and clicked the Send button. "Okay. Just sent it."

"Hang on." A second passed. "I've got it. Give me a chance to read it."

A few seconds passed. "Okay, it doesn't look like a direct threat, but I suppose it could be construed as an indirect threat."

"Exactly. That's one of the reasons I didn't call 911. The local cops would say it's not a direct threat, and they'd be too obtuse to see the subtlety of the definite indirect threat."

"Can't disagree with that. What is this Grape and Bean place?"

"Oh, just kind of a local bar in Alexandria."

"What? Were you on a date or something?"

Why did he have to ask this question? Then again, she wasn't surprised. "No," she said, lying. "Just out drinking with some JAG officers. That was it."

Silence.

"Mark? You there?"

"Yes, I'm here. I was just thinking."

"What should I do?"

"You know, Norfolk's not that far. Do you want me to drive up? Just say the word. I can be in DC in four hours."

"No. That won't be necessary. But thanks anyway."

A pause. She could tell he wanted to come. And even though she didn't want him here, she had almost said yes. Which was why she was reluctant to call him to begin with.

"Okay, listen. This is probably some kind of practical joke by some crackpot. There's probably nothing to worry about. And because there's technically not a threat, you're right, the local cops wouldn't even consider it a threat, and even if this crackpot had specifically threatened to do something to physically harm you, they couldn't figure out how to track the guy anyway.

"But here's what I'm going to do. I'm going to call our NCIS branch in Washington, and we'll have some agents come out and watch your place for the evening. You won't know they're there, but we have agents available for protective detail of naval personnel, and if I make the call, they'll comply."

She sighed with relief. "Thank you, Mark."

"I'll need your address to tell them where to go. You can just shoot me an email with it if you'd like."

"Sure. Thanks."

"And there are just a couple more things I need you to promise me."
She hesitated. "Okay. What?"

"First, if you see or hear anything tonight, call me immediately, and I'll notify our NCIS guys on the ground. You promise?"

"Yes. Of course."

"And the second thing is this. Do you still have that little 9-millimeter you used to have when we were dating?"

"Yes. It's in the drawer beside my bed."

"Well, if you haven't done it already, I want you to load it and keep it nearby tonight, wherever you are in your apartment. If anybody tries to enter your place without your permission, I want you to use it. Can you do that for me?"

"Sure."

"So give me a call if you suspect anything at all is out of the ordinary. Okay?"

"Okay."

"Don't worry," he said. "I miss you."

"Thank you," she said.

"Talk to you soon?"

She hesitated again. "Sure, and thanks for everything, Mark. I need to go check my gun."

"Okay, be safe. Night."

"Good night."

She picked up the 9-millimeter Glock from the drawer beside her bed and stepped over to her dresser. The ammunition clip already had ten rounds preloaded. She popped the clip into the base of the pistol grip and chambered a bullet, then walked back into the living room and plopped into her leather club chair, keeping her eyes glued on the door.

It was going to be a long night.

CHAPTER 8

• • •

RACQUETBALL COURTS
CONGRESSIONAL GYMNASIUM
BASEMENT OF RAYBURN HOUSE OFFICE BUILDING
CAPITOL HILL
TUESDAY MORNING

"Come on, move your feet!" United States Senator Charles E. "Chuckie" Rodino, D-NY, screamed at the top of his voice. Then he smashed the ball hard against the front wall, unleashing a furious reverberation against the spit-polished walls of the enclosed racquetball court inside the mysterious congressional gym.

The lightning-fast pace of the ball, rocketing against the back and side walls and off the varnished wooden floors, required quick footwork and hand-eye coordination to master the game. In this sport, understood by few and enjoyed by the privileged, the junior senator from New York excelled as one of the best in the United States Congress.

His opponent today—or rather, his "next victim"—the term Rodino preferred—was the brash, outspoken Democrat congressman from Boston, William O. "Mackey" Milk.

"Twelve-eight!" Rodino shouted, announcing the new score just as the ball he'd smashed against the side wall sailed beyond Milk's reach.

"You're killing me, Chuckie!" Milk squeaked in a frustrated voice.

"Shut up and take your medicine, Mackey," Rodino quipped.

"Oh? You're going to give me some medicine?" Milk gave him a mischievous wink.

Rodino stepped up to the service line, bounced the rubber ball three times, and shook his head. "Play ball like a real man, Milk."

"Like a *real man*? Chuckie, if I didn't know about your pro-gay voting record, I could swear that you're bullying a gay man!"

"I *am* bullying a gay man." Rodino chuckled. "And don't be fooled by my pro-gay voting record. I need the votes from all your cousins and boyfriends from Lower Manhattan."

"I love you, Chuckie Rodino!" Milk chuckled.

Rodino shook his head, bounced the ball on the floor again, and said, "Take this, Milk." Then he smashed another serve against the front wall.

This time Milk got his racquet on the serve, setting off another flurry of exchanges, back and forth, back and forth, extending the rally, like a couple of Ping-Pong players locked in a game of waiting for the other to make the first mistake.

Chuckie Rodino was possessive of his early-morning time in the once-obscure congressional gym, located in the murky, windowless basement of the Rayburn House Office Building.

But the mysterious gymnasium wasn't the well-kept secret it once had been, ever since a sexaholic former Democrat congressman from New York made it notorious by taking pictures of his disgustingly half-naked body and sending texts to young interns, or when a half-naked White House chief of staff, with just a towel wrapped around his waist, would emerge from the congressional showers beside the courts and, screaming and cursing, poke his political opponents and even his fellow party members in the chest and demand that they fall in line and cooperate with whatever Obama wanted.

Despite the fact that Anthony Weiner's and Rahm Emanuel's actions had lifted the veil of obscurity shrouding this place, Rodino found something mesmerizing about the history of it all, and found something attractively brash about what Weiner and Emanuel had done. Even in Weiner's case, there was something about his brashness, his boldness, his swagger that Chuckie admired.

"Senator Rodino!"

The ball sailed past his racquet, causing him to lose serve, which set off a guttural string of unfettered profanity. He turned toward the staffer who was about to get blamed.

"Louie! What are you doing here? You know I've got this 8:00 a.m. time blocked for play with my buddy Congressman Milkey." Milkey was the half-affectionate, half-sarcastic pet name Chuckie sometimes used to razz his buddy. "Now you've caused me to lose serve!"

"Sorry, sir," the skinny young staffer said. "But you've got a phone call I thought you may want to take."

"Look, Louie," Chuckie snapped, "unless you've got either Bill or Hillary or Obama himself on that line, it will have to wait until I finish polishing off Congressman Milk here. Got that?" He tossed the ball to Milk. "Your serve."

"It's from a guy named Vinnie, Senator. He said Phil told him to call." Chuckie turned around and, with bricks suddenly in his stomach, looked at his staffer.

"He called on your private line, sir. And since we know only a few people have that number, we assumed you gave it to him. He insisted that he talk to you. He said you would want to talk to him. But I can tell him you aren't available."

"No. Hang on! Don't hang up." He turned to Milk and held up his index finger. "Mackey, give me a minute."

"Sure, Senator."

"You got him on the phone now?"

"Right here." The staffer held up the iPhone, wagging it in the air.

"Tell him I'll be right with him."

"Yes, sir."

Chuckie waited as the aide asked the caller to hold a second, then took the iPhone. He stepped outside of the racquetball court, leaving Louie and Milk inside, and walked into the congressional locker room.

Chuckie looked around to make sure he had privacy, then brought the phone up to his ear. "This is Senator Rodino. May I help you?"

"Chuckie!" The caller stretched out his pronunciation as if they were lifelong bosom buddies. "This is Vinnie! What's up with all the formal 'This is Senator Rodino' stuff? I thought we were best pals."

"Vinnie." He spoke in a hushed voice. "I told you never to call on this line."

"Chuckie. Hey. What are friends for? I mean, a true friend reminds us of our roots, right? I mean, take our mutual buddy Phil. He said you would understand. He also said his uncle Sal said you would understand."

Blood boiled in Chuckie's neck, and his stomach knotted into a twisted mess.

"Ya still there, Chuckie?"

"I'm still here. What do you want?"

"I need to see you face-to-face. Meet me in two hours. Hank's Oyster Bar on Pennsylvania Avenue."

"Vinnie, it's eight in the morning. Bars on Capitol Hill don't open until later in the day."

"It'll be open for you, Chuckie. It's a seafood bar. We got connections. Remember?"

The line went dead.

CHAPTER 9

...

P.J. sat at his workstation. At nine o'clock in the morning, his eyes were already burned into the screen of his laptop as he conducted more legal research on Fourth Amendment issues.

Which way to go?

Already he'd written two different drafts of his opinion letter, one with one result, one with the other.

Part of him wanted to get it over with already. He knew what they all wanted. They wanted him to buck his own conscience and rubber-stamp this thing.

Part of him hoped a case would come down from the Supreme Court that would give him enough legal cover to kill the project before it got started.

At the moment, he was studying a recent U.S. Supreme Court opinion favoring the good guys. That is, if one defined the good guys as anyone interested in preserving the Constitution and opposing turning America into a police state.

But on June 25, 2014, the United States Supreme Court, despite an inconsistent, spotty track record on constitutional questions in the last ten years, finally got one right. In *Riley v. California*, the high court ruled unanimously, in a 9–0 vote, disagreeing with the Obama Justice Department, holding that police must get a warrant before snooping on people's cell phones.

What a rare, refreshing victory for the Fourth Amendment. The same justices who mucked up the Obamacare ruling in a divided 5–4 split were, finally, on the same page.

"Let's see," he mumbled under his breath. "Could I cite this case to argue that random drone surveillance would require a warrant? I mean, nine to zero is a strong vote." He moved his mouse over the court's opinion, copied it, and pasted it into his research file.

His desktop phone rang.

"Code 13. Legislation, Regulations, and FOIA. Lieutenant Commander MacDonald speaking. This is a nonsecure line subject to monitoring. May I help you, sir or ma'am?"

"Boy, that's a mouthful. Is that the way I'm going to have to answer the phone when I report for duty?"

Instinctively he looked over at Victoria, who sat in her cubicle about twenty feet away. Victoria's eyes shot over at him as if she knew who was on the other line.

With the final draft of this opinion due in less than forty-eight hours, the last thing he needed was a looming, hissing catfight on top of everything else. But what could he do about it? It wasn't his idea to station both at the same duty station with him, at the Pentagon, in the most elite, selective appointment in the Navy JAG Corps.

It *was* his idea to ask Victoria out to wine.

But the long kiss wasn't his idea.

But he'd done nothing to stop it either.

In fact, he'd very much enjoyed it, which at the moment compounded the gut-wrenching flood of guilt drenching his stomach.

"Well, whether you answer the phone like that depends on if you want to kiss up to the captain."

She giggled. "P.J., you know I've never been much on kissing up. Especially not to a captain."

"You got that right." He glanced at Victoria, who thankfully had turned her eyes back to her computer screen. "The Caroline McCormick I know never kisses up to anybody."

She laughed again. He had almost forgotten how he enjoyed that velvety laugh of hers. "Hey, what are you doing around 1300 tomorrow?"

He checked his watch. "Same ole routine. I'll do lunch, probably grab something from the Center Courtyard Café and bring it back to the office, then maybe PT if I have time."

"Did you get my text?"

"Ah . . . yes." *Why do I have the feeling you could have been watching me just before you texted me?* "Sorry. I was going to respond, but one thing led to another."

"Same ole P.J." She laughed. "You're still using that old flip phone that gets delayed messages, aren't you?"

He forced a chuckle in return. "I know. But you know me. One of the last holdouts resisting the peer pressure to stick a minicomputer in my pocket."

She laughed again. "Now, P.J. MacDonald, I thought for sure when you moved to Washington they would have made you move into the twenty-first century."

"Not quite yet. I'm still rebelling because of all those people and teenyboppers who always keep their noses glued to their smartphones. Those things are turning us into a nation of sheeple. One of these days this old flip phone will wear out, and then they won't be selling them anymore. Because they'll all be obsolete, I won't have any choice. Heck, it was the last one in the store when I bought it."

"Well . . . as a matter of fact, if you got my text, you know I'm going to be at the Pentagon tomorrow afternoon to see Admiral Brewer and then pop into the offices at Code 13 to say hi to everyone."

"Super. I heard you might be stopping by soon." An awkward pause. "So when are you officially reporting for duty?"

"Friday, it looks like. Unless Captain Guy has other ideas. I'll be in Section 134 handling Command Authority Issues."

"Super. That's what I heard." *At least they're not putting her over in Ethics with Victoria.*

"But listen," she said. "I have a proposition for you."

"Oh really? What kind of proposition?"

"Well, you said you might PT later on. Think you could delay your PT to about 1300 and maybe take me out for a run?"

He checked his watch. "You said 1300? Well, the problem is I've got this legal opinion due to SECNAV in less than forty-eight hours."

"Aw, come on, P.J. If I know you, you've already got the draft done of whatever you're doing, and you've probably already edited it several times and don't want to submit it before you have to because you want the final draft to be perfect."

He chuckled. "You do know me, don't you?"

"Some things a girl doesn't forget."

"I've got a feeling there's not much you forget."

She laughed. "Okay, I'll stop by around 1300, say hello, then maybe we can go down to the locker room, change, and you can take me out for a jogging tour of Washington."

P.J. glanced at Victoria's darting eyes. "Okay, that would be great. See you then."

CHAPTER 10

• • •

Richardson DeKlerk brought the glass to his lips, sipping his first spot of brandy for the day. He checked the clock on the wall. *9:30 a.m.*

Normally he didn't start drinking until noon so he could get in a full morning's work without being under the influence. But the utter incompetence of both Jack Patterson and Bobby Talmadge had driven him to an early-morning swig. He drained the liquor down his esophagus and thought some more.

Perhaps Jack wasn't all that incompetent. At least he had gotten a dossier on these Navy lawyers who were holding up his billion-dollar contract in the cryptic office in the Pentagon called Code 13.

Of course, Jack *should* have gotten the dossier on the obstructionist bureaucrat JAG lawyers for the hourly rate that he'd been paid. A thousand dollars an hour should have gotten more than a dossier. In fact, Richardson could have hired four or five private detectives to dig up the same information.

But in Jack's expensive defense, at least he got the job done. Information costs money. And in many cases, it costs a lot of money.

With another swash of the intoxicating brew, Richardson picked up the dossier, provided by Jack's firm today, and glanced over it again.

From: Jack Patterson, Esq.
To: Richardson DeKlerk, CEO AirFlite Corp
Subj: U.S. Navy Internal Legal Procedures for Approval of Contract—Project Blue Jay
Classification: Confidential

a. You asked us to investigate internal U.S. Navy legal procedures for legislative approval of contracts and, in particular, the top-secret project known as "Blue Jay." As a result, the following is provided:

b. Internal U.S. Navy regulations require full legal vetting of acquisitions contracts for major military systems to ensure full legal compliance.

c. Within the Office of the Navy Judge Advocate General, the legal division responsible for providing such advice is the JAG's Administrative Law Division, also known as Code 13.

d. Based upon reliance on strategic contacts in the Pentagon, we have learned that the action officer assigned to write the opinion letter to the Secretary of the Navy on the legality of the proposed deployment of drones under the contract is Lieutenant Commander P.J. MacDonald, JAGC, USN.

e. A graduate of the College of William and Mary and the University of Virginia School of Law, LCDR MacDonald has been instructed to provide an opinion letter to the Secretary of the Navy on the legality of the proposed usage of the drones under the contract, if approved by Congress.

f. Principally at issue, and under consideration by LCDR MacDonald, are (1) *posse comitatus* implications of the

Navy overseeing the drone project for use by domestic law enforcement (Homeland Security) over U.S. territory, and (2) Fourth Amendment sustainability under the federal government's self-declared Constitution-Free Zone.

g. LCDR MacDonald has been ordered to clear up these issues in anticipation of libertarian and Tea Party opposition in Congress to the project, with the expectation that opposition may be raised on these grounds.

h. Intercepted emails from classified sources in the JAG chain of command indicate that LCDR MacDonald may be wavering in his opinion. Should MacDonald recommend to the Secretary of the Navy that the projected purposes are illegal or unconstitutional, the effect upon the Secretary would be unclear.

i. Recommend continued correspondence with congressional liaisons to apply political pressure on MacDonald's superiors.

Sincerely yours,
Jack

Richardson leaned back in his chair and tossed the memorandum on his desk. The two-page letter probably cost AirFlite twenty-five thousand dollars. That would be twelve and a half grand a page! Maybe more.

He decided not to glance at the invoice when it arrived. He would let Ivana read it and tell her to pay the bill without even telling him.

He picked up the telephone. "Ivana."

"Yes, sir."

"Would you come in here, please? And bring me another drink. Then I need your help with something."

"Certainly, sir."

He glanced at the twenty-five-thousand-dollar memorandum

again, for the third time, and made a decision. Something needed to be done about this P.J. MacDonald character. No midlevel naval officer was going to stop this contract. Not now. Not ever.

A knock on his office door.

"Come in."

The door cracked open. Ivana, wearing a fitted white-and-gold dress that ended above her knees, smiled at him.

"Your drinks, sir." Her voice was cheery, and she carried a silver tray holding another glass, a glass pitcher of ice cubes, and two different liquor flasks. He loved her walk almost as much as he loved her velvety, Czech accent.

"I know you were drinking cognac, sir. So I brought you another flask of that. And in case you wanted to switch up, I also brought you a flask of scotch."

"Set it on the desk, Ivana."

At that point he noticed it. The gold ankle bracelet dazzled against her tanned ankle, just above her white pumps.

She stepped over toward his desk. "Certainly, sir."

Was that flirtatiousness in her voice?

"Would you like another glass?"

"Sure." When she stepped behind his desk to pour his drink, he caught a whiff of her perfume. The rock on her finger glistened as she drained the drink into his glass. Perhaps a half carat at most.

What a waste for a woman so enticing to be tied up with a boring engineer.

She turned and started walking away. "Ivana?"

She turned around. "Yes, sir?"

"May I ask you a question?"

"Certainly, sir."

"Did anyone ever tell you that you bear a striking resemblance to the former Russian tennis star Anna Kournikova?"

Her pretty face brightened. "You think I resemble Anna Kournikova?"

"Actually," he said, "the resemblance is quite striking."

"Thank you." A kittenish grin crossed her lips. "She is a beautiful lady."

He responded quickly. "She has nothing on you, my dear."

Her smile broadened. Her eyes glistened with a sparkling bluish hue.

"I think you are a handsome man." Her velvety accent thickened. "So much in control." She put her hand on his shoulder. "Such a strong visionary."

He stood up and pulled her close to him. Their kiss was instant, electric. Why had he waited this long? He did not wish to stop, but the thought of the unexecuted contract distracted him from the excitement of the moment, and he pushed her away.

"Is something wrong?" A look of longing settled into her eyes. "You do not like my kisses?"

"Nothing is wrong. I love your kisses. And I hope to kiss you again."

"Do you promise?" She moved in, closer to him, as if coming for more.

"Yes. Of course." He stopped her advance with his hands. "But we have work to do. First I want you to get me Senator Talmadge on the phone. Then, after that, I want you to get Jack Patterson on the line."

"Yes, sir." Her face looked both disappointed and starry-eyed. "I shall get the senator for you right away."

She turned and walked toward the door, and he gazed at her as she left the room. Why had he pushed her away? She was there for the taking. Right in his office. Then he remembered. As much as he loved women, he loved money and power more. The more he poured into a woman, the more money he would lose.

Best to enjoy them in spurts but keep them at a healthy distance.

Her intoxicating voice, this time with a bit more spark than usual, oozed through his intercom. "Senator Talmadge is on the phone, sir. Line one."

Richardson picked up line one. "How is my favorite United States senator today?"

A chuckle from the voice on the other line. "I hope you're referring to me as your favorite senator, Richardson." Another nervous-sounding, bookend chuckle.

Not a good sign, this nervousness in Talmadge's voice. "Well, let me put it this way, Bobby. If I was in fact referring to you when I used the phrase 'my favorite United States senator,' then the continued use of that phrase might well depend upon the status of the little project I've asked you to work on."

"Well, I—"

"Put it this way, Bobby," Richardson interrupted. "For some of us, there's a fine line between having a favorite senator and having a senator we are determined to see defeated in the next election, and are prepared to spend millions of dollars either way."

"I know, Richardson. You're calling about the drone project."

"Actually, ole boy, I thought you would have already called me with some positive news. But the sound of your voice doesn't seem so jolly."

"My apologies. I've not forgotten you, and I understand what this AirFlite project means to the economy in Savannah and southeastern Georgia. I hope you'll give me the privilege of being part of that ribbon-cutting ceremony. It's going to be a great day for the Peach State, Richardson. And I'm going to recommend that the governor put you in for the Governor's Economic Development Award."

Richardson pulled out his desk drawer, extracted his .38 caliber revolver, popped open the empty cylinder, and started spinning it. "My dear senator, you should know that I couldn't care less about any feel-good political award the governor of Georgia, or any other politician, for that matter, might bestow on me for political purposes." He started loading bullets into the chamber. "I can buy my own awards anytime I want."

He finished loading the gun and popped the cylinder back into place, then brought the gun to his mouth and blew his breath onto the barrel, caressing the barrel with his finger, allowing the touch of his finger on the barrel to ignite an irresistible tingling that spread throughout his body. "What I want is an executed contract."

He aimed the gun at the door, imagining that either Senator Bobby Talmadge or that meddlesome Navy officer from the Pentagon who was playing the dangerous role of obstructionist to Richardson's aims would dare walk through the door at that moment.

"Don't worry, I—"

"Don't worry? Did you just tell me not to worry?"

"Well, yes. Look, I have an appointment to talk with Senator Fowler today. You know, he's the most powerful member of the U.S. Senate. He's the chair of the Armed Services Com—"

"Yes, I know who Fowler is. Spare me the patronizing. What I want is action. So tell me why I don't have a signed contract yet."

"They . . . Look, I expect the Navy to approve within the next couple of days. Then it's clear sailing. Don't worry."

Richardson took a swig of liquor. "Do you even know who in the Navy is responsible for pushing it along?"

"Yes, of course. The Secretary of the Navy. And I expect—"

"Do you know what's holding up the Secretary of the Navy?"

"Uh, I believe he's waiting on approval from the Navy JAG."

"Why is the Navy JAG delaying?"

"I, uh, I'm sure it's a matter of processing some paperwork. Look, everybody wants this project—"

"A matter of processing paperwork?"

"Could I please finish, Richardson?"

"You're going to be finished if you don't get this contract through the Navy and then through Congress. Since your people don't know as much as my people, let me enlighten you."

"Richardson—"

"Don't Richardson me, Senator."

"Okay, okay."

Richardson picked up the twenty-five-thousand-dollar memo, but his fingers shook with anger to the point that he couldn't even read it. "Give me a second, Senator."

"Okay, Richardson. Take your time."

Richardson inhaled, then slowly exhaled, then repeated the process. "Okay, Bobby. Let me educate you, since my own private sources seem to be superior to the offices of your almighty United States Senate office. So let me see." There. He saw the name. "The officer who seems to be causing all the problems is a Lieutenant Commander P.J. MacDonald in an office under the Navy JAG they call Code 13. Our sources say this MacDonald chap is wavering on this contract and may be planning to recommend to the Secretary of the Navy that it's not legally defensible. Did you know that, Bobby?"

"Well, I . . ."

"Don't stumble around on me, Senator. Did you know that, or did you not know that?"

Talmadge hesitated. "Well, we knew it's in the JAG's hands, but we didn't have that level of detail."

"I didn't think so. I'm more than disappointed at your inaction and ignorance. So my patience is running out." He waited a second. No response. "Let me ask you, Bobby. Have you heard of Georgia State Representative Billy Ray Oliver, Republican of Fayette County?"

A delayed response. "He's a rookie representative. I don't know him personally, but I hear he's a fine young man with a bright future in the party."

"Yes, well, but from what I'm hearing, that fine young man, as you call him, may have his eyes set on becoming a United States senator from the great state of Georgia."

Another hesitation. "Well, if he's conservative enough, we need to be grooming bright political talent up through the ranks so they're ready when the time's right."

"I'm glad you feel that way, because from what I'm hearing, the kid may be ready to become a senator sooner rather than later."

"I don't follow you, Richardson."

"Oh, I think you understand. Because of his conservative voting record in the State House, he's catching the attention of the national Tea Party. Some are even saying young Billy Ray ought to take a shot at you in the primary."

Silence on the other end. "Are you threatening me, Richardson?"

"It's taken you this long to figure that out? Yes, I'm threatening you. You can either serve your constituents or expect a challenge."

"Look, there's no reason to feel this way. We're gonna get this done. I promise."

"You'd better get it done!" Richardson slammed down the phone, half satisfied that he was among a small handful of people in the state of Georgia who could slam down the phone on a United States senator and get away with it, but at the same time boiling with anger that his handpicked choice for United States senator had not delivered.

At the moment, his rage at Talmadge exceeded his self-satisfaction in having hung up on him.

He punched his desk intercom.

"Ivana."

"Yes, sir?"

"Get Jack Patterson on the phone now."

"Yes, sir. Right away, sir."

Richardson stood, picked up his liquor glass, and walked over to the bay window overlooking the Savannah River. In perfect V formation, three seagulls swooped in from the right, from the direction of the Atlantic toward the port facilities downtown, their white feathers a bright contrast to the river's blue water and the marshes swaying in the breeze along the way.

Soon his drones would be flying in formation over every major river in the nation. There would be no political prejudices in his marketing, no limits to his customer base. Like the Bank of England, the Federal Reserve, and other international banks that had financed both sides of wars since the 1700s, AirFlite would sell drones and other airborne weapons to all sides!

But first, this obstructionist commander in the Pentagon would need to be dealt with.

His desk intercom buzzed. "Mr. DeKlerk, Mr. Patterson is on the line for you."

"Bring me a portable phone and another drink, Ivana. Make it a bourbon."

"Yes, sir."

Ivana walked in with a portable phone and a glass of bourbon, handed them to him, and turned around and walked out.

"Jack, you cost me almost as much money as what it cost me to buy elections to get some of these idiot Georgia bozos elected to federal office. But I'll say this. At least you get things done."

"Thanks, Richardson. Does this mean I should raise my rates?"

"Don't push your luck. I'm not in a joking mood."

"Yes, I can hear that in your voice. What's up?"

Richardson sipped his liquor, then stepped out onto the balcony.

"Still there, Jack?"

"Still here, Richardson. Take your time."

"That's part of the problem. Too many people are taking their bloody good time. Like that ungrateful rookie Republican U.S. senator I put into office. I don't have any time to take, Jack. Do you understand?"

"Bobby Talmadge giving you a hard time? I'm sure he wants this contract as much as we do."

"I'm sure he wants the project, because it will make him look good politically. But he isn't moving fast enough, and I still don't have a contract."

"When did you last talk to him?"

"A few minutes ago."

"What did he say?"

"Cheesy political talk. He promised to talk to Roberson Fowler and assured me everything would be okay."

"I'm sure he'll talk to Fowler. Fowler's a powerful guy in the U.S. Senate. He's the oldest rat in the Republican barn. Get him on board, and this project is a done deal."

"I don't have time for all that!"

"How can I help?"

"I got your memo about the problem we're running into with this Navy commander."

"Right. From what I understand, this MacDonald guy is a maverick officer who more or less marches to his own tune."

"Excuse me, but tell me how a midlevel officer in the Pentagon can wield such power. To me this makes no sense. Why doesn't some admiral order him to write this paper—or whatever it is—to push the contract through?"

"Well, you know, I never served in the military. That was a fantasy I never fulfilled. I always wanted to be a Navy JAG. But after the NFL didn't work out, I got married, went to law school—"

"I'm not paying you to reminisce about your unfulfilled professional fantasies!"

"Sorry. Here was my point: I've researched the JAG and know a little about it. To answer your question, the JAG officers are charged with rendering independent legal opinions. Now, this MacDonald is an action officer at the Pentagon. His job as part of this Code 13 group is to provide independent legal opinions to the Secretary of the Navy. He's been ordered to research the legality of this project. Once he submits his opinion, the Secretary is free to accept it or reject it. And other JAG officers get to comment on it too."

"Will the Secretary of the Navy accept MacDonald's recommendation?"

Jack hesitated. "Richardson, I don't know. I don't know the Secretary of the Navy. I do think the Navy wants this contract, though. It would be a major coup to be awarded the largest drone contract in the history of the world, and especially over the Air Force.

"But on the other hand, a negative opinion from MacDonald is not good. My concern is this: While I don't think a negative legal opinion from the action officer will kill the project from the Navy's standpoint, I think it could put the brakes on the project. The Navy might delay and demand tweaks in the operational plans until they feel like they can deal with the objections of these Ron Paul–worshipping libertarian types in Congress who will oppose this contract from the day it's announced like white on rice."

"Unacceptable!" Richardson stepped back inside and flung the glass of liquor across the office, smashing it into the far wall, sending shards of glass everywhere. Raindrops of liquor rolled down the wall. "Delays cost millions! Delays will not be tolerated!"

Three quick knocks on the door. "Sir, is everything okay?"

"Yes, I'm fine, Ivana!" he yelled. "Hang on, Jack."

"Sure, Richardson."

He waited a second to check his composure, then lowered his

voice to just above a whisper. "Jack, what do you know about this MacDonald?"

"Probably more than his own mother knows, unless he's told his mother that he's falling into an embarrassing love triangle. Recently broke up with another JAG officer, a Lieutenant Commander Caroline McCormick. They were hot and heavy when he was stationed in San Diego. Now he's playing footsie with a new potential love interest, a Lieutenant Victoria Fladager, a hot little firecracker of a redhead JAG officer. McCormick doesn't know about Fladager, and this could get interesting, because they're all about to be stationed at the Pentagon at this Code 13 together."

Richardson thought for a second. "You've certainly done your homework."

"That's what you pay us for. I've not even sent you the full dossier—only what we intercepted about his thinking on the drone contract. We know more. His immediate boss made the mistake of sending a couple of confidential emails up the chain, which we intercepted. My sources leave no stones uncovered, Richardson."

"I take it since your firm has managed to gather data by whatever means on this MacDonald that you could, for example, track his movements anywhere, anytime?"

Patterson snickered. "Put it this way. As long as you're willing to spend the money, we can track him anywhere, anytime, as long as he's not inside a U.S. military installation or on a warship out to sea."

"I don't even want to know what I had to spend for this dossier."

"No, you don't," Patterson quipped. "But at least I got you results, unlike your buddy up there in the senate. Just proves you can get a lot more done by hiring a lawyer than hiring a politician."

Richardson did not immediately respond. As high-priced as Jack was, he had a point. And Jack's services went beyond legal services. Quarterbacking investigations. Numerous private investigator contacts in every city in America. Experts capable of intercepting emails, texts, and cell phone conversations.

Jack had already given him more information about this MacDonald character than Talmadge had, but there was no point in acknowledging that Jack got results. No point in stroking his ego. That might encourage him to raise his rates even more.

"Listen, Jack. Since you're bragging about your contacts and such, I want you to take care of this MacDonald so he's not a problem blocking this contract anymore. Do you think you can do that?"

No immediate response.

"Is something wrong with your phone, Jack?"

"I'm here." Another pause. "Uh, what do you mean when you say you want me to take care of him?"

"What I mean is that we have millions, maybe billions in profits riding on this contract. That's a ton of profits not only for AirFlite, but also for Patterson & Landry, assuming Patterson & Landry remains principal counsel to AirFlite. I'm sure that thought has crossed your mind. Am I right?"

"Of course. I understand there's a lot riding on this. What are you suggesting, Richardson?"

"I'll leave that up to you. And you're smart enough not to ask questions like that over the phone. But I don't care what you do as long as MacDonald doesn't write a negative legal opinion to the Secretary of the Navy. You take care of MacDonald from your end, and I'll take care of Talmadge from my end. Do you understand me?"

"I understand, Richardson."

"Good. Then let's get to work."

He slammed down the phone, then punched the intercom and told Ivana to bring another drink.

CHAPTER 11

• • •

"I think this is the place, Kristina," Chuckie Rodino said from the back of the nondescript white Ford Taurus used by low-level members of his senate staff. Remaining unrecognized while traveling around Washington, DC, was a challenge for a United States senator.

Yet anonymity was often essential, for various reasons. Chuckie learned early on from some more seasoned members of the Democratic Caucus that scrapping a senatorial-assigned black limo for an unostentatious staff car helped reduce suspicion.

"When should I pick you up, Senator?" The enthusiastic young intern had gotten the job of glorified taxi driver by virtue of her position as vice president of the District of Columbia Young Democrats, and also by the fact that she passed Chuckie's looks test for his intern staff.

"I'll give you a call."

"Yes, sir. I'll be here for you, Senator."

One had to be careful with interns. Some of his foolish colleagues had not been. But Chuckie had not been caught. He was too smart for that.

He stepped out of the passenger side of the car onto the brick sidewalk. Holding his head down, he quick-stepped past the handful of small, black, wrought-iron tables and chairs, entering the hole-in-the-wall joint that was no more than twenty feet in width, called Hank's Oyster Bar.

Inside, a long, single bar with forty or fifty bar stools ran deep into the joint.

A figure sat alone down at the far end, perhaps a hundred feet from the Pennsylvania Street entrance.

"Chuckie!"

"I'm here. What do you want?"

"Come talk to me! The bartender made you a drink. On the house!"

It was the subtle, classic power move. Vinnie wasn't coming to the front to greet him, and in fact wasn't even going to stand.

He hated kissing up to wormy maggots like this. But it was part of the price of power.

Hopefully one day he would be sufficiently powerful that he would never have to kiss up to such scum again.

He walked alongside the long bar, his eyes fixed on the rat sporting the cheese-eating grin. Approaching the human rodent, he stuck out his hand for a shake, a politician's innate instinct whether approaching friend or foe.

"That's all I get?" Vinnie stood up. "A handshake? I thought we were like family." He opened his arms wide. "How about giving your main man a great big bear hug?"

Vinnie wrapped his arms around Chuckie, hugging him like he was a big, fat, Italian teddy bear. As he broke the bear hug, the senator caught a whiff of Vinnie's cologne, which smelled like a mixture of ammonia and mint julep.

"Have a seat." Vinnie pointed to the bar stool right beside his.

Chuckie obliged. "Okay, tell me how I can help you."

"First things first before we start talking business, Chuckie boy. I mean, we're friends. Right?" Another cheesy grin. A jovial, man-pal punch in the arm.

"Yes, Vinnie. We're friends."

"That's more like it. So listen. There's one thing I gotta know."

"What's that?"

"I mean, being such a big, powerful senator, you must get all the women. Matter of fact, the way I hear it, there might be a little switch-hitting involved. You know?" Vinnie laughed. "Maybe a little congressional boy action, too, once in a while?"

Chuckie fumed at the notion of these animals spying on his intimate sexual practices.

"I wouldn't know."

"Hey, hey."

More smiling. More cheese-eating grins. Chuckie would punch this guy, except that would end his political career.

"I hear you can get the pick of the litter, Chuckie!"

Chuckie glanced down at his watch. "So how can I be of service?"

"Relax. We'll get to that." He patted Rodino on the shoulder and swigged his liquor. "So tell your man about these interns. I hear they're among the best perks of being in Congress! And I hear they love Democrats. Gary Condit, Mark Foley, Anthony Weiner, Johnny Edwards. Hey, even the big kahuna, ole Slick Willie himself, had one! Huh? Huh?" More backslapping. "Come on, bro. Give me something juicy!"

Chuckie wanted to punch the guy. "It's not just a Democrat problem, Vinnie. Plenty of Republicans have gotten into trouble too."

"Oh, come on, man. I hear the interns are hot. These young babes are hot. I know you've got a little side thing going with a bunch of 'em, right? It stays here. You can trust your man!"

"There's nothing to say."

"Come on. How about that hot little brunette babe who drove you up here? What's her name? Kristina, ain't it?"

Rodino felt his blood boil with rage. "How do you know who drove me here? And how do you know her name?"

"Chuckie! Chuckie! We're family, bro! Family keeps up with family!"

"Look, let's get to the point. I have a busy schedule. Tell me how my office can help."

"I hear she's a good kisser! Huh? Huh?"

"I'm not sure what Kristina or any other intern—"

"She sure looks good for the camera! Huh?" The rodent plopped a yellow envelope on the bar and slid it over in front of Chuckie. "Huh? Check it out!" Laughter.

His heart pounded at the sight of the envelope. He wanted to rip it to shreds. Sweat beaded on his forehead.

"Go ahead, Chuckie. Check it out. She's a babe. And a great kisser, from what I hear."

What to do? Chuckie followed his instinct. The first photo had been taken inside his senate office. Time mark: 11:15 p.m. The still shot showed him in a white shirt with sleeves rolled up, pushing Kristina McRaven against the wall and kissing her. Her arms were wrapped around his back, and he was clearly cooperating.

The picture had been snapped through his office window, obviously with a telephoto lens.

The second picture showed them in the front seat of his car, at night, in front of her apartment, kissing again. The photo had been enhanced through infrared photography.

Chuckie stuffed the photographs back into the envelope and slid them back to Vinnie. "Very cute."

Vinnie pulled out the first photo, looked at it, and laughed. "So, hey, she looks like a great kisser to me. What do you say, Senator?"

"What's your point?"

"No point. Just that you're a lucky guy."

"You're not planning to let anybody see those pictures?"

"Now, why would I do such a thing? In fact, once you help us the way we need to be helped, we might just forget all these little bitty pickies. Ha-ha!"

It was a classic mobster blackmail power play. Chuckie had heard of it a hundred times. The Washington rumor mill had it that someone had gotten to Republican Chief Justice John Roberts with some sort of threat or blackmail, which was the only rational explanation Chuckie could think of for Roberts's strange switch to author a bizarre opinion upholding the Affordable Care Act on a "taxation" theory that not even the Obama administration lawyers had advocated.

Now Chuckie was staring a blackmail power play right in the face. Come what may, he had to play a cool hand. He couldn't let this slimeball see his forehead sweat or detect any other signs manifesting his inner turmoil.

"Okay, you've made your point. What do you want me to do?"

"Now that you mention it . . . See, the family is worried about a certain piece of legislation about to float before Congress."

"What legislation would that be?"

"Well, as you may or may not know, a lot of our business depends on deliveries by sea into the great ports of this nation, and even the lesser ports of this nation. So this drone project we've been hearing about? This ain't good for the family business. Know what I mean?"

"Yes, I think I know what you mean."

"And this Navy commander at the Pentagon . . . what's his name?" Vinnie reached into his shirt pocket and extracted an index card. "Ah, yes. This Lieutenant Commander MacDonald who might be writing some opinion to the Navy Secretary supporting this project, well, we don't need none of that. We need that project opposed. Do you hear me, Senator?"

"I hear you."

"So do your job, Chuckie." Vinnie pulled out the black-and-white picture of the kissing scene in Chuckie's office and smiled. "Your job is to provide excellent constituent services and kill this contract at all costs. Nip it in the bud so the Secretary of the Navy doesn't even want it. Am I clear on the family's needs here?"

"Loud and clear."

"All right. I think we're done, Senator. Failure on your part ain't an option. And remember, I bet there's more pictures where those came from. Kristina's making more on the family payroll than you can afford to pay her." He looked at his watch. "Now, your car should be out there in front of the bar waiting for you right about now. I don't need you here no more. Not for now, anyway. You'd better get going. You got some work to do."

Chuckie stood and looked at the tattooed human reptile. "Don't worry, Vinnie. I'll take care of it."

"Good. That's what I like to hear." He flashed another sarcastic grin, then slapped Chuckie on the back. "You know, Chuckie, you help us pull this off, and ole Phil's going to be a happy camper. In fact, he might even help you become president, where you could really do a lot of good for business. Know what I mean?" A disgusting guffaw. Another cheesy slap on the back. "Okay, Senator. I think you've got a hot little twenty-five-year-old intern waiting for you outside."

Chuckie turned from him and walked down the long, narrow bar, out the front door, and onto the sidewalk, where, just as the scum said, Kristina McRaven was already waiting for him.

Obviously she had been a plant, albeit a very hot-looking plant. And he had taken the bait.

He should have known better.

He got into the backseat of the Taurus.

"Did you have a nice meeting, Senator?"

The phoniness in her voice made him want to puke, reminding him of the pact he had made with the devil from the beginning. Politics in modern America was about selling one's soul. Democrats morphed into Republicans. Republicans morphed into Democrats. They talked a different game on the outside, but they were all the same behind closed doors.

With few exceptions, the implicit Washington mantra was more power, more money, more freewheeling sex. More service from sycophantic staffers, more attention and adulation from the common minions over whom one lorded, more extraction of the ignorant commoners' wages, all to fulfill the Washington mantra, swirling without end to achieve for the politician more, more, and even a greater more. The goal was taking more of all that could be grasped and to enjoy a life of an intoxicating power-money-sex-dom before the devil came to claim what had been bargained for in the beginning—the politician's soul. He had been warned many times that the politician's soul would die long before the body was laid in a casket.

Senator Charles E. Rodino, D-NY, like most of his colleagues on both sides of the aisle, had taken the deal, had mortgaged his soul, and gambled that he would enjoy the pinnacle of power and riches before the devil filed mortgage on his collateral.

If good fortune chose to shine before the soul was gone, perhaps a cabinet position, as had happened with former senators Bobby Kennedy, Hillary Clinton, and John Kerry. Or perhaps even vice presidential consideration, as happened with former senators Johnny Edwards and Joe Biden.

That was the goal—before the final sale of the soul.

But now, unfortunately, it appeared his career might be cut short of all that. Now the agents of the devil with whom he'd made his pact held photographic evidence that could end his career tomorrow. With a snap of the finger, they could make him the next Gary Hart, or Eliot Spitzer, or Mark Sanford, or Johnny Edwards.

They already thought they owned him from the campaign contributions they had arranged. But now all doubt had vanished. Now it was become their full-time lackey or bust.

If he didn't deliver, Chuckie Rodino would become a first-term bust like Johnny Edwards.

He had to stop this drone contract, come hell or high water, and he would pull out all the stops.

"Take me to the office, Kristina. I've got some calls to make."

• • •

FORT BELVOIR OFFICERS' CLUB
5500 SCHULZ CIRCLE
FORT BELVOIR, VIRGINIA
OVERLOOKING THE POTOMAC
TUESDAY AFTERNOON

In most cases, United States naval stations and bases around the world, from a standpoint of beauty, scenery, desirability, and weather, beat all other duty stations from the four other armed services hands down.

But to every rule there was an exception. And while places like Fort Bragg and Fort Campbell and Fort Benning and Fort Dix could not compete with anything the Navy offered, duty-station wise, the Army did contain a couple of well-kept secrets.

Unfortunately, one of those secrets, the gorgeous Fort Ord Army base on the breathtaking Monterey Peninsula in California, was closed in 1994.

The other, located on the other side of the continent, just outside of Washington, DC, and sitting above the Potomac River, five miles downriver from Washington's estate at Mount Vernon, was the breathtaking U.S. Army base at Fort Belvoir.

When Caroline had received orders to go to Washington from San Diego, she had expected a substantial drop in the scenery quotient. But then when she arrived at her temporary quarters at the BOQ at Fort Belvoir, she discovered, inadvertently, the Army's best-kept secret.

Frankly, she wished she would be able to stay at Fort Belvoir a bit longer, to enjoy the idyllic setting, if nothing else. But Gunner had made a call in advance to a realtor buddy of his in the DC area who had located a furnished townhouse within the next couple of days.

Sitting at her table in the officers' club, overlooking the dogwood flowers blooming down the green banks all the way to the gorgeous blue Potomac River, Caroline found herself awash in thought.

So much to do, so little time.

Let's see, she was scheduled to report to Code 13 at the Pentagon by Friday.

P.J.

Tomorrow she would see him. The circumstances would be harmless enough. The run from the Pentagon into DC and back would provide a venue they both would enjoy while participating in an exercise they both enjoyed.

Running had a way of removing pent-up anxiety, and running with a partner almost always generated a bonding effect to one degree or another between the runners. If tomorrow's scenic jog led to a reignition of their relationship, then so be it. If there was no new spark, then so be it. Either way, she had decided to leave it all to the Lord.

Still, the mere thought of P.J. caused her heart to skip a beat.

How she wished this weren't the case, but just being in the same area with him again, even before she had reported for duty, had an unexpected effect on her psyche.

Even when they were a continent apart, even with no commitments either way, the thought of him had been enough to stave off advances from the ultra-handsome skipper of the USS *Cape St. George*, Paul Kriete.

What a handsome, rock-solid hunk Kriete was. Without the still-lingering memories of P.J., she would have gone out with him in a heartbeat.

How ironic that the three of them would wind up serving in Washington together now that Kriete had accepted his new position as commander of the Navy's newly minted drone project, Operation Blue Jay.

Even still, Caroline had no worries that things would become awkward between the three of them. Kriete's responsibilities would demand all his time and set him running in circles at the highest echelons of the Navy. Commander Rob Turner, the new interim CO of the *Cape St. George*, had been right about one thing: Paul Kriete would soon become a rear admiral.

How easy it would have been to hitch her wagon to a shooting star. *And how tempting.*

"Care for more water, Commander?"

She looked up. Her waiter, a distinguished, late-sixtyish-looking silver-haired gentleman, was holding a silver tray and spoke in a rural Virginia brogue.

"Ah yes, George. Thank you. And you can also bring the check, please."

"Certainly, Lieutenant."

Caroline forked her grilled chicken salad, lamenting the fact that she had paid for it but eaten little of it, in part because a nervous stomach had quelled her appetite.

Her phone rang. She fished it out of her purse.

Capt. Paul Kriete, USN.

What? Her heart shifted into sudden overdrive. "Good afternoon, sir."

"Caroline. How are you?"

"Fine, sir. How about you?"

"Okay. Just got to Washington and I miss my ship already. I know this is a big job and all, but the Navy isn't for landlubbers."

The waiter returned and put the check on her table. "Well, you were a great ship commander, Captain, and I know you'll be superb in this job as well."

"Hey, thanks. How about you? Have you reported to the Pentagon yet?"

"Not yet, sir. End of the week, on Friday."

"Well, the JAG has picked an excellent officer to serve in the Pentagon."

"Thank you, sir. Have you reported yet, Captain?"

"Oh yeah. I'm up on the interior of the E-Ring, fifth deck, across from the Secretary of Defense's office. You gotta have stars on your collar to get on the outside ring."

"I'm sure that first star will be coming to you soon, Captain. The drone project is huge."

"Hey, enough about me. Listen, I want to go for a run. Maybe take a little hike from the Pentagon over the Memorial Bridge, then down to the Washington Monument and back. What do you say?"

What was he asking her? "That sounds like a pretty good run, Captain."

"Yes, that's what I hear. So what do you think?"

Was he suggesting . . . ? "I think you should go for it, sir. Go ahead and get that running route established. I think it would be a great stress reliever for your new job."

She heard him laughing. "You're going to make this hard on me, aren't you, Commander?" More chuckling.

"I'm sorry. I don't follow you, sir."

"How about if I can get a running partner? How about tomorrow?"

"Ah, I can't tomorrow, sir. I already have plans." She almost added "with P.J."

"Okay. I understand. How about Friday?"

"From the Pentagon?"

"Sure. I hear it's a great run. Unless you're ashamed to be seen with a drone driver."

What to do? Maybe a little jog wouldn't hurt. "I think I could work that out. I mean, I'm checking into Code 13 on Friday, but I hear Captain Guy is pretty flexible about PT time."

"Super. I'll see you outside the Pentagon at the beginning of the jogging trail at 1300 on Friday."

"Look forward to it."

"Me too." The line went dead.

Great. Now what? So much for her notion about all this not getting awkward. This she could say for Paul Kriete, though: at least he would go for what he wanted. Why couldn't P.J. be as aggressive?

Maybe he would be.

Then she decided. If things went well with P.J., she would call Paul and cancel their run.

If P.J. seemed disinterested, she would go forward with the run with Paul.

Her grandmother often said the Lord worked in mysterious ways.

Her grandmother never mentioned the confusing part.

CHAPTER 12

• • •

Captain Paul Kriete walked down the long corridor of the E-Ring of the Pentagon, passing the office of the Secretary of Defense on his right. The clicks of his white uniform shoes echoed off the wide tile floor as he reached the next angled bend, just past SECDEF's offices.

A moment later, he turned through a large double-door office on the left.

"Attention on deck!" the new command master chief in the newly formed U.S. Navy Drone Command barked. Four officers and three enlisted men jumped to immediate attention as the commander of the U.S. Navy Drone Command walked into the room.

"Everybody at ease," Paul said.

"Welcome aboard, sir."

"Sir, welcome aboard."

"Good to be here, everybody. Now, let's get to work. What have we got on the agenda? Commander Wong?" He looked over at a short Navy commander with Asian features. The commander wore the wings of a U.S. Navy pilot and had been assigned as Paul's second in command at Drone Command, the functional equivalent of the executive officer on board a ship.

"Sir," Wong said, "the first thing I see on our schedule is a written brief for you from the Secretary of the Navy outlining our proposed operational sharing between the Navy and Homeland Security in Project Blue Jay."

"Between the Navy and what?" Paul said.

"Between the Navy and Homeland Security."

"What are you talking about, Wong?"

"I'm sorry, sir. I forgot that you'd not been briefed on that portion of the project, Captain."

"Come into my office, Wong. And bring that report."

"Aye, sir."

Paul stepped from the foyer area of the offices back into his new but basic-looking personal office, complete with a window view of the outside alley separating the E-Ring and D-Ring of the Pentagon. He had not yet taken time to, nor did he care to, decorate. No diplomas or military commissions on the wall. No photographs of himself and all the admirals for whom he had worked.

He wasn't much on "I love me" walls and would get to all that stuff later. Right now, his new chief of staff had piqued his curiosity. And he didn't like the direction of the pique.

"Have a seat, Commander."

"Thank you, sir."

"So . . ." Paul sat for the first time behind his new desk. "What were you saying about Homeland Security?"

"Yes, sir. As you will see from the briefing papers, for political reasons, there is a proposal that the Navy and Homeland Security share operational control of the drones operated under Operation Blue Jay. The Navy would have ultimate control, and you would, of course, remain overall commander. Homeland Security would assume operational control over the drones operating over domestic areas of the United States, while we assume operational control at sea."

Paul shook his head. "You've got to be kidding me, Commander."

"I wish I could say I am, Captain. Homeland Security has been pushing hard on all the political buttons here, because they feel trying to sell a drone project to Homeland Security for purposes of conducting domestic surveillance would run into trouble getting passed by Congress."

"I could see why."

"So they want to piggyback in under a drone contract sold to the Navy, which they think has a better chance of passing in Congress."

Paul shook his head. "I love last-second surprises."

"I don't know what their thinking was in not telling you until you arrived, sir. But I know they're trying to keep a lid on the Homeland Security part and emphasize the Navy part of the operational plan. But the Homeland Security component has been the most controversial part of the internal debate. In fact, as I understand it, Navy JAG here at the Pentagon is expected to deliver a legal opinion to the Secretary evaluating the Homeland Security component."

Paul looked at Wong. "JAG?" His mind moved to Caroline.

"Yes, sir."

"*The* Admiral Brewer himself?"

"They've assigned it to Code 13 here in the Pentagon. Last I heard Admiral Brewer was waiting on the opinion."

"Interesting. We just had a JAG officer transfer to Code 13 from San Diego who was doing a ton of work on my ship getting us ready to deploy."

"Well, sir, maybe he'll be able to give us some insight on what they're thinking."

"Not he. She."

"I see, sir."

"Anyway, let me see that briefing paper."

"Aye, Captain."

Paul opened the yellow envelope and extracted the three-page, top-secret briefing paper, titled "Operation Blue Jay—Joint U.S. Navy–Homeland Security Operational Plan."

Paul read down the brief, outlining the plan to give the Navy ultimate operational control over Blue Jay but to "loan" Navy drones to Homeland Security, under ultimate Navy authority, for "domestic surveillance operations."

The more he read, the more he felt his blood boil. Finally he tossed the memo down on his desk. "Are these people crazy, Charlie? What kind of horse-manure proposal is this?"

Wong adjusted his glasses. "Homeland Security has their lobbyists, Captain. On the political front, the Navy Legislative Affairs Office tells us the Republicans in Congress would favor allocation for drones to the Navy but would be reluctant to purchase them for Homeland Security. With the Democrats, it's the opposite. They spend tons on Homeland Security but want military budget cuts.

"Right now, as you know, the Democrats control the senate and the Republicans control the House. So I'm told that to make this fly politically, we've got to throw in the Homeland Security component."

Paul shook his head again. Why wasn't he informed about the proposed Homeland Security component when he was ordered to take this job? Of course, he already knew. That was the Navy way—keep a lid on things until there was an absolute need to know.

What could he do about it anyway? Walk into the Secretary of the Navy's office and pick an argument based on philosophical grounds? Bottom line, as a naval officer, he was duty-bound to obey the orders of his superiors and to go where the Navy ordered. But still . . .

"Charlie, why do I feel like I need to take a hot shower?"

Wong smiled. "I understand, sir. If it makes you feel any better, and I'm sure it won't, the general consensus on the Navy side of the house is just like yours. There's not a lot of appetite for sharing anything with Homeland Security. But it's all about politics."

"I hate politics and I hate politicians. I should have stayed with my ship."

Wong laughed. "Unfortunately, sir, Washington's full of politics and politicians."

"Roger that, Charlie. The largest cesspool of rats in the country." He picked up the memo again. "So as a practical matter, how the heck is this going to work?"

"Well, as a matter of fact, I'm supposed to take you down to Pax River tomorrow for a joint demonstration flight of one of the drones. As you know, Pax River will be the operational command headquarters for the Navy's East Coast drone ops, with San Diego the operational headquarters for West Coast ops. The Homeland Security operators will be on base, and we'll launch from Pax River, swing out over the coastal waters, then fly inland over Washington and bring the bird back into Pax River. We should be able to get a feel for how it will work then."

"Sounds like we're going to have to have both Navy operators and Homeland Security operators in the same operational facility."

"Yes, sir, which is the reason for part of the controversy. But I think we'll get a better feel for it tomorrow."

"Okay, Charlie. May as well make the best of it. Where'd you say that hot shower was?"

"I didn't, sir. But it's down in the locker room."

CHAPTER 13

• • •

Wearing her summer white officer's uniform and smelling French fries, Caroline walked past the short-order grill in the basement of the D-Ring. That told her the Code 13 spaces were somewhere in the area.

Today marked only the second time she had been in the building, and frankly, the endless corridors that all looked the same, except for the upper decks of the E-Ring, made for a confusing morass that would take some getting used to.

She made the turn at the next corridor. The sign to her left on the wall proclaimed "Navy JAG Code 13—Administrative Law."

She checked to make sure her belt buckle was aligned, her medals were aligned properly, and there were no runs in her hose. Today she would stop in, say hello to the captain, meet a few of her fellow officers, and return to administrative matters inherent in a permanent change of duty.

Friday would mark her first day on the job. Today she would see P.J.

A dual sense of anxiety and excitement pervaded her on both accounts.

She put her hand on the door and then saw she needed the security code.

"Oh, that's right." She had forgotten. Her sponsor had told her about the security code and in fact had provided it to her in her welcome packet.

"What did I do with that thing?"

She stepped back, away from the door, because she didn't want anyone to see her fidgeting in her purse.

There.

4-2-1-2.

She stepped back to the door and punched the code.

The locks unlatched, and she pushed the door open.

"Afternoon, ma'am."

The Code 13 command master chief, LNCM Richard Magadia, sat at the duty desk just inside the door.

"Afternoon, Master Chief. I'm Lieutenant Commander Caroline McCormick."

"Oh yes, ma'am." The master chief's eyes brightened. "We're expecting you Friday, as I recall."

"That's right, Master Chief. I'm visiting the captain today and then hopefully going on a little run with Commander MacDonald."

"Yes, ma'am," the graying master chief said. "Most of our officers are out right now for PT or lunch. But the commander and Captain Guy are here. Let me take you back to the captain, and then we'll find Commander MacDonald."

"Great, Master Chief. Let's do it."

"Right this way, ma'am." Caroline stepped in behind the master chief, and as she followed toward the captain's office, she sensed someone staring at her. She glanced to her left as they reached the captain's office.

A redheaded female lieutenant with fiery green eyes hit her with a stare that screamed first-degree murder. Then she looked down at her desk just as Caroline heard Captain Guy's voice.

"Commander McCormick. Welcome aboard." Her new skipper

stood, extending his hand for a warm handshake. "I thought you were reporting on Friday."

"I am, sir. I wanted to stop by and say hello, and then Commander MacDonald is going to take me out for a run."

"Oh, that's right." Guy's eyes lit like a lightbulb had turned on. "You and P.J. were at RLSO San Diego together."

"Yes, sir. We used to PT along the San Diego waterfront, and the commander offered to show me this famous running route across Memorial Bridge over into the District that everybody's talking about."

"Great run. I think you'll enjoy it."

"I'm looking forward to it, sir. And I plan to be in first thing Friday morning to report officially."

Guy's phone buzzed. "Captain Guy, Admiral Brewer is on line one."

"Excuse me, Commander. Duty calls."

"See you Friday, sir."

They stepped out of the office. Caroline noticed the redhead's laser-beam stare again.

She was distracted when a smiling, handsome young officer, wearing the shoulder boards of a Navy lieutenant and who could have passed for Tom Cruise, walked up from another direction. "Good afternoon, ma'am. I'm Lieutenant Ross Simmons. I'm over in 133. Welcome aboard."

The master chief interjected, "The lieutenant works with Commander MacDonald over in our legislative affairs subcode. He's just been deep selected for lieutenant commander."

"Congratulations, Lieutenant," Caroline said. "I'll look forward to working with you."

"My pleasure, ma'am. Commander MacDonald speaks highly of you, and we look forward to having you at Code 13. Now, if you'll excuse me, I'm headed out to PT."

"Nice to meet you, Lieutenant." Simmons walked away. She looked at the master chief. "Speaking of Commander MacDonald, where is he, Master Chief?"

"Right this way, ma'am."

"Did I hear a familiar voice calling my name?"

She caught a whiff of his Geoffrey Beene cologne, a fragrance that tantalized her, even before she saw that irresistibly appealing face.

She wanted to hug him. But that would breach military protocol and professionalism, especially at the Pentagon.

Her heart raced in her chest.

"Long time no see, stranger." She blurted the only thing she could muster, unable to suppress her smile. "Where is everybody?"

"Everybody is either out to lunch or still at the gym or on a run. Only ones in right now are me, Captain Guy, the master chief, and Lieutenant Fladager."

"Well, are you going to introduce me to your friend, P.J.?" The ice-cold voice came from over her shoulder. Caroline turned, and there stood the gorgeous redhead, flashing a superficially fake smile, casting a stare that burned with apparent anger.

"Uh, yes. Excuse me." Squeamishness saturated P.J.'s voice. "Lieutenant Commander Caroline McCormick, meet Lieutenant Victoria Fladager. Victoria is an action officer in our Ethics Division, Subcode 132."

"Nice to meet you, Victoria," Caroline said.

"And likewise. A pleasure to meet you, ma'am."

"Please, call me Caroline." She extended her hand.

"Yes, ma'am." Victoria shook Caroline's hand with a handshake that felt as cold as an ice cube.

What was up with this lieutenant? Wait a minute. *Could she and P.J. be . . . ?* Caroline dismissed that thought.

"Anyway," P.J. interjected, "since we're all going to be working together, I volunteered to take Caroline out on our jogging route."

"Oh, I see." The lieutenant cut her eyes at P.J. "That's very nice of P.J. to volunteer to take you out. He's a hospitable guy. But, P.J., I'm surprised you have time to PT today, with your big paper due to the Secretary tomorrow."

"Well, I—"

"You know, I've been trying to get P.J. out on the running circuit all week, but he's been bogged down with this sensitive project. So I'm not sure how you convinced him, ma'am."

"Please," Caroline said. "It's okay to call me Caroline. I'm sure you'll be picked up for Lieutenant Commander soon anyway." She looked at P.J. "From what I hear, Code 13 pretty much guarantees it."

"Thank you, Caroline." She looked at P.J. "Say, P.J., if you're in a big-time jam today because your opinion letter's due tomorrow, I'll be glad to take the commander out for a run." Victoria shifted her eyes back and forth between P.J. and Caroline. Something was going on here. "I'm sure the commander and I could spend the time getting to know each other."

"Thanks, Victoria." P.J. looked guilty. "But the opinion letter's almost ready to go. In fact, I've got two different letters ready to go, so all the work has been done. It might do me some good to get out and run to clear my head."

Victoria beaded her eyes like a viper ready to strike, all the while smiling coyly. "Well then. I suppose you have a point. Anyway, Caroline and I will have plenty of time to get acquainted."

"Yes, I'm sure of it." Caroline forced a smile.

"Well," P.J. said, "we should be going. I'll be back in an hour."

"Have fun." A sarcastic tone.

P.J. opened the door and Caroline, with her purse and a small blue gym bag over her left shoulder, stepped out into the D-Ring. The door to Code 13 shut behind them.

"This way to the locker rooms," P.J. said, and they turned left, walking in the direction opposite from where she came in. She thought he might comment on the lieutenant's behavior, but he seemed to clam up, clearly uncomfortable with the encounter that had just taken place. Something was up with those two, which was fine with her. After all, she and P.J. had broken up, and they both were free to date whomever.

Whatever. "Okay, here's the ladies' locker room. Meet you in a few."

"Okay, I won't be long," she said.

CHAPTER 14

• • •

Sitting on the peninsula at the convergence of the sparkling blue waters of the Potomac River and Chesapeake Bay, the massive and picturesque Patuxent River Naval Air Station, known as "Pax River" within U.S. Naval circles, provided for the United States the principal base for land-based U.S. Naval air power in the middle Atlantic.

Located sixty-five miles from the center of American military power, the Pentagon, the Pax River Naval Air Station, like the Pentagon, entered service to the U.S. military in 1943, in the middle of World War II. But that was about the only commonality between the Pentagon and Pax River.

None of this was lost on Captain Paul M. Kriete, the newly appointed commander of the U.S. Navy Drone Command. The physically chiseled, cleft-chinned captain, who years ago had passed up an appointment to the Coast Guard Academy to pay his own way to Duke, where he entered into the Naval ROTC, looked out the passenger window as the car began to slow on its final approach to the base. His mind raced with thoughts of his action-packed agenda for the day, even as the Navy lieutenant driving the car that contained Kriete and his chief of staff, Wong, pulled up to the main gate.

Paul exchanged salutes with the SP at the gate, then unloaded on Wong as the staff car rolled through the gate. "Makes a heck of a lot of sense, doesn't it, Wong? You set up the operational command for all these drones here at Pax River but put the commander of the operation back at the Pentagon."

Wong shook his head as the car rolled through the gate.

"No kidding, Captain. When did anybody in Washington propose solutions that made sense economically?"

"Yeah, well, I've been told they've got the command at the Pentagon for political purposes, until we can get this contract finally approved by Congress. Once that's done, all the operation commands will be at Pax River and San Diego. Right now, Charlie, it looks like we're going to have to put up with a bunch of bull until we can get this baby off the ground."

"I hear you, sir."

"Okay, here we are, gentlemen," the driver said.

Paul looked up at the blue sign outside the three-story stucco building.

U.S. NAVY DRONE COMMAND
EAST COAST OPERATIONS
TEMPORARY OPERATIONAL HEADQUARTERS

"Home sweet home," Paul said. "They should be waiting for us. Let's check it out."

Paul and his party stepped out of the staff car, and he paused to enjoy the refreshing, salty Chesapeake Bay sea breeze.

For a Navy man, nothing proved more refreshing than taking in the scent of the sea and breathing ocean air deep into his lungs. Already the stark contrast of the sea versus Washington's smells of asphalt and exhaust fumes made him long for his ship.

Perhaps he should have stayed with his ship. Yes, the appointment was an honor, and yes, it would fast-track him to admiral. But would it be worth it?

Yes, Washington wanted him to take the job. But he had enough seniority as a senior captain that if he had pushed hard enough, they would have passed him over and selected another officer.

He almost told the detailer to find another officer to command the first-ever U.S. Navy Drone Command. After all, he was a ship driver. Not a remote-control airplane pilot.

But he had to make a decision, and in a now-or-never decision that might be his only chance to ascend to admiral, he took the now.

But more than once he had already second-guessed himself.

Would he ever even return to sea in command? Or would he trade his love of the ocean for stars on his collar, swanky cocktail parties, and the classic butt-kissing and bull manure that one had to endure to move up in the ranks?

Of course, one redeeming quality might make Washington worth enduring: the most gorgeous blonde he'd ever laid eyes on. And the fact that she wore a naval officer's uniform made her even hotter. And the fact that she was a lawyer wearing a naval officer's uniform shattered the thermometer as far as he was concerned.

Of course, it remained to be seen whether Lieutenant Commander Caroline McCormick would ever give him the time of day. Of course, if she didn't give him the time of day, his Washington tour could prove quite boring and even more regrettable. But he wasn't too worried about that possibility at the moment.

Captain Paul Kriete usually got his way, as Caroline McCormick would soon find out.

That thought made him smile.

Enough daydreaming about her. Time to get back to work.

As they stepped into the entry area of the building, they were greeted with a barrage of sailors and junior officers jumping to attention.

"Attention on deck!"

"Attention on deck!"

"At ease," Paul said.

"Good afternoon, sir. I'm Master Chief Gonzales, your operations master chief."

"Master Chief." Paul nodded.

"Sir, Commander Jefferies sent me down to escort you up to the ops center on the second deck."

"Very well. Lead the way, Master Chief."

"Right this way, sir."

The master chief led the triumvirate into an elevator, where he entered a code and then punched 2.

"The commander's been looking forward to having you aboard, sir, to give you a firsthand idea of what we can do once this drone fleet gets fully developed."

"I've been looking forward to that myself, Master Chief."

The elevator stopped and the doors parted. The master chief stepped out and shouted, "Attention on deck!"

Officers and enlisted men jumped to attention at Paul's entrance, with one exception: six middle-aged-looking men, two with potbellies, two more balding, all with short-sleeved white shirts, turned in their chairs, and only one stood. And the one who stood was slowest to get up and showed no semblance of any military bearing.

Homeland Security. Paul's stomach twisted in disgust.

"At ease, gentlemen," he said.

"Welcome aboard, sir." A slim, enthusiastic-looking commander approached him with a smile. "I'm Commander John Jefferies. I'm your officer in charge of the East Coast detachment. Glad to have you here, sir."

Paul extended his hand and discovered Jefferies's handshake proved firm and confident. "So you're the lucky guy who gets to run this place and fly all these drones while I'm back in Washington having to kiss butt and raise money so you'll have more drones to play with."

Jefferies smiled. "I feel lucky and privileged, sir. But frankly, we're looking forward to the day you can join us out here. That would mean the fleet is up and running as envisioned, and of course, we'd need to expand our personnel to operate that fleet."

"Okay, Commander," Paul said, changing the subject. "What are you going to show me today?"

"With pleasure, sir." Jefferies nodded enthusiastically. "Do you mind if I give you a tour of the ops center as I brief you?"

"Whatever it takes to bring me up to speed."

"Very well, step this way with me." He motioned to three officers sitting front and center. "This is our command and control for U.S. Navy ops. As you know, sir, currently the Navy has purchased a total of one hundred drones for our experimental fleet, with fifty of these blue babies stationed here at Pax River and the other fifty stationed at North Island Naval Air Station in San Diego."

"Technically Coronado," Paul added. "But no biggie."

"Yes, sir." Jefferies nodded. "Anyway, sir, from this command and control center here at Pax River, we can control the drone activity of the fifty drones stationed here at this air station, and we can also control takeoffs, landings, and all operational aspects of the fifty drones flying out over the Pacific from North Island. Not only that, but we can launch and recover drones on both coasts at the same time and monitor live television feeds from both coasts at the same time. All this television feed is being fed into our computer for digital recording, and the computer can also flag areas of concern that we might miss with the human eye. Now, we already have two drones in the air, one over the Pacific and one over the Atlantic, and we'll be demonstrating our capabilities for you momentarily, sir."

"Impressive, Commander." Paul smiled.

"Thank you, sir. It's fairly easy through remote control right now, given the small number of drones in our experimental fleet. Once Congress passes the bill authorizing development of the entire fleet, our personnel requirements will explode and we'll be juggling hundreds of balls in the air at the same time."

"Let's hope I can get you these balls sooner rather than later. JAG's supposed to be taking a look at it in the next day or so, then the legal opinion goes to the Secretary of the Navy and hopefully to Congress and we get the green light."

"Hopefully, sir. Now, if you'd follow me over to the left side of the control center." They stepped over toward the short-sleeved civilians, who finally stood as Paul approached. Not that Paul would expect a civilian to stand. But the one potbelly who stood a moment ago was the first to stand again, and displayed a friendly countenance as he approached Paul. Perhaps the head Homeland Security guy?

"Sir," Jefferies said, "I'd first like you to meet Mr. Roger Cullipher. Mr. Cullipher is the AirFlite representative who taught us all how to fly these things, and who helps us maintain them when they're down."

"So you're the manufacturer's guy?" Paul said, noting Cullipher's strong handshake.

"That's me, Captain. And I'm here to help in any way I can."

"Tell ya what. Want to swap jobs? You go up to DC and wine and dine the admirals, and I'll come down here and breathe the salt air of the Atlantic and feel like I'm back where I belong. With the fleet."

"Well, Captain, I hope we can get you out here soon. I've heard great things about you."

"Thanks," Paul said. "Okay, everybody. I'm enjoying the chit-chat, but let's get this show on the road. Show me what I need to see so I can go back and try to sell this project to all those senators and congressmen up on the hill."

Commander Jefferies spoke up. "Sir, as your OIC here at Pax River, it's my honor to serve as your tour guide. Here's the plan, if it's all right with you, sir. First, we'll take you down to the flight line so you can examine the drones up close. We'll have Mr. Cullipher here explain the technical components, including the aircraft's high surveillance capabilities. Then we'll put two of the birds up in the sky and let you observe the launch from the flight line. We'll bring one of the birds back in for a landing. After that, we'll come back up into flight control and establish the live video monitor for the birds already in the air, one over San Diego and one headed over toward DC. How's that sound, sir?"

"Sounds like a plan to me, Commander. Like I said, let's get this show on the road."

"Aye, sir."

• • •

ARLINGTON MEMORIAL BRIDGE
SPANNING THE POTOMAC RIVER
BETWEEN VIRGINIA AND WASHINGTON, DC

Under the warm midday sun, the sky above and river below sparkled in a bright light blue, a remarkable contrast to the great white marble of the Lincoln Memorial on the other side of the bridge. A warm breeze swooped in from the left, reminding her that while the sunshine and blue waters might have been reminiscent of San Diego, in DC the mild humidity, even in late spring, had a moist feel of its own, and she already felt the sweat beads dripping from her nose.

The pedestrian walkway alongside the traffic lanes of the historic memorial bridge was sufficiently wide, leaving enough room for three or four people to walk abreast without feeling threatened by traffic whizzing by in both directions. Caroline fell into single file behind P.J., jogging along at a comfortable seven-minute-mile pace. They hugged the right side of the walkway, jogging up next to the bridge railing to the right of the green gas-lamp-replica light poles erected between the walkway and the road.

Ahead of her, P.J. motioned with his left hand, and from all those months of jogging with him along the San Diego waterfront, she knew what that meant: pick up the pace.

He kicked it into higher gear and she followed, reaching the DC side of the river.

As they reached the end of the bridge, to the east of the Lincoln Memorial, they jogged past one of a pair of neoclassical bronze sculptures depicting a warrior on a horse, titled *The Arts of War*; the sculptures flanked each side of the bridge.

They crossed the street and came to the base of the white-marbled Lincoln Memorial. In front of the Memorial, P.J. slowed for a minute as Caroline caught up. As they began to run side by side, a sense of déjà vu overcame her. It was like she'd been here before.

"So what do you think of the run so far?" he asked.

"Beautiful. But more humidity than San Diego."

"If you think it's humid now, wait till the middle of summer. This is nothing. But it's good for you. You'll get used to it."

"We'll see. Where to now?"

"We're going to follow the circle here in front of the base of the Lincoln Memorial, then follow the walkway along the reflecting pool up to the monument, then loop it, then turn around and come back."

"Let's do it," she said.

"You okay with the pace?"

"I'm with you. Let's roll."

• • •

OPERATIONAL HEADQUARTERS
U.S. NAVY DRONE COMMAND
U.S. NAVAL AIR STATION "PAX RIVER"
LEXINGTON PARK, MARYLAND

Following the lead of Commander John Jefferies and his civilian counterpart, Roger Cullipher, Paul and his entourage reentered the drone air traffic control center overlooking the long Pax River runway.

Down below, two F/A-18 Hornets were lined up on the flight line, preparing to take off. Two Blue Jay Navy drones followed in line, prepared to launch after the Hornets.

"All right, sir," Jefferies said, "we're going to show you some aerial views now to give you an idea what these babies can do surveillance wise. The first will be a shot over the Atlantic, and the next two will be interior shots over land. Lieutenant Watson, your show."

"Yes, sir," the lieutenant said. "Captain, if you would turn your attention to screen one, and we should have that shot up in three . . . two . . . one . . . there."

The screen flashed on, showing blue waters below. "All right, sir. You're looking at a shot of the open waters of the Chesapeake Bay, forty miles southeast of here. Now, if you'll stand by just a second . . . here we go!"

The screen now showed a full-length shot of a U.S. Navy warship, and Paul recognized it as being the same Ticonderoga-class type Aegis cruiser as his former ship, the USS *Cape St. George*.

"What a beautiful sight," Paul said.

"Just for you, sir," Jefferies said. "We thought you might like our ship selection."

"Making me homesick, Commander."

"This is the USS *Monterey*, CG-61, served up especially for you, sir."

"Oh yeah." Paul battled a flash of nostalgia, wishing for the moment that he was aboard the bridge of the *Cape St. George* on her way to the Western Pacific. "Beautiful piece of floating firepower. Under the command of Captain Scott Basnight, as I recall."

"Your memory serves you correctly, Captain. Not only that, but keeping in mind that we're flying three thousand feet over the ship, meaning that they can barely see or notice us, the *Monterey*'s crew has a special message for you. Ensign Simpson, close-up."

"Aye, sir."

The screen blinked. A second later the camera showed a close-up of six sailors on the forward deck, looking up, smiling, and giving a thumbs-up. One sailor held up a small sign proclaiming, "Welcome, Captain Paul Kriete, Commander, U.S. Navy Drone Command!"

"That's some pretty impressive photography, Commander Jefferies. You can almost see the hairs up their noses."

"Remember, this is from three thousand feet. And actually, Skipper, if you wanted to see the hairs up their noses, I can have Ensign Simpson here do a next-level close-up. Would you like to see, sir?"

"No." Paul laughed. "I trust you, Commander. That's a little too up close and personal for me."

"Aye, sir," Jefferies said. "Next we're going to switch over to one of our West Coast drones, and we'll start over navigable waters and then transition over land so we can practice, and you can observe, the switch from U.S. Navy to TSA air traffic control."

"Fair enough."

"Okay, Skipper, if I could invite you to have a look at screen four here and, Ensign Simpson, go ahead and see if you can get a shot up there."

"Aye, Commander."

Screen four blinked, and a second later rolling blue waves appeared, much like the scene that had initially appeared on screen one.

"Okay. Ensign, give us a wider angle for a second so the skipper can get a better view."

"Aye, sir."

The screen widened, and suddenly a gray warship, larger than the *Monterey* and with a large helo pad in the aft, came into view. The ship had triangular twin stacks, one over the bridge and one just forward of the aft helo pad, the distinct look of the new amphibious support ships belonging to the San Antonio class.

"Looks like one of our LPDs," Paul said.

"Correct, sir. This is the USS *Green Bay*. She's steamed out of port for the afternoon. Ensign, widen her out a little more."

"Aye, sir."

The next level wide-angle showed a geographic landmark all too familiar to any American sailor who ever served on the American West Coast. To the left, the large, mountainous, thumb-like peninsula stretched from the north into the ocean, overshadowing the other flat peninsula stretching, with a large air strip on the end, to the north.

The visually contrasting tips of the Gibraltar-like Point Loma peninsula from the north and the flat Coronado peninsula from the south came close enough together in the water to form the majestic entrance into San Diego Bay, which was now, after base closures in the early nineties, the only remaining major U.S. Naval facility in California.

Paul knew this harbor like the back of his hand. He could navigate it in his sleep.

"You guys are taking the old man on a sentimental journey, aren't you?"

"Thought you might like this, Skipper. Okay, so here's what we're going to do. We're bringing the bird down low, to five hundred feet, to avoid air traffic out of Lindbergh Field and North Island. Then we'll fly her straight down the center of the bay, making the same turns any warship entering the harbor would make. We'll fly over the San Diego–Coronado Bridge and then fly her down to the beginning of the 32nd Street Naval Station, and when we're even with Pier 1, we'll turn her inward, flying east over the base. Once we cross the border from the base to civilian airspace, we'll switch to the Homeland Security controllers so you can see how we do the transition over civilian airspace, still subject, of course, to our overall supervision. Questions, sir?"

"Negative, Commander. Let's do it."

"Aye, sir. Ensign?"

"Moving forward, sir."

On the screen, the shadow of the drone could be seen skimming over the sunlit morning waves of the bay as the drone turned right, catching a glimpse of the supercarrier USS *Ronald Reagan*, moored at Naval Air Station North Island to the right. Sailboats and several small craft crisscrossed out in the bay, cutting wakes in their sterns. Off to the left, Paul recognized Shelter Island and the U.S. Coast Guard facility. And with another turn to the right, the downtown San Diego waterfront came into view on the left. Farther up to the left, the clipper ship *Star of India* came into view, followed by the World War II carrier USS *Midway*, permanently moored along the waterfront as a military museum.

A moment later, the familiar, curve-shaped San Diego–Coronado Bridge came into view. A second after that, the first of some thirteen piers of the San Diego Naval Station, known as the 32nd Street Naval Station.

"Very well, prepare to execute turn niner-zero degrees," Jefferies said.

"Preparing to execute. Aye, sir."

"Execute turn niner-zero degrees."

"Executing turn niner-zero. Aye, sir."

The drone turned and began crossing over the government buildings of the naval station, its shadow passing from building to building.

"Prepare to switch to DHS control."

"Preparing to switch. Aye, sir."

"Switch to DHS control."

"Switching to DHS control."

"Homeland Security now has control of the aircraft."

"We have control of the aircraft."

Paul watched as the U.S. Navy controllers leaned back from their monitors and the white, short-sleeved air-traffic controllers from Homeland Security leaned forward, pushing a variety of buttons and turning knobs.

"Okay, got it," a bald-headed man said.

"Your bird, boss," another DHS controller said.

"This should be fun," said the lead DHS controller.

"Hey, boss, there's Interstate 5!" a third white-shirt remarked.

"Okay, let's turn the bird to the north and follow the interstate awhile," the lead controller said. "I want to see the park!"

"Great idea, boss."

Paul stood behind the civilian DHS controllers with his arms crossed. The civilians acted like starry-eyed kids who had just unwrapped a new toy found under the Christmas tree. Why did it seem like the JV team had just taken the field? Whoever came up with this idea had to be a lamebrain bureaucrat with no grasp on reality.

Bureaucrats, politicians, and lawyers: probably a committee of that worthless group of bloodsuckers had come up with the notion of putting DHS paper pushers in command, or even in partial command, of U.S. military assets. No class of human beings came closer to epitomizing cold-blooded slugs and vermin than these three people groups.

Of course, there were exceptions to that rule. Very rare exceptions, but definite exceptions.

He smiled as he thought of Caroline. Her blood was anything but cold. This he knew, though he'd never held her close enough to feel her pulse and know for sure.

But still, he knew.

Time was on his side. Soon he would hold her close to him. Soon and very soon. He knew it in his gut.

The screen showed the view from the drone flying north up Interstate 5.

"Hey, there's Balboa Hospital," a short-sleeved white-shirt said.

"Yep." The lead controller spoke with a sense of satisfaction in his voice. "We're coming into the southern end of the park."

Why did this fat-belly have an obsession with Balboa Park?

"Hey, I see the Air and Space Museum," one white-shirt said.

"And there's the Friendship Garden and the Old Globe!" another said.

"It all looks so green from the air," a third controller said.

"Hey, Stewart. Get me a close-up of the Friendship Garden," the lead controller said. "I thought I saw something."

The drone circled in the air, and already Paul felt like he'd seen enough. As the DHS controllers played with their toy, he whispered to Commander Jefferies, "You got any coffee?"

"Coffee mess is in the back, sir." He pointed. "Right back there."

"I'll be right back, gentlemen," Paul said.

He turned and headed toward the coffee mess. But before he made it out of the room, cackling laughter erupted from the civilian controllers.

"Go for it, dude!"

"He's getting started early!"

"She looks like she's ready."

He turned to see what all the commotion was about, and when he turned, he saw a close-up image of a man and a woman on a park bench, kissing, making out, and apparently about to do more than that.

"Okay, get that off the screen!" he snapped, his blood boiling.

The civilian controllers complied, and the close-up was replaced by a large overview of the park, with the kissing couple no longer visible.

"I'm gonna step into the coffee mess for some battery acid. Let me know when the drone is in position over DC. Commander? Want to join me?"

"Aye, sir."

• • •

NATIONAL MALL
WASHINGTON, DC
CIRCLING THE WASHINGTON MONUMENT

The breeze had cooled down a bit, and the circle of American flags flapping in the breeze gave a sudden boost of patriotic adrenaline.

The monument marked the halfway point of the run, P.J. had told her. From here they would run the loop around the monument, then run back down the Mall, past the World War II Memorial, past the Lincoln Memorial, back across the Memorial Bridge, then skirt the edge of Arlington Cemetery and head back to the Pentagon.

This was her first run on the Mall, and she didn't want to look like a tourist. But still, something about the size and grandeur of that great obelisk, the Washington Monument, compelled her to stare upward.

"You're going to get dizzy if you keep looking up," P.J. said.

"I know. I feel like a stupid tourist."

"Don't feel bad." He showed no sign of being winded. "I did the same thing for the first week."

They circled around the back side of the monument, the U.S. Capitol side, then approached the Lincoln Memorial side.

"Hey, wanna kick up the tempo a little bit?" she said.

"Let's do it."

He jumped out ahead of her a little, looking fabulous in navy blue running shorts and a white T-shirt. She took in the view for a second, then responded with an extra burst of speed and caught up with him, now on the down stretch toward the reflecting pool.

"Trying to make me look bad, are you, big boy?"

"You're the one who wanted to pick up the pace."

"I figured you needed to get back to do some finishing work on your big brief."

"Thanks for reminding me." He sounded less than enthusiastic.

"Sorry. Didn't mean to bring up a sore subject."

"No worries. I'll just be glad to get it over with. The whole thing is a stupid idea, if you ask me."

They approached a young couple holding hands, coming down the gravel walkway in the opposite direction. Caroline split right. P.J. split left. A second later, past the couple, they reconverged, running shoulder to shoulder, and jogged across 17th Street, now almost at the beginning of the World War II Memorial.

"Hey, you know what?" P.J. said.

"What?"

"We should slow down a little bit when we circle the World War II Memorial out of respect. This is the most hallowed ground in DC, if you ask me. I don't want to be a distraction to people trying to get in here."

"Agree."

They slowed their tempo to almost a jog as they took a semicircle path to the right around the World War II Memorial.

Caroline looked to her left at the large, oval-shaped monument. It was surrounded by fifty-six granite pillars and a huge fountain out in the middle. P.J. was right. People milled within the monument, moving slowly, with a solemn respect for the sacrifice of four hundred thousand Americans who gave their lives for the liberation of Europe and the Pacific. She felt the same goose bumps she had felt when they jogged past Arlington Cemetery.

They said not a word until they had cleared to the west of the Memorial, with the beginning of the reflecting pool now in front of them.

"You mind if I change the subject?" she asked.

"Please do. Anything other than my writing assignment."

"Sooo . . ." She hesitated. "What's going on with Victoria?"

"What do you mean?"

"Well, the first time she laid eyes on me, she shot me the look of a cobra ready to strike."

"You think she looked like a cobra?"

"Okay, more like a jealous paramour determined to protect her property."

"So what are you getting at?"

"You know what I'm getting at."

"Are you asking if there's anything between me and Victoria?"

"Like I said. You know what I'm getting at."

The sound of an airliner roared overhead. P.J. responded, "Okay, so we went out once. No big deal."

"I didn't hear an answer to my question, Counselor."

"Do you care?"

"Don't know about care." She picked up the pace, moving about a half step ahead of him. "But I can be curious, can't I? I mean, we were almost engaged."

"You know what they say about curiosity, don't you?"

"Yes, curiosity killed the cat. But you still didn't answer my question."

"I'll put it this way. There might be something there from her perspective. But for me? I'll be honest. I'm glad you got orders to Code 13."

"Really?"

"Really."

"Race you back to the Pentagon," she said.

"You're on."

She picked up the pace again, pulling now a full step ahead of him, taking in the glorious sight of the Lincoln Memorial ahead and the sparkling waters of the reflecting pool just to their left.

The single, popping sound at first seemed like a sharp clap from the traffic along Constitution Avenue over to their right. No, maybe it came from the cherry and elm trees above.

A moment later, when it seemed like she was running alone, she glanced back over her shoulder.

He was down, face-first in the gravel walkway beside the pool, and his right hand beat against the ground.

Blood rushed from a gaping hole in his temple.

She stopped, turned around, and screamed at the top of her lungs. "Help! Somebody help me!"

She sprinted to him and kneeled, weeping, screaming. "No, please! No! P.J.! Wake up! Please! P.J., please! Not this way! No! Please!"

• • •

Paul sat in the coffee mess chatting with Commander John Jefferies, drinking coffee and snacking on a handful of dry-roasted almonds.

"So, John, level with me. You've done some dry runs with these DHS guys. What are your thoughts?"

Jefferies hesitated. He sipped his coffee. "Permission to speak freely, sir?"

"That's why I asked you."

"I think this drone project, for purposes of allowing us to patrol coastal waters, gives us an opportunity to enhance national security, sir. But when it comes to domestic surveillance"—he took another sip of coffee—"the chemistry with these Homeland Security controllers is awkward, to say the least."

"Exactly my thoughts. Plus, they act like a bunch of voyeurs from what I can see. Like perverts with a new spy toy." A sip of coffee. "Leave it to the lamebrain politicians to come up with a proposal that is neither practical, nor workable, nor compliant with the Fourth Amendment," Paul said. "All for the sake of money and power. And my orders are to go help sell it to Congress."

"I hear you, Captain. I think everybody on the military side of the house has grave reservations about the civilian use of the drones. And frankly, no one has been impressed by anything we've seen from Homeland Security so far. But as far as the military mission goes, we're big-time vulnerable to maritime terrorism attack. ISIS or some group like that could sail a ship into New York Harbor and set off a nuclear bomb on board, and *kaboom*. You know as well as I do, sir, that our radars can't see over the horizon. So we've only got about a seven-mile window of alert before they're on top of us. But with this drone fleet on patrol, we've got a chance to see them hundreds of miles out to sea."

"I know, Commander. Which is why I'm willing to hold my nose and do all I can to get this passed. Because you're right. We're vulnerable to maritime terrorism attack. Anyway—"

"Excuse me! Captain. Commander." Paul looked up. Ensign Simpson stood at the door with a look of bewildered excitement on his youthful-looking face.

"What is it, Ensign?" Jefferies asked.

"Drone 1 is now over DC, and there's something I think you might want to see."

"Not the DHS bureaucrats getting excited about spying on a sex party, I hope," Paul quipped.

"No, sir," Simpson said. "Something's happened on the National Mall, sir. Down off the reflecting pool. Flashing blue lights. Ambulances. Hopefully not a terror attack, but we can't tell yet."

"Let's check it out," Paul said.

"Aye, sir."

They stepped out of the coffee mess back into the adjacent control room.

Five large flat screens mounted on the bulkhead above the civilian controllers showed the same image. The drone circled in an orbit over the western section of the National Mall, its shadow making a wide loop on the ground between the Washington Monument and the World War II Memorial.

The growing crowd burgeoned along the portion of the Mall from 17th Street to the west, in and around the World War II Memorial and spilling down toward the eastern end of the long, ruler-shaped reflecting pool. Already, police cars were parked along 17th Street in the shadow of the monument, and police could be seen roping off the street as ambulances and fire trucks poured in, their red lights swirling.

Inside the command center, every naval officer, every enlisted man, and every civilian stood with eyes glued to the scene on the ground.

"Are we video-recording all this?" Paul asked.

"Yes, sir, Captain," the lead civilian controller responded.

Unlike the cackling from a few minutes ago at the spectacle in Balboa Park, every man now seemed stunned, soberly watching the real-time drama unfolding on the ground.

"Look, Captain. They're carrying somebody out on a stretcher."

"Where?"

"There."

"I see it," Paul said.

Four paramedics surrounded a stretcher with a man on it in the area near the end of the reflecting pool. One paramedic applied chest compressions. When they lifted the stretcher, they began moving, first at a brisk walk, and then almost at a jog, toward an ambulance waiting by the World War II Memorial. Six DC policemen circled the paramedics, clearing the crowd out of the way as the paramedics moved toward the ambulance.

"Can you get a close-up on that?" Paul said.

"Yes, sir," the lead DHS controller replied.

The screen flashed to a closer view, then flashed to a still-closer view.

The man on the stretcher was motionless. His mouth hung open, with tubes going in, and the pillow behind his head was bloody. His eyes were closed, and his skin looked white as a ghost.

One paramedic continued chest compressions on the man, even as they all rushed toward the ambulance.

"That guy on the stretcher looks familiar," Paul said.

"Yes, he does," Jefferies said.

"Is he Navy?"

"Not sure, sir, but he does look familiar."

"I don't like the looks of it," Paul said.

"Me neither, sir. If that guy makes it, it'll be a miracle."

"Gentlemen," Paul said, "if you are into prayer, I think now is the time to pray for that guy."

The paramedics arrived at the back of the ambulance. As they prepared to slide the stretcher inside, a slim woman wearing jogging shorts and a T-shirt could be seen running toward them from the direction of the reflecting pool.

Three policemen stepped in to stop her, but she pushed against them, trying to force herself past the cops and toward the back of the ambulance.

"Look at the woman," one of the drone controllers said.

"What's she doing?" said another.

"She looks like she's screaming," another said.

"She must know the guy," still another said.

"Can we get a closer shot of the woman?" Paul asked. "Maybe a still frame?"

"Sure, Captain," the DHS controller said. "Let me see what I can do."

The screens went black.

A second later, the word *recalibrating* appeared in white lettering in the middle of the black screen, and then the screen reappeared with an even-closer view of the scene.

The woman appeared in the middle of the screen, and she was still being restrained by police. Her blonde hair was pulled back in a ponytail, and her arms reached out desperately toward the ambulance as it began pulling away.

Who was this woman? It was hard to tell from images, even live images, showing mostly the top of her head. But still.

Then, in her flailing, she glanced up for a split second and then back down again. The screen shot of her was so fast that he couldn't really tell, but long enough to accelerate his heart. Could it be?

"Can we do a playback and do a freeze on that woman when she looks up?"

"If the computer decides to cooperate, I think we can, Captain."

"Do it, please."

"Yes, sir."

Again, a black screen. A second later, the word *recalibrating* appeared in white lettering. And then she appeared.

Paul froze. His heart fell into his stomach.

"Oh dear God, please no."

"You know her, Skipper?"

"She's Navy. Navy JAG. Stationed at the Pentagon. And I have a feeling the guy they just put into the ambulance might be JAG too."

"Doesn't look good for the guy," Commander Jefferies said.

"John, do we have any choppers on the flight line available for transport?"

"I think the squadron has three Sea Stallions on standby at the moment, sir."

"Call the squadron commander. Tell him I need a lift to the Pentagon. Now."

"Aye, sir."

• • •

EMERGENCY ROOM
WALTER REED NATIONAL MILITARY MEDICAL CENTER
BETHESDA, MARYLAND

The second hand of the clock on the wall swept past twelve again, and Caroline could do nothing except pace back and forth and watch it sweep another loop around the numbers of the dial.

Two nurses and several orderlies had crisscrossed in the spaces behind the admitting area, behind the corpsman chief who manned the desk. Several other visitors milled about in the waiting area, as if trying to avoid stepping on a bridge to nowhere.

What was taking them so long?

P.J. had been in emergency surgery now for almost thirty minutes. Still nothing.

"Dear Jesus, please save him," she whispered, then realized that no one even knew where they were. She needed to call Captain Guy. But she didn't have a cell phone. What to do? Without her cell phone, she didn't even have the Pentagon number for Code 13.

"Commander McCormick?"

She turned around. The rear admiral, standing there in summer whites, wore a burnished cross on his right collar, signifying that he was a Christian chaplain in the U.S. Navy. His name tag pinned to his shirt said "Lettow."

"Sir . . . I . . ."

"I'm Rear Admiral Lettow. Chief of Navy Chaplains."

"Sir, how did you know?"

"We got a call from a Captain Paul Kriete. Somehow he knew."

"Paul? I mean, Captain . . ."

"It's all right. Captain Kriete saw some photographs of the scene and alerted JAG. Some members of your command should be here anytime. Admiral Brewer, who is a longtime friend of mine, called me immediately. I was here at the hospital visiting a senior officer who just had surgery. When I found out, I wanted to come down here and wait with you, and pray, if that's okay."

"Thank you, sir. That would mean a lot."

He looked around and then motioned to a couple of chairs over in the corner. "Why don't we go over there and wait. Might be a little more private."

"Good idea, sir."

They walked over and sat in two corner chairs separated only by a small coffee table with a vase of flowers. Her stomach was torn, her eyes watering. But something about the chaplain's presence brought her comfort.

"Looks like you could use this." He handed her a handkerchief.

"Thank you, sir."

"You're welcome. You know, it's kind of chilly in here. They jacked up the air-conditioning. Want me to find you a blanket or something to cover you up?"

She nodded, wiping her eyes. "That would be nice, sir. Thank you."

"Let's see what I can do." Lettow got up and walked over to the desk, prompting the senior chief who was sitting behind it to rise. They talked for a moment, then the senior chief stepped away from the desk.

Caroline needed to get herself together. She was a naval officer. People were looking. People were watching. Thank goodness she wasn't in uniform at the moment. Maybe the nurses and corpsmen and other military personnel milling about wouldn't know. But Admiral Lettow knew. And if anyone from Code 13 showed up, as the admiral hinted, the last thing she needed was to make a lasting first impression of a crybaby. P.J. would agree.

She bit her lower lip, and the admiral returned.

"Look what the chief scrounged up." He handed her a gray sweatshirt.

"Thank you, sir." She took the sweatshirt and pulled it over her body. A baggy fit, but the fleece trapped the heat in her body and felt good against the cold air-conditioning in the waiting area.

"What's your connection to him?"

"To P.J.?"

"Right."

"We had a relationship in San Diego. We talked about getting married. Almost got engaged. Seemed like it would happen. Then . . ." She looked down, then up at him. She tried fighting her emotions, but the tears flowed again. "Thank you for this." She dabbed her eyes with the handkerchief he had given her. "I wish I didn't need it."

"I understand." His voice filled with compassion.

"Anyway," she continued, "you know how it is in the Navy, sir. He got his orders here. It looked like I was going to be sent to Europe or Japan. Anyway, we were a world apart. We never got engaged."

"But I take it the feelings never died?"

"No, sir. At least not from my standpoint. I mean, others were interesting, but I never could fully shake P.J. And then . . ." She dabbed her eyes again, but at least her voice remained under control, thank God. "And then I got these orders to Code 13 here at the Pentagon, the very same duty station where P.J. was stationed. And to be honest with you, sir, I'm thinking, 'Is this the hand of God?' And now this. I may never know."

"Has the doctor told you anything about his condition?"

"At first they weren't going to talk to me at all because of HIPAA. They said they could only talk to immediate family members. So to be honest, I sort of embellished the truth. I told him P.J. and I had been engaged. The doctor even said that wasn't enough until we were married. But I kind of begged and he relented. He said P.J. is critical. That he'd taken a bullet to the brain and they were going to have to perform surgery to remove the bullet. Even still, he said P.J. had lost lots of blood, and there could be massive damage to the brain, and I . . ."

Her lips began quivering, and her voice cracked. The tears flowed again. She couldn't finish her thoughts. She brought the handkerchief to her eyes.

"It's okay," Lettow said. "Don't say any more. I get the idea."

"Thank you, sir."

"You know, Caroline, I don't always know the will of God. But I do know this. This very moment is in the hands of God, because everything is in his hands. Unfortunately, we still have to deal with sin and strife and division and, yes, even death in this fallen world. But despite the pain and despair we all feel, it's all in his hands. Do you know if P.J. knows the Lord?"

She nodded. "Yes, he told me he gave his life to the Lord at age thirteen. He talked about his faith often when we were together, and I know he prayed."

"You know what?" Lettow said. "If he was praying to God, and if he confessed his faith in Jesus, that makes me feel better about him, no matter how this turns out. Would you feel comfortable letting me lead us in prayer right now?"

"Please do, Admiral. Please pray for him before it's too late."

"Let's pray."

She bowed her head.

"Dear Lord in heaven, you have said where two or more are gathered in your name, there you would be also. And so we gather now in your name and know you are here with us. And you have also said that in all things we should pray, and about all matters we should pray, and at all times we should pray. You have said your burden is light and your yoke is easy. So we come to you with our heads bowed, in obedience to your instructions, believing you will hear us and trusting that you have all things under your control.

"Now in this critical hour, and in this critical moment, we pray for our shipmate and for Caroline's friend, Lieutenant Commander P.J. MacDonald. Lord, P.J.'s life is in danger, as you already know, as the doctors you have appointed for this hour work to save his life."

Caroline reached out and took the chaplain's hand. He responded with a warm squeeze.

"Lord, we don't know the full extent of P.J.'s injuries, but you do. And so we ask that you would sustain him, and give him strength, and give him life. We pray that you would watch over the doctors who are treating him. Give them wisdom and steady their hands as they work to remove the bullet from his brain.

"And, Lord, you say we can ask you for anything. And so even as the doctors perform surgery, we ask that you would not only save P.J.'s life but bring about full healing, as only you can do. We believe you can heal and save P.J., if only you will, and if only you so choose.

"Lord, you have said that you have appointed for everyone a time to die. None of us knows when that hour may come. You've appointed that hour for me, you've appointed that hour for Caroline, and, yes, you've appointed that day and hour for P.J. too. So though we are asking you for a miracle, we also ask that if you have made a decision to take P.J., that you not take him, please, until his salvation is assured. Caroline has said that he has professed your Son, Jesus, and I pray that this is true, because there is no way to heaven without a personal relationship with Jesus.

"And as I close, Lord, I ask that you will be here for Caroline, too, and comfort her with your Holy Spirit. Thank you for hearing our prayers and being with us. May your will be done. In Jesus' name, amen."

Caroline released the chaplain's hand and opened her eyes. From behind her she heard another voice, a man's voice that sounded familiar, say, "Amen."

She turned around. "Captain."

"It's okay. You can call me Paul," said the handsome U.S. Navy captain who had followed her from San Diego. "I thought maybe you could use some support."

"Admiral, this is . . ."

"Sir, I'm Captain Paul Kriete. I'm the one who called in the report. Caroline did some excellent legal work on my ship when I was the skipper of the *Cape St. George*. Thank you for being here, sir."

"A pleasure to meet you, Captain, although I wish it was under more pleasant circumstances."

"Likewise, sir. Do we know anything yet?"

"Commander McCormick?"

Another man's voice came from behind, interrupting the conversation between Paul and Admiral Lettow. Caroline's heart instantly shot into overdrive. The doctor was coming to tell her P.J.'s condition. She stood and turned, her stomach feeling sick.

The sight of the Navy captain standing there, in summer whites, calmed her soul. For a millisecond she didn't recognize him, until her eyes found the gold mill rinde, the symbol of the Navy JAG Corps, on his black shoulder boards.

"Captain Guy." Delayed recognition caught up with her. She heard the relief in her own voice that he wasn't the doctor.

"Do we know anything?"

Thankfully, Admiral Lettow stood up and provided the necessary responses. "Captain, I'm Rear Admiral Lettow, Chief of Navy Chaplains."

"Yes, sir. Thank you for being here, sir."

"You're welcome," Lettow said.

"What do we know?"

"I haven't spoken with the doctors, but the surgeons did come out and speak with Commander McCormick earlier. It sounds real touch and go, Captain."

Captain Guy turned to Caroline. "Commander, can you talk about what happened?"

Caroline bit her lip and tightened her stomach. She would not fall apart in front of her superiors. No matter what, she would remain strong for P.J. "We were jogging, sir. Just talking back and forth. We circled the Monument and started back down the Mall. We had just passed the World War II Memorial. I pulled ahead of him and heard a pop. I didn't think much of it. But a second later, I sensed that he wasn't there. I turned around and he was lying on the ground, bleeding. Someone called 911. The rest was a blur. They lifted him into the ambulance, and a DC police officer drove me over here."

"Did you see where the shooter was?"

"No, sir. The detectives came in earlier and asked me the same thing. It seems like I heard the popping noise from behind, and the detectives think the shooter might have been at an angle behind us. It all just happened so fast. None of it makes any sense."

"No, it doesn't."

"Commander McCormick?" Another male voice. Caroline looked over and saw Commander Bill Dockerty, Medical Corps, United States Navy. Dr. Dockerty was P.J.'s surgeon.

Dr. Dockerty hadn't uttered a word, but Caroline already knew. His head hung. The somber look on his face said it all.

Shakespeare said the whole world was a stage, and we were but actors upon it. If only life were that simple. She'd once seen a movie called *The Truman Show* where everything was staged. Everything was televised. Everything was preplanned.

If only life were so choreographed. If only the world were really a stage, as Shakespeare said. If all that were true, then pain could also be choreographed. Like water streaming from a faucet in a kitchen, tears could be turned on and off. In the words of the song, "No more pain. No more tears."

She mustered all the strength within her to embrace what was coming.

"I'm sorry. We did everything we could." His voice reflected an aloof professionalism yet also carried a strain of compassion. "He . . ." Dockerty adjusted his glasses. "We lost him about five minutes ago. He'd lost too much blood. On top of that, the bullet severely damaged his brain. And anytime a vital organ sustains that kind of tearing, survival can be nothing short of a miracle. I'm very sorry for your loss, and I'm sorry that we could not save him."

Her stomach churned and her heart cried, but she would not allow the tears to flow. Not here. Not now.

Still, she was grateful when Captain Guy stepped in.

"Doctor, I'm Captain David Guy. I'm Commander MacDonald's commanding officer. I'll need to make the call to his family. Is there anything at all you can share with me that might bring them words of comfort?"

The doctor looked at Caroline, as if calculating his answer to project a special sensitivity toward her. "Tell them he was a strong man who fought to the end. Given the severity of the gunshot wound, ninety-nine out of one hundred people would have died on the spot. Lieutenant Commander MacDonald was strong, in fact incredibly strong, to survive as long as he did. He was a fighter."

CHAPTER 15

. . .

The breakers coming in at low tide broke into whitecaps. The ocean along this stretch of Georgia's Golden Isles was anything other than blue, and the beach not exactly golden. In fact, the surf and the beaches, at least around the luxurious resorts of Sea Island, St. Simons Island, and Jekyll Island, were notoriously brown in color. If it came down to beachcombing and venturing into the water, Richardson Wellington DeKlerk preferred the wide white beaches and blue waters of Hilton Head and Llandudno Beach in his native South Africa, on the Western Cape.

But the luxury of the old five-star resort they called the Cloister and the alluring history of the Golden Isles still made the place curious and desirable. Draft legislation creating the U.S. Federal Reserve was written just down the coast at the Jekyll Island Club in 1910, and President Jimmy Carter assembled his first "kitchen cabinet" right here at the Cloister in 1976.

Plus, for a splendid opportunity to get away for a day with Ivana, Sea Island was perfect. Hilton Head was too close to Savannah and thus proved a likelier place for someone to see them together. And Jack Patterson, who was expensive enough already, had already warned him about the added expense should he find himself in the midst of divorce litigation. Not that Richardson worried about Ivana's husband, Harold Martin, whom he could either crush in court or buy off at a price.

The other thing about the Cloister that separated it from other locations was that it was a five-star expense, which, frankly, put it out of reach of most of his employees and most residents of Savannah.

Indeed, wealth had its privileges, and pending legal approval of the AirFlite contract from the Navy JAG, Richardson DeKlerk would claim as much wealth, privilege, and power as any man in the world.

He pushed up on his beach towel and looked over at Ivana as she sunned on a green towel beside him, lying on her back in a dark-blue bathing suit, a shock of her blonde hair blowing in the wind across her face.

He couldn't see through her designer shades whether she had made eye contact, but the smile on her face, which came when he leaned up and looked at her, and the tilting of her head as she smiled, let him know that she could see him and she was pleased with what she saw.

Richardson usually got whatever he wanted, and right now, with the hypnotic, lulling sound of waves washing up on the beach just a few yards from their feet, with the sporadic chirping of seagulls overhead . . .

He leaned over to her just as a cool breeze whipped in from the ocean. When their lips met, the instant electricity proved any risk of being seen was worth it.

"You are incredible, Richardson. Harold doesn't have a clue."

He didn't respond but instead leaned in and kissed her again. Just as the second kiss was about to turn from electric to something more, his cell phone rang. He cursed, then opened his eyes and looked down.

Jack Patterson.

"Pardon me, my dear, but I need to take this."

"I understand." Her pretty face reflected disappointment.

"Jack. What do you have for me?"

"It's taken care of, Richardson."

"What do you mean?"

"I'm talking about the uncertainty over this legal opinion about Project Blue Jay. I just got a call from our contact in DC. Let me put it this way. We don't have to worry about this Lieutenant Commander MacDonald authoring any legal opinions that will influence the Secretary of the Navy against us."

Richardson smiled. "Excellent work. What did this cost us?"

"No need to worry about that."

"You're right. Plausible deniability. It works for your Democrat friends. Why not us?"

"It's not just the Democrats who use it."

"Point well taken. Anyway, whatever they do, that legal opinion must give the Secretary of the Navy an excuse to rubber-stamp recommended approval of this contract. Then we need to get it before Congress ASAP. Billions are riding on this, Jack, and we pay your firm a ton of money to lobby for us. So I expect no more road bumps. Are we clear on all this?"

"Perfectly clear. We're on it."

"Excellent. Now, unless you have an emergency situation, I'm going to be detained for the rest of the afternoon."

"Tell Ivana I said hi."

"You weren't supposed to know about that."

"You pay me to know everything, Richardson. Besides, it's attorney-client privilege. I can't say anything about it even if I wanted to."

"Just get that bill through Congress, Jack." He hung up.

"Is everything okay, Richardson?"

"Just lovely, my dear. Everything just got a bit rosier." He pulled her close to him and kissed her.

CHAPTER 16

. . .

HEADQUARTERS
NEW YORK CONCRETE & SEAFOOD COMPANY
EAST 161ST STREET
THE BRONX
WEDNESDAY AFTERNOON

"Mr. D'Agostino, you got a call!" The woman's voice, resonating in a thick Brooklyn accent, blared through Phil's office phone.

"Who is it, Vivian?"

"It's Vinnie, sir. On line one. He says it's important."

"Tell him to hang on a second."

"Yes, sir."

Phil took a last, satisfying drag from the Marlboro cigarette, sucking the nicotine into his lungs, then snuffed it out in an ashtray alongside the six other ash-tipped cigarette butts he had smoked this afternoon alone.

"Vivian!" He raised his voice loud enough to be heard through the open door out to his secretary's office. He didn't believe in the intercom. Yelling was the Italian way.

"Yes, sir, Mr. D."

"Come get this ashtray and empty it, will ya? I've gotta take this call from Vinnie."

"Yes, sir."

Vivian walked in and picked up the ashtray as Phil punched line one and picked up the phone. "Vinnie. Whatcha got?"

"There's some good news, boss. Big Sal is going to be happy."

"Talk to me."

"You know that naval officer threatening to write that paper approving this contract? MacDonald?"

"What about him?"

"We got him."

"You mean . . . ?"

"I mean he just got a promotion to captain of the morgue."

"Are you serious, Vinnie?"

"As dead serious as that guy is dead."

Phil smiled and extracted another cigarette from his shirt pocket as Vivian returned and put a clean ashtray on his desk. "Excellent work, Vinnie. You're turning into a smart son-in-law. Maybe I'll tell my daughter, who you don't deserve and never deserved to begin with, that there's hope for you after all." He took a first satisfying drag from the new cigarette.

"Thanks, boss. Coming from you, that means a lot."

"Listen, Vinnie, I don't need to know details, but I want you to monitor this situation, find out who gets to write this memo now that this MacDonald guy is gone, and make sure it gets written like we want it. Go back to Chuckie Rodino's office and get them involved if you have to."

"I'm on it, boss. I already met me a friend from Rodino's office. I think I'll pay him another little visit just to make sure we're all singing from the same song sheet. Know what I mean?"

"I never know what you mean, Vinnie. Sometimes, the way you talk, it's impossible to know what you mean. But here's what I mean. I want you to stay on the ground and do whatever you need to do, and work with Chuckie Rodino's office to make sure this drone contract project gets killed as cold as this MacDonald is. We got that clear?"

"Perfectly clear, boss."

"Excellent. You get to work on that now, and I'll break the news to Big Sal."

"You got it, boss."

CHAPTER 17

...

DIRKSEN SENATE OFFICE BUILDING
UNITED STATES CAPITOL
OFFICE OF ROBERT TALMADGE (R-GA)
WASHINGTON, DC
WEDNESDAY AFTERNOON

United States Senator Bobby Talmadge looked up just as Tommy Mandela rapped three times on the outside of the senator's office door. He walked in before Talmadge could even say a word. Talmadge could tell by the serious look on Mandela's face that whatever he had in mind, it wouldn't be jovial political chitchat.

"Need to talk to you, boss."

"By the look on your face, Tommy, I'm not sure I'm gonna want to hear it."

"Maybe you will. Maybe you won't."

"Spit it out."

"That JAG officer from Code 13, the one Richardson was worried about writing that opinion letter, was shot this afternoon."

"What?"

"Yep. Bullet to the back of the head. Took him to Walter Reed for emergency surgery. Died on the table."

"Holy crap."

"Want me to put you on the line with Richardson to tell him that problem's taken care of?"

"Let me think." Bobby felt a twisting in the pit of his stomach. He had hired Tommy Mandela for his reputation as a ruthless political operator, as one who would make things happen without the necessity of specific direction, a take-no-prisoners operator whose goal was the political advancement of his boss. In fact, Bobby had hired Mandela at the joint recommendation of Richardson DeKlerk and Joe Don Mack of the Georgia Political Victory Fund. "He'll be the perfect balance for you, Bobby," Joe Don Mack had said. "You can be the nice guy and he can be the bad guy. Every smiling politician needs a cutthroat operator in the background where you won't want to know about stuff he did."

Why did the smirk of satisfaction on Tommy's face and his piercing black eyes make Bobby's stomach feel sick?

"Tommy, do we know what really happened to this officer?"

Mandela hesitated. A knowing grin. A look of self-satisfaction.

"You really want to know the answer to that question, boss?"

Something didn't feel right about all this. "Do you think I should know?"

"Not if you want to claim plausible deniability, boss."

Mandela's words jolted him, and Bobby felt his stomach being knotted like a tightly twisted washrag with all the water being wrung out of it. "I guess it doesn't matter. Tell you what. Leave it alone with Richardson for the time being. If he doesn't already know, he'll find out soon enough. And the last thing we need is for him to get another shot at razzing me about the status of the drone contract."

"Ya know what, Senator?" Mandela didn't give Bobby enough time to answer. "For a rookie senator, your political instincts are pretty darn good."

"Thanks, Tommy. Let's leave it at that. Meanwhile, let's arrange a meeting with Senator Roberson Fowler. We need to call in the big guns to get this contract through. Gotta make sure we stay on DeKlerk's good side. Joe Don Mack's too."

"As I said, Senator, for a rookie senator, your political instincts are pretty darn good. I'll get that meeting arranged ASAP. But understand, sir, we're gonna have to go to him. He's not coming to us."

"I understand. He's been in the senate since Ulysses S. Grant's inauguration. He's the king of Washington. I'm the new kid on the block."

Mandela laughed. "With a learning curve like that, Senator, we'll have you in the White House faster than a bullet can take out a troublemaker."

"Don't know if I like the analogy, Tommy. But thanks for the compliment."

CHAPTER 18

· · ·

"Okay, look, Chuckie." Phil sucked on his third cigarette in the last hour. "Now that the problem of that troublemaker JAG officer has been eliminated, we need some action on this contract. You know, I've been patient. Big Sal has been patient. But we need this contract squashed. You know, the family didn't get you elected just to go down to Washington and drink caviar and sip champagne. So what's going on, Chuckie? What am I gonna tell Big Sal? I mean, Big Sal ain't gonna be patient forever!"

"Don't worry, Phil." Rodino sounded nervous. "This drone project bill hasn't even been brought to Congress yet. Tell Big Sal it will never see the light of day. And if it does see the light of day, it'll get squashed in committee."

"Wait a minute. Are you telling me it won't get called for a hearing, or are you telling me it will get called but won't pass? What are you telling me, Senator?"

A pause.

"Hey, tell Big Sal the bill hasn't been passed, and if I have anything to do with it, it won't be passed. Tell him I guarantee it."

Vivian stepped into the office.

"Mr. D'Agostino, it's Vinnie on the line again."

"Look, Senator, I'll pass it on to Big Sal. But right now I gotta go. Just do your job. Okay? Talk to you later."

Phil slammed down the phone and picked up the blinking line. "Vinnie. What have you got for me?"

"We got a problem, boss."

"Talk to me, Vinnie."

"Our computer geek just called."

"Which computer geek? We got several of 'em."

"Tony, boss. You remember Tony?"

"Oh yeah. Tony. What about him?"

"Well, you know we've been watching emails coming out of this Code 13, right?"

"Right. What did we have to spend? Thirty thousand cash for some civilian clerk at the Pentagon to give us log-on info?"

"More like forty grand, boss."

"Okay, whatever. So you're telling me Tony's found something?"

"Yep. So he says."

"Spit it out."

"Seems like this MacDonald, before he got taken out, finished his legal paper and emailed it to another officer who works in the same section, this Code 13, for safekeeping. Except he didn't email it to a government computer. He emailed it to a private email address. Which means it's probably at the officer's residence. And it gets worse, boss."

Phil rocked back in his chair, fuming, and tempted to scream at his son-in-law lackey who, as much as he hated to admit it, wasn't as stupid as Phil wanted him to be. But there was no point in killing the messenger, even though nobody ever made that point to Big Sal, who would take Vinnie's bad news out on him. "Okay, Vinnie. How does it get worse?"

"Well, the opinion that he wound up writing? From what Tony says, it ain't good. He wrote it against us, saying that the drones would be legal. And then he wrote that he might send another opinion, saying the drones would be illegal, but he never sent it. He got bopped off instead."

"So, Vinnie. Let me see if I can get this straight. You're saying our computer guy intercepted an email this MacDonald wrote to another naval officer, working in the same division, with a legal opinion saying the drones are legal so the Navy can go forward with the contract?"

"Right, boss."

"But in the body of the email, he said he might be sending the officer a contradictory opinion, saying the drones are illegal, which is what we wanted him to say?"

"Actually, boss, he said he *would* be sending another opinion after he got back from his run. In other words, if he hadn't got bopped off down on the National Mall, it looks like he would have come back, taken a shower, put on his uniform, and sent the second opinion, saying the drones are illegal, which is what we wanted him to say. But he got hosed out on the Mall."

"So let me get this straight again. There's one opinion floating around out there that cuts against the family, and it might be in some other officer's hands by now. And there's another opinion out there, but it's still sitting in the Pentagon, because MacDonald got hosed before he could come back from his run and send it."

Phil cursed. "Why'd you have to work so fast, Vinnie?"

"I was just doing what I thought you wanted me to do, boss."

Phil shook his head, drummed his fingers on his desk, and thought.

"Who did MacDonald send this email to?"

"Hang on. Let me check the name." A pause. "To another officer. A Lieutenant Ross Simmons, who is also a JAG officer at Code 13. In the same division. Apparently this Simmons worked with or worked under MacDonald."

"Did MacDonald say anything in that email about why he sent his legal opinion to Simmons?"

"Hang on. Let me look." Another pause. "He said, 'In case something happens to me, they'll probably reassign this to you. Wanted to make it easy for you to pick whichever opinion you would want to go with.'"

"Son of a—!" Phil drew on his cigarette. "The sucker knew somebody might take him out."

"Right, boss. And my guess is it ain't just us who wanted to see him get iced."

"You're smarter than I like to give you credit for, Vinnie."

"You gonna tell Big Sal?"

The backhanded compliment about being smarter than given credit for seemed to have blown over Vinnie's head.

"I don't know yet. I don't want to bother Big Sal if we can handle it in-house."

"What do you want me to do?"

"We gotta find this Lieutenant Simmons and get that opinion back. We can't have that thing floating around out there. And talk to Tony and see if there's any way we can get that email erased."

"You got it, boss. I'm on it."

CHAPTER 19

...

ARLINGTON NATIONAL CEMETERY
SECTION 60
ARLINGTON, VIRGINIA
SATURDAY AFTERNOON

The late-afternoon sun, blazing through the cloudless, deep blue sky, lit the wind-ruffled cherry tree blossoms standing guard above the still-empty grave. All across the massive acreage of the sprawling tree-dotted cemetery, the sun seemed to lend a deeper lushness to the green grass carpeting on the hallowed plains and hills.

Perhaps the perfect weather and picturesque beauty was God's way of telling them that P.J. was now in a better place. Because if it weren't for the sight of thousands of simple grave markers rising from the grass, this place might be a future glimpse of heaven.

At least that's what Caroline told herself. For the beauty gave her comfort in the midst of sorrow and a surrealistic reprieve from the surrealistic shock.

Though she had been ordered to report to work yesterday, all that changed with P.J.'s death. Captain Guy had told her to take off a couple more days and meet them at the service.

Now here she was in full uniform, standing at parade rest with the other members of her new command, the prestigious Code 13.

In the distance, they heard the *clip-clop* of horses' hooves on the asphalt cartway just behind them. Then from around the bend, about a hundred yards away, down by the old oak tree, two white horses appeared. They approached at a slow gait, walking side by side.

On the left horse was a rider, a United States Army sergeant in service dress blue uniform. The right horse bore only an empty saddle.

A second pair of horses followed the first pair, and then a third, all tethered together in pairs of two, clipping and clopping against the grief-laden silence awaiting their arrival.

There were six white horses altogether, commanded by three Army sergeants in service dress blues.

As the third pair of horses rounded the bend, the red, white, and blue of the flag covering P.J.'s casket appeared atop a caisson pulled behind the third pair of horses.

Walking just in front and to the right of the caisson was a United States Navy admiral in full choker white uniform. Caroline recognized him as Rear Admiral Jeffrey Lettow, the Chief of Navy Chaplains who had prayed with her at the medical center. He would officiate.

Six U.S. Navy petty officers, in service dress white jumper uniforms and white Dixie cup caps, marched two by two in exact precision behind the caisson.

The sight brought tears to her eyes and chills to her body. Fighting the compulsion of her emotions, she cast her eyes away from the caisson, although she could not erase the haunting sound of the *clip-clop* of the horses as the procession drew near.

By the open grave a few yards away, three rows of empty seats awaited the family, who were still sitting in black limousines along the cartway, waiting for the casket-bearing caisson to arrive.

Other friends and family members, mostly civilians, were gathered in a semicircle behind the row of empty seats. To the right of the empty seats, a Navy commander who would serve as funeral director stood at parade rest.

Behind and to the right of the civilians, about thirty yards from the grave, a U.S. Navy bugler stood at parade rest. Another ten yards or so behind the bugler, six U.S. Navy riflemen—the firing party—also stood at parade rest.

The *clip-clopping* drew nearer, now so close that Caroline could hear the squeaky sound of the caisson's wheels turning and a snort from one of the horses.

A moment later, the horses stopped. The caisson had reached its debarkation point only a few yards from the gravesite.

The sound of car doors opening. Car doors closing. More opening and closing.

Navy-enlisted men led family members in single-file columns toward the reserved seating, where they began filling the back row. A moment later, all but the front row had been seated.

The Navy commander, who had been standing just a few feet from the front corner of the grave, and who wore a ceremonial sheath and sword holstered to his uniform, turned and walked toward the cartway. With sunshine reflecting off the stainless steel sword, he changed direction slightly, walking to the front of the team of horses pulling the caisson, which had stopped just behind three black limousines, their engines still running. The commander gave a hand signal, and the front and back doors of the first two cars opened. Men, women, boys, and girls, all looking solemn, some wiping their eyes with handkerchiefs, emerged from the lead cars.

A lieutenant, also bearing a sword at his side and who had been standing guard by the parked cars, led them in a solemn, single-file procession across the grass.

Some looked off to the right at P.J.'s flag-draped casket. Others looked away, staring straight ahead. One little girl with curly blonde locks, her hair fluttering in a gust of breeze, took her mother's hand.

A young couple clasped hands.

The lieutenant directed them to the front row, where they sat, leaving three seats on the end vacant. The lieutenant nodded at the commander, who opened the back door of the third limousine.

Gabrielle Barnes MacDonald stepped from the car and took the commander's arm. Even in mourning, wearing a simple black dress that accentuated her slim body, P.J.'s sixty-three-year-old mother looked gorgeous and elegant in the afternoon sun. Her face bore a grim look with all the grace that Jacqueline Kennedy had displayed so courageously all those decades ago in this very cemetery for another former naval officer struck down by an assassin's bullet.

P.J.'s father, William, and his younger sister, Delia, fell in behind Gabrielle and the commander. They were a graceful family who projected strength and reassurance among dozens of sniffling mourners displaying emotions of sorrow around the grave. The MacDonalds were class personified, and Caroline had hoped to become a part of this family.

Now that would never happen.

The commander led the MacDonalds to their seats, and they sat in silence, absorbing the sounds of chirping birds and the breeze rustling through the treetops.

Caroline noticed for the first time several high-ranking naval officers behind the family. There stood her friend, Captain Paul Kriete. She felt a sense of comfort and appreciation that he had come. Beside Paul, Vice Admiral Zack Brewer stood with his wife, Diane Colcernian Brewer, her auburn hair gleaming in the sun, wearing a dark-blue dress and large designer shades. Just beside the Brewers was the Secretary of the Navy, the Honorable H. Lawrence Anderson, with his wife, Amy.

Gabrielle MacDonald looked up at Admiral Lettow and nodded her head, signaling the chaplain to step forward.

"Ladies and gentlemen, the Lord giveth, and the Lord taketh away. Blessed be the name of the Lord.

"We gather here in this gorgeous place, on this hallowed ground, in the midst of God's natural beauty, to say our final good-bye to Lieutenant Commander P.J. MacDonald, who was an officer, a gentleman, a servant of his country, and, most important, a servant of our Lord and Savior, Jesus Christ.

"As we prepare for the final portions of this military ceremony, to render honor to this strong man whom we lost too soon, a patriot who loved his country, the family has requested two passages of Scripture that were P.J.'s favorites, one from the Old Testament and one from the New, each marked in his Bible.

"The first is from the book of Psalms, from Psalm 29:3–9 to be precise, and reflected P.J.'s love of the sea.

"The voice of the LORD is upon the waters;
The God of glory thunders,
The LORD is over many waters.
The voice of the LORD is powerful,
The voice of the LORD is majestic.
The voice of the LORD breaks the cedars;
Yes, the LORD breaks in pieces the cedars of Lebanon.
He makes Lebanon skip like a calf,
And Sirion like a young wild ox.
The voice of the LORD hews out flames of fire.
The voice of the LORD shakes the wilderness;
The LORD shakes the wilderness of Kadesh.
The voice of the LORD makes the deer to calve
And strips the forests bare;
And in His temple everything says, 'Glory!'"

Lettow paused, looked up, and cast a reassuring glance at the family. "And then there are two short verses from the New Testament, which in so many ways go to the very heart of who P.J. was, and indeed of who he still is." He looked down. "The first is from Saint Paul's letter to the church at Ephesus, chapter 2, verses 8 and 9. 'For by grace you have been saved through faith; and that not of yourselves, it is the gift of God, not as a result of works, so that no one may boast.'

"And finally, from Paul's letter to the church at Rome, chapter 10, verses 9 and 10. 'If you confess with your mouth Jesus as Lord, and believe in your heart that God raised Him from the dead, you will be saved; for with the heart a person believes, resulting in righteousness, and with the mouth he confesses, resulting in salvation.'"

Lettow closed the Bible in his hand and looked up.

"This concludes the reading of the true and everlasting Word of God. Blessed be the name of the Lord.

"The words of Holy Scripture remind us that even in death, there is yet life. The promise of the great Savior, Jesus Christ, is that if we have placed our trust in him, though we should die, so also shall we live. P.J. placed his hope and trust and confidence in that great Savior, who is the only way to God the Father, and because Jesus lives, so, too, does P.J. live.

"If you do not know Christ Jesus as your Lord and Savior, if there is doubt in your mind, doubt in your heart, if you don't know your destination should earthly death come upon you, suddenly and unexpectedly, as earthly death came quickly for our brother-in-arms, then I invite you today to place your faith in Christ. Only in him, only through him, only by him, may we escape the fiery bondage of eternal death and be assured of life forever, on streets of gold, by precious running waters, in the presence of our glorious Savior under the wings of God the Father.

"Accept Christ now, before it is too late.

"Even so, come quickly, Lord Jesus.

"In the name of the Father, and the Son, and the Holy Spirit, amen."

Another moment of silence, as the chaplain's words resonated against the peaceful sounds of nature.

The commander turned to the family members seated by the grave and gave them a silent hand signal to rise, and they all stood.

The sight caused Caroline's heart to pound. She knew what was coming, and she dreaded it with all her heart.

"Attention on deck!"

Caroline snapped to attention, along with every other member of the United States military standing by the grave.

"Present . . . arms!"

Every naval officer flashed a sharp salute.

The commander withdrew his sword, bringing it to a tight vertical position, gripping it just below his chin, holding it in alignment straight in front of his face, the sun glistening off the sharp, stainless steel blade.

The pallbearers moved in perfectly executed half steps to surround the casket. In somber silence, with their hand movements in exact unison, they began to lift the casket up off the caisson. In precise half steps, they stepped back with it, now clearing the caisson.

"Mark time, march!" the squadron leader called.

They marched in place as they executed a pivoting maneuver, turning the casket, feet first, at an angle lined up with the grave.

"Forward, march!"

In hallowed silence, they stepped forward, the squadron leader out front, carrying the casket across the green grass to the grave. In a reverent unison of motion they brought the casket over the grave and laid it onto the lowering device, then stood at perfect attention, guarding P.J.'s body in respect.

"Order . . . arms!"

The officers dropped their salutes.

"Parade . . . rest!"

Captain Guy stepped forward, to a position just away from the head of the casket, as the six pallbearers lifted the American flag off the casket. Caroline watched the flag. They started from the feet of the casket, the end covered only with the red and white stripes of the flag.

They worked in a slow, robotic, dignified fashion, wearing white gloves, as if they were handling the most precious commodity on the face of the earth, something more valuable than gold or silver or rubies. One perfect fold followed another, a third fold, then a fourth.

Searching for a mental exercise to help her fight tears, Caroline counted folds. And when they reached the head of the casket, they folded the flag for the fourteenth and final time, compacting Old Glory into a perfect triangle. The last pallbearer turned with the flag tucked in the crook of his elbow and faced the squadron leader. With his right hand he gave a slow-motion salute, bringing his white glove to the bill of his cap.

The squadron leader, a Navy lieutenant, slowly returned the salute, reciprocating the slow-motion dignity with which it was rendered, and received the flag.

The squadron leader then did an about-face, took two steps toward Captain Guy, and commenced another slow, reverent salute, bringing his white glove to the black bill of his cap.

As Captain Guy slowly returned the lieutenant's salute, then received the flag, a tear rolled down Caroline's cheek.

The lieutenant did a slow about-face, took two steps toward the casket, and came to attention, standing watch over it with the other pallbearers.

A warm breeze swept in, lasting about two seconds, then died down. A second later, Captain Guy walked alongside the casket, past the pallbearers, past the squadron leader, and approached P.J.'s mother.

He went down on one knee just inches in front of her, with the folded flag resting on his knee.

"On behalf of the president of the United States, the United States Navy, and a grateful nation, please accept this flag as a symbol of our appreciation for your loved one's honorable and faithful service."

Lifting the folded flag in his white gloves, he handed it to her.

Caroline could see that she smiled, nodded, and said, "Thank you," although her voice could not be heard in the breeze.

Captain Guy stood, stepped away, and walked back to his position.

"Attention on deck!"

All military personnel snapped to sharp attention.

"Present . . . arms!"

Caroline and the others saluted.

"Ready . . . fire!"

The first rifle volley cracked the air with a stinging fury. Caroline winced.

"Fire!"

The second volley echoed across the cemetery, bouncing off white gravestones.

"Fire!"

The third boomed like distant thunder.

When the echo from the rifles died, with a slow, melodic strain, off in the distance, the Navy bugler began to play taps, and her mind remembered the words.

Day is done, gone the sun
From the lakes, from the hills, from the sky;
All is well, safely rest, God is nigh.

The long haunt of the bugle ended.

"Order . . . arms!"

The officers dropped their salutes.

Admiral Lettow, Captain Guy, and the commander in charge of the funeral slowly filed by the family members, shaking hands and offering condolences, and then the commander invited the family to stand and led them off to the waiting limousines.

"Parade . . . rest!"

"Company dismissed."

That was it? Just like that?

Caroline felt numb. Some mourners chatted, and some started to leave. She wished the family had stayed, but they'd elected to leave and not mingle.

She stepped forward, walked over to the casket, and put her hand on it.

"Good-bye, P.J. Until we meet again."

She turned and walked away.

• • •

ARLINGTON NATIONAL CEMETERY
SECTION 60
BRADLEY DRIVE

Victoria strolled across the lush green grass of section 60, looking for her car, which she had parked somewhere at the intersection of Bradley Drive and Marshall Drive. She was glad that Mark was here for the funeral. She found his presence comforting in a way that surprised her.

Still, as he walked with her across the cemetery, ever the gentleman he always had been, she didn't feel like engaging in small talk.

Her whole relationship with P.J. MacDonald had come and gone as fast as a whirlwind—a compacted representation of life itself—here today, gone tomorrow.

In the brief time she'd known him, his magnetism had enticed her imagination almost day and night, and their kiss just a few nights ago was the most electric thing she had ever experienced.

In many ways P.J. had been everything Mark wasn't. Exciting. Super brilliant, über handsome. Unpredictable.

Yet here was Mark. Steady. Dependable. Mildly handsome, but no Adonis like P.J. But ever the gentleman.

Still, she knew she couldn't soon shake the images of the afternoon. The horse-drawn funeral caisson. The folding of the flag. The firing of the rifles and the final rendition of taps, all in honor of P.J.

But the image that she would never forget came after all that. The image of Caroline standing alone by his casket, her hand lovingly placed upon it, tears streaming down her face.

Lieutenant Commander Caroline McCormick was the woman who still loved P.J. MacDonald more than anyone in the world. And now Victoria felt a tinge of guilt that she had made a play for him.

But then again, what red-blooded single woman wouldn't have been drawn to him? And besides, it wasn't like he and Caroline were still together at the time.

But the image of Caroline at the casket?

Victoria felt her eyes watering.

And now here was Mark, by her side again, which compounded her guilt.

A moment later, they reached Bradley Drive, which was one of several streets inside the boundaries of the cemetery, all named for great American war heroes.

"I parked around the corner, over on Marshall Drive. Not much farther," she said finally. But before Mark could even respond, she spotted the woman, who within a matter of days, had both brought out her jealous anger and then brought her to tears.

"Caroline!"

The blonde naval officer, her black Volkswagen Passat parked along Bradley Drive, looked up. "Victoria?"

"Wait a second?"

"Okay," Caroline said.

"Is that the officer who was standing by P.J.'s casket?" Mark asked.

"That's the one. Give me a second, will you?"

"Sure."

Victoria stepped out ahead of Mark and walked across the last two gravesites over to the street where Caroline stood by her car. She walked right up to the woman she had thought would become her rival. "Caroline, I just want to let you know how sorry I am. I think I can see how much he meant to you. I didn't realize it before. It's so obvious."

Caroline smiled and nodded. "That's very gracious of you. Thank you for your kind words."

"I also want to apologize that I didn't come across in a warm manner when we met. Please forgive me."

"No worries. It's all such a blur anyway."

"You know, I hope we can be friends. I mean, we're going to be working together, and although you knew P.J. a lot better than I did, I have a feeling that's the way he would have wanted it."

Caroline looked up. Her eyes were still watery. A kind smile crossed her face. "I think that's a great idea. And I think you're right. P.J. certainly would want us to be friends." She reached out, and they embraced.

"I've got someone I want you to meet," Victoria said.

"Okay."

She turned and motioned Mark over. "This is my friend, Special Agent Mark Romanov, from NCIS in Norfolk. We go back a long way. He heard about P.J. and came up to offer his support."

"Hi, Mark," Caroline said.

"My pleasure, Commander."

"Please, Caroline is fine."

"It's nice to meet you," Mark said, "but I wish it could have been under different circumstances."

"Thank you."

"I want you to know we are going to get to the bottom of this, and whoever is responsible will be brought to justice."

"Mark's the NCIS's best investigator," Victoria said, "and they've brought him up from Norfolk to nail whoever did this."

"Actually," Mark said, "they're assigning me up here for six months

TAD." TAD was the military acronym for temporary active duty. "Just to work this case until we get some answers. I've leased a furnished townhouse in Alexandria."

"Oh really?" A ton of bricks hit Victoria's stomach. "I didn't know that part. I mean, the part about you getting a TAD assignment."

"Just found out myself," Mark said. "I didn't get around to mentioning it yet."

"Anyway, thanks for the words." Caroline looked at Victoria. "Was everybody here today from Code 13?"

"Everybody except Lieutenant Ross Simmons."

"I thought he was missing," Caroline said. "I remember meeting him just before our run."

"Was he supposed to be here?" Mark asked.

"I thought Captain Guy ordered everybody to be here to show full support from the command."

"Strange," Mark said, turning to Caroline. "Anyway, Commander—"

"Caroline," she interrupted.

"Yes. Caroline. Would it be okay if I give you my card, just in case you need me for anything?"

She smiled. "Yes, of course."

He handed her his card.

"Thank you."

"My pleasure. And I hope to see you under more pleasant circumstances next time."

"You too."

Caroline got into her car, cranked the engine, and drove away.

Victoria watched as Caroline's car turned off onto a side street, then disappeared.

"You can tell she's taking this hard," Mark said.

"We're all taking it hard. But no doubt, she's taking it the hardest."

"Tell ya what," Mark said, "I don't like hanging around cemeteries. Let's find your car, then go get a drink and grab something to eat. Maybe Old Town Alexandria? Or maybe Georgetown? What do you say?"

She studied his face. She didn't want to rekindle their relationship. Not now, anyway. Not with P.J. just being buried.

On the other hand, he had played the role of the perfect gentleman, and she didn't want to be alone after spending the afternoon in a cemetery.

"Okay. All right. But just as friends for the time being. Okay?"

"Okay." He flashed the same handsome smile that had attracted her from the beginning. "For the time being."

"Deal," she said.

"Deal."

CHAPTER 20

• • •

The drive from Arlington down the Shirley Highway, past the Capital Beltway, and then to Old Keene Mill Road in Springfield had taken forever, or so it seemed.

Washington's traffic nightmare, no matter the time of day or day of the week, was far worse already than anything she had experienced in San Diego.

And another problem with Washington was exorbitant housing prices. DC was even more high-priced than San Diego. Junior officers had to live out a ways from the Pentagon because senior officers, lobbyists, and high-paid government bureaucrats snapped everything closer to the Pentagon and closer to DC itself.

Caroline took comfort in the fact that the Judge Advocate General of the Navy, Vice Admiral Zack Brewer, although he could afford something closer, had elected to live out in Springfield, "to be with the men and women with whom I serve," he had often said.

She had already heard that the admiral's townhouse was off Old Keene Mill Road, about a mile from her rented townhouse in Oxford Hunt.

Brewer was a legend and JAG Corps hero. And to a lesser degree, so was his wife, Diane, once among the top JAG officers in the Navy before she married Zack and left active duty.

She turned left on Huntsman Boulevard.

Her townhouse community sat near the intersection of Huntsman and Sydenstricker Road. She wheeled into her short driveway, turned off the engine, sat a moment, and stared at the townhouse.

She got out of the car, locked it, walked to the front door stoop, and unlocked the door. She tossed her purse onto the sofa in the den, went into the kitchen, and grabbed a bottled water from the fridge, then went to her bedroom to check her email.

The computer on her desk had lapsed into sleep mode. She tapped the space bar and was back in business.

That's what she needed now. To get her mind off this.

She opened AOL and was greeted with an immediate, "You've got mail."

She smiled at the sound. Even an electronic voice at the moment was better than no voice.

Let's see. Junk. Delete. More junk. Delete. What's wrong with my spam filter?

She scrolled down a bit.

What's this?

From: Ross Simmons.
Subj: Caroline, P.J. asked me to contact you.

What?

The email had been sent two days ago, but with the shock of P.J.'s death, frankly, she had missed it.

She opened the email.

LCDR McCormick,

I met you the day you first visited Code 13. I was working with P.J. on several projects. He gave me your personal email address and asked me to contact you if something happened to him. He didn't want me contacting you on government email.

Captain Guy assigned the Blue Jay project to P.J., and P.J. emailed me a draft opinion that he completed the night before he died. He wanted me to show it to you if something happened, but not at the Pentagon.

My address is 4024 Lafayette Drive, Alexandria. My cell is 704-555-3141, but it's best not to call me to avoid anyone who might be monitoring. Can you come as soon as you get back from P.J.'s funeral? It's important.

Very respectfully,
R. D. Simmons
LT, JAGC, USNR

How strange.

She picked up her phone and started to dial the cell number provided.

No, if Simmons asked her not to, there must be a reason. And if P.J. had asked Simmons to deliver something to her, he must have had a reason.

She hit the Print Screen button on her computer, then snatched the address off the printer. She grabbed her purse and bolted out the door to her car, got in, and, trying to control her shaking hands, punched the address into her GPS.

With a twisted feeling in her stomach and with her heart racing, she backed into the street and stepped on the accelerator.

CHAPTER 21

• • •

APPROACHING LIEUTENANT ROSS SIMMONS'S CONDO
ALEXANDRIA, VIRGINIA
SATURDAY AFTERNOON

The GPS showed Ross Simmons's condo was three hundred feet on the left. Her heart accelerated as she slowed the car, turning onto the short street that was Lafayette Drive.

The street was off a main road, in what looked like a quiet, low-traffic neighborhood. She strained to look at the gold house numbers on the black front door of each condo. Even numbers on the left. Odd on the right.

4016 Lafayette Drive . . .

4018

4020

4022

The next condo's front door was wide open, blocking her view of the house number.

4026

4028

Caroline tapped the brakes, stopping the car. She shifted into reverse.

4028

4026

The driveway was empty. This had to be 4024 Lafayette Drive.

Caroline glanced down at the paper with Simmons's address printed on it and double-checked.

Just what she thought. 4024 Lafayette Drive, Alexandria, Virginia. This had to be it. But why would Ross Simmons leave the front door wide open?

She pulled into the drive and got out of the car, but instinct told her to proceed with caution. The silence coming from the condo seemed overpowering. No cars were parked along the street. No one was on the sidewalk. A few birds chirped over the distant roar of traffic out on Kings Highway, the main thoroughfare intersecting Lafayette Drive.

A small front sidewalk, maybe ten feet in length, connected the driveway to the front stoop. She stepped onto the stoop and heard the silence give way to classical music coming from inside. Orchestra music. The grand strains of Beethoven's "Ode to Joy."

She knocked on the door three times and then rang the doorbell. When there was no response, she instinctively pulled out her cell phone, but realized that she didn't have his number in it.

She stepped off to the left and looked behind the front door.

4024.

"Ross!" she called into the condo. "Ross Simmons?"

She heard a noise like the sound of a door closing. Maybe Simmons had been out in the backyard and was coming back in.

"Is anybody home?"

No answer.

"It's Caroline!" A pause. "Lieutenant Commander Caroline McCormick from Code 13."

Still nothing.

Was the music getting louder? Was someone inside turning up the volume? Or was she imagining things? Maybe it was her imagination. Should she leave?

Something deep inside told her to run and not look back.

She turned and started to step back onto the sidewalk, but something stopped her.

Ross Simmons missed P.J.'s funeral today. And he had gone to the trouble of sending a private email to her personal account.

What was going on?

Whatever it was, it was related to P.J. Perhaps Ross had discovered information on P.J.'s murder. Perhaps he could provide a clue about what happened and who did it.

She couldn't leave. Not now, anyway. She decided to call out once more.

"Ross? Are you there?"

Caroline stepped across the threshold into a small, modest foyer area with vinyl flooring. Off to the left was a small den area with a sofa and two chairs. The walls displayed no artwork. No pictures. Typical bachelor pad.

"Ross? Anybody home?"

A small, narrow hallway, dimly lit, led back from the foyer. Stepping gingerly, she followed it straight back, passing a small head on the right before stepping into the kitchen.

The kitchen, lit by an overhead fluorescent light, looked like a wreck, with pots and pans stacked in the sink. The classical music was coming from a room off to the right.

She followed another hallway to the entrance of an office. The music grew louder and louder, and she stepped inside.

"Dear Jesus, no! Ross! Ross!"

She sprinted across the room toward where the lifeless body of Lieutenant Ross Simmons was slumped in a chair in front of a computer monitor, his head fallen forward onto his desk, resting sideways on a blood-drenched keyboard. His mouth was frozen open and his tongue hung out. It appeared that a bullet had gone through his temple.

Caroline froze in her steps.

She had to be living a nightmare. Not again!

She ran out of the office and back into the kitchen and started scrambling through her purse for her cell phone.

The NCIS agent. Victoria's friend.

What was his name?

Wait a minute. He'd given her his card.

"Lord, help me."

Found it! Thank God!

She held her fingers to the screen and punched in the number.

One ring.

Two rings.

"You have reached the voicemail of NCIS Special Agent Mark Romanov. Please leave a message after the tone and I'll get right back with you." *Beeeep.*

"Mark, this is Lieutenant Commander Caroline McCormick. Please call me back now! It's an emergency."

She hung up and took a moment to clear her head. Before she could punch in 911, the phone rang.

Special Agent Mark Romanov.

"Mark. Thank goodness!"

"What's going on?"

"Lieutenant Ross Simmons! From Code 13! He's been murdered!"

"Okay, calm down. What do you mean murdered? Where are you?"

"Here! I'm here! It looks like somebody shot him in the head! There's blood everywhere. It's worse than when they shot P.J."

"Okay. Try to calm down. Where is here?"

"I'm at Ross's condo."

"Okay, where is it? What's the address?"

"Hang on. I wrote it down." She fumbled through her purse for the computer paper. "Here. I've got it." She unfolded it. "Okay, I've got it. It's 4024 Lafayette Drive."

"Okay, which city? Arlington? Springfield?"

"Alexandria."

"And you're still in the house with the body?"

"Yes, it's awful."

"Is anybody else there with you?"

"I haven't seen anybody."

"Okay, listen. I want you to get out of the house now. The killer could still be in there for all we know. And I want you to go out to the street where you're clearly visible. Have you called 911?"

"No."

"Okay. I'm on my way, and I'll call 911. Got it?"

"Got it. I'm heading outside right now."

She took a last look at Ross's body, then stuffed her phone in her purse and dashed down the hallway, through the foyer, and out the front door into the late-afternoon sunlight.

"Caroline?"

She instinctively screamed and turned at the sound of her name.

"Paul! What are you doing here?"

He stood near a blue Suburban, still in his white uniform. "Are you okay?"

"They killed Ross Simmons!" She wiped her eyes.

"Who? Where?"

"He's inside. Somebody shot him."

"Stay here. Don't move."

Paul darted into the house.

Caroline stepped down off the porch onto the sidewalk and then moved to the driveway. She found herself shaking.

Why should anyone have to suffer through two murders, so quickly, with one of the victims being the man she loved? What had she done to deserve this?

Of course, there were those fellow service members who had come back from places like Iraq and Afghanistan who had seen more death than she had.

But then again, those deaths occurred in combat.

But these? These were unexpected murders.

She wished someone would come hold her right now. How she wished P.J. could be here.

Where was Paul? What was taking him so long? Maybe she shouldn't have let him go in. She remembered what Mark Romanov said. The killer could still be in there.

Dear Jesus, please. No more murders.

She should go check on Paul.

No. Maybe that would be stupid.

Maybe she should call 911.

No. Wait. Mark said he would call 911.

Caroline felt breathless, like she had finished the last sprint of a five-mile run.

Water.

She needed water.

How long had Paul been in there? She checked her watch. That didn't help. Where was Mark Romanov?

She had to check on Paul. She walked back onto the porch.

"Paul? Are you okay? Captain!" No answer. "Dear Jesus, please. Not again."

She heard the sound of a helicopter buzzing in the skies. She turned around and looked up but saw nothing.

Hands touched her shoulders from behind. She jumped.

"It's okay. I'm right here."

"Thank God."

Paul's voice was soothing, but not enough to quell her raging emotional hurricane.

"I think we should back off from the house and call 911."

"I just talked to Special Agent Mark Romanov from NCIS. He's on his way. He said he would call 911."

"Excellent."

Sirens blared in the distance. Paul led Caroline away from the porch.

"How did you know I was here?"

"I have my ways," he said. "I was worried about you."

"I don't understand."

He looked into her eyes. "Look up there." He pointed up and at an angle.

The light-blue drone, with the insignia proclaiming U.S. Navy, buzzed off to the right, just over the tree line, and then disappeared. "We had a couple of our test drones overhead covering the funeral, just in case. With all the uncertainty and with P.J.'s killer still on the loose, and with the top-ranking brass in the Navy there, our people were monitoring certain persons of interest just in case."

"What persons of interest?"

"The Secretary of the Navy. Vice Admiral Brewer and his wife. Captain Guy. You."

"I'm a person of interest?"

"You are to me."

"So you had the drone watching me?"

"A drone was assigned to you and the others. We had four of them in the sky. My orders were to maintain surveillance until sundown. You were with P.J. when he was shot, and I wanted to make sure you were okay. You didn't know it, but I've been close by since you left the funeral."

"Captain—"

"Paul."

"Paul, this is terrifying."

"I know it is. But we're gonna get to the bottom of it."

His voice faded into the blare of sirens, and off to the right flashing blue lights approached. Four police cars raced down Lafayette Drive, one behind the other.

They screeched to a halt, two on one side of the street, two on the other. Officers poured out with guns drawn.

"Freeze!" one of them yelled. "Captain Johnson! Alexandria police."

"Better put our hands up, Caroline," Paul said. "We'll get this sorted out."

"We got a report of a shooting! What's going on here?"

"We're naval officers from the Pentagon," Paul said. "The victim is inside. Nobody else is in the house as far as we know."

"Check it out!" Johnson said. Four of the officers, guns drawn, charged into the house. "Liles, check 'em for weapons."

"Yes, sir."

"Keep your hands up, please, sir," the officer said to Paul, then conducted a pat-down. "He's clear, Captain."

"Check her."

"Hold still, ma'am." The cop started with her shoulders and came down. "She's clear too, sir."

"You can put your hands down," the cop said.

Just then another car came up, quickly stopping behind the police cars. Out popped Mark Romanov, flashing a badge. "Federal agent, NCIS!" Victoria Fladager, still in her service white uniform, got out of the other side of the car.

Mark walked straight toward the police captain, his badge out in front of him, repeating his credentials. "Federal agent! Special Agent Mark Romanov! NCIS. I'm the one who called 911. The deceased is a U.S. Navy JAG officer. One of these officers notified me of the homicide. There's no reason to draw weapons."

The police captain dropped his gun. "My apologies, Captain. Commander. Standard procedure. We often draw weapons on arriving at a homicide scene, not knowing who is who."

"Not a problem, Captain," Paul said.

"I will need to see some identification, though. Do you have your armed services identification card?"

"Here you go," Paul said, drawing his wallet from his pocket.

"Mine's right here," Caroline said, lifting hers from her purse.

The captain took a moment to scan each piece.

"Captain!" Just then, one of the police officers ran out of the house. "We got a homicide! One male victim. Single bullet through the temple. Bad-looking exit wound. Blood everywhere. Looks real bad, sir."

"Okay. Get the scene secure. Call forensics. Call the morgue for an ambulance. I'll be right there."

The police captain turned to Paul, Caroline, and Mark. "Okay, so what happened here? Agent Romanov? I believe you said you called 911?"

"That's right, Captain. I got a call from Lieutenant Commander McCormick here, who was first on the scene."

The police captain turned to Caroline.

"And you say you were first on the scene?"

"I'd say the killer was first on the scene. But I was the first one of any of us here."

"And when did you get here?"

"I don't know. It's all a blur. Maybe ten minutes?"

"Maybe ten minutes? You're not sure?"

"It wasn't long. I didn't check my watch."

"And what did you find when you arrived?"

"The door was open."

"The door? What door?"

"The front door. It was wide open."

"What did you do next?"

Caroline didn't like anything about this guy. Why did she feel like a criminal suspect? Perhaps she should stop this interrogation and demand her right to counsel. She dismissed that thought. For now.

"The sound of music was coming out of the residence. So I hesitated."

"What kind of music?"

"Classical music. Beethoven's Ninth."

"And you hesitated because music was playing?"

"I hesitated because I thought someone was home."

"What did you do next?"

"I called out to Ross, but there was no answer."

"Is that the victim's name? Ross?"

"Yes, Lieutenant Ross Simmons, U.S. Navy."

"You knew him?"

"I had met him, yes."

"You have anything against him?"

"Of course not! I don't know what you're insinuating. I only just met him."

"Okay. Calm down, ma'am. Just doing my job. What happened next?"

"Sorry, Officer."

"Captain! I worked a long time to get these bars, ma'am. The guys going in and out of this crime scene are officers."

"Sorry, Captain. It's been a rough day."

"What happened next?"

"Next, after I called out several times and didn't hear anybody, I decided to go inside. I walked through the house, toward the source of the music. That's when I found P.J. Excuse me. That's when I found Ross."

"Who's P.J.?"

Mark Romanov spoke up. "A little background, Captain. P.J. was Lieutenant Commander P.J. MacDonald. He was the JAG officer who was gunned down on the Mall a few days ago."

"I saw that on the news."

"Lieutenant Commander McCormick was jogging with Commander MacDonald when he was shot. We all just came from Commander MacDonald's funeral, which finished two hours ago. Commander MacDonald, Commander McCormick, and Lieutenant Simmons, the deceased, all worked in the same division of Navy JAG at the Pentagon."

"So let me get this straight. We've got two JAG officers working in the same section of the Pentagon murdered within a seventy-two-hour span?"

"You're reading that correctly, Captain. NCIS has already opened an investigation into the murder of the first officer. That's why I'm here. As you may know, we get involved in investigating criminal matters in which United States naval personnel are victims."

"Well, as you may know, Special Agent Romanov, we exercise jurisdiction for crimes committed in the city of Alexandria outside of federal property, which this is."

"And as you know, Captain, I am a federal agent, and to the extent that there is a conflict between federal and state matters, federal jurisdiction controls. Having said that, we're always happy to work with local law enforcement on matters like this."

The police captain looked half irritated and half miffed. Just then a large, dark-blue van rolled up with "Alexandria Police—Mobile Crime Forensics Lab" on its side.

"I'm going to go inside and have a look," Mark said. "Since we will be cooperating on this, Captain, you're free to join me."

"Sure," the police captain said, even as his men were erecting yellow crime-scene tape all around the house. Mark turned to Caroline and Paul. "Captain Kriete? Commander? Would you mind waiting just a few more minutes? I'd like to chat with you just a second, and the captain here might have another question too."

"Not a problem," Paul said.

"Sure," Caroline said.

As Mark and the police captain turned to walk into the house, Victoria stepped forward, held open her arms, and, without saying a word, hugged Caroline. She held her for a few seconds, then with her hands on Caroline's arms, she stepped back and looked into her face. "Are you okay?"

"I'm so stunned that I can't even answer that question, to be honest."

"You don't have to answer it. We're all in this together." Victoria released her.

What a transformation Caroline had seen in Victoria in the days since P.J.'s death, from the catty stares and snotty remarks of a jealous woman to warm and genuine affection.

Death sometimes had a way of changing people. Sometimes for the best. Sometimes for the worst. Whatever Victoria's motivation, Caroline was grateful.

"Thank you for being here. I'll get it together. What a blessing that your friend Mark is here. Having NCIS get here so quickly makes it seem a little safer, anyway."

"Yes, well," Victoria said, "Mark's a good guy."

"I take it you two know each other well?"

"Yes. We dated when I was at RLSO Norfolk."

"I see. Was it serious?"

"I'd say so. He took it hard when I left for DC. But you know how it is in the Navy. Here today, gone tomorrow."

Caroline nodded. "Yes. Do I ever know."

"I'm sorry," Victoria said. "That was a horrible comment."

"It's okay. I know what you mean."

Two more police cars rolled up, followed by a television crew. Caroline looked over and saw Mark Romanov and the police captain walking in their direction. The police captain spoke up first. "Okay. As far as I'm concerned, you're free to leave. But, Commander"—he eyed Caroline—"our detectives will need a statement and will probably want to interview you. You may want to consult with an attorney."

"What?"

"Just precautionary. You're not a suspect at this point."

"At this point?"

"Here's my card. If you see a call coming through from this number, please answer."

She exchanged glances with Paul.

"Now, if you'll excuse me," the police captain said, "I've got to get back inside to check on the forensics team."

He tipped his cap and walked off.

"He's treating me like a suspect!"

"I wouldn't worry about it," Paul said. "You've got an alibi. You were with us."

"I agree," Mark said. "Plus, you have no motive for shooting Simmons."

"Of course I don't."

"But somebody did," Mark said. "And somebody also had a motive for shooting P.J. And somehow I have a feeling there's a linkage."

"Makes sense," Paul said.

"Look," Mark said. "Victoria, you were working with P.J. last. Caroline, you went back a long way with him. Why don't we all get together, maybe for dinner, and brainstorm to see if we can figure all this out. Are you all okay with that?"

Victoria nodded. "We were planning to have dinner anyway. So why not?"

Caroline didn't feel like going out. Not when they had just buried P.J.

On the other hand, P.J. was a fighter, and so was she. And whoever killed him would not get away with it. "Whatever it takes to bring P.J.'s killer to justice," Caroline added.

"Captain, would you care to join us?"

"Sure. Why not?" Paul said. "When and where?"

"How about the Sequoia over in Georgetown? Say, eight o'clock? Might be a nice change of scenery."

"Okay. I'll be there."

"Good," Mark said. "Then let's get out of here. I'll see everybody then."

CHAPTER 22

· · ·

At this time of night, with the warm breeze whipping in from the east, from the direction of the Atlantic, the moonlit ripples on the surface of the Savannah River created a ghostly foreground against the silhouette of miles of uninhabited marsh fields at the edge of the opposite bank. To the untrained eye, or to a Northerner or Midwesterner not accustomed to the marshes of the low country, the moonlit tips of the marshes across the way, swaying in the wind, might resemble a sea of rolling cornstalks.

But down to the left, the vibrant lights of downtown Savannah proved a colorful contrast of modern southern civilization abutting a salt-marsh habitat of snakes and alligators.

Standing on his office balcony, and now distracted by the wisp of wind tossing a strand of Ivana's blonde hair, Richardson pulled her to him and kissed her. The extra shot of champagne he had just gulped down made the kiss more pleasurable. They disengaged, only for a moment, then turned, arm in arm, to relish the romantic vista and ambience.

"Richardson, what would Harold say?" She spoke in that velvety Eastern European accent that he found so delectable.

"No need to worry about Harold." He pulled her into him and kissed her again. "I've made sure he's working so hard that he will be too tired to notice. Besides, you know these engineering types. They're oblivious to anything beyond the end of their noses and their mathematical theorems."

She giggled. "Yes. My husband was my ticket to America. But it is true. He is boring with all of this math and engineering talk. Totally opposite of my powerful, charming, brilliant, and exciting boss."

"Perhaps you will find this somewhat exciting."

He leaned in and kissed her again, and she cooperated. But when the cell phone in his pocket rang, he pushed her away and cursed. Business before pleasure.

He pulled out his cell phone.

Jack Patterson.

"Excuse me, my dear. I have to take this."

"Certainly, Richardson."

"Hang on, Jack." He waved Ivana back into the office. She stepped through the glass doors and strutted over to his desk, going straight for the champagne bottle. He closed the sliding glass doors, insulating his conversation from earshot. "Sorry about that. I had to shoo off Ivana. Your timing is impeccable."

"I hope you're making sure nobody sees you with her up there."

"So what if they do? She's my secretary. And corporate executives cannot stay ahead by working nine to five."

"Okay, Richardson. I suppose you have lots of dictation to take care of after hours."

"I hope you're not charging me for this little mini-lecture of yours."

"Don't worry. You're not on the clock until I get to the point."

"Okay. Let's get to the point. Has my drone bill been introduced in Congress yet?"

A pause.

"Are you still there, Jack?"

"I'm here."

"Well?"

"On the bill, there's been a slight delay."

"What now?"

"Well, you know how you wanted the problem with the JAG officer, MacDonald, taken care of?"

"Yes. He was threatening a negative legal opinion."

"Well, this is one of those cases of being careful what you ask for."

"Does that mean I'm closer to getting my bill passed?"

"Should be a bit easier now, Richardson. We've just got to remove one impediment at a time."

"Get it done, Jack. Right now I'm preoccupied with other things." He hung up.

• • •

SEQUOIA RESTAURANT
3000 K STREET NW
GEORGETOWN
WASHINGTON, DC

The modern-looking restaurant, with a full two-story glass front wrapping around the building, sat on the banks of the Potomac River. The lights surrounding the restaurant proved vibrant. The shoreline, with a clear view of the Kennedy Center, Roosevelt Island, the Key Bridge, and the red, white, and green lights of the Virginia skyline across the way, proved spectacular.

People strolled about with a casual nonchalance outside the restaurant, and couples held hands along the waterfront, giving the place an electric atmosphere, full of life and energy.

How could such a vivacious setting feel so lonely?

Just outside the entrance, a small plaque proclaimed that the restaurant had been named for the former presidential yacht, the *Sequoia*.

She was early.

Paul had called and offered to pick her up, but that didn't seem right. At least not yet. The night had a surrealistic feel. A numbness hung in the air. She was here, yet she wasn't here. She wanted to be with someone, yet she wanted to be alone.

And now? The notion that the police captain might suspect her of being involved in the murder of Ross Simmons weighed heavily on her.

How she wished she could see P.J. right now. If only he could walk up and give her a hug.

She wiped a tear from her cheek, for the mere thought of him caused her to cry in an instant. She didn't want to be here, but she was here because of him. She had to find out who had murdered him, and she would go to her grave if necessary to bring his killer to justice.

"You look like you could use a friend."

She turned around. "Paul." She hoped he hadn't noticed the tears in her eyes.

"I take it the others aren't here yet?"

"I haven't seen anybody." She wiped her eye, trying to avoid the obvious. "I just got here."

"I wish you'd have let me pick you up—"

"Captain! Commander!"

Caroline looked around to see who had interrupted Paul. Mark walked up with Victoria, who now sported a nicely fitted pair of designer jeans and a little green top. "Have you been here long?" Mark asked.

"Not really," Caroline said.

"I just got here," Paul said.

"Glad you weren't waiting long," Mark said. "Let's step inside. I called for reservations."

Mark held open the door for the ladies, waited for Paul to step into the restaurant, and then followed them in.

"Good evening. I'm Kay. Welcome to Sequoia. Do you have reservations?" the hostess asked.

"Yes, I called in under Romanov. We have reservations at eight o'clock for four."

"Yes, Mr. Romanov. Right this way."

The hostess, who looked to be in her early twenties, led the foursome off to the left, bringing them to a table that sat right beside the massive window front, with an exquisite view of the river. Two bottles of red wine, already uncorked, sat on the table with four empty glasses.

"Will this table be acceptable?"

"This okay?" Mark looked to the others.

Caroline and the others responded with a blend of "This is fine," "Okay," and "Fine with me."

"We'll take it, Kay." Mark got the chair for Victoria, and Paul did the same for Caroline. "And please ask the waiter to give us some time. We need to discuss something."

"Certainly, Mr. Romanov." The hostess smiled and nodded. "I'll alert the waiter. If anyone would like to change out the wine, just let me know."

"Thank you, Kay."

She smiled and stepped away.

"What a beautiful setting for such a sad occasion," Mark said.

"So true," Caroline said.

"I hope you all don't mind, but I know we've all had a long day. So I took the liberty of ordering a little red wine in advance. Should be Malbec."

Victoria spoke first. "I don't mind at all. I could use a glass or two."

"Caroline?"

At first she hesitated. "Sure. Why not? Maybe it will help deaden some of the pain."

"Captain?"

"No. I think I'll pass. For the time being, anyway."

Mark picked up the bottle and began to pour, first Victoria's glass, then Caroline's. Victoria had said Mark was a good guy, and he obviously had good manners too. Of course, Mark's good manners and gentlemanly demeanor still hadn't stopped Victoria from apparently pursuing P.J.

As much as it irritated her, Caroline couldn't blame Victoria for that. After all, Mark Romanov was cute, but he was no P.J.

Caroline watched Victoria take a sip of wine as Mark filled his own glass and cast a quick glance at Victoria. His face reflected that he was still in love with her. But Victoria did not seem overly interested in the gentlemanly NCIS agent.

"Since we're all here," Mark began, "because of what's happened to our two shipmates in these last few days, I hope it's okay if I propose a toast."

"Well, if we're going to have a toast," Paul responded, "I'd better at least pour a splash in my glass."

"Let me do the honors, Captain." Mark lifted the bottle and poured Paul's glass half full. "Now then, my friends, may I begin by raising a toast to the life and service of Lieutenant Commander P.J. MacDonald, Judge Advocate General's Corps, United States Navy. May he live forever in our hearts, and may we resolve to do all we can to bring his killer to justice."

"Hear, hear!" Paul said.

Caroline raised her glass, clinked it against the three others, and brought it to her lips and imbibed, in honor of the man she loved. She suddenly felt less guilty that she had allowed herself a drink on the night of his death.

"And likewise"—Mark raised his glass again—"may we also toast Lieutenant Ross Simmons, Judge Advocate General's Corps, United States Navy. May he live forever in our hearts, and may we resolve to do all we can to bring his killer to justice."

Caroline raised her glass again, tapping it against the others', then brought it against her lips. The wine went down smoothly and generated a sense of warmth within her. She felt grateful and comforted to be among friends.

"Friends," Mark said, "I want to thank all three of you for coming tonight. I know it must be hard to be here, considering the shock of what we've been through these last few days. But I know these two officers were friends of yours, and even close to you in some cases. And that makes this case personal to me. I want to nail these animals. And I hoped we could meet for a brainstorming session to focus our emotions and our intellect in the right direction. Are y'all up to it?"

"Let's do it," Caroline said, speaking up. "I want to grease up these animals with gasoline and then throw them in the furnace."

"Attagirl," Mark said.

"In fact," Caroline said, "there's something I need to show you all."

"What is it?" Mark asked.

She looked at them, hesitated, then pulled the email out of her purse. "Ross sent me this email just after P.J. died. P.J. had apparently sent him a copy of the opinion. My guess is this is why they went after Ross."

"Let me see that," Mark said. He took the email and studied it, then passed it to the others. "Incredible," he said. "Ross had been sent the opinion P.J. wrote. Somebody knew that, because they must have monitored his email, and that's why they took Ross's computer and killed him. They didn't want the email out."

"That's exactly what I think," Caroline said.

"This is starting to get out of control," Victoria said.

"The plot thickens," Paul said, "and I don't like the sound of it."

Mark spoke. "It's out of control only if we let it get out of control. We need to cut these people off at the knees, and do it now." He looked at Caroline first, then at the others. "Are you guys with me on this? And before you answer, there's no pressure. This is what I do for a living. But I might need you all to trap these animals."

They all looked at one another.

"I'm in," Victoria said.

"I'll do whatever I can to help," Paul added.

"Good," Mark said. "Well then, let's start with the obvious. What did P.J. and Ross have in common that might have placed a target on their backs?"

"That's obvious," Victoria said. "P.J. was assigned to write a legal opinion, which, no matter which way the opinion broke, could have meant millions or even billions of dollars to certain interest groups. And Ross had P.J.'s memo, which was like holding a deadly stick of dynamite to someone if the memo cut against their interest."

"Precisely," Mark said. "Now, what groups might have an interest in the outcome of this legal opinion?"

Caroline felt her mind engage as she pondered the question. How bizarre, yet how curiously refreshing, even in the midst of sorrow, that a sense of purpose to avenge P.J.'s death could arise so quickly, even hours after they had laid him into the hallowed ground at Arlington.

Yet deep down, this was what P.J. would want. She knew it in her gut. He wouldn't want her wallowing in sorrow but would want her to get up off the mat and engage. To engage her mind, her heart, to find something to fight for.

That's what P.J. would have done. Had their plights been reversed . . . How she wished she had taken that bullet for him. But if she had taken the assassin's bullet, and if he were sitting here tonight in her place, not only would he be fighting like heck, but he would be leading the charge to avenge her death.

And that's exactly what she was going to do. She would fight to avenge his murder with all her intellect, strength, and courage, all consistent with her duties as a naval officer.

"Isn't it obvious?" She spoke up.

"What are you thinking, Caroline?" Mark asked.

"It seems to me, assuming they knew of P.J.'s involvement in this project, that two groups would have a strong interest in influencing his legal opinion. And these two groups would have the same interest in influencing Ross Simmons's opinion too."

"Let's hear it," Mark said.

"The first is the most obvious. The defense contractor stands to make billions, or even lose billions, depending on whether Congress approves the acquisition of these drones."

"Wait a minute," Paul said. "I'm the naval officer directly in charge of the program. I've met some of the representatives of the defense contractor. They look like typical nerdy engineering geeks. But nothing about them makes them seem like killers."

A pause. Glances exchanged.

"Question, Captain." This was Mark.

"Sure. Anything."

"The defense contractor is AirFlite, out of Savannah, correct?"

"That's correct."

"Sir, have you had a chance to meet either the CEO of the company or any of the top-level executives yet?"

Paul sipped his water. "Well, I've only been on this job a few days, so no. I haven't yet met the CEO. But that's on the agenda within the next week or so."

"Okay," Mark said. "So what do we know about this guy?"

"Hang on. I'm checking." Victoria had her nose in her iPhone.

"While she's checking," Paul said, "the CEO's name is Richardson DeKlerk. I understand he's South African—"

"Got it," Victoria said. "Excuse me, Captain. I didn't mean to interrupt."

"It's okay, Lieutenant. Tell us what you found."

"You sure?"

"Sure. Go ahead."

"From Wikipedia. 'Richardson Wellington DeKlerk is a South African–born business executive, currently living in the United States. He is CEO of AirFlite, an international defense contractor known for the manufacture of military aircraft, air-to-air missiles, and drones. Mr. DeKlerk, who is divorced, and who became a United States citizen in 2015, resides in Savannah, Georgia, where he oversees AirFlite's North American operations, which includes fifteen thousand employees working at the company's headquarters in Savannah and at various manufacturing facilities around the country.'

"Then there's a section entitled 'Project Blue Jay.'"

"I'd like to hear what Wikipedia says about that," Caroline said.

"Okay," Victoria said. "'Richardson's company, AirFlite, is known for having secured several substantial contracts with various military groups around the globe. Most recently, the company was awarded a contract with the United States Navy for the deployment of one hundred thousand drones, to be deployed along the east and west coasts of the United States and the Gulf of Mexico.

"'The contract, however, is contingent upon approval by the United States Congress and has sparked some controversy as to the legality of the arrangement. It is believed that the legality of the contract is currently under review by the U.S. Navy JAG.

"'If approved, some military analysts say Project Blue Jay would be the largest military contract awarded to a single defense contractor in history.'"

Glances were exchanged around the table. Mark spoke up. "It also looks like we have someone who would be highly motivated to influence the outcome of the legal opinion."

"But here's what doesn't make sense," Paul said. "First, AirFlite, or whoever did this, would have to know who was writing the legal opinion, and that wouldn't be known outside of the JAG Corps."

"Captain," Mark said, "money can get you that information."

"Okay, I'll give you that. But even if these officers' names were leaked out, I don't see how they'd become a target unless somebody thought they were going to write an opinion that might influence the contract in a direction opposite of what the assassin wanted."

"That makes sense, Captain," Mark said. "So that brings us to the question, which way was P.J. leaning on this position paper? Because whichever way he was leaning, that could give us a clue as to who wanted him alive and who wanted him dead. We need to go back and take a look at the attachment to the email Caroline just showed us. Caroline, can you pull it up on your phone?"

"Hang on." She got it from her purse, swiped the screen, and went into her email. "Here it is."

"Would you read it?"

"Sure." She felt her heart pounding as she started reading the email.

LCDR McCormick,

I met you the day you first visited Code 13. I was working with P.J. on several projects. He gave me your personal email address and asked me to contact you if something happened to him. He didn't want me contacting you on government email.

Captain Guy assigned the Blue Jay project to P.J., and P.J. emailed me a draft opinion that he completed the night before he died. He wanted me to show it to you if something happened, but not at the Pentagon.

My address is 4024 Lafayette Drive, Alexandria. My cell is 704-555-3141, but it's best not to call me to avoid anyone who might be monitoring. Can you come as soon as you get back from P.J.'s funeral? It's important.

Very respectfully,
R. D. Simmons
LT, JAGC, USNR

"Was there an attachment to it? With the legal opinion?" Mark asked.

"No," Caroline said. "Just this email that said Ross had the opinion."

"I can't believe that idiot police captain didn't even ask why you were there so he'd know about this," Victoria said, but then looked sheepish. "Well, I guess we didn't ask you either, although I wondered if you were simply checking up on Ross because he'd been missing from the funeral."

"One of the many reasons NCIS is involved," Mark said, "is that local law enforcement misses more than they catch, and they, by the way, didn't have any emotional attachment to Ross. Give me a second to look at this."

All eyes turned to Mark.

"So," Mark began, "P.J. emails an opinion to Simmons, and it's a draft of the opinion about the legality of the drone contract. I mean, what else can it be? Everybody agree?"

All three nodded.

"Okay, and then he's careful to use his personal email, instead of the Code 13 email, because he's afraid someone may be monitoring his Code 13 email at the Pentagon," Mark said.

"It looks like somebody was monitoring his personal email as well," Paul said, "which likely is why the killer arrived on the scene. Because they wanted to see or control whatever opinion was attached to that email."

"Precisely," Mark said.

"How do we know this isn't a coincidental random act of violence?" Victoria asked.

"Because the strong linkage in subject matter between Ross's murder and P.J.'s murder makes that theory, the random act of violence theory, almost impossible to believe," Mark said.

"Not only that," Caroline added, "but when I found Ross's body, he was slumped over onto his computer desk, and there was a keyboard and a monitor but no computer."

Mark spoke up. "Because whoever shot the lieutenant wanted

to make sure any opinion that had been downloaded was physically removed from his house."

"Makes sense," Paul said.

"Not only that," Mark said, "but if whoever did this was monitoring P.J.'s personal email traffic, that means they knew who he was, knew what he was doing, and probably were monitoring his government email at the Pentagon."

"Could they do that?" Victoria asked.

"In a heartbeat, if they have enough money to hire the right kind of hackers," Mark said. "Fighting enemy hackers and maintaining cybersecurity are some of the main tasks NCIS agents are involved with."

"Sounds like the killer was well financed and well connected," Paul said.

"Precisely," Mark said. "And there's one other thing we have to be concerned about." He looked at Caroline.

"What's that?" Paul asked.

"Lieutenant Commander McCormick here has been specifically identified. That puts you on the radar screen, Caroline." He kept his eyes on her. "They don't know what you know. For all they know, you may have been given a copy of P.J.'s opinion. I'm afraid that makes you a target."

Caroline's stomach knotted.

Mark continued, "I'm going to have to recommend some sort of security detail for you."

"I don't want a security detail."

"You may not have a choice."

"One thing's for sure," Paul said. "Tonight you're coming home with me."

"Paul—"

"I won't take no for an answer. I'll sleep on the sofa. I'll be a gentleman. But until Mark can look into this more, I'd be crazy to let you go back to that townhouse."

"I think the captain's suggestion is prudent," Mark said.

"I'll think about it," Caroline huffed. "But in the meantime, how are we gonna catch these people?"

"Okay," Mark said. "Here's what we're going to do short term. First, I'm going to have some of my guys in NCIS computer forensics check into P.J.'s email traffic, both his official email traffic at Code 13 and his private email. I want to know what P.J. sent to Ross Simmons, and I want to figure out what's on that stolen computer. My hunch is that P.J. sent a draft opinion that rubbed somebody the wrong way, and that somebody intercepted the email and didn't want that opinion to get sent or to ever get out in the public."

"I've got a feeling you're right about that," Paul said.

"How can I help?" Victoria asked.

"Tell ya what," Paul said. "Since you've already pulled up some information on this Richardson DeKlerk character, why don't you start with an informal background on him? You know, a printed dossier of public stuff on the net from Dunn & Bradstreet, Wiki, stock holdings he may have, a list of former spouses, business associates. Just get us some names and issues that we can follow up on. I want to know everything I can about DeKlerk and his associates. That would be a good start."

"Will do," Victoria said. "How soon do you need it?"

"Sooner rather than later. How about 8:00 a.m.?"

Victoria looked at her watch.

"In fact," Mark said, "I hate to break up the party, and I know we all just got here, but how would y'all feel if we break now and get to work, and then reconvene at 8:00 a.m. at la Madeleine over on King Street in Alexandria. I can get the tab for the drinks, but I want to jump on this before the killers get too far away. Is that okay?"

Caroline looked at Paul, who nodded at her. She spoke up. "If it takes cutting dinner short to get these animals, I say let's do it. What can I do to help?"

"Here's what you can do to help. For tonight, go home with Captain Kriete and stay safe."

"I'll drink to that," Paul added.

"Then let's reconvene in the morning and see what we have."

Paul looked at her. "Are you going to be okay with that?"

She hesitated, then decided that spending the night on Paul Kriete's sofa might be just what the doctor ordered.

CHAPTER 23

. . .

At times, serving as a member of the United States Senate, even serving as a junior member of the senate, proved to be the world's most glamorous job. At other times, however, when under pressure for high-money constituents who expected a junior senator to play the role of miracle worker, the job felt like a thankless sentence to permanent purgatory.

And tonight, sitting in his office with only a skeleton crew present, Senator Bobby Talmadge had decided that today had been more gut-wrenching than blissful.

At issue was how to get the massive Blue Jay contract out of the bowels of the Pentagon and onto the floor of Congress for passage. Not only were thousands of jobs for his home state of Georgia hanging in the balance, but his biggest financial contributors, the Georgia Political Victory Fund and AirFlite CEO Richardson DeKlerk, had been breathing down his neck with threats to support another candidate if he didn't deliver.

The matter had been complicated by the shooting of the JAG officer assigned to write the internal legal memo on the project. Bobby

Talmadge didn't know what had happened with the JAG officer, and frankly, he didn't want to know.

In politics, as Tommy Mandela had indicated, they called that plausible deniability.

"Okay, boss. We've got some movement on your meeting with Senator Fowler."

Bobby looked up. Tommy walked into his office holding a legal pad. "When?"

"In two days."

"What? Two days? Tommy, you know I can't wait two days."

"I understand, boss. But not only is this Saturday, but Fowler's in New Orleans and won't be back in Washington until then. His staff didn't offer a phone conference, but they're insistent he's not available until then."

"Well then, how about if we just fly down to New Orleans? My political future depends on this legislation, Tommy."

"I already floated that idea—of us going to Louisiana—but Fowler's staff insists he's out-of-pocket until Tuesday."

"Out-of-pocket." Talmadge cursed. "What's her name?"

"You said it, boss. I didn't."

"Crap." He folded his arms, twirled around in his chair away from Mandela, and looked out the window at the lights of the capital city.

"Excuse me, Senator." A woman's voice.

Bobby turned around again. His secretary, Maryanne, stood at the door.

"Whatcha got, Maryanne?"

"Sir, we just received a package."

"A package?"

"Actually, an envelope."

"From who?"

"I'm not sure, sir. But the senate courier hand-delivered it. It's marked confidential."

Talmadge looked at Mandela. "Maybe something positive from Fowler's staff?"

"Could be, sir."

"Let me see it, Maryanne."

"Yes, sir."

She handed the senator a large yellow envelope, delivered by the U.S. Senate Courier Service. It was addressed to *U.S. Senator Robert Talmadge, Personal & Confidential*, with no return address.

Bobby opened the envelope and fished out a sheet of white paper with a handwritten note on it. He reached for his reading glasses.

Dear Senator Talmadge,

Here are some pictures I thought you might enjoy. There is a school of thought that these snapshots might motivate you to help get the Blue Jay legislation out of the hands of the Navy and passed by Congress.

We hear you might have an opponent in the next Republican primary. How interesting.

But of course, if the Blue Jay legislation passes in Congress in the next week, there's no reason for these little masterpieces to fall into the hands of either your primary opponent or your liberal Democrat opponent in the upcoming election!

Anyway, thought the glossy 8x10s would evoke some fond memories! Maybe Mrs. Talmadge will like these too?

Enjoy!

A Friend

Bobby's heart pounded with a furious rage against the inside wall of his chest. His fingertips felt the glossy photographic finish of several photos.

Cold sweat broke out on his forehead, and the pit of his stomach felt like a sandbag had been dropped into it.

"Uh, Tommy, Maryanne, give me a second, will you?"

"Sure, boss."

"Sure."

He waited as his secretary and chief of staff stepped out of the office. They had learned that "Give me a second" was Bobby's polite way of saying, "Get the heck out of my office, and now."

"Dear Lord, no."

The first photo brought more cold sweat to his forehead. His hands shook as he stared at it.

The invitation to the Christmas party at the oil-and-gas lobbyist's home in Arlington had come at a time when Molly Sue McGovern Talmadge, who as a former Miss Georgia was a looker in her own right, had flown home to Savannah for a few days to take care of some personal business. Bobby's vote was crucial for the approval of a pipeline along the Savannah River near Augusta, and some old-money property owners and environ-wackos had opposed it.

That night he met for the first time twenty-seven-year-old Marla Moreno, the red-hot Italian model. Their meeting was no accident. They all had sipped liquor and watched a brief runway show put on by Marla in the lobbyist's home. She worked the runway with mesmerizing skill, grace, and beauty.

At first he thought her eyes noticed him as she worked the room. But he decided it was his imagination. Then, when she modeled her final outfit, a little red "Santa's helper" number to capture the festive mood of the season, perhaps it was the liquor talking, but he was sure she was making eyes at him.

And he didn't mind that. She accepted applause, and then, when the band struck up a mix of big band and yuletide music to start the party, he turned around.

There she stood. Smiling.

"Excuse me, Senator Talmadge, but I'm an admirer of your work, and I've always wanted to meet you."

That was all it took.

The first photograph documented what happened about fifteen minutes later, when she sat on his lap on the end of a sofa, showing lots of leg, provoking a delighted smile on his face as she nuzzled her nose into his neck. But if the first photograph wasn't bad enough, the second was a killer.

The cameras had obviously been prepositioned in multiple hiding places in the bedroom before she coaxed him under the sheets.

Now, sitting there staring at photographic evidence of the night he so foolishly compromised himself, thoughts of suicide danced through his head. Not only did the oil-and-gas lobbyist now own him forever, for he would always have to vote the way they told him to vote, but whoever possessed these photographs owned him too.

He couldn't bear to look at the third photograph. But when a morbid curiosity overcame him, he saw that it was as bad as the second, showing them embracing, compromised in multiple ways in the bedroom after the act.

The encounter had been ecstasy, at least for the time that the alcohol still controlled his faculties. But later that night, back at his apartment, he lay alone in his bed. The liquor's effects began to subside, yielding to the reality of his moral downfall, and an internal hell on earth besieged every inch of his body. The space from the pit of his stomach running all the way up to his heart and then his throat felt like someone was twisting his organs.

Why?

Why had he done this?

It haunted him in the dark of night. All the times he had condemned the political womanizers of the world, the Bill Clintons and the Johnny Edwardses and the Teddy Kennedys and the Mark Sanfords. He had often declared self-sanctimoniously, even to his wife, that he was "not like them."

And now he had fallen from his high-and-mighty pedestal and, like them, entered into a world of moral sewerdom.

He was a tortured man that night, alone in his bed, two days before Molly Sue would return. Unable to sleep, he called out into the night, quoting the God-man he professed to follow: "My God, my God, why have you forsaken me?"

Rolling and twisting in the bed, he felt every bit the forsaken man, as if God had withdrawn himself from him.

Oh, he had known all about sin, at least in theory. Most Southern Baptists do. And as a deacon and a Sunday school teacher back at his home church in Augusta, he had talked the talk and talked a good game.

So far his secret fall from purity had cost him only one vote—in favor of a pipeline he probably would have voted for anyway—and a ton of sleepless and restless nights in the three months since it happened.

But now this.

Now his sins were coming home to roost.

Now, sitting alone in the inner sanctums of his palatial office, with his chief of staff and his secretary waiting outside for him to call them back in, he experienced every physical flashback he had felt that night in the aftermath of his dalliance with the hot young model.

They had him where they wanted him.

DeKlerk.

DeKlerk was responsible for this. From start to finish. His lawyers knew every lobbyist in Washington. All Jack Patterson had to do was make a call to the oil-and-gas lobbyist, who made a call to Marla Moreno and offered her enough cash, and they had him where they wanted him. And he'd fallen for it like a rat tempted with a huge glob of sharp cheddar cheese.

But now, with the murder of the JAG officer, things became even less certain.

What if his staff was involved in the shooting of the JAG officer?

He'd asked himself this question a dozen times over the last few days. And truly, he didn't want to know the answer to the question.

Yes, he had told Tommy Mandela to "take care of the problem," with the "problem" being, of course, the uncertainty as to which way the opinion would break.

"Back-channel sources," in the words of Tommy Mandela—and Talmadge didn't want the details about that—had intercepted some emails and other messages signaling that MacDonald could break either way in his opinion.

Bobby's money-backer constituents couldn't risk that MacDonald might, at the end of the day, author a legal opinion that could undermine the project, or undermine a part of the project. So Bobby had told Mandela to "take care of the problem" and left it at that.

What if the revelation of this tryst led to an indictment for conspiracy to commit murder?

How had things gotten so out of control? Why had he not had the strength to hold on to his morals? Since his election, things had happened quickly for him.

Marla Moreno wasn't the first opportunity to fall in his lap. From the moment of his election to the senate, women had thrown themselves at him in droves.

He began to heave, certain that he was about to vomit on his desk.

Another thought hit him. Was his own chief of staff involved in this? Had Tommy Mandela been planted in his staff by the GPVF or by DeKlerk?

Who could he trust?

He had lost all hope. He had lost all trust. And what had happened to his joy? Where was his boyhood joy? Joy at the simplest things, like his grandfather taking him deep-sea fishing at Hilton Head, or the times spent duck hunting in the lowland marshes of the Georgia and South Carolina coasts?

It was all for naught. He would never recover the simple pleasures in life he once had known.

U.S. Senator Bobby Talmadge, in all his glory and splendor, and wielding the power and influence that few people would ever attain, felt like he had struck a deal with the devil as his price for it all. Indeed, perhaps he had done just that.

He opened his right bottom drawer.

The long silver barrel of the Taurus .357 revolver glistened in the light from the lamp on his desk.

He picked up the gun, closed his eyes, and jammed the barrel against his temple.

As a professing Christian, he knew intellectually that suicide was wrong. But what he had done was even more wrong. What choice did he have? Once those photos came out, if they came out, his marriage would be over, his career finished, his name scorned and ridiculed, and very likely he would be indicted, probably for conspiracy to commit murder of a U.S. Naval officer.

There was no hope, no way out.

His mind raced in uncontrollable fury. He took a deep breath, uttered a quick, final prayer—"Forgive me, God"—and pulled the trigger.

The revolver responded with a single *click*.

Bobby cursed. He had forgotten to load the gun.

He laid it down on his desk, reached to the right bottom drawer, pushed some papers around, and found the box of .357 hollow points he'd had shipped in from Atlanta.

He popped open the chamber, pulled out a single bullet, kissed it, and slid it into the first cylinder. This revolver was a seven-shooter, unlike most six-shooters, and the senator loaded every bullet into place.

He needed only one bullet, but there was no point in risking a misfire.

He put the gun in his mouth this time, but something told him a head shot would seem more ceremonious, in fact more courageous.

He brought the barrel back to his temple and again asked God to forgive him.

Something white appeared in the air in front of his desk.

"What?"

A message chirped on his cell phone.

Whatever appeared was gone.

Was he going crazy?

He picked up the cell phone. A text.

Hi, Daddy!
Whatcha doing?
Wanna grab a late dinner tonight?
Love you!
Marybeth

"Oh crap."

He pulled the gun down.

Whatever he'd seen . . . Were his eyes playing tricks on him? There was no other explanation. He must be going mad!

Ah yes . . . the text . . .

He read the text again, then looked at the gun.

Maybe later.

Not now.

Maybe underneath it all, in some way, his kids still needed him.

He slipped the gun into the lower right drawer. Maybe later. The envelope with the pictures of Marla went into the same drawer.

He returned the text.

Sure Sweet Girl,
I'll call you when I leave the office.

He pressed the Send button and breathed out a sigh of relief, which did nothing to ease the turmoil in his stomach and chest and throat.

But he would fight a little longer. Perhaps he could deal with it in a way to minimize damage.

He hit the intercom on his desk.

"Maryanne?"

"Yes, Senator?"

"Send Tommy back in."

"Yes, sir."

A second later, Tommy reentered Bobby's office. "Are you okay, boss?" Bobby studied Mandela's face. Did Mandela know what the envelope contained? Bobby thought for a second about confronting him. But if Mandela didn't know, confronting him would simply give it away, and Bobby needed to play this close to the vest.

"Yes, I'm fine," he said, though nothing was fine. "Just communicating with my daughter about dinner. That's all." A half-truth following the lie. "Look, Tommy, we've got some powerful people breathing down my neck who want this contract out of the Pentagon and on the floor of Congress for a vote. So here's what I want you to do. I want a bill drafted, and I want it drafted by Monday, approving expenditures for Operation Blue Jay.

"Once it's drafted, I want you to send a draft copy to Richardson DeKlerk at AirFlite, and then I want it introduced on the floor of the senate. We'll send a copy over to Congressman Jones's office and encourage them to introduce a concurrent bill containing the same language in the House. I want you to call in my legislative staff and get on this. Now! Is that clear? We've got to deliver, or the results will be disastrous. All around. Do you understand me?"

Mandela responded with an evil-looking grin. "I understand more than you know, Senator."

• • •

LA MADELEINE COUNTRY FRENCH CAFÉ
500 KING STREET
ALEXANDRIA, VIRGINIA
SUNDAY MORNING

Caroline decided putting on her designer shades not only would block the bright early-morning rays from the sun but also might serve as a bit of a disguise to prevent her from being recognized.

Paul Kriete had been a perfect gentleman last night. He hadn't bothered her in the least, nor been suggestive that she had come to his apartment for anything other than chivalrous protection. For this she was grateful.

But, of course, hiding in the shelter of Paul's apartment-nest might work for a night or two, but she couldn't hide under his protective wing forever.

"So how well did you sleep last night?" Captain Kriete asked as he turned into the parking lot of la Madeleine.

"I had some trouble getting to sleep at first, but after an hour or so, I slept like a baby. Thank you."

"You should have slept in my bed and let me take the sofa." He parked his blue Suburban in a space just in front of the restaurant. "Tonight I'm going to insist on that."

"I don't know, sir. You can't be my personal bodyguard forever."

"Why not?"

"Sir, I—"

"Hang on. I'll get your door for you. We'll talk about this later."

He got out, walked behind the Suburban, came up to the passenger side, and opened the door for her.

"Thank you." She stepped out of the SUV just as a red Mercedes pulled into the parking space right beside them.

"You ready?" He closed her door and hit his remote clicker, causing the SUV to beep once as the doors locked.

"As ready as I'll ever be."

He rested his hand in the middle of her back and rushed her at a brisk pace toward the front door of the restaurant.

How strange, she thought as they walked across the asphalt, that she didn't object to the feel of his hand touching her back. Not that she felt some sort of electricity or magical romantic magnetism—especially not so soon after P.J.'s death.

But the touch of his hand exuded a firm certainty, a sense of security and safety. What else could she expect from a strong, confident man who had commanded a U.S. Navy warship? She would never admit this to him, but right now, with her head spinning and her emotions swirling, Paul Kriete's masculine strength was exactly what she needed.

"Here ya go." He opened the door for her just as a light breeze brought the scent of his cologne, distracting her in a way she had not expected.

"There they are." She pointed across the restaurant. Victoria and Mark sat in the far corner, both waving at Caroline and Paul. They walked over to the table, and Victoria and Mark stood as they approached.

"Everybody okay?" Mark asked, waiting for them to sit.

"We're here," Paul said as a server approached.

"Sir? Ma'am? Would you like coffee?"

"Yes, cream and sugar," Caroline said.

"Black," Paul said.

"Be right back."

"So did you find out anything?" Paul asked.

"Our computer forensics folks were able to trace Commander MacDonald's emails, both personal and business." Mark sipped his coffee. "Here's what we know. P.J. wrote two legal opinions: one saying the proposed project is legal in its entirety, and one concluding that the project as proposed is not legal because of *posse comitatus* and Fourth Amendment issues.

"The email he sent to Simmons concluded that the project was legal, and he said he planned to send the second opinion to Simmons later, but he only sent the opinion that would have legally cleared the project for passage by Congress."

"Your coffee?"

Caroline looked up. The server stood there holding a silver tray with two coffee cups, milk, and sugar. She and Paul both thanked her and she left.

"Let me see if I can get this straight," Caroline said. "The opinion P.J. sent to Ross Simmons would have green-lighted the project legally?"

"That's right, Commander," Mark said.

"So it's a reasonable deduction that whoever killed Ross and stole his computer didn't want that opinion to get out in the public domain or to wind up on the Secretary of the Navy's desk?"

"I think you're all over it, Commander." Mark again.

Silence.

Glances were exchanged.

Paul spoke. "So it's reasonable to assume that the AirFlite folks wouldn't be suspects here?"

"Maybe," Mark said. "Maybe not."

"Why maybe not?"

Victoria responded, "Can I take that?"

"Sure," Mark said. "This is a brainstorming session."

"Maybe not," Victoria continued, "because P.J. said in his email that he was getting ready to send the opposite opinion—that the arrangement is illegal—and it's possible that someone wanted to ensure that Ross Simmons didn't search P.J.'s computer at the Pentagon for the opinion that cut in the other direction."

"Agreed," Mark said. "We can't yet rule out either side."

"I see your point," Paul said with a tinge of disappointment in his voice.

More silence.

"One thing is for sure," Caroline said.

"What's that?" Victoria asked.

"Well, it seems to me that whoever is assigned to write this opinion is going to have a target on her back."

Paul spoke up. "You mean a target on his back. Captain Guy hasn't reassigned this to another officer, has he?"

"Not yet," Caroline said.

"I don't know if I like the sound of this," Paul said.

"Whether we like the sound of it or not," Mark said, "Caroline's right. Both officers, Commander MacDonald and Lieutenant Ross, had one thing in common. They both had access to this legal opinion. P.J. wrote the opinion, and Ross later had it in his possession. The opinion became a dangerous hot potato. Whoever killed Ross didn't want it to see the light of day."

Caroline locked eyes with Mark.

Paul spoke up again. "It seems like for the safety of the officers of Code 13, maybe this job should be assigned to another legal team."

Caroline spoke up. "Maybe. Then again, maybe not."

"What are you saying, Caroline?" Mark asked.

"I'm saying if we're going to catch whoever killed these guys, we're going to have to bait the killer."

"I don't follow you," Paul said. "And I'm not sure I want to follow you."

"What do you have in mind when you say 'bait the killer'?" Victoria asked.

Caroline looked at Paul, who cut his eyes at her. But his disapproving look would not deter her defiance toward the worthless maggots who killed the man she loved. She would do this, or at least try to do it, for him.

"I'd like to know too," Mark said. "What do you mean by 'bait the killer'?"

"What I mean is this. I'm going to go to Captain Guy and see if he will appoint me to finish writing the opinion—"

"No!" Paul interrupted.

"Yes!" Caroline shot back. "And not only that, I'm going to ask if we can do some sort of press release so the public will know."

"I can't let you do that!" Paul said.

"Sir, with respect, I'm not in your chain of command. It's not your choice."

"That puts too big of a target on your back."

"That's the idea, sir," Caroline said. "Draw the rats to the cheese and then kill the rats. Of course, I think we would need NCIS's cooperation to make this work." She cast a glance at Romanov. "Mark?"

All eyes turned to Mark. He waited a couple of seconds to answer. "The captain's right, Caroline. You'd have a huge target on your back. NCIS could try to protect you, and we would try. But any bait-and-trap plan can be highly dangerous, and there are no guarantees."

"Why can't we find some other officer for this?" Paul said.

"No!" Caroline snapped, then felt sorry for her tone. "I apologize. I didn't mean to raise my voice. No. This has to be me. I have a personal interest vested in this. I want to do this. If I get killed, I get killed."

Mark looked at Paul. "Looks like she's made up her mind, Captain."

"Just because she thinks she's made up her mind doesn't mean I have to like it."

Caroline insisted, "It's not a matter of *thinking* I've made up my mind. I *have* made up my mind. I want to nab this piece of trash who killed P.J., and Ross too. And if that means putting my life in danger, then so be it. I don't care!"

She could feel their stares boring into her. And somewhere in the background, she heard the low rumble of conversation and the occasional clanking of utensils. She had stated her position, and that would be that.

"Wow." Mark broke the silence.

"Excuse me, sir." The server had returned. "You ordered a variety pack of bagels?"

"Ah yes," Mark said. "Just put them down there. And we're fine for the time being."

"Yes, sir." The server stepped away.

"I took the liberty of ordering these before you arrived."

"Thanks, Mark," Paul said.

"So, Caroline," Victoria said. "I admire you for your determination and your bravery, but don't you think Captain Guy might have something to say about this? What if he selects someone else to write it?"

Caroline looked over at the woman who just one week or so ago had appeared to be her newfound rival for P.J.'s affection. "Look, Victoria, that opinion letter needs to be written. Code 13 is the one department within JAG tasked with researching and writing these legal opinions. Now whoever gets the job will be a target. I might be new to the party, but with respect, I outrank you, I outranked Ross Simmons, I've got a personal interest in this, and I'm willing to take the risk.

"Plus, this isn't just a legal opinion anymore. It's also a sting operation." She looked at Mark. "Hopefully I'll get some help from NCIS in persuading Captain Guy to let me go forward with this."

"Don't look at me," Mark said.

"You are exactly who I'm looking at, Special Agent Romanov. Now, I want you to man up, talk to Captain Guy, and let's get this done!"

Mark just shook his head. "Your courage and determination are astounding, Commander."

Caroline bit into a chocolate-chip bagel, then washed it down with coffee. "Don't know about courage and determination." She looked at Paul, who shook his head. "Maybe more like anger and determination." She shifted her gaze from Paul to Mark. "So, Special Agent Romanov, you dodged my question. I'll try this again. You are going to help coordinate this, aren't you?"

Mark looked at Paul, then at Caroline. "At the risk of Captain Kriete launching a drone strike against me," he said hesitantly, "yes, I'll see what I can do."

"Thank you."

Paul cursed. "This is so unnecessary."

"P.J.'s murder was unnecessary," Caroline replied. "What is the specific game plan, Mark?" she asked.

"Well, first we've got to get Captain Guy to go along with it, to assign the project to Caroline. Then we've got to find a way to leak this out to set the trap. I'll see if we can leak it at the Pentagon's daily press briefing tomorrow afternoon. Then we've got to keep an NCIS tail on Commander McCormick and hope we nail the bad guys before . . ." He looked at Caroline.

"Before they nail me. I know."

"Right," Mark said.

"I'm ready to go," Caroline said.

"Now?" Paul asked.

"Now. If I'm going to become rat bait, let's get the show on the road."

Mark spoke up. "Let me at least make a call to get an NCIS tail on you."

"Tell you what. The captain here is going to take me to his home for one more night, and that's all the time I'm giving you. You can have your tail start following me there. And then I'll be back at my townhouse tomorrow. Meanwhile, I've got a legal opinion to write once this all gets set up and I get P.J.'s research." She stood up. "Shall we, Captain?"

"You're crazy."

"You don't know the half of it."

They stepped out of the restaurant into the parking lot, and as they walked toward Paul's Suburban, the red Mercedes parked beside it pulled out and screeched its tires, speeding out of the lot, making a left on King Street.

"That was weird," Paul said.

"Everything about this is weird," she said. "Let's go, Captain."

"As you wish."

CHAPTER 24

• • •

HEADQUARTERS

NEW YORK CONCRETE & SEAFOOD COMPANY

EAST 161ST STREET

THE BRONX

SUNDAY MORNING

Phillip D'Agostino sucked on another cigarette and glanced at the headlines of the sports section of the *New York Times*.

Another loss for the Yankees. This time to the Sox again. Great. Big Sal would take it out on everybody around him.

He yelled at his secretary as he snuffed out his cigarette. "Hey, Viv! I'm headed down to the dockyard."

"Got it, boss. Good luck. Be careful!"

"Yeah, sure."

Phil walked out the back of the offices, got into his black Porsche 918 Spyder, and started the engine. He pulled out his 9-millimeter pistol, racked the slide, and laid it on the seat.

The Porsche, which he had purchased for a cool $940,000 just last year, purred like a cat and jumped like a leopard when Phil hit the accelerator, peeling out onto East 161st Street.

A minute later, he took the ramp up onto I-278 West and pushed down on the accelerator again.

The drive down to the Brooklyn dockyards would take half an

hour or so, depending on traffic. As he blew past a slow-moving U-Haul in the right lane, Phil's mind raced through his pre-docking procedures to make sure there would be no problems in landing and distributing the stuff.

Let's see . . .

Bribes to Port Authority police.

Check.

Bribes to the right NYPD officers patrolling the area.

Check.

Hush money to the three federal DEA supervisors working the area.

Check again.

Coordination with company seafood trucks to pick up the stuff and run it to various rendezvous points up and down the East Coast.

Check.

Keeping Big Sal happy?

Only a perfectly executed operation would keep the big guy happy. The family needed to do everything within its power to make sure those drones never took to the skies. And while some progress had been made when the wise-guy JAG officer got waxed, Phil remained unconvinced that the bill was dead.

His cell phone rang.

Phil checked the caller ID.

"Vinnie, what's up? I'm getting ready to see Big Sal. Tell me I got nothin' to worry about with this drone contract."

"I wish I could tell you. But we got another problem."

"What are you talkin' about, Vinnie?"

"What I mean is we got this JAG—"

Silence.

"Vinnie?"

Nothing.

"Vinnie!"

Phil cursed and hit Redial.

"Hey. You've reached Vinnie. I can't answer now, so leave me a message and I'll get back with ya."

Phil cursed. The idiot had let his phone die again.

Just when he started to think there was hope for Vinnie, the bone-head inevitably did something stupid.

Approaching Exit 31, he wheeled the Porsche onto the off-ramp, merging onto Williamsburg Street, and then, under sunny morning skies, entered the old Navy Yard through the Clymer Street gate.

The old Navy Yard had once been used for many years by the United States Navy. But now, having been turned into an industrial park with the help of money from the city, the old Navy Yard was no longer a hub of activity as it was in World War II. Now it had become a mish-mash of light industrial use and warehouses, and took investment money from just about any business enterprise willing to chip in a few bucks.

It was also a perfect transit point for the New York Concrete & Seafood Company, which had leased two piers, Pier J and Pier K. They jutted out into Wallabout Bay and the East River.

The company also owned several warehouses, fishing boats, and vessels carrying various other types of goods and merchandise crucial to the profitability of the family business.

The fishing business was, indeed, a legitimate family enterprise and was the face of the enterprise to the public, and the ostensible reason for the need of a presence down at the old Navy Yard.

Phil turned right onto Railroad Avenue, heading out toward the warehouses situated between the two piers.

He slowed the Porsche to a crawl, approaching two armed, black-clothed, and big-bicepped private security guards standing at the end of the pier.

The guards, with their forearms, biceps, and necks covered with tattoos, stood straight, almost coming to military attention. When they saw the Porsche, they enthusiastically waved it through.

They knew who paid their salaries.

Phil rolled down his window as he slowed past the guards.

"Heya, boss!" the guard on the left said.

"S'up, Joey?" Phil said. "The big guy here?"

"Yes, sir. He's in da warehouse. Right over there."

"He in a good mood?"

"Don't know, boss. They've had a little commotion."

"What commotion?"

"Oh, you know," the guard said. "Some dockworker with his hands caught in the cookie jar."

"That's just great," Phil said. He looked in front of the Porsche. Seven big rigs, company trucks with the New York Concrete & Seafood Company logo, with a big red crab painted on the side, were lined up over on the right side of the pier, one behind the other. "Hey, Joey. Go park my car. I'm gonna step in and talk to Big Sal."

"You bet, boss." A sparkle lit the goon's eyes.

"Hey. Don't scratch it. Got it?"

"I ain't gonna scratch it, boss."

Joey opened the door of the Porsche, and Phil stepped out and pulled out a cigarette. He had a feeling he was going to need it. He struck his lighter, but the wind whipping from across the East River flattened the flame.

"Here. Let me help ya, boss." The guard stepped in and cupped his hand over the flame as Phil sucked the satisfying nicotine into his lungs.

"Appreciate it, Joey."

"You bet, boss."

"Take care of my baby."

"Will do, boss. Like she was my own."

"Ya better."

Joey got into the Porsche and drove down toward the end of Pier K, heading to a parking spot almost right across from the freighter *Occidental*, where dockworkers were unloading cargo, some of it fish, some of it other stuff, as Phil took a second satisfying drag from the cigarette.

Phil hated having Big Sal around because of blurred lines of authority. Sure, Sal was the big-daddy godfather of the business. But Sal himself had made the decision to retire to Palm Beach and leave Phil in charge of the day-to-day operations.

That meant with Sal in Florida for the last five years, Phil had been *the* man in the company, and especially in New York. But every six months or so, sometimes every nine months, Big Sal would trek his way back up to New York and stay just long enough to get into the middle of things, muddying the lines of authority.

The men were used to taking their orders from Phil, and all of a sudden the big cat's on the scene, barking orders of his own. Every time it happened, you could see the confusion on the men's faces.

Then, after a few days, Sal and his entourage, which usually included a harem of hot-looking models young enough to be Sal's granddaughters, would disappear back down to Florida, leaving Phil to clean up the mess.

Frankly, Phil just wished the ole guy would stay in Florida and stay the heck out of the way.

But that hadn't happened yet.

And now, this latest thing with the drone contract had gotten the old guy stirred up, precipitating his latest trip.

Not that Phil could blame Big Sal for worrying about the drone contract. Phil himself had lost a night or two of sleep over the whole thing.

Oh well. May as well get it over with. Sal would be ornery enough without the commotion, but now? What the heck.

The refrigerated warehouse stood only a few paces in front of him, maybe twenty feet across a short alleyway. He stuck the cigarette back into his mouth, walked across the alleyway, opened the side door, and stepped inside, where the cool, refrigerated air immediately embraced him.

NYC&S employees, in jeans and sweatshirts, lifted boxes and loaded them onto forklifts. Others were driving the forklifts over to an assembly line, dropping crated boxes onto conveyor belts that ran the boxes outside to company trucks.

Out in the middle of the concrete floor, the body lay sprawled facedown, blood gushing from the head.

Phil walked over and stood over the man, nonchalantly blowing cigarette smoke as he looked down at the body. The exit wound had made a bloody mess of the back of his head. Phil didn't recognize him, but what a waste.

"Got his hand caught in the cookie jar."

Phil recognized the gruff voice that he'd dreaded hearing and looked up at the big-bellied, six-foot-four-inch balding hunk of an aging man. He wore khaki pants and a light-blue, short-sleeved shirt, shirttail out, and held a long-barreled revolver in his hand.

"Big Sal!" Phil forced a smile and feigned a voice of excitement. "How's my favorite uncle?" Not waiting for an answer, he continued, "You look nice and tanned."

"Yeah, and I bet you everybody else around here wishes I'd stayed in Florida. Especially him."

"Your handiwork, Sal?"

"The foreman offered to take care of it, but the ole man needed some target practice." He held the barrel of the revolver to his lips and kissed it. "She's my baby. Obliterates the back of the skull every time."

"Looks like you ain't lost your touch, Uncle. How much did he have on him?"

"He stashed five kilos in his pocket. Close to a hundred fifty thousand bucks' worth street value," Big Sal said. "Caught him on camera."

"These idiots never learn." Phil took a draw from the cigarette. "They see us wax three or four of 'em in here a year, pay 'em a great salary, and they still are stupid enough to think they can get away with it."

"A new hire," the godfather said. "He found out what we do to thieves around here. Got one of those?"

"A cigarette?"

"What else do you think I'm talkin' about? Sheesh. Sometimes I think you're as dumb as that idiot son-in-law of yours."

"That hurts, Uncle." He handed Sal a cigarette.

"Thanks. Gotta light?"

"Yes, sir. Here ya go."

"Thanks." A second later, Sal blew smoke in Phil's face. "Hey, Marco!" His voice thundered across the concrete floor.

One of the workers about twenty yards away, standing over by the conveyor line, turned and looked in their direction. "Are you talking to me?"

"Who do you think I'm talking to?" Big Sal thundered. "Get your butt over here!"

The man started a quick pace toward them. "Sorry, boss." He directed the comment to Sal, not Phil, and Phil bit his lip.

"I thought you said Mario. I misunderstood you, boss."

"If I had wanted to say Mario, I would have said Mario!"

"Sorry, my bad." Marco looked apologetic.

"Hey." Sal pointed down at the bleeding body. "I want you to get a couple of guys and get this scum off my floor. Cut the body up and use it for crab bait, and throw the bones to the dogs. Got it?"

"Got it, boss," the sycophant said. "Hey, Stefano! Fredrico! Get over here and help me get this goon off the floor!"

"Hey, nephew. What do you say we take a walk while these boys clean this mess up?"

"Sure, Uncle Sal."

"Why don't we step outside? You know, it's a little chilly in here. I've gotten used to the warm sunshine in Florida. And you know, your uncle gets queasy at the sight of blood and dead bodies."

"I see you've kept your sense of humor, Uncle Sal."

"Well, ya know"—the godfather sucked on his cigarette—"it's just this blood thing. Sometimes it takes a little blood to get the juices flowing."

They stepped out of the warehouse into the sunlit alleyway, out where the two armed guards were standing. Sal tossed his cigarette and pointed down at the company trucks being loaded by dockworkers. "You know, this is gonna be a pretty big haul for us, Phil."

"I can see that, Uncle."

"Hey! Mr. D.!"

Phil and Sal turned around.

Marco, the dockworker Big Sal had just assigned cleanup duty, had stepped out of the warehouse and was walking in their direction.

"What are you doin' out here?" Sal said. "I thought I told you to clean up the mess."

"We're workin' on it. But there's something I needed to tell you."

"What is it?" Big Sal contorted his face. His voice sounded irritated.

"We caught another one with his hand in the cookie jar."

Sal cursed. "How much this time?"

"Three kilos, boss."

Sal cursed again.

"What do you want to do, boss?"

Big Sal looked at Phil, then at Marco. "Hey, I gotta talk to Phil. You take care of it, Marco. But call everybody around and make sure everybody sees what you're doing. We need to reinforce the message. You steal from your employer, and you get waxed."

"Yes, sir." A grin of satisfaction crossed Marco's face. He turned and headed back to the warehouse.

"Anyway," Big Sal said as they turned and started walking again toward the end of the pier, "this looks to be a pretty big haul."

"Looks that way," Phil said. "What are you thinking? Maybe twenty million?"

"At least," Big Sal said. "Maybe thirty."

"Did you say thirty million?"

"Possible. The foreman on the ship tells me they got some high-quality stuff. And lots of it."

"That's one of our biggest hauls to date."

Sal stopped walking as they approached the ship's bow, just short of the transoms where company dockworkers were moving crated boxes down the catwalk, loading some onto the NYC&S trucks and carting others into the warehouses. He turned and looked Phil in the eye.

"That's right. And the next one due in here two weeks from now could be even bigger than that. So things are looking quite rosy . . . except for one little problem."

Phil knew where this was going, but he also knew Sal, and he had to play along to keep the big guy from going ballistic. "What would that be?"

"The problem is the possibility of drones swarming up in the air"—he pointed into the blue skies—"and busting up all the fun we've been having. Now, don't you see that as a problem, Phil?"

"Yes. Of course, Uncle Sal. It's a potential problem."

"Well, I thought that by now you would assure me we got nothin' to worry about!"

"Well, we've been working on it, Uncle Sal. We sent Vinnie down to Washington—"

"That, in and of itself, worries me," the godfather said.

"I know, Uncle Sal. Vinnie ain't winnin' no Einstein awards. But he's loyal and he does what you tell him."

"You got a point. But we gotta have more than just the absence of screwups here." Sal pulled out a big cigar. "Give me your lighter!"

"Here, I'll get it for you."

More smoke.

"So what's Vinnie been doing down there, and what's going on with our boy, the distinguished Senator Chuckie Rodino?"

"Well, Vinnie already paid ole Chuckie a visit. Made him visit him in a bar down there and laid down the line that we expect them to kill this thing."

The sharp clap of a single gunshot rang out, echoing inside the warehouse.

"Another one bites the dust," Sal said.

"We need to start making these boys use silencers," Phil said.

"What's the big deal?" Sal said. "It ain't like the cops don't know what's going on." He puffed on his cigar. "They're getting paid a ton of money to keep their mouths shut."

"That's a fact."

"So back to the point. I need to know this genie with the drones ain't comin' out of the bottle."

"Well, we're watching it, boss. The Navy had this JAG officer who was about to write a legal opinion against us. Put it this way. That JAG officer ain't a problem anymore."

They stopped at the end of the pier. Sal looked out over the East River, appearing to gaze across the way at Lower Manhattan.

Phil kept his mouth shut and decided to enjoy the view. The views of Manhattan from across the East River never got old. As much as he wished Big Sal would stay in Florida, Phil couldn't blame the old man for wanting to come back as much as possible. Once you got New York in your blood, there was no place like it on earth. Not Palm Beach. Not LA. Not Vegas. Not Chicago.

Hopefully Sal would get his fix of the Big Apple and then get the heck out of town.

Big Sal spoke again but didn't look at Phil. "Okay, so the JAG officer ain't a problem. But these officers are a dime a dozen. Ya wax one of 'em, they just replace him with another."

"Hopefully the replacement gets the message that it ain't a good idea to say there's anything okay with this contract," Phil said.

"You mean like these bozos in our own warehouse get the message?" Sal asked. "You bop off one, and another does the same stupid thing."

"That may be true, Sal, but our idiots stand to profit a lot more from being stupid than some JAG officer. They get away with it, and they make more in one haul than a JAG officer makes in a year."

Sal took a draw from a big, fat cigar. "That's true. We need to make sure the Navy stays in line."

"We will, Sal."

"But we also need to make sure our handpicked senator stays in line."

"Like I said, Sal, we've been working on him."

The godfather looked at him. "Well, working him ain't good enough. I want guarantees this bill never sees the light of day."

Phil flicked his cigarette out into the East River. The wind lit into it and blew it over the water, out to the right toward the United Nations Building, before it splashed down. "A guarantee is a big thing, Sal. What do you want me to do?"

"Here's what I want you to do." Sal's voice grew resolute. "I want you to get the good senator and that congressman friend of his . . . What's his name? Milkey Mack or somethin' like that—"

"I know who you're talking about. Mackey Milk, I think they call him. Definitely light in the loafers."

"Whatever. Anyway, I want you to get 'em both and bring 'em

right up here to the warehouse, and I want to have a chat. They've gotta understand. Either they kill the bill, or it ain't gonna be pretty. And by the time I'm done with 'em, I don't think we'll have anything to worry about. Ya got that, Phil?"

"Got it, Sal."

CHAPTER 25

• • •

Caroline stepped through her front door, dead-bolted it behind her, and then walked over to her front window. The black Taurus off to her left, parked twenty yards or so away from the corner, was NCIS, and two armed agents sat inside. Two more armed agents were sitting in a blue Chevrolet right around the corner and out of her view.

Mark Romanov had wasted no time in pouncing on her idea, despite Paul's objections on grounds of chivalry, and she appreciated Mark's cooperation and his fast action in getting NCIS protection for her. The guy was on the ball. Victoria may have had the hots for P.J.—who wouldn't?—but if it worked out for them, Mark would be an outstanding catch.

Of course, again, he could not compare to P.J. Who could?

Her mind raced to another thought.

Why, with NCIS protection watching her twenty-four hours a day for the foreseeable future, did she feel so vulnerable?

Was she crazy to have volunteered for this?

Of course she was crazy—crazy in love with P.J.

Why couldn't they have just gotten married and stayed in

California? They had talked about pooling their money and buying a small bungalow up on Mount Helix.

But the Navy.

The Navy!

Like P.J. had, she both loved it and hated it. She loved the adventure. She loved the sense of service. She loved the call of duty. And she served for the love of country.

But she also hated it. She hated the way it separated families. She hated the long hours of loneliness it caused.

But as it had with P.J., her love for the Navy won out over her hatred for it. The Navy was all she knew. It was the only thing he knew. No job in any private law firm, regardless of big salaries and fat bonuses, could ever compare.

P.J. gave his life in service to his country, and if necessary, she would do the same.

She turned, walked over to her sofa, and sat. She felt herself beginning to tremble. A moment later, the tears started again.

Thank God for the privacy of her four walls. Thank God no one could see her in such an emotional state, for a commander in the Navy could never show such vulnerable emotions in public.

"Why, God? Why me?"

She got up, walked over and got a tissue, dabbed her eyes, and looked out the window again at the NCIS car down below.

Why had God put her here? Why had he allowed her to endure such passionate love and then such passionate loss? And now, why was he placing her in the line of fire?

Actually, perhaps it wasn't God who was putting her in the line of fire. After all, she had volunteered to make herself a target to trap P.J.'s killer.

But then again, maybe he was putting her in the line of fire after all.

Her mind wandered back to a Bible study she had attended as an undergraduate at the University of North Carolina. Something they had discussed from the book of Romans. She remembered the chapter, but not the specific verse.

Was God trying to tell her something?

She walked into her bedroom and found the Bible sitting on her nightstand. When she picked it up, somehow the feel of the leather binding against her palms made her realize she needed to pick it up more often. Something, or Someone, told her, in a voice that was silent yet clear in her mind and heart, that she needed to call out to God for protection, especially now.

She sat on the side of the bed, opened the old Bible to the book of Romans, and found chapter 8.

"Now, where was it?" she asked aloud, and then, seeing it, she said, "There!"

At first she read it silently.

But again a thought entered her mind from out of the blue. *There is power in the spoken word.*

She decided to read aloud, starting with verse 28.

"'And we know that in all things God works for the good of those who love him, who have been called according to his purpose. For those God foreknew he also predestined to be conformed to the image of his Son, that he might be the firstborn among many brothers and sisters. And those he predestined, he also called; those he called, he also justified; those he justified, he also glorified. What, then, shall we say in response to these things? If God is for us, who can be against us?'"

She closed the Bible, and when she did, a sudden calmness overcame her.

She looked at the wall clock. It was time.

She walked into her living room, turned on the flat screen, and switched to Fox News.

It had all been arranged.

Fox would televise the Pentagon's daily press briefing on the topic of the safety of U.S. military personnel in the DC region.

The trap would be set.

On the screen, the familiar visage of longtime Fox anchor Tom Miller appeared.

Caroline sat back down on her sofa and upped the volume.

"This is Tom Miller in New York, where we are about to join the daily Pentagon press briefing, live, where we expect Rear Admiral Bill Cameron to address a number of topics.

"But the topic that seems to be on everyone's mind at the moment is the murder of two U.S. Navy JAG officers, Lieutenant Commander P.J. MacDonald and Lieutenant Ross Simmons, both of whom were assigned to the Navy's secretive and prestigious Code 13, which is part of the Office of the Judge Advocate General at the Pentagon.

"Not only have condolences been pouring in from all across the country, but now we've had members of Congress raising concerns about the Pentagon's ability to protect its own officers.

"Still others are asking whether this could be terror-related, or even somehow related to a proposed drone project the officers were working on.

"And as we await the briefing from Rear Admiral Cameron, we bring in Fox News military analyst, retired U.S. Marine Colonel Sam Beckett.

"Colonel, welcome to you."

"Good to be here, Tom."

"So what's going on here, and what do we expect to hear from Admiral Cameron?"

"Tom, that's a good question. What we know is this: We have two dead U.S. Navy JAG officers who, as you pointed out, were both assigned to the same division of the Navy's Office of the Judge Advocate General at the Pentagon.

"The division they were assigned to is a secretive, selective division of the JAG, that is, Code 13, which bears the rather innocuous title of the Administrative Law Division. And up until now, no one would have heard of it unless they were involved at the top levels of the government and the upper echelons at the Pentagon. And that was by design.

"Now, I'm not NCIS and I'm not law enforcement, but the fact that we have two JAG officers assassinated just days apart, both working at a selective, secretive division of the Pentagon, suggests that these terror attacks against our Navy personnel are not coincidental but were, for whatever reason, coordinated.

"The question is, why target two officers from a small and heretofore unknown and secretive JAG division in the Pentagon?

"Well, no one can say for sure, and I'll be interested in hearing what Admiral Cameron has to say. But as you know, I have a few contacts in the Pentagon, and here's what I've been hearing.

"Both officers were doing work on a proposed military acquisitions project known as Project Blue Jay. Now, that project is for a large drone purchase the Navy may be placing before Congress. At this point I don't know all the details, but there is yet another common element between these two officers."

"Colonel," Miller said, "what about rumors circulating that these killings are terror-related?"

"Good question, Tom. Well, certainly these are acts of terror, in one way or another. But if by terror-related we are talking about Muslim-Islamic terror, which is the biggest threat to international peace in the world, my sources haven't been able to confirm that. Frankly, I'm not convinced Islamic fascism is involved. It's more likely domestic terror."

The screen cut back to Tom Miller. "Thank you, Colonel. Sorry to cut you off, but we see that Rear Admiral Bill Cameron is entering the Pentagon press briefing room. And this is a surprise. It looks like Admiral Cameron is being accompanied by another flag officer. Who's that?"

Colonel Beckett interjected, "That's Vice Admiral Zack Brewer, Judge Advocate General of the Navy."

Caroline smiled at the sight of Zack Brewer on the screen.

"Yes, of course," Miller said. "How could I have not recognized him? Admiral Brewer is one of the most recognizable figures in the U.S. Navy. But seeing him in an unusual setting threw me off. And now, let's listen in as Admiral Cameron steps to the microphone."

The camera zoomed in on the two-star U.S. Navy Admiral, wearing a summer white uniform with black-and-gold shoulder boards and with a bevy of colorful medals and service ribbons above the pocket on his left chest.

On the bottom of the screen flashed the caption "RADM Bill Cameron, Pentagon Spokesman."

"Good morning, ladies and gentlemen. As you know, I am Rear Admiral Bill Cameron, currently serving as Pentagon press secretary. I'm honored to have with me today Vice Admiral Zack Brewer, who, as many of you know, is the Judge Advocate General of the Navy.

"Admiral Brewer will make a brief statement, and then I will also make a brief statement and follow up with your questions." Cameron looked at Brewer. "Admiral?"

The Judge Advocate General stepped behind the podium, nodding and sporting a confident smile. He was a hero to the JAG community, and even before he spoke a word, his very presence brought a sense of comfort to Caroline.

"Good morning," Brewer said. "As Admiral Cameron said, I will be brief. As many of you know, the U.S. Navy JAG Corps has, within the last few days, lost two of its best and brightest officers to senseless and inexcusable acts of murder. We don't know the details of who, what, or why. At least not yet. I'm confident that we will know, however, and I'll leave that to Admiral Cameron to discuss.

"But I just wanted to say a few words in tribute to these officers, because the nation needs to know who they were. Lieutenant Commander P.J. MacDonald was the best of the brightest. He served his country and he served the Navy with honor and distinction. I wish we had a thousand others like him, but he was one of a kind."

"Yes, he was, Admiral." Caroline wiped a tear from her eye.

Brewer continued, "Lieutenant Ross Simmons was a bright rising star in the JAG Corps. Ross was one of the top officers in his Justice School class, and he won the prestigious New York City Bar Association Trial Advocacy Award, which is given to the winner of the Navy Justice School's trial advocacy competition.

"Ross Simmons possessed unlimited potential, having just been deep selected for lieutenant commander ahead of many of his peers.

"I have expressed my deep condolences to the families of P.J. and Ross, and expressed our great sorrow for their loss. But today I am announcing that both Lieutenant Commander MacDonald and Lieutenant Simmons are being awarded posthumously the Meritorious

Service Medal for outstanding meritorious service to the United States, to the U.S. Navy, and to the JAG Corps.

"I will be presenting the medals to the families of these officers in a more private and intimate setting in the near future. But today I wanted to take this opportunity to acknowledge their service before the nation and to thank them, and thank their families, for their service."

Brewer looked at Rear Admiral Cameron. "Thank you, Admiral."

Cameron stepped back to the podium as Brewer stepped down. "Thank you, Vice Admiral Brewer, for those comments," he said. "And let me add that on behalf of the Chief of Naval Operations, the Secretary of the Navy, the Secretary of Defense, and of men and women in uniform in every branch serving this country all over the world, we are all grateful for and salute these two officers, Lieutenant Commander MacDonald and Lieutenant Simmons, and we offer our condolences to their families, with our assurances that they will not be forgotten."

Cameron paused, slipping on a pair of reading glasses. "Now, I know a lot of questions have arisen concerning the deaths of these officers. The Secretary of Defense is aware that questions also have arisen concerning the safety of our sailors and troops.

"But we want to assure not only the American people but also our men and women in uniform, particularly those serving here in the National Capital Region, that their safety is of our utmost concern.

"As far as the attacks on these officers go, we have been working with NCIS every day, and of course the JAG Corps has been cooperating with NCIS and also local law enforcement, and we expect the killers to be apprehended.

"I have time for just a few questions." The admiral paused, then pointed. "Yes. Karl."

"Admiral, Karl Rogers, Associated Press. We've heard that both of these officers were working on the same contract. Could you comment on that?"

Cameron glanced at Brewer, then said, "Karl, that is accurate. Other questions?"

Multiple hands were raised.

"Yes. Lisa."

"Admiral, Lisa Rogers, Reuters. Sir, we've heard these officers were both working on a legal opinion for that contract that might pave the way for a mammoth-sized drone acquisitions project for the U.S. Navy. Could you comment on this, and will the Navy now assign another officer to this project? And are you concerned about the safety of officers working on this project?"

"Wow, Lisa. That's about ten questions wrapped into one."

Laughter.

"Which one would you like me to answer first?"

"Whichever one you would like, Admiral."

Cameron sipped from a glass of water. "Okay. Yes, your sources are correct. It's no secret that the Navy has been considering an experimental rollout of a drone fleet to protect our coasts against potential adversaries and terror threats. Both officers were in fact working on a legal opinion for a drone project. So yes, they were working on the same project. Yes, we will assign the project to another officer, and while we are always concerned about the safety of all our personnel, we're confident in the ability of NCIS to keep our officers safe."

Rumbling in the gallery. "Yes. Mary."

"Mary Warren, *Washington Post*. Admiral, has the Pentagon issued any warning to U.S. personnel about terror threats in the wake of these attacks on the two officers?"

Another sip of water. "At this point, we have no evidence to suggest these attacks were coordinated terror attacks. So we want our people to be cautious and vigilant as always, but not to overreact. Bill?"

"Bill Scheiffer, CBS News. Admiral, you say you have no evidence to suggest these killings are terror-related. But don't you find it beyond coincidental that we have two officers murdered from the same division working on the same project?"

Cameron nodded. "Bill, I see and share your concern. But no, at this point, we aren't aware of any terror threat or coordinated attack."

"Quick follow-up, sir," Scheiffer said.

"Sure."

"Are you at liberty to give the name of the JAG officer who will now be handling this project?"

Cameron hesitated. "Sure. Why not? The new JAG officer assigned to the project is Lieutenant Commander Caroline McCormick. And we expect that she will complete the JAG phase of the project and will do an excellent job."

"Admiral . . ."

"Admiral . . ."

"Sir, just out of curiosity . . ."

Caroline cut off the television. She had heard all she needed to hear.

Her name had just been broadcast to millions of people all over the world. Soon, most of the world, perhaps even the killer, would know.

The question had been a plant and the answer deliberate.

The bait had been set on the trap.

And the idea had been hers.

She got up off the sofa and walked into the kitchen.

A lone bottle of pinot noir sat in a rack atop the fridge.

She reached for it, took it out, and brought it up to her face. Though she liked her red wines at room temperature, the wine bottles remained cool. The glassy exterior of the bottle, chilled by the air conditioner, felt refreshing rolled against her cheeks.

She set the bottle on the table and reached into a drawer for a corkscrew. She held it up against the light and examined it. Even the corkscrew reminded her of him. In a sense, it had linked them together that Saturday when they lounged in the plush green grass of Coronado Tidelands Park, celebrating his deep selection to lieutenant commander. The corkscrew had sat on their checkered red blanket on many occasions at La Jolla, too, as they lounged on the grass above the cove, their toasts and celebratory sips of wine enhanced by one of the most romantic sights in the world—the orange sun, a big, benign, lazy ball, dipping below the horizon and into the Pacific.

The corkscrew had gone with them to the Southern California mountains that day when they opened the bottle of Castle Rock that had accompanied the warm, luscious apple pie they bought from Mom's Pie House, the quaint little pie-baking shop just off Main Street in Julian.

How odd, and how amazing, that something as insignificant as a corkscrew could evoke such powerful and emotional memories of love forever lost.

She worked the corkscrew once again, this time popping the cork off the pinot noir.

She poured herself a glass of wine and took a sip. Another sip followed the first.

Then words flowed from her lips, words she had memorized at Camp Caroline, a Christian Bible camp in North Carolina she had attended years ago as a teenager.

"'Yea, though I walk through the valley of the shadow of death, I will fear no evil: for thou art with me; thy rod and thy staff they comfort me. Thou preparest a table before me in the presence of mine enemies: thou anointest my head with oil; my cup runneth over.'"

She raised her glass in the air and said softly, "Good-bye, P.J. I'll love you forever."

As she took another sip, the wine went down smoothly, leaving a warm sensation in her esophagus.

She let the effects go to her head and let her thoughts linger on him a few seconds longer. Then she walked to her bedroom, sat down at her computer, and closed her eyes.

When she opened her eyes again, thirty minutes had passed.

That should be enough time.

She opened her email and began to type.

From: LCDR Caroline McCormick, JAGC, USN
To: Captain David C. Guy, JAGC, USN
Divisional Director, Code 13
Office of the Judge Advocate General
United States Navy
Subj: Acknowledgment of Assignment: Legal Opinion, Project Blue Jay

1. Acknowledge assignment for completion of legal opinion letter, and understand my assignment to draft a legal opinion to the Secretary of the Navy with no predetermined directions on determining the proposed legality of the contract and bill presented to the United States Congress.

2. Acknowledge my assignment to present a legal opinion on the legality of the proposed joint use of Project Blue Jay drones to be shared between the U.S. Navy and the Department of Homeland Security, with a focus on (1) whether the proposed use would be legally permissible under the doctrine of *posse comitatus*, and (2) whether domestic surveillance proposed under the joint use would be legally permissible under Fourth Amendment prohibitions against illegal search and seizure, as well as whether such surveillance would be in violation of the Constitutional right to privacy, also under the Fourth Amendment.

3. After having reviewed the files left behind by both LCDR MacDonald and LT Simmons, the undersigned has discovered that LCDR MacDonald drafted two separate opinions, one opining that the proposed project was legally permissible and another opining that the proposed project was not legally permissible, based on *posse comitatus* and Fourth Amendment principles.

4. The undersigned is committed to a thorough and independent review of all research conducted by LCDR MacDonald on these issues. However, based on a review of Commander MacDonald's notes on this issue, and based on an original draft of an opinion letter sent from LCDR MacDonald to LT Ross, it appears that LCDR MacDonald had come to the conclusion, or was coming to the conclusion, that joint use of Project Blue Jay drones, as proposed jointly, for budgetary reasons, by

the Departments of the Navy and Homeland Security, was legally permissible.

5. Based on my preliminary review of LCDR MacDonald's work, the undersigned will finish and complete both legal opinions, *acknowledging that each legal opinion contains conclusions contradictory to the other*, and will, based on additional legal research, submit one or the other to the Secretary of the Navy.

6. As directed by your instruction, the undersigned will choose and send a final opinion letter within 72 hours.

7. Please acknowledge and submit further instructions as necessary.

Very respectfully,
C. M. McCormick
LCDR, JAGC, USN

Caroline took a moment to read over what she had written, then took a deep breath, uttered a silent prayer, and hit the Send button.

There was no turning back. The trap had been set. And she just might have signed her death warrant.

CHAPTER 26

• • •

NEW YORK CONCRETE & SEAFOOD COMPANY
MID-ATLANTIC OFFICES AND WAREHOUSE
ANACOSTIA RIVER
SOUTHEAST WASHINGTON, DC
MONDAY AFTERNOON

Vinnie Torrenzano sat in the back office of NYC&S's Washington warehouse, which, like the larger warehouses in New York and other sections of the country, had served the family in a variety of ways.

On some days, maybe once a week, fishing trawlers coming in off the Chesapeake would dock at the piers down by the waterfront and dump tons of lobster and crab into the company's refrigeration boxes for packing and shipping to fish markets and groceries in the Mid-Atlantic region.

Of course, if seafood were the only enterprise in which the family held an interest, then the family could have selected other, more logistically efficient locations for the company's Mid-Atlantic location.

But neither seafood nor concrete constituted the bulk of the company's off-the-books profit margin, and thus the selection of the nation's capital as the site of the Mid-Atlantic headquarters reflected the company's need to conduct certain other aspects of the business. The "other-than-seafood" operations, shortened to "OTS," as those operations were known to the company's accountants and corporate bigwigs, constituted a large part of the reason for the location of the warehouse in DC.

Today was one of those "other ways" in which the conveniently located facility would serve the family, supporting one of those OTS enterprises.

Vinnie rather enjoyed his business jaunts to DC. For in DC, he got a lot of the well-deserved respect he often missed out on in New York.

In fact, he was so respected around this place that they called him Mr. T.

The boys on payroll here, even the nerdy computer wonks, understood that *he* was their meal ticket and that *he* was their connection with New York.

Vinnie took a sip of bourbon, sat back, alone, and tinkered with his laptop. He had grown to enjoy these temporary assignments to DC. They gave him a chance to get away from the wife.

Have a little fun.

What Maria didn't know wouldn't hurt her.

No reason for her to know.

And certainly no reason for Phil or Big Sal to know.

Plus, with the boys working down here in the DC warehouse giving him the respect he deserved, knowing that he was from New York and was part of the family and all, they knew to keep their mouths shut.

Anyway, he hoped the job here would be wrapped up soon, which would give him more time for a little rest and relaxation on the ground before having to head back up I-95 to company headquarters.

Only one more work-related task remained. And he should be putting the finishing touches on that anytime now.

But in the meantime, time to lay a little groundwork.

He struck up a cigarette, sucked a warm cloud of satisfying nicotine into his lungs, mixed the nicotine with another big swig of bourbon, then typed www.hotflightattendants.com into his browser. He always had a thing for blonde stewardesses wearing a nice little hot navy blue skirt as part of their flight uniform.

A moment later, he was online and back in business.

"Yes!" He pumped his fist into the air when he saw that target number one had sent him a reply.

Her name was "BuffytheDCgirl."

At least that was her screen name.

She purported to be a leggy flight attendant for American Airlines, and if she looked anything like her photos, she was red-hot smoking. Based on her profile, she was looking for someone to take her out who was "red-hot affectionate," but she wasn't ready for any commitments.

Perfect. Fun with no strings!

He grinned and let his Italian mind race to faraway places that only a brain oxygenized by Sicilian blood could imagine.

Her reply came up, and he took another sip before he started to read.

"Here we go," he said to himself.

Dear SeafoodMagnate,

I loved your profile and am flattered that you would reach out to me! Thank you for the nice comments.

Such a gentleman! What a way with words!

Can you see me blushing already? Haha!

Seriously, I work out every day to try and keep my legs toned, and stay in shape so I can enjoy my red wine in the evenings when I go out LOL!

I also loved the pic of your car. I've found that you can tell a lot about a man from his wheels LOL!

J/K!!! Hehe!

But even better than your car, I LOVED your profile pic. What a handsome man! I LOVE your salt-and-pepper hair.

I think I might have to go turn down the air conditioner to about 58! LOL!

Are you really a seafood magnate? I love men who take charge in business. The magnate notion is a real . . .

Well, I've said enough already.

Seriously, you sound like someone I'd love to get to know a little better.

I don't fly again until Wednesday.

I'm not normally this forward, but I'll just put it out there if that's okay.

Wanna meet for a drink?

Can't believe I said that haha!

Anyway, lemme know!

XO
Buffy

"Good golly! Let's do this." Vinnie refilled his glass with bourbon, took a sip, and started to write.

Dear Buffy,

Glad you like my car. I'd love to take you for a spin in it. It's gonna be a ride you'll never forget!

BTW, my name's Vincent, but my friends call me Vinnie.

So am I a magnate? Well, depends on how you define a "magnate." Let me put it this way. I'm a guy that's got a lot of guys who work for me. I'll let you decide when we meet for a drink.

I'd like to . . .

"Hey, Mr. T.!"

Vinnie cursed and looked up. "What is it, Guido? I'm in the middle of something!"

"Sorry, boss. But the senator's here."

"Already?" Vinnie checked his watch.

"Yes, sir."

He saved his message to Buffy and put the computer in hibernate mode. "Okay, send him in."

Vinnie looked up as Rodino, wearing a blue blazer, khaki slacks, and no tie, walked in, surrounded by three of the boys from the warehouse.

"Chuckie! Welcome to our Washington hangout!"

"Whatever this is about," Rodino said, sporting a scowl on his face, "did you have to insist that I travel into the slum section of the city? What if a member of the press sees me over here?"

"Chuckie! Chuckie! You hurt my feelings. I thought you'd appreciate our local digs. A great place for the boys to hang out. Know what I mean?"

"Vinnie—"

Vinnie held up his hand. This would be a one-way conversation. After all, he had other business to attend to. "Have a seat, Chuckie. Make yourself at home." He looked at a warehouse goon. "Giuseppe, take everybody else outside. Me and the senator, we got some business to attend to. This won't take long."

"Sure thing, Mr. T."

"Mr. T.?" Rodino crossed his arms and raised an eyebrow as the warehouse goon ushered everyone else out of the office.

"It's an affectionate name, Chuckie. *T* is for Torrenzano. Know what I mean? Hey, want a drink?"

"No," the senator snapped. "You know I'm happy to help any way I can, but my time is limited. So can we please just get to the point?"

"Patience, Senator Grasshopper. And sit down, sit down!"

The senator, still scowling, pulled up a chair and sat. "You've got my attention. What's this about? Did Phil ask you to call me in here?"

Vinnie took a drag from his cigarette and blew smoke in the direction of the high-priced political prostitute. He once heard Big Sal say at a family reunion, after Big Sal had had a few too many, that politicians are nothing but puny, punk prostitutes all pimped up in pickle-threaded pinstripes.

They could be bought and paid for with election contributions and controlled with bad dirt that, if the political pimp didn't cooperate, could be fed to the press.

Big Sal was right. More smoke blown at the wimp.

"Actually, Senator, this ain't got nothin' to do with Phil. Actually, Big Sal wanted me to call you in for a little chat."

At the mention of the name Big Sal, the senator-wimp's face morphed from slight irritation to a near ashen-gray.

"Big Sal?" The senator's eyes shifted. "What's Big Sal need? Is everything okay?"

"Is everything okay? Well, that just depends on your perspective, I suppose."

"So what's going on?" he asked in a nervous, high-pitched tone.

"What's going on is Big Sal wanted you to see these." He slid the envelope across the desk.

"What's this?"

"How would I know?" Vinnie threw up his hands, feigning ignorance. "Have a look for yourself."

Vinnie couldn't contain his sense of self-satisfaction, nor could he suppress the grin that crawled across his face as the junior Democrat senator from New York squirmed.

As the senator's bony-looking fingers started to shake, he opened the envelope and slowly fetched the glossy 8x10 color photographs. His face turned red, and veins popped from the blood pressure in his neck. Rodino protested in a shrill voice that made him sound like a screeching cheetah.

"This is an outrage!" Rodino threw the photos down on the desk. "This is an inexcusable invasion of my privacy. And I object! In fact, I vociferously object!"

Vinnie laughed. "Who you gonna object to, Senator? You don't think we got all the judges in our pockets too?"

"It's still an inexcusable invasion of privacy. And I never thought the family would stoop to something this low!"

Vinnie abandoned all pretenses of hiding his cheese-eating grin. "Oh, I dunno, Chuckie. I thought the one of you and your boyfriend holding hands on the beach at Martha's Vineyard and kissing under the moonlight was cute. And the one of you two in the sauna. What's his name?" He smirked. "Milkey Mark? Markey Milk? Something like that?"

"He is Congressman William O. 'Mackey' Milk, the distinguished Democrat from Boston, and one of the most brilliant members of the United States Congress!"

"Easy there, Chuckie. I mean, look on the bright side. Those pictures, if they get out, would mean ole Markey boy would get reelected every time in Boston, where that stuff is a badge of honor. Probably even help you in New York. Hey, you're guaranteed to carry Greenwich Village."

"That's not funny."

"But for those national presidential aspirations of yours, well, this stuff will definitely help you in California, but you're gonna need to carry a few southern states, and at least run well in Texas."

Rodino glared at him. "What do you want?"

"And if Eleanor Claxton gets the nomination, she ain't gonna want nobody on the ticket who will hurt her in the South. And this definitely ain't gonna help you in South Carolina or Mississippi or Texas. Or even Florida, for that matter, whether you're at the top of the ticket or in the second spot."

Silence.

"I said, what do you want?"

Vinnie inhaled the Marlboro cigarette. "It ain't what I want, Senator. It's what Big Sal wants."

Another look of fear at the mention of Big Sal. "Okay, then what does Big Sal want?"

"Well, he told me to tell you two things. First, he wants to make sure that drone contract gets killed."

"That contract is as good as dead in the water. It hasn't even gone to Congress yet."

"Hey, don't tell me." Vinnie threw up his hands again. "Tell that to Big Sal."

"What do you mean?" Rodino looked over his shoulder as if expecting someone to walk into the room.

"Don't worry. At least not today. Big Sal ain't here. But he wants to see you in person."

"Me?"

"Yes, you."

"When? Where?"

"Tomorrow morning. Company headquarters in New York. We'll arrange for transportation. And tell your boyfriend he's invited too. Now get out of my office!"

"But I—"

"We'll have one of our boys pick you up from out in front of the Capitol Building. You and your boyfriend, Congressman Milkey. Be ready around seven thirty and wait for our call. We'll fly you up in one of our private jets, bring you before Big Sal, and then, depending on what he says, we'll fly you back."

"But—"

"But nothing. Look on the bright side. The family's paying your travel up. And if Sal don't cut you up and throw you to the sharks, you might get your way back paid, too, if you're lucky."

"But—"

"But that's it, Chuckie."

"There must—"

Vinnie hit the intercom. "Giuseppe! Escort the senator out of here."

"Yes, Mr. T."

Rodino stood, wearing a permanent scowl, and pulled his arm away when Giuseppe came in and touched him.

Vinnie turned back to his computer, eager to get back to his message to Buffy. If he got lucky, maybe even tonight . . .

"Excuse me, boss."

"What is it now?"

"One of the programmers needs to see you."

"About what?"

"About the drone project."

Vinnie took another glance at the profile picture of the hot-looking flight attendant, then looked up at Giuseppe. "Send the senator on his way, then send the guy in."

Rodino left with Giuseppe under no further protest.

The programmer, a wimpish-looking figure wearing a short-sleeved shirt and black plastic-rimmed glasses, looked like a character from *Invasion of the Nerd Snatchers* as he walked into the office.

"Mr. Torrenzano," the nerd-man started, "I'm Marvin Dorn. I'm one of the new IP associates from Georgetown. There's something I need to speak with you about."

"I'm in the middle of something important. Spit it out."

"Well, sir, this morning the Navy held a press conference and announced that this Lieutenant Commander McCormick is being assigned to finish working on the part of the project MacDonald and Simmons were working on."

"We thought it would be one of the officers at Code 13," Vinnie said. "But I'm surprised she's the one. She's one of the two women MacDonald was having a fling with."

"Agreed, sir," the nerd said. "But not only that, not long after the press conference, we monitored Commander McCormick's email. And there's something I think you should see." The weasel handed a sheet of paper to Vinnie. "This is an email McCormick sent to her commanding officer, Captain David Guy."

Vinnie took the email and read it.

"What the heck is this supposed to mean?"

"Which part, sir?"

"The part where she says, 'Based on my preliminary review of LCDR MacDonald's work, the undersigned will finish and complete both legal opinions, acknowledging that each legal opinion contains conclusions contradictory to the other, and will, based on additional legal research, submit one or the other to the Secretary of the Navy'?"

"I don't know what it means," the computer geek said. "But it sounds like she may be thinking about writing an opinion that cuts against our position, which is why I thought you might want to see it."

Vinnie pounded his fist on the desk. "Dang it!" He unleashed a string of profanity. "And I thought we about had this problem under control."

The geek stood there nonresponsively, staring blankly like a dead fish lying on a bed of crushed ice at the fish market.

"Okay, thanks, Miller. That will be all."

"Marvin."

"Say again?"

"My name is Marvin. Marvin Dorn."

"Okay, whatever. Thanks. Look, I need to make a phone call. If you don't mind, just step out and close the door. Maybe go back to your computer or something. I'll let you know when I need you again."

"Yes, sir."

Miller . . . or Marvin . . . or whatever his name was, walked out of the office and closed the door behind him, as instructed.

Vinnie turned around and crossed his arms. Buffy would have to wait. Besides, there were a million Buffys out there who would swoon over the family money and power and do whatever he wanted them to do.

Right now, he had bigger problems.

Phil wasn't going to like this.

Neither would Big Sal, if it percolated up that far.

This would need to be nipped in the bud, and sooner rather than later.

Oh well. May as well get this over with. He pulled out his cell phone, went to the stored numbers, and hit autodial.

The phone rang once . . . twice . . . then an answer.

"Yo. Phil. This is Vinnie."

"I know who you are. You get everything set with Chuckie and his Milk boy? Like Sal wanted?"

"Yo. Just took care of it. But listen. Phil. We got us another problem."

"What did you screw up this time, Vinnie?"

"I ain't screwed up nothin', Phil."

"Then who screwed what up?"

"The Navy put this woman JAG officer on the case. Looks like she might write an opinion against us."

Silence.

"Phil. You there?"

"Yes. I'm here. But we sent you down there for a reason. And that's to kill this contract. Big Sal's already on my back, and if you don't perform, you ain't gonna be there much longer, or anywhere else, for that matter. If this new Navy lady or whoever gives us a problem, I want you to take care of it. Ya got it?"

"Got it, Phil. Loud and clear."

CHAPTER 27

· · ·

ELIZABETH ON 37TH
105 EAST 37TH STREET
SAVANNAH, GEORGIA
MONDAY EVENING

The quaint, romantic restaurant, occupying an elegant two-story mansion built in the early 1900s, sat inconspicuously in Savannah's Thomas Square Streetcar neighborhood.

The five-star Elizabeth on 37th, considered by many to be the finest among all of Savannah's exquisite dining establishments, was a favorite of AirFlite CEO Richardson DeKlerk.

At Richardson's direction, AirFlite had reserved the place many times, including for the company's Christmas party, New Year's Eve party, and Fourth of July bash. He had also reserved the place for annual board meetings and had hosted numerous dignitaries here.

With the money AirFlite had spent, the company almost had a snap-the-finger relationship with the exquisite dining venue, with Richardson having standing priority to reserve the restaurant almost anytime he wanted, for any reason he wanted.

Elizabeth on 37th also served as his venue of choice whenever he decided it was time to take home some hot blonde for the first time, since the restaurant staff would be tipped more than enough to give them incentive to keep their collective mouth shut. He had reserved the place tonight and was sipping wine alone with his latest fixation in the elegance of the exquisite dining room, gazing into the sparkling blue eyes of his irresistibly sensual, smiling, and very much married Eastern European secretary.

He reached across the table, and when her hand touched his, he felt an instant spark. So when his phone rang in his pocket, he decided to ignore it, for their burgeoning affair remained in the electric stage. Of course, he knew in the back of his mind, from the many affairs he had experienced before, that eventually the electricity would morph back into a dull thud, like the magic of Cinderella's coach morphing back into a pumpkin surrounded by rats at midnight.

That stage would come, he knew from experience. And when it arrived, because she was his secretary, he would need to take special measures in dealing with it.

He wouldn't fire her. He might have to take harsher measures than a mere job termination if she went ape-ballistic on him once he eventually ended it.

But he hoped drastic measures wouldn't be necessary.

Perhaps he would resolve the post-affair awkwardness by transferring her to another department, or perhaps even to one of AirFlite's satellite locations on the West Coast.

Of course, if she talked, threatened him, or tried to cause trouble, he would deal with all that too. Hers would be a scenario in which she could not win.

But for the time being, until that time came, they would both enjoy the mutual exhilaration and excitement that ignited each time their hands touched or whenever their legs brushed together.

He caught a whiff of her perfume, and it proved so intoxicating that he ignored the phone when it rang a second time. She had taken the time to make herself hopelessly attractive for the occasion in every way, from her perfume, to her little black dress with simple white pearls, to the luscious, subtle pink color of her lipstick. So ignoring the last ring and letting it go to voicemail, he instead leaned into her. Their lips met. He reached behind her head and, feeling her hair, pulled her face in closer to his.

When their kiss ended a moment later, she giggled and gazed at him. "You are such a naughty boss to send my husband to South Africa for two weeks."

He laughed. "You look so heartbroken, my dear Ivana."

She smiled, and her hand felt his face.

"I wanted to suggest that you might extend his two weeks to two months."

"Only two months?"

She unleashed a naughty little laugh and grinned. "You are a bad man, Richardson DeKlerk."

"Thank you for the compliment."

As he started to kiss her again, his phone rang again.

He pulled away from her and cursed. "Excuse me, my dear."

"Don't stop kissing me, Richardson."

"This must be important. Hang on." He turned his shoulders from her and pulled the phone from his pocket. A 202 area code, a Washington, DC, number he didn't recognize.

He answered the phone. "DeKlerk here."

"Mr. DeKlerk, this is Tommy Mandela. Senator Talmadge's chief of staff."

"Tommy. Why are you calling me from a number I don't recognize?"

"I apologize, sir. It's a security measure. Under the circumstances, we use a computer-generated scrambler to change the numbers around to deter eavesdropping and surveillance. We never know who's listening, and frankly, we can't afford to take any chances. Anyway, you asked me to keep you informed, and the caller ID block got triggered. So I used the scrambler."

Richardson looked over at Ivana, who sipped her wine and gave him a come-hither look.

He winked at her, smiled, and then looked away.

"Very well. I suppose under the circumstances that's acceptable. Now, why are you calling? Hopefully to tell me that our good senator has done his job and gotten us a vote lined up to approve this drone contract."

"Unfortunately, sir, the senator still hasn't been able to make that happen. He's requested a meeting with Senator Fowler, but that hasn't materialized yet."

"Unacceptable!"

"I agree, sir. But I do know he's trying."

"We didn't get him elected to try, Tommy. We got him elected to deliver. There's too much money at stake for this contract to get bottled up in Congress. Now, I'm paying you a lot of money to make sure he does what we need him to do, and I expect you to deliver."

"Yes, sir."

"Does Talmadge know you're calling?"

"No, sir. I wanted to check with you first about something."

"Does it have to do with the drone contract?"

"Yes, sir. Potentially it does."

"Don't tell me more delays."

"Potentially, sir."

Richardson felt the steam coming from his ears. He got up and walked away from the table.

"What do you mean, potentially?"

"Sir, the Navy reassigned the legal opinion to another JAG officer, a Lieutenant Commander Caroline McCormick. We started routine surveillance of her email. It looks like she may be wavering on writing the correct opinion letter. We've also learned there may be another seventy-two-hour delay, and we don't know which way the opinion will break."

Richardson cursed under his breath. "So what you're telling me is that we've just replaced one problem with another, that we've got another rogue JAG officer we can't count on to deliver?"

"That appears to be the case, unfortunately."

He had to be careful about what Ivana heard. He nodded at her, held up his hand, mouthed, "I'll be right back," and stepped out of the dining room.

"Okay. I don't care how you do it. But take care of this problem. Now. Got it?"

"Yes, sir."

"And one other thing. I've lost patience with Bobby Talmadge. He has not delivered on what he was hired to do, and now we are back to square one. Once you take care of this problem, you tell Talmadge that if the Navy appoints yet another JAG officer who might have any inclination to opine that this contract is anything other than legal, then his political career will be over. In fact, you can tell him I've already put in a call to Joe Don Mack at the Georgia Political Victory Fund, and we are ready to designate Talmadge's replacement if he isn't going to deliver. Are we clear on that?"

"Perfectly, Mr. DeKlerk."

"Excellent. Now, if you will excuse me, I have some unfinished business I must attend to."

CHAPTER 28

. . . .

The single-shot Remington Model 700P light tactical rifle lay in the backseat of the car, which was parked in a cul-de-sac across the street and catty-corner from the target's residence.

One of the best things about this rifle was its short barrel of only twenty inches, which made it ideal to carry out an assassination in tighter quarters, say from the inside of a car. But also, when firing a single .223 bolt-action round, the light recoil made the weapon easy to handle.

The shooter glanced at a photo of his target.

Female.

Blonde.

Blue eyes.

Expected to emerge in a white female naval officer's uniform with a white skirt.

What a waste.

But hey, business was business. And there were other good-looking women in the world. Sometimes you had to waste something good to get to something better.

From this distance, the shot would have to be just right. He knew that. But the 700P was accurate enough to pull this off, even at this distance, if the babe didn't move too fast and he could nail her at a good angle.

But even if he didn't get the angle he wanted, hey, it wasn't like this was his only opportunity. If he didn't get her today, he would get her eventually.

He tightened the silencer on the end of the barrel.

Check.

He then removed a single NATO-round .223-caliber bullet, held it up against the morning light, and studied it for a second, then brought the round to his lips and kissed it for good luck. Kissing the bullet was a ritual he had started years ago, after his first kill.

The idea of a pre-execution ritual with a bullet came from a story he had read about General John "Black Jack" Pershing, who in the early 1900s was dealing with the problem of Muslim extremism in the Philippines.

Shortly before World War I, there were a number of terrorist attacks against the United States and its interests by Muslim extremists. Some things never change.

Pershing knew Muslims detested pork because they believed pigs were filthy animals. Some of them refused to eat pork, while others wouldn't even touch pigs at all, nor any of their by-products. To Muslims, eating or touching a pig, its meat, its blood, and so on, was to be instantly barred from paradise and doomed to hell.

So to set an example against Islamic extremism, and to set an example for the Islamists as to what could happen to them if they kept up their terrorist tactics, General Pershing captured fifty of the terrorists and had them tied to posts execution style. He then had his men bring in two pigs and slaughter them in front of the now-horrified Muslim terrorists.

The soldiers then soaked their bullets in pigs' blood and proceeded to execute forty-nine of the terrorists by firing squad. Then they dug a big hole, dumped in the terrorists' bodies, and covered them in pig blood, entrails, and so on.

They let the fiftieth man go. And for about the next forty-two years, there was not a single attack by a Muslim fanatic anywhere in the world.

And so the personal bullet routine had been inspired by Pershing himself. The way Pershing had handled that situation was epic. If one planned to kill with a bullet, then it was fitting that the bullet be anointed.

And so, over the years, the actions of the man called Black Jack had inspired his own pre-hit ritual. The best assassin should bond, spiritually, with the death bullet. For an assassination to occur with honor, the bullet and the shooter must become one.

In a strange way, the sensation of the cold casing against his lips felt like a worship experience and brought an electrical surge through his body.

It was as if he and the bullet were one.

Yes! They were one!

He chambered the bullet into the rifle.

He rechecked the silencer to make sure it was secure. He couldn't take the chance that the rifle shot would crack the air. The car's engine would remain running for a quick getaway.

Sitting with the rifle in the driver's side, but pointing the gun across the interior of the car and out of the passenger's side, he hoped the barrel wouldn't be noticeable. That, plus the silencer muffling the shot, should allow him to accomplish the deed without much attention—if he could get off a good shot.

He held up the rifle, looked through the scope, and brought the crosshairs onto her front door.

All he could do now was sit . . . and wait.

• • •

LIEUTENANT COMMANDER CAROLINE MCCORMICK'S TOWNHOUSE
NEAR THE INTERSECTION OF HUNTSMAN AND SYDENSTRICKER ROADS
OXFORD HUNT
WEST SPRINGFIELD, VIRGINIA
TUESDAY, 6:05 A.M.

Caroline stood in front of the mirror in her bathroom, in her summer white uniform, checking the alignment of her medals and ribbons above the blouse pocket. She took a moment to adjust the alignment of her Navy Commendation Medal and her Navy Achievement Medal, then stood back.

In her mind, she knew her uniform was shipshape. But she also wondered, would this be the last day of her life? Yes, the NCIS agents were out there . . . somewhere. Yesterday she saw their cars. Today she hadn't stepped out to look. Stepping outside to look could be too dangerous. For in order to set the trap, to bait the rat to get close enough to come for the cheese, they could only be so close, making her decision to play the role of the bait a very dangerous proposition. Hopefully the rat would show and they would kill the killer before he killed her.

But nothing was guaranteed, except the fact that somebody was likely to get killed.

If it were the last day of her life, then maybe, at least, she would see P.J. again today.

Not that she felt fatalistic, but the morning had brought yet another radical and unexpected emotional shift. This morning there was little pain . . . little sorrow . . . mainly a strange sense of surrealism. It was as if she were an actress, suspended somewhere on some inanimate stage, and she had been given a catbird's view in the balcony of a theater, about to watch herself perform onstage, down below, under a bright spotlight.

Why did she feel like her personal balcony seat, to watch her own performance, was in the presidential box at Ford's Theater?

Enough internal philosophizing.

She had to get her head in the game. She had to do it not only for P.J. but also for herself.

He had spoken these words so many times as they kicked into high gear to finish their runs.

"You can do this. Bring it across the finish line, baby."

And now she could hear his voice again. So clearly. Here and now. If she didn't know better, she would swear he was right here. Right now.

Yes, she would bring this across the finish line, not just for him, but for herself, for the sake of justice, and for the Navy.

She could do this. She *would* do this.

She took a deep breath, said a quick prayer, and headed for the door.

CHAPTER 29

• • •

Did the doorknob move?

The assassin held the rifle still, refocused his eye, and took another look through the high-powered scope.

The front door cracked, but just barely. Maybe an inch or two.

His heart pounded with the excitement of a hunter closing in on his prey.

The target—he thought of her as a *target* because that made it easier to embrace the idea of shooting a woman—would be emerging any second, and hopefully he would be able to nail her right there on her front door stoop, dropping her like a stuck pig with a bullet to the head, and then he would be on his way, out of sight before someone noticed her lying there.

He pulled back on the bolt action and then pushed it forward, chambering the single .223 death bullet, and with his right finger he began caressing the trigger, waiting for the target to emerge.

He felt himself enter into a zone. Only a hunter-killer could relate. The seconds before a kill, the body of the killer was filled, from head to toe, with adrenaline-charged electricity that couldn't be replicated by any other human sensation known to man. Nothing else could satisfy the appetite of the professional killer. Not money. Not sex. Not fame. Not luxuries.

Only the kill could satisfy the greatest of all innate desires.

And when the target's head exploded from the bullet, an ecstatic ecstasy would explode within him like nothing describable, a sensation that most weaklings would never experience or understand.

Now she was so close he could taste her death, and his tongue salivated like a hound dog eyeing a rib eye steak.

"Come on, baby. Come home to Daddy."

• • •

LIEUTENANT COMMANDER CAROLINE McCORMICK'S TOWNHOUSE
NEAR THE INTERSECTION OF HUNTSMAN AND SYDENSTRICKER ROADS
OXFORD HUNT
WEST SPRINGFIELD, VIRGINIA
6:11 A.M.

"Where is the darn thing?" Caroline mumbled aloud. She had become so enraptured in her thoughts, so distracted by what she was about to do, that she realized she had forgotten her cell phone.

She had started to open the front door and was about to step out when she remembered.

Thank goodness she wasn't halfway to the Pentagon, when it would be too late to turn around and she would be stuck without it all day.

No luck in the bedroom.

She stepped into the bathroom.

"Thank goodness." She had left it on the counter as she checked her ribbons.

Already she had three missed calls from him.

She hit the speed dial.

Two rings.

Paul answered. "How are you this morning?" A tinge of concern filled the captain's voice.

"Fine. So far, anyway."

"I was worried about you."

"Sorry. I forgot to turn the phone off silent and then started out the door and realized I forgot it."

"Okay. I know you have a lot on your mind. Just call when you get to the Pentagon, will you?"

"Sure. If it will make you feel better. But you know, I'll be fine, and we can't keep this up every day."

"Just one step at a time. Just for the next few days, anyway," he said. "That okay?"

"Okay, I'll keep you posted for the next few days."

"Thanks. Be safe on the way to work."

"I'll call you in a few."

She hung up, put the phone in her purse, and headed for the door.

• • •

OUTSIDE LIEUTENANT COMMANDER CAROLINE MCCORMICK'S TOWNHOUSE
NEAR THE INTERSECTION OF HUNTSMAN AND SYDENSTRICKER ROADS
OXFORD HUNT
WEST SPRINGFIELD, VIRGINIA
6:12 A.M.

He held the rifle in firing position, his finger on the trigger, his eye peering through the high-powered scope.

The exterior of the door was painted black, making the small red laser-beam light that shot across the street, straight onto the outside of the door.

Any second now . . .

The door swung open, and there she stood.

She stepped out onto her front porch, looking hot in her white navy uniform, and turned her back to him as she locked the door. He could see her so clearly through his scope. Her legs were so toned and tanned. Her backside so shapely. She had the body of a runner. No doubt she worked out.

He gazed at her for a moment through the scope. What a colossal waste this would be.

He considered shooting her through the back. Then, when she turned, he moved the laser to the center of her heart.

No.

That would mean too much red blood seeping through that white uniform. What a shame.

He moved the laser back up to her head.

"Bye-bye, baby."

He pulled the trigger. The shot rang out, and instantly a Springfield Mass Transit bus pulled up on the street, blocking his view.

The assassin cursed, unable to see his kill because the blasted bus had rolled in the way. But he couldn't wait around. He tossed the rifle on his backseat and hit the accelerator.

CHAPTER 30

. . .

U.S. Senator Robert Talmadge walked into the front door of his office and nodded at his secretary.

"Good morning, Maryanne."

"Good morning, Senator. Your coffee is almost ready."

Bobby checked his watch.

He started to step into his office, then turned and looked at her. "Is Tommy in yet?"

"No, sir. But Mr. Mandela called a few minutes ago and said he's on his way."

"Any word from Senator Fowler's office?"

"Not yet. But Mr. Mandela hopes we hear something today."

"Okay, thanks. Just bring the coffee into my office."

"Yes, sir."

He watched as she turned and held his gaze pleasurably for a few moments as she gracefully stepped away from him, then disappeared off to the right, moving into the kitchen area.

Bobby stepped into his office, laid his briefcase on his desk, took off his jacket, and hung it up. He had already developed a well-deserved reputation for being one of the hardest-working rookie senators in the senate.

Bobby Talmadge, as a young college student, feasted on political bios, which had inspired him to study law and go into politics.

He had once read an article about Bobby Kennedy, who, albeit from a different political party, also had the reputation of a tireless workaholic.

When RFK had been attorney general, he would often work late into the night. When Kennedy left his office, if he drove by J. Edgar Hoover's office and saw the lights on, legend was that he turned around and drove back to his own office to work some more.

Bobby was determined to beat his colleagues to the office and routinely arrived before 6:30 a.m., beating even members of his staff into work, with the exception of his secretary, a forty-year-old single brunette named Maryanne Pendleton, who had been more loyal to him than his own wife.

In fact, once when he and Molly Sue had separated, discreetly, not long after he first was sworn into Congress, Maryanne had been there for him—in every way. Fortunately, despite the rumor mill, the story never hit the press in either Atlanta or Savannah.

In a way, Maryanne knew him better than anyone knew him. She had heard about what had happened at the Christmas party, and while she showed signs of jealousy, she had never judged him. Most important, she had never breathed a word of it to anybody.

If that ever got out, it would be all over.

Personally.

Politically.

Professionally.

He had gotten no sleep—none—since the photos showed up. And frankly, he wondered if there were more.

He had to deliver on this contract. Had to. It was now or never. Do or die.

Maryanne came back in, wearing a fitted dark-blue skirt, black heels, and a satin blouse, smiling and holding a cup of steaming black Maxwell House in his favorite Georgia Bulldogs mug.

"Here's your coffee, Bobby," she said softly. She often called him by his first name—a practice he rather liked—when she was sure nobody else was in earshot.

"By the way, where's my copy of the *Washington Post*?"

"The *Post*?"

"Sure. You know. That liberal rag Jesse Helms used to call the *Pravda on the Potomac*. Could I sweet-talk you into bringing me a copy?" He delivered an affectionate wink but did not receive the flirtatious, Marie Osmond–look-alike return glance, as he so often got in the early-morning hours with just the two of them alone in the office.

The look on her face.

Something was wrong.

CHAPTER 31

• • •

Even at the secretive and hush-hush Code 13, as was the case with most military stations around Washington, DC, military protocol demanded that junior officers and junior enlisted personnel be among the first to report to duty for a new workday, or a new shift, or any special or extraordinary assignments involving the military unit.

Although this was not a direct command from on high that was written in stone, the practice was true for naval and marine units in the National Capital Region. Junior officers and enlisted personnel understood that if they wanted to advance within the Navy, they would have to adhere to this rule, get to work before their bosses, and make the work space as accommodating as possible for their superiors.

Usually that meant starting the coffee mess, firing up lights and computers, checking overnight message traffic and making sure that all messages were delivered to the correct recipients, answering before-hours phone calls, and handling anything else that might pop up that would be of service to the command.

Lieutenant Victoria Fladager, still the junior officer at Code 13, had already started the coffee mess and was firing up her computer when the phone rang.

"Navy Judge Advocate General. Code 13. This is a nonsecure line subject to monitoring. May I help you, sir or ma'am?"

"Victoria? Is that you?"

At first Victoria wondered about the identity of the woman on the other end of the line. The Pentagon's landline, because of scrambling features to deter electronic eavesdropping, sometimes altered the pitch and tone of a caller's voice.

Then it hit her.

"Caroline?"

"Thank God I got through. I couldn't reach either you or Paul on your cells."

"Cells hardly work inside the Pentagon. What's going on? You sound terrible."

"Somebody just took a shot at me."

"What? Are you okay?"

"I'm okay for the time being."

"Where are you?"

"I'm in my car. On Old Keene Mill Road. On my way to work."

"What happened?"

"I was on my front doorstep. Locking my door. All of a sudden, out of the blue, this bullet whizzed right by my ear and went through my front door. Luckily I'd moved my head just before the guy shot, and this Metro bus pulled up in front of my townhouse. I didn't see the NCIS agents and didn't know if whoever it was would shoot their way in the house if I went back inside. I just wanted to get out of there as fast as possible. So I jumped in my car and took off."

"Is anybody following you?"

"I checked my rearview. There are cars behind me, but if the shooter's back there, I wouldn't have a clue."

"Did you get a look at him?"

"Negative. In fact, I think he may have used a silencer, because I didn't even hear a gunshot. Just my door almost exploding beside my head."

"Did you call 911?"

"No!"

"Do you want me to call them for you?"

"No. I want to keep the local cops out of it. They're a bunch of buffoons, and I don't trust them. If they get in the way, it might blow our chances of finding this guy. But I do want you to call Mark and let him know, if he doesn't know already. Let's keep NCIS on this. They've got a better chance of finding P.J.'s murderer than the Springfield police. And then call Paul and let him know. I should be there in about thirty minutes, assuming I don't get shot first."

"Okay. Consider it done. I'll call them right now, then I'll call you back. But please be careful."

"Thanks, Victoria."

The line went dead. Victoria felt her heart pounding inside her chest in a delayed reaction.

She punched the speed dial for the man who had been out of her life and now had come back into it.

"NCIS. Special Agent Mark Romanov."

"Thank God." She realized, for the first time, that the sound of his voice brought her comfort. "Mark, this is Victoria. Somebody tried to shoot Commander McCormick."

CHAPTER 32

• • •

DIRKSEN SENATE OFFICE BUILDING
UNITED STATES CAPITOL
OFFICE OF ROBERT TALMADGE (R-GA)
WASHINGTON, DC
TUESDAY, 6:18 A.M.

Maryanne stepped back into Bobby's office, looking both sumptuous and worried at the same time.

"You got the paper?"

She nodded, winced, laid it down on his desk, then turned and walked out.

He picked up the paper and felt his stomach drop through the floor.

CHRISTMAS SEXCAPADES:

THE ROOKIE SENATOR FROM GEORGIA
AND THE HOT ITALIAN MODEL

by Julian Morgan III, Staff Writer

WASHINGTON HAS BEEN ROCKED BY THEM SINCE TIME immemorial. JFK and Marilyn. Bill and Monica. Wilbur Mills and Fanne Foxe. Johnny Edwards and Rielle Hunter.

Powerful men in Washington, wielding more power than

a million other men combined, still growing discontent and wanting even more.

Theirs is an electric pattern of excitement that must live on the brink of self-destruction.

And so, in pushing themselves to a destructive brink, recklessly womanizing, what's not clear is whether they secretly want to be discovered.

"Deep down, these men get their turn-on by pushing their luck to the limit, hoping they will be exposed. It's both a macho thing and a masochistic thing at the same time," said Dr. Jim Bell, professor of clinical psychology at George Washington University and author of the book *Playboys of the Senate: Why the Men of the Upper Chamber Cannot Restrain Themselves*.

Now a new Romeo-boy has joined a long line of conquistadores, making himself eligible for inclusion in the update to Bell's book.

Meet rookie senator Robert "Bobby" Talmadge, Republican of Georgia.

Based on eyewitness reports and photos leaked to the press, the newest member of the senate's playboy club is rumored to have been involved in a tryst with red-hot Italian supermodel Marla Moreno.

The two were first spotted together at a Christmas party at the home of oil-and-gas lobbyist Hub Webster. The picture shown below, taken by a partygoer, shows Ms. Moreno, 27, in a short black leather skirt and Santa cap, sitting cozily on Talmadge's lap, flopping her arms around him and nuzzling her nose behind his ear.

And from the photographic evidence, it doesn't appear that the married Mr. Talmadge, who is shown turning his head toward Ms. Moreno and grinning like a satisfied Cheshire cat, is objecting to the attention.

Witnesses at the party report that the senator and the model, who had been carousing with one another under the influence of intoxicating beverages for a good portion of the party, disappeared at the same time, reportedly retiring to a secluded area of the house to be alone.

Fortunately for Talmadge, he doesn't face reelection for another two years, so it remains unclear just how news of this breaking scandal might affect his political future.

The *Post* attempted to contact Talmadge's office for comment, but his office did not return our calls.

Bobby dropped the paper on his desk.

His life was over. Politically. Personally. Professionally. His reputation had fallen into the sewer, and he could never get it back.

It was over. He was ruined.

How? How had this happened?

The phone on his desk rang.

Maryanne. He punched the intercom.

"Yes?"

"You okay?"

No response.

"Bobby?"

"I'm okay," he lied.

"You've got a phone call."

"Who is it?"

"Your wife. She said she couldn't get through on your cell."

Molly Sue had seen the article. He knew it. Or someone had called her about it. "How'd she sound?"

"Not good."

"Tell her, uh . . ." What to say? What to do? "Tell her I'll call her back."

"Yes, sir."

Like certain members of the U.S. Senate before him, including John Kerry and John McCain, Bobby Talmadge not only had married into natural beauty but also had married into a ton of money.

There was nothing wrong with marrying into an ultra-rich and powerful family, especially if all the parties were on the same page.

And in this case, Molly Sue's father, former congressman Steve Roy McGovern, had made his fortune in peanut brokerage and gone on to serve in Congress for nearly forty years, where he had chaired the powerful House Ways and Means Committee and become known as the "oldest rat in the Republican barn."

Long before Bobby ever met Richardson DeKlerk or came under the wing of the Georgia Political Victory Fund, Congressman Steve Roy McGovern took Bobby under his wing, recognized him as a political star, basically handed him the congressional seat in Buckhead that McGovern had held over four decades, and made sure the money got spent to ensure Bobby's success.

The payback would be to guarantee that McGovern's only daughter and only child, Molly Sue, who was so darn gorgeous and talented that she could have won Miss Georgia even without her daddy's money and influence, would be guaranteed the life of a high-powered political socialite wife, whether it be in Washington or as first lady of Georgia.

She inherited all of Daddy's money when he died, prompting the *Atlanta Journal-Constitution* to run a feature story dubbing her as the "Richest Woman in Georgia"—and she inherited all his meanness too.

In fact, the older she got, the meaner she got. She stayed on his case constantly. Criticizing. Nagging. No matter what election he won, no matter how far he climbed in the polls, no matter what accolades were bestowed upon him, it was never enough. She was always pleased to compare him unfavorably with other men—other senators, other members of Congress, other husbands, other professionals. Doctors, lawyers, ministers—whoever. "If only you were more like so-and-so," she would harp.

Once, he had surprised her for her forty-fifth birthday with a romantic trip to Paris. One would think the gesture would have been appreciated. And although at first she had seemed excited about it, from the moment they stepped off the plane at Charles de Gaulle Airport, she unleashed a torrent of nonstop criticism that proceeded to flow like hot lava from an angry volcano for the entire duration of their French getaway.

The five-star accommodations he arranged were not acceptable.

She complained about the taxi service.

He should have checked the weather to make sure there was no rain on the day he made reservations for their tour of Montmartre.

Like a Roman solider lashing a shirtless prisoner on the back with a skin-stripping bullwhip, her sharp tongue lashed him constantly. Night and day. Every waking minute. And she kept coming back. She would attack, starting her barrages against him about 8:00 p.m. after a couple of glasses of red wine. Then, after a brief respite while she switched to scotch, she would take a few gulps and allow herself to be worked up into another frenzy of verbal attacks. And her second barrage, usually commencing around ten o'clock, felt like salt tossed into the bloody wounds she had delivered in her first round of haranguing. Usually, in round two, she launched into an ultra-critical soliloquy about his body.

"I prefer slim, athletic men," she would say. "Of which you are not and will never become. You need to work on your body type to make yourself more attractive."

Granted, he expanded and contracted around the waist a bit, depending on the season of the year. And granted, he wasn't blessed with her superfast metabolism, as few were. But no one had accused him, ever, of corpulence, except her.

Of course, to the outside world, which saw none of that, Molly Sue was the perfect southern lady, gracious and fun-loving and attuned to the social mores. Moving graciously among country club circles. Appearing for cheery photo ops at charitable events.

Her self-anointed charity, "Yes, There Is Hope," targeted the poor, minority orphan girls of Atlanta and provided a network of volunteer tutors who were all more than willing to serve as junior ambassadors in Molly Sue's charitable domain.

She knew all the right things to say, all the right things to do. She knew the little idioms of the richest of aristocrats and moved attractively in all kinds of social circles.

Nobody would believe him if he told them.

Because behind closed doors, the sweet, sexy, demure Episcopalian aristocrat turned into the mother of all Tasmanian devils.

Her family money and her family power had brought him from the shadows of lower-middle-class suburbia, his father having been an uneducated mill worker, and she constantly reminded him of it.

"You'd be nothing without me. I could snap my fingers and destroy you in a heartbeat if you crossed me."

Of course, her appearances with him in public were all smiles and happy waving, and she seemed to be in active competition against him for the affection and admiration of her own followers.

His every step when they were together was like walking through a minefield. It had been that way for years and had only gotten worse with time.

His philandering had been wrong and he knew it. He had tried to stop it, but in his weakness he had failed.

But was life with a wife supposed to be this hard? Surely God hadn't intended it to be this way. Had he? Was there no hope for him? Was he forever condemned to this internal tortured existence?

He had prayed for relief from her, but frankly, there had been none. So now what was he to do?

His staff tried protecting him. And Maryanne was the anti-Molly, so unassuming and shy, with a natural ability to blend into the woodwork. Molly Sue had never suspected anything between them. That's what Bobby had loved about Maryanne. She was an opposite personality type from the overbearing socialite-debutante he had married. He found solace in her presence.

He often thought that had Molly Sue discovered the truth about Maryanne, he just might be able to survive that. It could be swept under the rug if discovered, and Maryanne would not be considered a splashy enough threat to Molly Sue's public domain.

Not so with Marla. The photographs in the *Washington Post* with the leggy, glamorous model would unleash an uncontrollable firestorm from hell, a torrent of obsession, rage, and destruction from the woman he had married.

In a word, Molly Sue would not consider Maryanne the object of threatening public competition. But Marla would be more than enough to ignite a fury that would burn hot and eternal.

And to make matters worse, there loomed the specter of P.J. MacDonald, the naval officer who had been gunned down in the streets of Washington. It was only a matter of time before his office became the subject of a public investigation about the shooting.

No, he would not live the rest of his life under such dark storm clouds of uncertainty. And not only that, he would not give Molly Sue another shot at him. He had already accomplished in his life more than the majority of men could even dream about. And he would end it all on his own terms. He reached into the drawer where he kept his gun, but then changed his mind, if only for a moment.

He stood up, walked over to his office door, and locked it. This would be hard enough on Maryanne, and there was no point in risking that she might walk in on him during the act. This way, with the door locked, perhaps the Capitol police would get to him first and spare her the agony of witnessing his body sprawled upon the floor.

He turned around, walked to his desk, plopped down into his large leather chair, and punched the intercom on his desk.

"Maryanne?"

"Your coffee has almost finished brewing."

"That's okay," he said. "I think I've changed my mind. No coffee for me." He hung up the phone.

His thoughts turned back to Molly Sue. Bobby Talmadge wasn't sure if it was jealousy, hatred, or an unrivaled sense of self-righteousness that drove her. But he knew if he returned her call she would announce that he would hear from her lawyer. And she would hire the top bulldog in Atlanta.

Then she would tell all and make sure he would never win another election. She would demand half of all he had. No, more. She would demand, and keep demanding, all that he had for the rest of her life, even though she didn't need it. She would do so solely for the sake of banishing him to permanent impoverishment.

Yes, that would be her only goal, to see to it that he lived the life of a cockroach.

Oh, she would go on to remarry. With her smile, her money, her looks, and her fake southern charm, she would hook herself a man. That would be for sure. And she would marry someone with either money or power. That would be a nonnegotiable prerequisite. But that wouldn't stop her from her sick obsession with him, or with hounding the living hell out of him until he drew his last breath as an old man.

Vengeance.

Revenge.

He would not be the object of her public ire for the rest of his life.

Nor would he be the serf-lackey of the oil-and-gas lobbyist who set him up with Marla to begin with.

Nor, for that matter, would he ever go to prison.

No, he would never be able to find peace again. She wouldn't allow that.

Never.

Ever.

He pulled out a pen and started to scribble a note on a piece of blank stationery with a royal-blue letterhead reading *United States Senate.*

Dear Molly Sue,

I'm sorry I wasn't able to please you. I did try. I tried hard. But I failed. I'm sorry it had to end this way.

I wish you the best for the rest of your life and hope that you find happiness. Please tell the kids I love them.

Love always,
Bobby

He slumped back in his big leather chair and looked around at the dark mahogany walls of the plush U.S. Senate office that would be the last sight he saw on earth.

He would miss his kids, but really, they were grown and didn't need him anymore.

Who needed him?

What good was he, at the end of the day?

Special interests owned him. The government might try to implicate him in the death of P.J. MacDonald. He had failed to shepherd a bill through Congress for his most powerful constituent, which was why he was being outed. And he had a wife who despised him.

Yes, this was the only way.

He reached down in the drawer and picked up the revolver.

"Senator?" Maryanne's voice through the door.

He put the barrel of the gun in his mouth, and the steel was cold to his lips and his tongue.

"Bobby? Are you okay? Bobby? Why's the door locked?"

With his thumb, he cocked the hammer into firing position.

"Bobby?" *Knock-knock.* "Are you okay? Please open the door!"

More knocking. Maryanne would not give up. But Maryanne could not save him. And there was nothing he could do for her. She deserved better.

Knock-knock.

"Bobby, if you don't open now, I'm calling security!"

He took the gun out of his mouth. "I'm okay. I'll be right there."

"Thank God. You're scaring me."

"Hang on."

He put the gun back in his mouth and pulled the trigger.

• • •

THE PENTAGON
SOUTH PARKING LOT
6:57 A.M.

Caroline swung around to the entrance of the large South Parking Lot of the Pentagon, one of four massive parking lots surrounding the building that housed the nation's Department of Defense.

The South Lot was reserved for the general public, for visitors who could get clearance to visit the Pentagon, but mostly for commuters who caught the Pentagon Metro Station for the easy subway trip to various points into the nation's capital.

But the lot also had spaces for low-level and midlevel military officers, and Caroline McCormick, who fell into the midlevel officer category, had been given a temporary parking pass there while waiting for her permanent pass to be assigned.

"Okay, I'm turning into the South Lot entrance now." She spoke into her car's Bluetooth to an anxious-sounding Captain Paul Kriete, who had been chatting on the phone with her for the last fifteen minutes. His voice—his strong, reassuring tone—had provided her with an unexpected level of comfort as she drove alone down the interstate and now into the Pentagon parking lot.

As she pulled into her space, she looked up and saw his cleft chin and reassuring smile, and felt a sense of peace surround her. Ever the gentleman, he reached down and opened her door, his handsome face showing a sense of relief.

"Thank God you're okay."

"I hope I'm okay," she said, her mind still in a fog from having survived a shooting attempt only thirty minutes ago. She caught a whiff of his cologne as the morning breeze rushed in from over the Potomac. "In a way, it was almost like when P.J. was shot, it happened so fast." She stepped out of the car, and he closed the door behind her and put his hand in the middle of her back.

"When P.J. was shot," she said as he began to accompany her across the parking lot toward the south entrance of the Pentagon, "I heard a sharp popping sound. But I thought it was the sound of a car backfiring on Constitution Avenue. But when I turned around and saw P.J. lying there on the ground, bleeding, I knew I had heard the sound of a gunshot. But this time I heard nothing. He must have used a silencer."

"Probably," Paul said.

"But know what the scariest thing about it was?"

"Tell me."

"I heard it whiz by my head, and I could feel the air from the bullet on my ear. That's how close it came to my head, Paul. Less than an inch, right past my ear."

She felt herself begin to tremble. "Give me a second, will you, please?"

The south entrance to the Pentagon was still about two hundred yards in front of them, but she had to stop walking for a second. Just to catch herself.

"You okay?" Paul asked.

"I . . . I . . ."

"Come here."

He knew what she needed. And as he put his big, strong arms around her, she fell into his powerful and soothing embrace, and the rippling muscles of his biceps felt like protective shields around her shoulders.

What a powerful man. No wonder he had succeeded so brilliantly in command.

She didn't even think about the dozens of military personnel walking around them, headed into the building. Nor did she think of, or even care about, the military's prohibition against public display of affection. For a fleeting half second, the safe feeling of his protection made her forget that someone wanted her dead, or at least her worries evaporated. If only for a second.

"You sure you want to do this?" he asked.

She glanced up into his eyes, at first uncertain what he meant by the question. Then she remembered.

She stepped back, away from his embrace, a new sense of determination steeling her soul.

"Yes," she said. "I made a vow to finish this, and I'm going to do it for P.J., and I'm going to do it because it's the right thing to do."

He winced. "Look. I have some friends at BUPERS"—the acronym for the Navy Personnel Command—"who owe me a favor. Or I could talk to Admiral Brewer. I'd hate it personally, but I think we should get you out of Washington awhile, until things blow over."

Her Scotch-Irish blood started boiling in a hot cauldron. "No, sir. That is not an option. I'm a naval officer, and just like you're called to do your duty, I'm called to do mine. And right now my duty is to write a legal opinion so just maybe you'll have a hundred thousand drones to command. Or maybe, depending on what I decide, I'll write an opinion that will kill the whole project," she said, feeling feisty. "Then you won't have any drones to command."

"I don't care whether you kill the project or not," he said. "I'll just go back to sea, which is where I'd rather be anyway. I just don't want you to get killed in the process."

"Captain! Commander!"

Caroline looked over her left shoulder. Mark Romanov was walking toward them, his face contorted in a worried look. "Are you okay?"

"I'm fine." Caroline spoke defiantly.

"She's as stubborn as ever," Paul said.

"I appreciate you gentlemen meeting me in the parking lot, but if I need bodyguards here at the Pentagon, we're in big trouble. Anyway, I've got to get inside. I've got a lot of work to do."

"Okay. I'll walk with you, if you don't mind," Mark said. "I need to ask you a few questions."

"I'm sure you do." Caroline stepped up her pace, walking again toward the south entrance.

"You guys can back off now! We've got it!" Mark shouted, which prompted Caroline to look over her shoulder.

"Who are you talking to?"

"Commander, meet Special Agents Carraway and Frymier."

She turned around and saw two well-cut younger men, one a balding black guy and one a white guy with a close-cropped crew cut, maybe in their late twenties. They were wearing pinstripe suits, Ray-Ban sunglasses, and earpieces attached to squiggly wires. "This is Special Agent Carraway."

"Ma'am," said the black guy, nodding at her.

"And Frymier."

"Good morning, ma'am," said the Caucasian, his cologne smelling a bit strong in the wind.

"Special Agents Frymier and Carraway are your overnight detail watching your place. They just followed you here."

"You were the guys who were on detail outside my house this morning?"

"Yes, ma'am. Plus, we had a couple of other agents stationed in the area also."

"Did you see anything?"

"No, ma'am," Carraway said. "When you came out of the front door, a bus pulled up and we lost visual contact for a second. Next thing we knew, you were in your car and on the road. We followed you as soon as you pulled out."

She looked at Frymier. "You didn't see anything either?"

"No, ma'am. We were stationed close to each other. I saw what Special Agent Carraway saw."

"Wow."

"Anything else, sir?"

"Not at the moment," Mark said. "Stay on standby until your shift changes. I want someone following her home this evening."

"Yes, sir."

She turned and started walking again. Paul and Mark flanked her on each side. "So, no offense to these guys, but what good are they if they let someone get off a shot and didn't even see the shooter?"

"Unfortunately, that's not always uncommon," Mark said. "Snipers sometimes aren't seen until long after the fact because they position themselves in obscure places. Sometimes they aren't seen at all. That's part of what makes this a dangerous business. And of course, when a sniper uses a silencer, it makes it even harder to know someone's even gotten a shot off."

They kept walking as a cloud passed over the sun, casting an ominous shadow over the great sea of asphalt.

"Frankly, I don't like it," Paul said. "When we've got NCIS agents out there and even they can't stop this, I think this is too much to ask of Caroline."

"Nobody's asking me to do anything, Captain."

"I know, but still—"

"Aaaaaahhhhhhhhhhhh!"

The parking lot spun like a whirlwind.

Sharp, burning pain.

Concentrated.

Instant.

Sharp.

Caroline fell forward. Her head hit the concrete.

"She's been shot! Hit the deck!"

CHAPTER 33

• • •

Richardson DeKlerk, wearing a blue designer blazer, rocked back in the chair behind his desk, sipped his morning bourbon, and was checking his email when Ivana popped into his office.

"Excuse me, Richardson," she said in that luscious Eastern European accent of hers, "but you have a telephone call from Washington, DC."

"I hope it's Bobby Talmadge with some good news about my contract."

"Actually, sir, it's Senator Talmadge's assistant, a Mr. Mandela. He said you know him. He says it's urgent."

"Urgent? It's already beyond urgent," Richardson said, then remembered that taking out his frustration over Talmadge's lack of action on Ivana would do no good. "Very well, my dear. Put Mr. Mandela through."

"Yes, sir."

Richardson picked up the telephone. "Tommy, I'm hoping you're calling to tell me our junior senator has gotten the proposal from the Navy he needs to bring Project Blue Jay as an up-or-down expenditures bill before Congress."

"Unfortunately, Mr. DeKlerk, it doesn't appear that Senator Talmadge will be bringing any more bills before Congress at all."

Richardson bottom-upped the last ounce of his morning shot. "What are you talking about, Mandela?"

"Unfortunately, Mr. DeKlerk, the senator shot himself early this morning."

"What? Did you say Talmadge shot himself?"

"Unfortunately, yes."

"Is he okay?"

"He's dead."

"What the heck?" Ivana appeared at the door with a bewildered look on her pretty face, obviously curious about the conversation. Richardson poured himself another shot of bourbon, then got up and started walking toward the riverview balcony. "What set him off?" A sip of bourbon.

"Well, the *Washington Post* somehow got hold of some of those pictures with the senator and Marla Moreno and wrote a juicy little exposé on the front page. That's all it took."

"Tommy, we weren't trying to get him to bop himself off, only to pressure him to act on this bill. How did this happen?"

"I don't know the answer to that yet, Mr. DeKlerk. But I'm sure the pictures run by the *Post* didn't originate from our camp. Somebody else was trying to get to him. He was three sheets to the wind at the party by the time she jumped on his lap. Anybody could have taken those pictures."

DeKlerk cursed. "This presents a problem. I've got to make some calls to get this seat filled, and fast. Maybe it's a blessing in disguise. Hopefully we'll find someone a little more compliant when we have a legislative request. Gotta go." He hung up. "Ivana?"

"Yes, sir."

"Get me Joe Don Mack over at the Georgia Political Victory Fund. Tell him it's urgent."

"Yes, sir."

"And bring another bourbon, please."

"Yes, sir."

Richardson stepped out on the balcony and looked down at the blue waters of the Savannah River. How had something that should be so bloody simple become so bloody complicated?

Ivana stepped out onto the balcony holding a cordless telephone. "Mr. Mack is on the line, Richardson."

"Thank you." He took the phone. "Joe Don. Have you heard the news about Talmadge?"

"Yep. Just got a call from the director of the Georgia Republican Party." Joe Don Mack spoke in an elongated southern drawl. "I'm shocked. What a waste. The *Washington Post* did a hit piece with him and that hot little Italian chick. Like ole Harry Truman said, if you can't stand the heat, get out of the kitchen. But this is one heck of a way to get out of the kitchen."

Richardson checked his watch. "Look, Joe Don, I don't have time to hear about Harry Truman. Right now I need to know what the procedure is for finding a replacement for Talmadge."

"Well, the governor makes the appointment. Then whoever the governor appoints has to stand for reelection at the same time Bobby would have been up for reelection."

"You've got a couple of names in mind?"

"Of course, Richardson. We always have a short list. A couple are from the Georgia State Senate."

"Okay, listen, Joe Don. I want you to go to your short list and pick the lackey who's going to pick up the ball where Talmadge dropped it, and I want you to have a specific conversation with him and tell him what we expect, and tell him that this drone project is vital to the state's economy, and to his general election chances, and to his health in general. Got it?"

"Got it, boss."

"Good. And then I want you to get this appointment through within forty-eight hours. Tell the governor that Georgia cannot afford to be without a United States senator and that his own chances for reelection or other political aspirations he may have will depend on him acting fast."

"But—"

"There's no but to it, Joe Don. Got it?"

"Got it."

"And as far as the Victory Fund goes, I'm prepared to spend whatever amount of money it takes, but only if you make it happen."

"We'll make it happen. I'll get the governor on the line—personally—and tell him how much this means to you and to the state of Georgia. We know how important AirFlite is to the Victory Fund. We won't let you down."

• • •

NEW YORK CONCRETE & SEAFOOD COMPANY
BROOKLYN NAVY YARD WAREHOUSE
OVERLOOKING THE EAST RIVER
KAY AVENUE
BROOKLYN, NEW YORK
10:15 A.M.

The last time he stood on this concrete floor in this cavernous warehouse, a dead body had been sprawled on the floor, oozing blood from a bullet hole to the temple, compliments of the long-barreled revolver of the "big guy" himself, the still-too-meddlesome godfather of the family, Sal D'Agostino.

But the company's cleaning crew had done a marvelous job spicking-and-spanning the place, Phil thought, taking a drag from his cigarette.

"Phil!" Sal shouted, barreling like a bouncing bear across the warehouse. "Hey, looks like all the blood and guts got scrubbed up good." He laughed. "Unless we decide to take out one of these limp-wimp, congressman-senator types." He laughed at himself again. "Hey, come give your favorite uncle a little affection, will ya?" The big guy held out his arms in a gimme-a-bear-hug gesture and wrapped them around Phil.

"How are you today, Uncle?"

"Great! Now that I've seen my favorite nephew."

"I'm your only nephew, Uncle Sal. That's the only reason I'm now running the family business."

"You'd be my favorite nephew even if I had a hundred nephews," Sal said. "Give me one of those, will ya?" Sal snatched the cigarette before Phil could even say "Sure thing," lit it, and started talking again. "So, are our two Washington lover boys almost here?"

"Joey just called. They're at the gate now."

"Good." Sal released a smoke ring. "Tell ya what. Let's go over and wait for 'em in the side office. Call Joey and tell him to bring those boys in to us as soon as they get out of the car."

"You bet." Phil punched the speed dial and relayed Sal's instructions.

They walked across the concrete door to an industrial-looking office with a plain wooden desk, several plain wooden chairs, and a few filing cabinets.

Mostly the office was used for foremen to sign off on receipts of inventory—catches—brought in from the fishing boats. Big Sal sat behind the desk and kicked up his feet. "So how's my boy Vinnie?"

"Still in Washington. So far, so good, I guess."

"The boy might get used to the lifestyle, Phil. Maybe we could buy him a congressional seat! That way we could get stuff done more efficiently." Sal doubled over, cackling at himself. The notion of Vinnie in Congress struck a funny nerve even with Phil.

"You got me on that one, Uncle."

Phil's phone rang. "It's Joey." He tried containing his laughter. "Yeah, Joey?"

"We're here, boss."

"Bring 'em in."

A moment later, Joey rounded the corner wearing a black T-shirt, his big, tattooed biceps naturally flexing. The two weasels from Washington walked in behind him, all decked out in their pinstripe-suit congressional attire, the senator in blue and the congressman in gray, and both looking rather unhappy.

"Senator! Congressman!" Sal bellowed. "Welcome to my humble abode."

"Glad to be of service." Rodino plastered a fake smile on his face.

"Joey, round up some chairs for our distinguished guests."

"Yes, sir."

"After all, it ain't often that we get visited by such . . . by such . . . what am I trying to say, nephew? Help me out."

"By such distinguished members of Congress?"

"No. That ain't it. It's more than that. What am I—" A sudden look of recognition. "Yes. It ain't often that we're in the esteemed presence of such esteemed political royalty! It's like having the king and queen of England in our presence." A cackling laugh. "Although I must ask, under the circumstances, which one of you plays the queen?"

The congressman snapped like an angry queen bee. "Do I detect a homophobic tone in that question?"

"A homo what-ic?" Sal was having fun toying with Milk and Rodino.

"You know," the congressman said, "England doesn't have a king."

Joey reentered the room. "Here are your chairs, Sal."

"Ah. Set 'em there, Joey. One for the king and one for the queen."

"What, boss?"

"Just set the chairs there, Joey. Maybe they're both the queen type."

Rodino and Milk exchanged angry glares with each other.

"Well." Big Sal spoke again. "I hear you gentlemen may have lost a colleague this morning. Sorry for your professional loss." Sal chuckled.

"Are you referring to Talmadge?" Milk asked.

Sal laughed harder. "Forgive me. The thought of more than one Washington maggot getting wiped out on a single day got me excited." More chuckling. "Of course I'm talking about Talmadge."

Rodino responded. "Talmadge was a right-winger. But you don't want to see that happen to anybody." Milk cast his eyes to the side.

"Maybe the moral of the story ought to be that it doesn't pay to get on the wrong side of the family when it comes to federal legislation that the family's interested in."

Milk looked at Big Sal. "What does that mean?" He sounded like an irritated female cat.

Phil spoke. "I think Sal means Talmadge was pushing for this drone project pretty hard. Not a smart move."

"So what did you do?" Milk snapped. "Just kill him?"

"Hey!" Sal held up his hands in a don't-shoot surrender gesture. Then he pulled out his shiny, long-barreled revolver, holding the barrel straight up into the air.

Milk jumped back, horrified, which made the sight worth the price of admission. "I—I—"

"Easy. Easy there, Congressman." Sal made no effort to hide his delight at watching Rodino's lover boy twisting on his seat. "You should know the family don't kill nobody." Sal formed his mouth in an O shape, as if about to blow smoke rings. But instead he blew a gust of breath on the gun and then wiped the barrel with a rag.

Milk jumped back again with another look of horror on his face.

Big Sal snickered. "I wouldn't hurt nobody with this gun, Congressman," Sal lied. "We just sometimes arrange for certain types of publicity to help nudge you political types along."

More confused looks, and Sal laid the gun down on the desk.

"What Sal means," Phil said, "is that Talmadge was pushing too hard on the other side. We have contacts everywhere. Lobbyists. Congressional staffs. You name it. One of our contacts turned over some fascinating photographs of the good senator, and we determined that it would be best if the senator turned his attention to something other than this drone project. Our friends at the *Washington Post* were happy to oblige." Phil allowed himself a grin. Silence.

"Okay," Rodino said. "So I'm confused."

"So what is it you might be confused about, Senator?" Sal asked.

"Well, the bill hasn't passed. Now its principal proponent, Bobby Talmadge, is dead. And Talmadge was pushing it because it would have brought a ton of jobs to Georgia. Mackey and I are good Democrats"—he looked over at Milk, who nodded in agreement—"and we've already been working behind the scenes against it. If you've brought us up here to tell us to oppose this thing, I'm not sure what more we can do, Mr. D'Agostino."

"Joey?"

"Yes, Mr. D."

"Bring shots of bourbon for everybody, will ya?"

"Yes, sir, Mr. D."

Sal looked at Rodino, then at Milk. "What I want, gentlemen, is assurance that this thing is dead on arrival. And I haven't gotten that yet."

Joey returned with two bottles of Evan Williams bourbon and four whiskey glasses. He poured the glasses full, and Sal took a sip before continuing.

"I know you can't stop some right-winger from introducing this legislation. But I want a legal opinion that this project is illegal, and I want that opinion from the Navy, before this bill ever sees the light of day. And I want it now." He smiled and looked at the political scum. "Care for a drink?"

Milk spoke again with the shrillness of a squealing hyena that got on Phil's nerves. "Look, Mr. D'Agostino, I understand that you have been a big contributor to Senator Rodino's campaign, and also to various Democratic Party causes. And for all that, you're to be commended. But my question is this." Milk paused, glanced at Rodino, then back at Sal. "What exactly do you want?"

With a slight smile, Sal seemed to ignore the question. "Give me a second, will ya?"

He extracted a large cigar, lit it, took a drag on it, and blew smoke at the two men.

"You know, I like you, Milk." Another smoke cloud. "But don't get too excited. Know what I like about you?"

"I have no idea."

"Well, I think the real question here is, what does the senator want?"

"What do you mean?" Rodino asked.

"You want to be president, don't you, Senator? At least that's what I've read in the paper."

Rodino's face reddened. Veins popped out in his neck. "Even if that were true, what's that got to do with anything?"

When Sal grinned, he set off two deep grooves on his bald forehead. Like his bald head was flashing three evil smiles, one below the nose and two above his eyebrows, giving him the sinister look of the Joker in the Batman comics. Except Sal looked more like a three-hundred-pound Joker. Right now, both Rodino and Milk were on the squirming end of Sal's famous glazed-over, crazy look.

"Well, you know . . ." He puffed again on his big stogie, then chomped it in his mouth and, with his finger, powerfully flicked the barrel of the .357 revolver. The gun spun round and round on the desk, as if in a game of Russian roulette. The liberal lover boys jumped again, drawing another chuckle from Sal.

Sal removed the cigar from his mouth. "As I was about to say, we here at the New York Concrete & Seafood Company are quite peaceful. We are a peaceful company and a peaceful family. But"—he wagged his index finger in the air—"I must say that we do believe in the Fourth Amendment right to freedom of the press."

Milk's eyes seethed. "It's the First Amendment that gives freedom of the press. And just what are you getting at?"

"Well, now. Gentlemen!" Sal said. "It appears that we do have a constitutional scholar in our midst." He leered at Milk, and his voice trembled with anger. "Let me tell you this, Mr. Constitutional Scholar. This old guy might sometimes get the First Amendment mixed up with the Fourth Amendment, but let me assure you of this." He picked up the long-barreled revolver. The two politicians flinched. "I always make sure I understand the Second Amendment."

Silence.

He set the gun down on the desk.

"But we here at NYC&S believe in the First Amendment freedom of the press. And if some well-known public newspaper, say the *New York Times* or the *Washington Post*, wanted to, you know, post certain pictures . . . I mean, who are we to object?" Sal threw up his hands and shrugged.

"What pictures are you talking about?" Milk snapped.

"Oh, I don't know." Sal was clearly enjoying the moment. "Maybe some you should ask your buddy Senator Rodino about. See what he thinks about it all."

Milk glared at Rodino. "What's he talking about, Chuckie?"

"They've got pictures of us."

"Pictures of us?" Milk's face reddened. Veins bulged in his neck.

"Yes. Private pictures. Last summer at Martha's Vineyard."

"What?"

"I saw the photos yesterday."

"That's blackmail!" Milk raised his voice.

"Blackmail?" Big Sal grinned. "What makes you think such a thing, Milkey? You haven't even seen the pictures."

"Nobody was supposed to know about Martha's Vineyard!"

Phil spoke up. "Well, it seems to me, Congressman, that if you didn't want to be spotted on a romantic weekend with your boyfriend here, then you should have picked someplace a little less public than Martha's Vineyard. Like, maybe Alaska or something!"

Milk shot back, "Still, I resent having my privacy violated!"

"Hey, Congressman," Sal said. "Ain't nobody violated your privacy. Not yet, anyway."

"Well, it sounds to me like you're threatening to run these embarrassing photos in the *Post*!"

"Let me ask you this, Milkey."

"It's Milk. Congressman William O. Milk. And my nickname, for only a select few in my inner circle, is Mackey. Not Milkey."

"All right, Congressman. Let me ask you this. Do you want to see your boyfriend here have a shot at being the vice president of the United States? Maybe even president?"

Milk looked over at Rodino, his eyes wide and his mouth open, as if coming to the realization that his lover from the U.S. Senate might actually have a shot at becoming the next president of the United States.

"Of course I would love to see Chuck become our next president. He has a certain strength and virtue about him that would make him one of the greatest ever to hold the office." An adoring dreaminess appeared in his eyes as he gazed at his senatorial lover with a look that made Phil want to vomit.

"Well, if these pictures got out, the irony is that they might help you get reelected in Massachusetts. Not that you would need any help getting reelected. The word's already out on you, and that lifestyle has always flown pretty well in Boston.

"But they don't know about you and Senator Lover Boy here, and I've got a feeling that won't fly too well down south, even in the Democrat primaries down there. And those pictures will kill his chances in a general election. And as far as vice president goes, if Eleanor Claxton gets the Democrat nomination, and she might, there's no way in hell Eleanor puts Chuckie here on the ticket." Sal leaned back and crossed his arms over his belly. "So it seems to me that keeping those pictures out of the paper would be a good thing for your friend's political chances."

"He's got a point, Mackey." Rodino reached over and touched his hand.

"So," Sal continued, "if you want Senator Lover Boy to have a shot at the presidency, then get on board with what we need. Milk, you're on the Armed Services Committee. I need you to spearhead opposition to this drone bill in the house and kill it." He looked at Rodino. "And same for you in the senate. I want to know this bill is dead on arrival! Do you hear me?"

"You have my cooperation," Milk said. He turned and nodded lovingly at Rodino. "But I'm doing this for him. Not you. You're not my constituent."

"I don't care who you're doing it for. You've got three days, or it's going to be a shark-feeding frenzy and you'll wish you had it as easy as Talmadge had it. Now get out of my office!"

CHAPTER 34

• • •

He walked into the room and, as he always had done, filled every corner of it with his charismatic presence. Women dropped what they were doing and turned their heads at the sight of his broad shoulders and muscular chest nicely filling out his summer white Navy uniform shirt. That hadn't changed. And neither had his broad, white smile and that jutting, rock-solid chin.

A golden glow surrounded his head, and over each of his black-and-gold shoulder boards appeared a strange golden light, almost like little golden clouds hovering behind him.

Her heart soared at the sight of him walking into the room; joy overcame her. She pushed herself up on her bed.

"Thank God! I thought I'd never see you again."

"You knew you'd see me again. How could I leave my running buddy behind?"

"I—"

"Shhh." He held his finger up to his lips. "Save your energy. Try not to talk."

His smile melted her heart, and when he stepped over to her and touched her arm with his hand, her soul started to burst from her chest.

The last time she had been with him, she had felt such ecstatic exhilaration, eager for a new beginning, only to have her hopes dashed forever in a cold, cruel moment on a heartless hot day.

She had always known it. At least, conceptually she had known. And her faith taught her that there was life after death for those who trusted in the Son of God.

But now . . . now she knew heaven was for real. Seeing him come in, feeling his touch, knowing he would take her with him as they walked out of this place into the afterlife . . . She was about to cross chasms of time and space to a promised land of milk and honey, whose streets were paved with gold, where holy light always shone, with no more tears, no more pain . . .

"I need you to take care of yourself." His voice was gentle and loving.

"I—"

"No, don't talk," he said. "Stay strong." She caught a whiff of his cologne. But it was like nothing she had ever experienced before. Like a fragrant, tranquilizing smell from another world. "Your work isn't done, Caroline. Not yet, anyway. I'm proud of you, and I'll be back for you. Know that I love you." He turned and started to walk away.

"P.J.! No! Don't leave me! P.J.! P.J.!"

The room went into a spin, and everything turned into a whirling, twisting blur as if she suddenly were in the midst of a funnel cloud.

"P.J.!"

"Are you all right?"

Caroline did not recognize the man's voice.

She opened her eyes to bright lights and saw a middle-aged man with curly hair and a receding hairline speaking in a warm, compassionate voice. "I'm Dr. Berman. You're in the recovery room at Walter Reed. Can you hear me?"

"Doctor?" She pushed herself up and looked around. "P.J.! Where is he? He was just here."

"You've been under some powerful medications, but you're going to be fine."

She laid her head back down on the pillow and let her heart pound for a second. She looked for him again. She knew he was there. She saw him. He was so real. She still smelled his cologne. Yet no one was there except the doctor and two nurses. Nothing was in the room except sterile medical equipment.

"What happened?"

"You took a bullet in the shoulder. Then you hit the asphalt and took a blow to the head and went lights out. You've been out for a couple of hours, but we removed the bullet and you're going to be fine."

She rubbed her eyes. "Was . . . Did I have a visitor?"

"A visitor?"

"Yes." She didn't say his name. They might think she was delusional and hold her longer. "A JAG officer?"

Dr. Berman, who wore on his collar the gold oak leaf of a lieutenant commander in the Navy Medical Corps, smiled. "No. Not in here. Just the medical staff. You do have some visitors from your command in the waiting area. Your commanding officer and another captain, and some officers from your command. You can see them if you'd like."

"But I . . ."

"It's okay," Berman said. "You're not the first patient who has had a visitor the rest of us couldn't see." He gave her a knowing wink.

"When can I get out of this place?"

"Oh, I think sooner rather than later. Let's see . . ." He turned away and looked at a computer screen. "Checking your chart here. I just want to monitor that concussion overnight, and I don't see why we couldn't let you go home sometime tomorrow."

"Doc, I'm okay. I need to go home now. I've got work to do."

He turned and looked at her. "Commander, with respect, you seem determined for a lady who's just taken a bullet in the shoulder."

"You don't know how determined I am." She winced as a sharp pain that felt like a hot knife shot through her shoulder.

"You okay?"

"I'm fine."

"You're going to feel some discomfort for a few days from that entry wound. We've closed it with dissolving sutures, so the good news is that you won't need to have stitches removed. But you may have some painful flare-ups for the next few days, which is another reason I'd like to keep you overnight for observation. If it flares overnight, we can treat you with painkillers."

"Thank you, Doctor, but I'll be just fine."

"Suit yourself." He shook his head. "Do you feel like company?"

"Sure," she said. "Send them in."

"Be right back."

Berman stepped out of the room, and so did the two nurses, leaving her alone and conscious.

She knew it hadn't been an illusion. He was so real. And the fragrance of his sweet cologne . . .

Or was her mind playing tricks on her? Like the doc said, she was under powerful medications and had been in surgery. Maybe she wanted to see him so badly that, combined with the drugs, it was all a dream, a hopeful figment of her imagination.

A tear came to her eye.

But then again, she had read accounts of near-death experiences when loved ones who had long ago passed away—a spouse, maybe a parent—returned, in some cases perhaps to tell their loved one it wasn't their time. Maybe in other cases they came to take their dying loved one to heaven to see Jesus. At least that's what the articles she had read claimed.

Illusion or not, she would choose to believe, and she would stay strong because of what P.J. had told her.

The door opened.

A naval officer in summer whites, wearing black shoulder boards with the four gold bars of a U.S. Navy captain, stepped in.

"Captain Guy?"

"Mind if I come in?"

"Please do."

"Glad to see you're alert."

"I feel great," she said, lying about the fact that her head felt like it was being squeezed in a vice and that her shoulder had started throbbing with a hot, wrenching pain. "Just ready to get back to my duty station, sir."

Her commanding officer, a tall, lanky man with thinning hair, nodded and smiled like an uncle determined to bite his tongue to avoid saying what was really on his mind.

"Do you feel up to a little more company?"

"Who's here?"

She asked the question, hoping against all hope that somehow the last week had been a horrible nightmare from which she had just awakened, and that Captain Guy would include in his answer the name of Lieutenant Commander P.J. MacDonald among the list of guests. For she had just seen him. He had been so real that she could at least hope once more. Couldn't she?

"Captain Kriete and Lieutenant Fladager, and you also have a surprise guest."

"A surprise guest?" Yes! She knew he hadn't been an illusion. He had come in to see her earlier, and now he was back again. She pushed herself up again, enduring the knifing in her shoulder. Her heart raced with excitement.

"You bet. Somebody close to you. I think you'll be glad to see him." The captain smiled. "Shall I bring them all in?"

"Oh, yes, sir!" Caroline could not contain her own smile, and the sharp shoulder pain was suddenly gone.

Captain Guy stepped out of the room and a second later returned with Captain Kriete. "How are you, kiddo?" Paul asked.

As soon as she said, "Doing great, sir," Victoria walked in, also in her summer white uniform. "You had us worried, Commander."

"I'm fine and I'm ready to get back to work. Thanks for coming."

"So are you ready for your surprise visitor?" Captain Guy asked.

"Can't wait."

Captain Guy stepped into the hallway. "Commander. She's ready for you."

She heard steps in the hallway, and her heart pounded because she now knew it was true. It hadn't been an illusion after all. He was alive. This had all been a bad dream! Praise God!

Her commanding officer stepped back into the hospital room, and with him there appeared a handsome lieutenant commander in summer whites, strong and broad chested, and smiling from ear to ear.

Her heart jumped.

And then . . .

"Gunner?"

"How's my favorite cousin?"

How could she tell him that she would be delighted to see him, except that he wasn't P.J.?

She knew at that moment that if P.J. had actually been there, or even if it had been a dream, he wasn't coming back.

"What are you doing here?"

"We finished our ops off Point Loma. *George Washington* pulled into North Island for a few days. Then they called a meeting of all the carrier Intel officers at Suitland, so I happened to be in the area for a few days anyway. Then Captain Rudy called me and told me what happened."

Caroline smiled. Despite her disappointment that Gunner wasn't P.J., she loved her cousin like no other man except P.J. himself. "Gunner, you're too good to me."

"Hey. You know what they say. Blood's thicker than water. You know nothing would keep me away. But"—he walked over to her and put his hand on her good shoulder—"you still didn't answer my question. How are you doing?"

"I'm doing great. I'm ready to get the heck out of here."

Gunner smiled. "You look great, cuz. But you don't look like you're ready to get out of here."

"What are you?" she snapped. "A medical officer now? Just because you're a super action hero doesn't mean you know jack about medicine."

"Well now." Gunner turned and shrugged at the others. "She seems to have that little trial lawyer bite of hers." He chuckled. "I guess convincing her is above my pay grade. You want to try, sir?"

Paul stepped over to the other side of her bed. "Look, Caroline. We're worried about you."

"There's nothing to worry about, sir." She saw instant irritation on his face that she had called him sir instead of Paul. "I feel absolutely fine."

"Well," he said, "for someone who's been through what you've been through, you look fine. In fact, you look great. But frankly, I'm . . ." He paused and looked over toward Victoria, who apparently took his glance as her cue to chime in.

Victoria also stepped toward the bed and like Gunner and Paul gave one of those well-meaning but sympathetic smiles that made Caroline want to scream at the moment.

"The captain's right, Caroline. Even in a hospital gown after some nut's shot you, you still look like a movie star. Gosh, I wish I had your looks and charisma." Another smile.

"Most guys I know wouldn't throw you off the turnip truck, Victoria."

That brought chuckles from the three officers, and then Victoria continued.

"I'm glad to see you've not lost your sense of humor after all this. But, Caroline, we're more worried about your safety than your physical condition."

Caroline glanced at Paul and Captain Guy, then looked at Victoria. "My physical condition is fine. My safety is fine. Thank you all for your concern. Where's Mark?"

Her three visitors glanced at one another, all looking surprised at her sudden change of subject.

"Mark," Victoria said, "sends his best. Right now he's doing his best to try to figure out who took this shot at you."

"He's a good man, Victoria. Don't let him go. Cherish every minute you have."

Victoria nodded. "He is a good man."

Paul spoke again. "Caroline, we're concerned about you being out in public. Frankly, what happened this morning was too close for comfort."

"I appreciate your concern, Captain, but I'm not concerned in the least," she said. "I knew this could be dangerous when I spoke to Mark about it. We need to stop this guy." Her blood boiled, igniting another hot, sharp pain where the bullet had entered her shoulder. "And we need to stop him dead in his tracks."

"But I don't—" Paul caught himself. "We don't want you dead in your tracks."

"I'll be fine."

"How can we know that?" Victoria asked.

"I just will be. I'm not afraid of dying. This is the right thing to do."

Silence.

"Caroline." Paul again. "I'm thinking about talking with Special Agent Romanov."

"About what?"

Captain Guy. "This might be too dangerous, Commander."

"Sir, this is nothing compared to what our guys have faced in Iraq and Afghanistan. It's nothing compared to what our SEALs face every day. We had seventeen Navy SEALs go down on Extortion 17. Thirty Americans were sacrificed in that flight alone, and for their sake, and for others who have given their all, I'm not backing down."

"I'm thinking about asking Captain Guy to take you off the case," Paul said. "If the captain won't agree, I may go to Admiral Brewer."

"You can't do that! You're not in my chain of command."

"I know I'm not in your chain of command. But I can still ask him."

"You do that and I'll never speak to you again." A menacing glare. "Sir."

The tension in the room thickened like the early-morning fog on San Francisco Bay.

Dr. Berman stepped in, almost as if on cue.

"I think," the doctor said, "that it's probably best if we keep the patient as calm as possible, as long as possible."

"Sorry, Doctor," Paul said. He looked at Caroline. "I apologize. We didn't mean to upset you. We just care. That's all."

Captain Guy looked at her. "Just promise you'll obey the doctor's orders. I'll see you back at the Pentagon when you're released."

"Aye, sir. Sorry if I was out of line."

"No worries." Captain Guy nodded. "We'll see you soon."

As quickly as they had come, they all left. And once again she was alone, in the sterilized antiseptic callousness of an impersonal hospital room.

Alone with her memories of P.J. and with her determination to avenge his death—or join him in the afterlife.

• • •

Why did she have to be so stubborn?

Paul had asked himself this question a hundred times on his drive from the Pentagon to Lexington Park, and he asked it once again as he drove the staff car up to the main gate of the air station.

"Evening, sir." He accepted a sharp salute from the Navy shore patrolman who had jumped to an exceptional level of attention at the sight of a U.S. Navy captain approaching.

"Evening, Petty Officer." Paul snapped a return salute from the driver's seat of the U.S. Navy Taurus and drove alone onto the base, on his way to the headquarters of the command he had been given, even though for the time being he had been forced to spend most of his time at the Pentagon and in Washington schmoozing.

And now, in the midst of the murders of two JAG officers and the attempted murder of Caroline, it seemed that he would be glued to Washington for the foreseeable future.

Frankly, he wished she would resign her commission and marry him. If she would agree, he would request a transfer out of Washington. Or maybe he would soon be transferred out anyway, once Congress approved the money for a hundred thousand drones. Perhaps she could accompany him to Lexington Park after his temporary schmooze-fest had ended.

Or if he had to stay in Washington for a while to continue nursing the incubation period of this project, perhaps they could move far enough out of town to get her out of the rat race of it all.

Of course, he knew in his gut that she was probably a pipe dream.

She hadn't gotten P.J. MacDonald out of her blood yet, and might never get over him.

Still, whether or not she eventually married him, or whether she would ever even give him the time of day, his feelings for her had become real, and he would do everything possible to keep her alive so that one day, just maybe, she would have a chance to change her mind about him.

This idea was a long shot, and he'd probably wasted gas driving over here. But it was worth a try.

The sun hung low in the sky now, about to set in the west and casting an alluring, late-afternoon orange glow over the windswept base that sat on a peninsula jutting into the Chesapeake.

Paul slipped his officer's cover on his head, then got out of the car, pausing just a second in the parking lot to allow the air of the sea to fill his lungs. He noted off to his left that the color guard had already moved into position to de-hoist the flag for the evening. He would have to hurry, lest he got caught outside.

He turned and started a brisk walk into the breeze across the near-empty parking lot to the entrance of the building. But seven steps into his short journey, a chorus of long, shrill whistles, like the sound of a hundred NFL referees blowing their whistles at the same time, descended upon the base.

Cars, trucks, and SUVs driving along the road pulled over. Naval officers and enlisted men still outside stopped in their tracks.

Paul, too, came to a stop and pivoted toward the flagpole.

A solitary trumpet began sounding the colors, a long, lyrical bugle call that sounded like a slow, melodic rendition of taps. Everything on base froze. Paul rendered a salute toward the flagpole, holding it reverently as Old Glory descended through a flapping breeze into the white-gloved hands of the color guard members, who began folding it into a tight triangle.

The call to colors ended as whistles blew again, signaling that it was okay to resume activity on base. Paul dropped his salute and turned, walking toward the entrance of the temporary headquarters of the new U.S. Navy Drone Command.

"Attention on deck!"

"Good evening, Chief. At ease. Looks like you and Petty Officer Martinez are the skeleton crew down here tonight."

"Aye, Skipper. Good to see you. Commander Jefferies gave us a heads-up that you were coming over."

Paul nodded. "Last-minute thing. Is he up in flight control?"

"Yes, sir. Would you like me to accompany you up, sir?"

"No, I'm okay. Maintain your post. Second deck, right?"

"Yes, sir."

"Very well. Carry on."

"Aye, sir," the duty chief said just as Paul stepped into the elevator.

When the door opened on the second deck, this time, unlike the last time he was here, the place was almost empty. Only a light crew remained.

That would change if the drones were purchased and deployed into the fleet. This place would become a hubbub of round-the-clock activity if Congress ever passed the bill that was currently the subject of Caroline McCormick's legal opinion—if Caroline lived long enough to finish the opinion.

"Evening, Skipper." Paul heard the voice of Commander John Jefferies to his left as he stepped off the elevator. Wearing a working khaki uniform, Jefferies approached with two mugs of coffee, one in each hand. "Chief called and said you were on your way up. As I recall, you like yours straight black?"

"Appreciate it, John." To be polite, Paul accepted the mug and took a swig, even though he didn't yet need his evening caffeine shot.

"Come on in, sir."

"Thank you."

"Have a seat."

"Appreciate it."

A long conference table sat in the middle of the room, just behind the flight control area, where only a couple of controllers were stationed. Paul set his coffee down on the table and took a seat, and Commander Jefferies followed.

"So, sir." Jefferies took a swig of coffee and continued, "You said you wanted to ask me something in person."

"Yes, John. You heard we had another shooting at the Pentagon this morning."

"I heard," Jefferies said. "Wish we'd have kept a drone on Commander McCormick."

"As a matter of fact, John, that's what I want to talk to you about."

"You want me to get another one up?"

"Well, that's a dicey situation, especially if we overdo it at this point. But you know how I had you get that bird up in the air to follow her after P.J. MacDonald's funeral?"

"Of course, Skipper. That's how we tracked her to the scene of Lieutenant Ross Simmons's shooting."

"Could I see the aerial video of her car approaching Simmons's house?"

"Yes, sir. Want to see it now?"

"That's why I'm here, Commander. Now's as good a time as any."

She wouldn't listen to anybody. And despite what anybody told her, despite all attempts to reason with her, she was going to get herself killed.

Of course, this determined, stubborn streak of hers was one of the many things he had grown to love about her.

"Something struck me. Wanted to check it."

"Fire away, sir."

"Remember my orders to keep the drone up on Commander McCormick the day of the funeral?"

Jefferies winced. "Of course, Skipper. How could I forget? Probably violated every FAA regulation known to man, and it would probably get us both court-martialed if word got out."

"Right," Paul said. "*Posse comitatus* issues. I got that. We're not supposed to be using military equipment in any sort of civilian law enforcement."

Jefferies nodded. "That's why they want us to turn these drones over to the Homeland Security weasels when the drones fly over CONUS."

Paul sipped his coffee. "Except it wasn't Homeland Security flying the drones that day. It was U.S. Navy."

Jefferies looked out over the runway. A U.S. Navy F/A-18 taxied down the runway, its running lights blinking, the roar of its twin turbojets audible, though barely, even through the supposedly soundproof glass of the newly constructed drone observation tower.

A second later, fire blazed from the back of the Hornet, and both men watched as the jet raced down the runway and lifted off into the twilight's last gleaming.

"John," Paul said, "I don't want you to worry about that flight at all. If anybody has any questions, I'll take full responsibility for it. I'm the one who ordered it, and if anybody says anything, I'll take the heat. Got a bottled water?"

"Yes, sir. Hang on a second."

"Sure."

Jefferies got up, stepped into the kitchen, and came back with a bottled water. "Here ya go, sir."

"Thanks."

Paul unscrewed the cap of the Dasani. "Anyway, I've been thinking."

"About what, sir?"

"Couple of things. One"—he took a sip of water—"if anybody asks, we'll . . . I'll argue that the drone flight that day was not for domestic law enforcement but rather was to protect members of the U.S. military from an internal domestic threat."

Jefferies raised an eyebrow in a knowing look. "Good point, Skipper."

"Exactly," Paul said. "We had FAA clearance for the demo flight the day P.J. MacDonald was shot. Correct?"

"Absolutely, sir."

"So as long as we're not flying the drones over land for law enforcement issues, frankly, I don't see the problem. At least I don't see a *posse comitatus* violation."

"I like your argument, Skipper."

"Which leads me to another question."

"What's that, Captain?"

"The day I had that drone follow Lieutenant Commander McCormick after the funeral at Arlington, was the drone filming anything?"

"Yes, sir, Skipper. Right now our test drones are programmed to make digital recordings on all test flights. I logged that as a test flight."

"Interesting." Paul scratched his chin. "How long do we maintain the video?"

"Indefinitely, sir. Digital recordings inside the drone transmit to a database here at Pax River. Our capacity to maintain those videos is virtually unlimited."

"Hmm." Paul pondered the situation, thinking out loud. "Going back to the day of P.J. MacDonald's funeral in Arlington, do you think you could go back and show me the aerial video?"

Jefferies nodded. "Shouldn't be a problem, Skipper. But that little Blue Jay was up in the air for at least a couple of hours. You want to see the whole thing?"

Paul sipped his water. "No. Just the last minute or so before Commander McCormick arrived at Lieutenant Simmons's house."

"Martinez!" Jefferies called to one of the petty officers manning the runway observation area.

"Yes, sir." Martinez turned around.

"Bring us two laptops. Key up to synchronize. I want the aerial video of the last sixty seconds of Lieutenant Commander McCormick's drive to Lieutenant Simmons's house."

"Aye, sir."

Jefferies looked at Paul. "This should only take a minute, sir. May I ask what you're looking for?"

"Not sure, John. I followed her in my car that day while you guys were keeping me apprised of her whereabouts by phone. I wanted to see if we could find any clues by looking at the aerial tapes."

"Good idea, sir."

A moment later, Martinez and another petty officer, both enlisted air traffic controllers, returned with two large-screen laptops and set one each in front of Paul and Jefferies.

The frozen screen showed an aerial shot taken from somewhere in the sky, above what appeared to be Caroline McCormick's black Volkswagen Passat.

"Okay, sir," Jefferies said. "This is an overhead shot of Commander McCormick's car, at this point headed south on Fort Hunt Road. Now before I play this, let me do a quick switch to the map just to help us get oriented. Then I'll flip back over to the video recording."

"Very well."

"Okay. At this point, sir, we're seeing a still shot of Commander McCormick's car, the black Passat, and it's headed south on Fort Hunt Road, just in front of this Wells Fargo bank. Now, when I roll the tape, we'll see the car move south past the Village Hardware, and then past the Rite Aid Pharmacy, and then it will slow just a bit and turn right on Lafayette Drive, the street where Lieutenant Simmons had leased a condo.

"And see this little balloon pin on the map? On Lafayette and almost in front of Hamilton Lane?"

"I see it."

"That's Lieutenant Simmons's condo. Ready to roll it?"

"Roll it."

Jefferies tapped his computer, and the screen morphed from the map back to the still photograph of the aerial view of the Passat. Just before Jefferies tapped the Play button, Paul noticed at the bottom right of the screen superimposed numbering.

U.S. NAVY DRONE COMMAND
PROJECT BLUE JAY
DRONE 003

The Passat started moving again and a second later wheeled right onto Lafayette, just as Jefferies said it would. A moment after that, the car whipped left into the driveway in front of Simmons's house.

A second later, the tape showed the car door opening, revealing blonde hair on the figure of a female naval officer in summer white uniform.

She looked great even from the air as she walked to the front steps of the house.

She started knocking on the door, then a moment later pulled out her phone.

"Okay, I've seen enough. Question."

"Yes, sir."

"Can we get a wider angle?"

"Oh yes, sir. We can pull it way back if you want."

"Okay. Go back and do that. Let me see the map of what we can do first."

"Yes, sir. Okay, here's the first map again."

"Okay, hang on just a second and we'll pull back on that."

"Very well."

Jefferies typed a few keys on the keyboard. A new map appeared.

"Okay, here's a wider-angle map, and this will correspond to the footage we'll look at for the same time frame. Now we'll start with Commander McCormick's Passat right in the same place again, right up here on Fort Hunt Road, just in front of Wells Fargo Bank.

"The difference here is that we'll be able to see a wider range of activities outside of the frame of the first shot, because we've pulled back on the angle and we're taking in Bunker Hill Drive, a block to the south of Lafayette, and also more streets to the north and east."

Paul sipped his coffee. "Okay, let's switch over to the video and watch the show."

"Aye, Captain."

The screen again morphed into the aerial photograph, displaying Caroline's car moving south in front of the bank.

But Paul wasn't so interested in Caroline's car. Instead, he focused on Ross Simmons's condo.

Just as Caroline's car turned right onto Lafayette, a figure emerged from the back of Simmons's house. The figure held something in his arms and started running, straight through the backyard and into an adjacent backyard.

"Do you see that, Jefferies?"

"I see him, sir!"

The figure—it looked like a man—ran past another house and emerged on the street behind Lafayette.

"Here's over on Bunker Hill," Paul said.

"What's he doing?"

"Look. He's setting that object on the hood of that red car."

"He's opening the door," Jefferies said.

"Yep. And he's putting that object in the backseat. Looks like a computer."

"I think you're right, sir. He's getting in the driver's side."

"Okay, now he's pulling out. Heading down Bunker Hill. Turning right. What's that street?"

"I think it's Wellington, sir."

"We lost him. Can we get a wider angle?"

"I'm afraid that's it, sir. We kept the drone over Lieutenant Simmons's condo."

Paul looked at Jefferies. "We just saw the killer, John. If we can just identify him and figure out where he is."

"Agreed, sir. But it's a step in the right direction. At least we've got an idea of what he's driving."

"That's a fact. Good work. I'll call Special Agent Romanov over at NCIS. Let's see if we can track this sucker down."

CHAPTER 35

· · ·

The narrow, dimly lit sports bar paid a historical tribute to the glory days of Georgetown basketball. Large black-and-white photos of the great John Thompson, the huge bear of a man with his trademark white towel wrapped around his neck. Photos of all the Georgetown greats of yesteryear, in uniform, adorned the walls. Patrick Ewing. Alonzo Mourning. Allen Iverson. Dikembe Mutombo.

Almost empty, the bar at first carried the aura of a smoke-filled room, except smoking had been banned in DC bars for years.

It was a place frozen in time, even in its music. The golden voice of Elvis softly caressing "Love Me Tender" would have little appeal to the mindless hip-hop generation of millennials interested in cacophonous rap.

Perhaps that explained why the place looked so empty.

"May I help you gentlemen?" The young hostess, a slim brunette, perhaps in her early twenties and wearing a navy blue Georgetown sweatshirt, approached them with a smile. She wore a name tag that read "Mindy."

"We're looking for a Mr. Romanov," Paul said.

"You mean Special Agent Romanov with NCIS?" The waitress smiled. "Agent Romanov and his friend are in the back."

"His friend?" Paul exchanged glances with Jefferies.

"I wanted to keep a tight lid on this, sir."

"Me too," Paul said. "I wasn't expecting a foursome."

"Would you like me to take you to them?"

"Sure." Paul turned to Jefferies. "I can always pull the plug on this if we need to."

"He's in the back. Right this way."

"Very well. Lead the way, miss."

The hostess led Paul and Jefferies to the back of the bar, where Mark Romanov sat in a booth with his back to the front of the bar. An attractive redheaded woman sat next to him.

"We're fine, John," Paul said. "She's a JAG officer. She's okay."

"Your guests are here, Agent Romanov."

Romanov turned and stood. "Good evening, Captain."

"Evening, Mark. Meet Commander John Jefferies, my XO at Drone Command and OIC at Pax River when I'm not around. I brought John because he knows how to run the computers, and I don't have time to get up to speed."

"A pleasure, Commander."

"You too, Agent Romanov."

"And, John," Paul said, looking at Jefferies, "I'd like you to meet Lieutenant Commander Victoria Fladager. She's at Code 13 along with Caroline McCormick. Victoria knows what's going on."

"Evening, sir," Victoria said.

"Commander." John nodded.

"Have a seat," Mark said. "You said it was urgent and you didn't want to go into detail over the phone."

"I think we have a break in the case."

"A break?" Romanov raised an eyebrow. "I'm all ears."

"Remember I told you that on the day of P.J. MacDonald's funeral, which was the same day as Ross Simmons's shooting, I had a drone in the air over the funeral?"

"Of course," Romanov said.

Paul glanced at Jefferies. "Well, we kept that drone in the air a little longer than the funeral. I was worried about Commander McCormick, and we kept the bird in the air and followed her all the way to Lieutenant Simmons's house."

A pause. "You have my attention, Captain."

"John," Paul said, "start the laptop. I want Romanov to see this."

"Aye, sir." Jefferies pulled out the laptop and positioned it so Mark and Victoria could both see it.

"Okay, Mark," Paul said. "We're going to start with an aerial clip of the last two minutes or so when Caroline was driving on Fort Hunt Road, toward Simmons's neighborhood. Pull the still shot up, John."

"Aye, sir."

"Okay, see? This is her car." Paul pointed to the screen. "But down here, in the lower left, is Simmons's condo. Now keep an eye on what happens."

"Okay."

"Roll it, John."

"Aye, Captain."

The car started moving south.

"Freeze it!" Paul said. "Look! See that guy coming out the back of Simmons's place?"

"Whoa," Mark said. "How'd you miss this before?"

"Because we were using a tighter angle and were only focusing on following Caroline's car. Now watch what he does. Roll it."

"Yes, sir."

"Okay, look!"

"He's making a run for it," Mark said. "What's he got?"

"The missing computer, I think," Paul said.

"Of course," Mark said. "Makes sense."

"Yep. Now watch what he does."

"He's headed to that red car," Mark said.

"Oh my gosh!" Paul said.

"What, Captain?"

"Freeze it, John."

"What?"

"Why didn't it hit me before?" Paul said.

"What, Captain?" Mark asked.

"That red Mercedes! I'm sure I've seen it before."

"Where?"

"In the parking lot!"

"What parking lot?"

"At la Madeleine. Sunday morning when we met there. Why didn't I put two and two together?"

"You saw the Mercedes in the parking lot?"

"I'm sure of it," Paul said. "I pulled into the parking lot, then got out of the car to get the door for Caroline. The Mercedes pulled in right beside us."

"Are you sure it's the same Mercedes, sir?"

Paul looked away. "Let me think." He gazed over at the large photograph of John Thompson. "Yes. An E-class. 350. I couldn't swear to it, but I know it in my gut."

The men looked at each other.

"Captain," Mark said, "you didn't happen to have one of those drones in the air this morning over either Commander McCormick's townhouse or the Pentagon, did you?"

Paul shook his head. "I wish I did. I was pushing it to justify an official training mission over Arlington the day of the funeral. And of course, as far as I'm concerned, it's legitimate to protect a United States naval officer."

Mark seemed to think. "Of course, you know if we turn this over to civilian law enforcement we run the risk of violating *posse comitatus*."

"How ironic," Paul mused. "The very issue these JAG officers like P.J. MacDonald were wrestling with, we may have already violated."

Commander Jefferies spoke up. "You mean using the military for civilian law enforcement?"

"It's a close line," Mark said. "That's the whole reason they want Homeland Security to operate these drones over civilian airspace. But right now, frankly, I'm more concerned about catching this monster than I am about *posse comitatus.*" He looked at Paul. "You know, I'm going to need her help again, and I'm going to need your help again."

Paul's stomach knotted. "Look, I'll be happy to help all I can. I'll even see about getting one of these drones up in the sky to support the operation, *posse comitatus* or no *posse comitatus.*" He looked Mark in the eye. "But can't we leave her out of it?"

Mark shook his head. "Captain, I know she's special to you. But if we don't get this guy, he might get her first."

Paul crossed his arms. "Look. Caroline's a real trooper. She has the mind of a JAG and the bravado of a Navy SEAL. But the difference is the SEALs get weapons, and we're asking her to put a target on her back like a sitting duck. There's only so much anyone can take. She only survived by the grace of God. She's so determined to trap this guy I'm just afraid she's going to get herself killed. I just wish there was another way."

Silence. "Maybe there is another way." Victoria spoke up.

Romanov looked at her. "What do you mean?"

"Captain." Victoria looked at Paul. "Can we keep Caroline in the hospital a few days?"

"Well, that's a medical decision. But as of today, I don't think Dr. Berman wants to cut her loose too soon because of that concussion, even tomorrow. She's stubborn and wanted to leave as soon as possible, but I think I could persuade Captain Guy to order her to follow doctor's orders."

"Do you have the keys to her townhouse and to her car?"

"No. But I took her purse to the hospital, and I think I could get the keys." Paul glanced at Mark, then at Victoria. "Why do you ask?"

Victoria grinned. Her green eyes sparkled. "You know, I wasn't always a redhead."

Mark responded, "I'm not sure I follow you."

"You do know that I was once a blonde, don't you?"

Mark raised his eyebrow. "Are you saying what I think you're saying?"

"How about this?" Victoria glanced at Mark, then at Paul. "Mark, how about if we plant a press release that Caroline has been released from the hospital, that she's safely home, and that she will be reporting for duty tomorrow morning. I can go home tonight . . . In fact, Captain, if you can get me into Caroline's place tonight, I can come out her door as a blonde in the morning, and we can get that drone in the air and see if this maggot falls for the bait."

The men exchanged glances.

Mark spoke up. "You want to play the role of Caroline?"

"Caroline's not in any kind of condition to be out there right now, and if she's willing to put her neck on the line, then so am I. P.J. was my friend too. We all want to know who killed him, and Ross." She looked straight into Mark's eyes with a steely determination that reminded Paul of Caroline. "Can you make it happen, Mark?"

Mark stared at her for a second, his face expressionless. "You really want to do this, don't you?"

She met his stare. "Mark, you know me. I've had two of my shipmates at Code 13 murdered, and a third who was almost killed." She paused. "I'm a naval officer, and this is my duty. This is personal."

Silence.

Paul spoke up. "I think she means it, Mark."

"Of course she means it," Mark said. "I've known her a long time. Okay. If it means that much to you, I can make it happen." He looked at Paul. "Captain, if you can get over to the hospital and get Caroline's keys and then get Victoria over to her townhouse tonight, I can get that story planted tonight. And of course we'll need drones in the air in the morning." He took a swig of beer. "We'll need to coordinate real-time communication between me and Pax River. If that sucker takes the bait, NCIS will be ready."

Paul nodded, grateful that Victoria had stepped up to the plate, and grateful that Caroline might be spared, at least for another day. "Sounds like we've got some work to do."

"Gentlemen, there is one thing," Victoria said.

"What is it?" Mark said.

"I hate to put any kind of a spoiler on this, but you know if this gets out, they may accuse us of violating *posse comitatus*, don't you?"

They all looked at one another.

"Look, it's okay if you change your mind," Mark said. "We understand. This will be a dangerous operation. Nobody's asking this of you."

"You misread me, Mark. I want to do this. Bad. But I wanted to put that bug in your ear in case I don't survive this mission. If they say we illegally used military assets for a civilian law enforcement exercise, your response has to be this: First, we didn't get civilians involved. This was solely an operation between the Navy and NCIS. Tell them you were given an opinion . . . As a matter of fact, I'm going to record my advice to you right now just in case." She pulled out her iPhone and began to speak into it.

"Therefore, I have advised these gentlemen that the operation planned is legally executable under *posse comitatus* solely as a military exercise to protect military personnel from attack, presumably by an enemy of the United States. It is not being executed as a civilian law enforcement exercise. Very respectfully, Victoria Fladager, Lieutenant, Judge Advocate General's Corps, United States Naval Reserve."

She stopped, punched a few buttons on her phone, and looked up. "There. I've emailed my recording to each one of you. If something goes wrong, take it to Captain Guy at Code 13."

The men glanced at one another. "Your courage is amazing, Victoria," Paul said.

"Thank you, sir, but it's not a matter of courage." Her dazzling green eyes flashed his way. "It's a matter of doing the right thing. I have to do this."

The pause gave Paul a second to reflect on the bravery shown by this young officer.

"Let's make it happen," Mark said. "Victoria, maybe you should go with the captain. I've got to contact Navy Public Affairs to get this press release out, and I need to coordinate with Captain Guy."

"That okay, Captain?" Victoria asked.

"Glad to have you," Paul said. "You are a courageous woman."

• • •

Victoria sat alone in thought in the backseat of the staff car. Captain Kriete and Commander Jefferies had headed up to Caroline's hospital room to try to get her keys.

She had declined to join them, on the theory that her presence in the room, if Caroline was awake, would slow them down even more. Time wasn't something they could waste.

She ticked off the things she needed to do to prepare. If they could get Caroline's keys, she would need to have the captain stop by her house to get her uniforms and other personal items. Then she would need to stop by Walgreens or Giant Food and purchase a box of hair color.

She had sworn to herself that she would never go blonde again. Mark had never seen her as a blonde, and it appeared now, if Caroline McCormick were any example, that P.J. preferred blondes.

A wave of guilt washed over her for even thinking the thought. Yes, she had experienced a foolish, silly, cat-like jealousy when Caroline arrived on the scene at Code 13. She had wanted to put her claws in the woman and scratch her face and stow her on the first plane back to California.

But truthfully, in just a few short days, she had come to admire the woman in ways never imagined. Her courage. Her commitment. Her patriotism. Her love for the Navy. The way she had carried herself with a serene sense of sublime dignity at P.J.'s funeral, even though deep down, Victoria knew, Caroline's heart was being ripped out.

No wonder P.J. saw something in her.

But P.J. was gone, and in the bittersweet aftermath, a new and strong resolve had descended over the officers at Code 13.

In a strange way, Victoria and Caroline had already become friends, baptized in a sudden and unexpected fire of love, petty jealousy, death, sorrow, fear, anger, patriotism, and unwavering determination.

Why was Victoria's life traveling at the speed of light?

She heard two electronic beeps, saw the car's headlights flash, then looked up and saw Captain Kriete and Commander Jefferies approaching.

The doors unlocked. The front doors opened.

"Any luck, sir?" she asked as each of the senior officers got into the front seat.

"Like taking candy from a baby," Captain Kriete said. "She just nodded her head and pointed to her purse. The nurse said she was drugged up for pain, and Dr. Berman came in when we were leaving the room and said they're going to hold her at least another day. So we've got a little bit of working room before she's up and causing trouble for us."

"But not much time," Victoria said.

The captain started the car, and as he began to drive through the hospital parking lot, his cell phone rang.

"It's Mark Romanov," he said. "Hang on. I'll put him on speaker." The dial tone blared twice over the Bluetooth as Kriete hit the Answer button. "Mark, I'm with Jefferies and Lieutenant Fladager. What have you got?"

"It's on, Captain." Mark's voice filled the inside of the car. "Navy Public Affairs just called me back. Starting at the top of the hour, Fox, CNN, and other outlets will be going with our press release."

"Excellent," Captain Kriete said. "We're coming up on two minutes to the top of the hour right now. Let me flip on Fox Satellite Radio and see if they run it."

"Good enough, Captain. Call me back if you don't hear it."

"Roger that."

The *click, click, click* of the signal light broke the silence as the car came to a halt approaching Rockville Pike Road.

Captain Kriete turned on the satellite radio just as the car swung out onto the pike.

"And now, this is a breaking Fox News alert from Washington. The U.S. Navy has just issued a press release concerning the status of the naval officer who was the victim of an attempted shooting this morning at the Pentagon. According to Pentagon spokesman Rear Admiral Kirk Foster, the officer, Lieutenant Commander Caroline McCormick, sustained only minor injuries and was treated and released earlier today. Commander McCormick has returned home and is expected to return to her duties tomorrow.

"Still no word on the identity or the motive of the shooter, and the Department of Defense is cooperating with local law enforcement in an ongoing investigation. So good news from the Pentagon that the officer injured in a shooting attempt earlier has been released and is expected to report to her duty station tomorrow. And now back to our regular programming."

Captain Kriete reached down and turned off the radio.

Silence followed as the car moved down the road.

"Well, I guess when Mark Romanov says he's going to deliver, he delivers," Captain Kriete said.

"Sounds like it's game on, sir," Jefferies said.

"Okay, Captain, if you can swing me by the drugstore to pick up some items, and then by my apartment to get my things, I'll just borrow Caroline's keys and become the next Caroline McCormick."

"Sounds like a deal," Paul said.

CHAPTER 36

• • •

LIEUTENANT COMMANDER CAROLINE MCCORMICK'S TOWNHOUSE
NEAR THE INTERSECTION OF HUNTSMAN AND SYDENSTRICKER ROADS
OXFORD HUNT
WEST SPRINGFIELD, VIRGINIA
TUESDAY EVENING

Victoria, her locks now having been transformed from auburn to blonde, sat alone on a simple sofa in a strange townhouse that she had never seen before.

It wasn't that the townhouse looked strange in appearance. Nothing about the color scheme, artwork, or furniture selection proved odd. Under different circumstances the place might have seemed homey.

The strange sensation, rather, was driven by the surrealistic realization that she was in another officer's home, without the officer's knowledge or permission, on the very day the other officer had a brush with death from an assassin's bullet. Now she was about to disguise herself as the other officer, possibly taking the assassin's bullet herself, to try to trap the worthless animal who had declared open season on JAG officers.

The imminent danger she would soon face should have been at the forefront of her mind, considering what had happened to three of her colleagues at Code 13 over the past few days. Two had been murdered and a third shot.

She should have been shaking. She should want to puke. For tomorrow morning there loomed the strong possibility she would meet the same fate as P.J. MacDonald and Ross Simmons.

Still, all she could feel was numbness. Her numbness was driven by a strange irony.

The poet Robert Frost once said, "The afternoon knows what the morning never suspected."

And what would the morning bring?

She got up from the sofa and went to the living room mirror. She stared curiously at herself with blonde locks now draping over her shoulders. The redness in her eyes from crying over the death of her two friends, and especially over P.J., whom she had hoped to know better, made her look like a hapless drunk coming off an all-night drinking binge.

She mouthed the words of the poet. "'The afternoon knows what the morning never suspected.'"

The words haunted her. For she feared, in the deep recesses of her soul, that she might never see another afternoon.

She would see the morning. That she knew. She would step out the doors of this townhouse and see if the animal had taken the bait. And if he took the bait, she could only hope and pray that Mark Romanov and his NCIS agents would spring the trap and break the rat's neck before her own skull exploded under the destructive force of a high-powered sniper's bullet.

Sitting alone, with a deep foreboding that this might be her last night on the face of the earth, she bowed her head and began to pray.

"Lord, it's been awhile since I prayed. I've not always acted as I should. I've been selfish, conceited. You've given me so many gifts and abilities. But too often I've used those gifts for my selfish ends.

"And now, with all this death, with all this senseless murder, it's like you've brought me face-to-face with my own mortality.

"Lord, I don't want to die. But yet, I want my life to mean something. Maybe someone is telling me to do this. To lay down my life for a greater cause.

"Lord, I should be scared. But somehow, I'm not. Maybe that's you." She wiped a solitary tear. "I feel sad that I've accomplished so little in my life.

"Whether I live or die, let this last act make a difference. Help us catch whoever is doing this and bring him to justice. And if you do take me, then please, tomorrow, bring me to rest in your arms, now and forever. In Jesus' name, I pray."

She set her alarm for 5:00 a.m., lay down on Caroline's sofa, and closed her eyes.

CHAPTER 37

. . .

Commander John Jefferies, operating on perhaps two hours of sleep, stood in the command center of the U.S. Navy Drone Command and sipped his black coffee. He was staring up at the center screen, which at the moment displayed a live-feed aerial view of the predawn suburban sprawl of Springfield, Virginia, about fifty-five miles by the flight of the drone to the northwest.

Jefferies knew they were all taking a chance of facing both legal and political blowback by flying this mission. He sipped more coffee and thought about that.

Not that the mission itself was the problem. Right now the command had only a handful of drones and a virtually unlimited budget for training missions in all kinds of conditions, including predawn hours as it was at present.

The problem was that this mission wasn't just a training mission. It was hands-on operational. And if the cat got out of the bag, it could be misconstrued as military interference in a civilian law enforcement operation, thus violating *posse comitatus*.

Personally, John felt satisfied with Victoria Fladager's legal explanation and defense, that by keeping civilians out of the loop, it remained a military operation only.

But what if the shooter wasn't a foreign national or member of a terrorist group? What if he or she turned out to be a U.S. citizen?

Wouldn't that make this a military operation to capture a civilian?

Maybe.

Maybe not.

Either way, John believed in his new boss, Captain Paul Kriete, who presented a confident, patriotic demeanor that would make any red-blooded patriot want to follow him. And if Lieutenant Victoria Fladager had bravely volunteered to put her neck on the line for the sake of stopping these attacks on naval officers, John Jefferies could at least put his career on the line. Even if Kriete had promised to step up and take all the heat, John Jefferies would stand with him on this.

"Hopefully we'll be able to see a little better in a few, sir," remarked the lieutenant serving as remote pilot of Navy Drone Flight 241. "Only fifteen minutes till sunrise."

"How much longer until we're in position over the target residence?" John took another swig of coffee and checked his watch. By "target residence" he meant, of course, the residence of Lieutenant Commander McCormick, where the morning aerial surveillance of Lieutenant Fladager would begin.

Unfortunately, even with all the advances in drone technology over the years, it was still difficult for a drone to see much in the dark, unless, like any aircraft, it was firing a bright spotlight down onto the ground. Part of the problem with firing a spotlight onto the ground was that the drone's position would be revealed, which would defeat the whole point of operating in the skies in relative obscurity.

"Two more minutes, sir. We'll go into orbit at one thousand and keep her there until the sun comes up or for as long as it takes. If anything moves down there, we'll see it."

"Very well." Jefferies took his last swig of coffee. "Steady as she goes."

"Aye, sir."

• • •

WALTER REED NATIONAL MEDICAL CENTER
BETHESDA, MARYLAND
5:45 A.M.

"P.J.!" Caroline sat up in bed, her eyes wide open, her heart pounding like a battering ram inside her chest. He had been there. She knew it.

"Victoria! Help her! Where am I?"

"Are you okay, Commander?" A Navy nurse rushed into her room.

"Yes, I . . ."

"It sounds like you were just having a bad dream."

"I . . . Somebody's going to get killed. I know it."

"You've been through a lot, Commander. Let me get you something to help you rest."

"No! Victoria! I've got a bad feeling."

"You're going to be fine, ma'am. You're suffering from a little post-traumatic shock."

A sharp pinching stung her upper arm. Caroline looked over at another nurse injecting medication through a syringe.

"Please relax, ma'am. Dr. Berman will be here in a few hours and he'll talk to you. We're here for you."

The hospital room started spinning, and she felt a foreboding desperation to stop it. "Please, someone warn her . . . please . . ."

She felt her head hit the pillow.

Darkness overcame her as she slipped from consciousness.

• • •

OUTSIDE LIEUTENANT COMMANDER CAROLINE MCCORMICK'S TOWNHOUSE
NEAR THE INTERSECTION OF HUNTSMAN AND SYDENSTRICKER ROADS
OXFORD HUNT
WEST SPRINGFIELD, VIRGINIA
5:52 A.M.

Mark sat behind the wheel of his government-issued Taurus and watched Caroline McCormick's home.

At a distance of a hundred yards or so, he would hopefully blend into the graying dawn, a gray lizard along the sidewalk, all in the hopes of not spooking the shooter, if this was the morning the shooter would take the bait, if the shooter were ever to take the bait.

Mark brought the Red Bull to his lips and took a swig. The caffeine jolted him immediately. Not that he needed the jolt. His adrenaline had been in orbit all night, since Captain Kriete had shown him the inadvertently captured aerial shot of the killer fleeing Simmons's condo.

Mark had studied the great heroes of law enforcement of all time. Wyatt Earp. J. Edgar Hoover.

But the greatest of them all, the hero Mark aspired to be like, was the greatest sharpshooter in the history of the FBI, a twentieth-century agent named D. A. "Jelly" Bryce.

Born in Oklahoma in 1906, Jelly Bryce became an FBI legend, drawing his gun faster than anybody on the planet and shooting with greater accuracy than anybody in the universe.

Wielding a long-barreled .357 magnum, Bryce had by 1945 gunned down at least ten bad guys in face-to-face gunfights and made the cover of *LIFE Magazine*. By the time he retired in 1958, Bryce's larger-than-life legend made him the envy of lawmen all over the country. If there were a Mount Rushmore for federal agents, Jelly would dominate the jutting granite on the far left, the position held by George Washington on the mountainous wall of presidents.

What had made Jelly Bryce such an unstoppable force?

Mark had considered this many times and had come to one inescapable conclusion.

Ultimately, though it was not a politically correct thing to say, a great lawman, at the end of the day and like a deer hunter tracking his prey, had to enjoy killing.

Killing.

Not the innocent, but the guilty.

The willingness to kill, and the necessary enjoyment of killing that fueled that willingness, separated a mediocre federal agent—and most were mediocre—from a great agent. Few were great.

Mark knew he had to embrace killing, in a controlled manner, in a limited manner, to become a great lawman. And he would do just that.

Mark looked at the long-barreled .357 revolver that sat on the passenger seat. Ah, yes. He had purchased it years ago on the street, for cash, from a witness who needed money. The serial number had long since been removed, making the gun virtually untraceable. And though he rarely fired it, he kept it with him, as both a reminder and an inspiration of the career of the great Jelly Bryce.

If he could pull this operation off, he would be positioned to fleet up from the NCIS to the FBI, achieving his lifelong dream. Once that happened, Victoria would take notice—that is, if she survived today—that as an FBI agent, he would have matched, if not surpassed, the professional status of the great P.J. MacDonald.

Yes, she would notice. He would make sure she noticed.

Enough reminiscing.

He needed to nail this guy. For a number of reasons. With him, and parked at triangulating positions around the neighborhood, were six other NCIS agents in three unmarked cars. One sat parked on Sydenstricker. Two others were parked on Oxford Hunt.

He would lead this operation, and the new agents hiring committee at the Justice Department would take notice.

"Task Force Leader. Drone Control." The radio message from Pax River broke his thoughts.

"Drone Control. Tango Foxtrot Leader. Go ahead."

"Task Force Leader. Be advised. Bird is on station. Waiting for the sun."

"Drone Control. Roger that. Bird is on station. You are our eyes."

"Task Force Leader. Roger that. We'll keep you posted. Drone Control out."

"Roger that. Task force out. Task Force Leader to all units. Acknowledge receipt of transmission from Drone Control."

"Task Force One. On station. Copy Drone Control. Ready to execute."

"Task Force Two. Also on station. Copy Drone Control. Ready to execute."

"Task Force Three. Copy that, sir."

"Very well. Stand by for further instructions. Leader out."

• • •

UNIDENTIFIED TOWNHOUSE
NEAR LIEUTENANT COMMANDER CAROLINE MCCORMICK'S TOWNHOUSE
NEAR THE INTERSECTION OF HUNTSMAN AND SYDENSTRICKER ROADS
OXFORD HUNT
WEST SPRINGFIELD, VIRGINIA
5:55 A.M.

Following the illuminated beam of the flashlight, the shooter stepped into the upstairs master bedroom for one last check before going downstairs. He wanted to double-check, to make sure they were fully dead. No point in risking faint breathing or a faint pulse.

He always double-checked, even when there was no doubt.

Quickly he swept the flashlight around the room.

The bed was a bloody mess, unfortunately, but the bullet hole through the skull of the man was clean.

Not so much for his poor wife.

Why did some heads seem to explode under the force of a bullet, while others endured the shot, revealing only a small hole, thus keeping bleeding to a more minimal level?

Heads, he had learned long ago, were like watermelons. Some punctured cleanly. Others burst like big watermelons splatting on concrete.

What a messy profession this could be.

He stepped out of the master bedroom and down the hallway, sweeping the flashlight into the first bedroom to the right.

The girl looked to be only about thirteen years old. Fortunately, her body remained intact. No one in the family ever knew what hit them. Sometimes he felt bad about doing what he had to do when such collateral damage was involved. But business was business. And war was war.

He headed back down the stairs to the lower floors from where he would commence his operation. The security on these dime-a-dozen townhouses was a joke, to the point that any amateur criminal could get in at any time by taking a screwdriver to the French doors on the back patio.

Of course, amateurs often set off the Dollar General–quality alarm systems the public thought would keep them safe. But most left-wingers, especially in Northern Virginia and all parts north up to Maine, being anti-gun for the most part, chose to remain unarmed. Like foolish sheep would remain defenseless against the slaughter. Thus, an activated burglar alarm simply alerted the police to come clean up the mess in the aftermath.

By contrast, professionals knew how to deactivate these pesky alarms in about five seconds, which he had decided to do—that is, to deactivate the alarm—because he needed to borrow these good people's home for a little while during the dark of night.

He had considered entering Caroline McCormick's townhouse through the back, while she slept, like he had here, popping a few rounds in her head, letting the police clean up the mess whenever they found her, and proclaiming to his superiors that his mission was accomplished.

But he was no fool.

He knew they had placed NCIS around her and that, in light of his first failed attempt, they would tighten the security noose. He could deal with NCIS, if need be. But they were more formidable than local law enforcement, and no point in getting too messy if it wasn't necessary to make a mess.

Of course, the fact that they would offer at least a semblance of protection energized him like electricity surging through a power grid.

Like a hunter chasing deer through the woods, killing was always amplified by the excitement of a challenge—and even more so by the excitement of danger—which would be posed by the FBI wannabe agents of the NCIS.

A professional always operated using the element of surprise.

The element of surprise ensured victory 99 percent of the time.

He was a professional. And they would be looking for him.

He would not make the same mistakes he had made last time.

He would not be spotted.

How foolish of the Navy to continue pressing this issue.

He may have missed the last time, but he would not miss this time.

He crept into the dark living room, pushed the curtains aside, and looked out the window. Across the street and five doors down, the light burned on the front stoop of Caroline McCormick's townhouse.

When news of the assassination hit the media later in the day, some would call it a "drive-by shooting." But in reality, this would be a planned execution.

This time his handiwork would result in a cold-blooded kill.

And the Navy would cooperate, or every officer who touched this project would meet a similar fate.

They had been warned, but they failed to realize who they were playing with.

Soon they would face, once again, the bloody consequences of their defiance.

• • •

LIEUTENANT COMMANDER CAROLINE McCORMICK'S TOWNHOUSE
WEST SPRINGFIELD, VIRGINIA
6:37 A.M.

The sun had risen forty minutes ago, and the bustle and activity of an early-morning commute began stirring this middle-class Fairfax County community just ten miles from the Pentagon.

Victoria stepped in front of the mirror in Caroline's living room for a final inspection of her summer dress white uniform.

The uniform looked sharp, so sharp, in fact, that she felt a wave of guilt for thinking that P.J. would have liked it. She adjusted the green-and-white Navy Commendation medal that she received in Norfolk and reminded herself that P.J. was never hers and that, despite their rather electric rendezvous at the Grape + Bean, P.J. had always been Caroline's.

Enough thinking about P.J.

Her father had gone to West Point, and though he feigned disappointment when she chose the Navy over the Army, he had reminded her on the day of her commission of the same creed that he had reminded her of a thousand times as a little girl.

"Duty. Honor. Country."

Now, for the first time, in the midst of so much death, turmoil, and uncertainty, she had finally come to the sudden, unexpected understanding of what her father, Colonel Stephen Fladager, had meant in the thousand times he had uttered those three words.

And now, duty called.

She checked the gold belt buckle of the white twill belt that held up her white skirt.

The sharp attractiveness of the white uniform had led her to the Navy over the Army. *"That's a silly reason to pick one branch over the other,"* her father had chided her.

He was right. He was always right. *But you're your own woman,* he also said. And he was right about that too.

Here, in this surrealistic moment, she had now become her own woman, having made a life-or-death decision that most women and most men would never have to make, and wishing that it were winter so she could wear her service dress blue winter uniform. The blue uniform, it occurred to her, wouldn't show her blood so badly as the white. And if she were going to take a bullet to stop this animal, she didn't want to give the animal the satisfaction of so easily seeing the blood that she was about to spill on behalf of her country.

She turned away from the mirror and picked up the earpiece communications device that Mark had given her.

"We'll be able to communicate with you when we see this guy," Mark had told her. "It'll help us keep you safe."

"The best-laid plans of mice and men," she mumbled aloud. She slid the two white earbuds in her ears, draped the small white cord down to a white communications box about the size of a man's wallet, and clipped it to her white belt.

"The white color will camouflage the communications device

so the shooter won't be able to see that you're wired," Mark had assured her.

She reached down and pressed the Talk button. "Testing. Testing. This is Lieutenant Fladager. Does anyone copy?"

Static buzzed in her ears.

Then, "Lieutenant, Drone Control at Pax River. Copy loud and clear. We've got a drone circling at one thousand feet over the townhouse. So far the coast is clear. Looks safe from here."

"Victoria, this is Mark. We've got four NCIS units in the area. The coast is clear, whenever you want to come out."

"Okay, that's good to know." A sick feeling weighed on her stomach. "I'm about to open the front door now."

"Roger that. We're watching for you."

"Okay. I'm opening the door."

She unlocked the deadbolt, then turned the knob and stepped out into the morning sunlight onto the front stoop. Why had their assurances that the coast was clear not soothed her stomach?

She put on her sunglasses and looked overhead to see if she could spot the drone.

Nothing there.

She reached for the keys Captain Kriete had given her for Caroline's townhouse. She fiddled with them, inserting the front door key into the lock.

• • •

UNIDENTIFIED TOWNHOUSE
NEAR LIEUTENANT COMMANDER CAROLINE MCCORMICK'S TOWNHOUSE
WEST SPRINGFIELD, VIRGINIA
6:38 A.M.

Peering through the garage door window, the shooter felt his heart racing faster than a lightning bolt exploding from a raging thundercloud.

With a jolt of adrenaline seizing his body, he punched the garage door opener, and as it raised the door, he worked the action on his

9-millimeter pistol, jumped into the driver's side of the Mercedes, and cranked the engine.

• • •

OPERATIONAL HEADQUARTERS
U.S. NAVY DRONE COMMAND
U.S. NAVAL AIR STATION "PAX RIVER"
LEXINGTON PARK, MARYLAND
6:38 A.M.

"Sir, we've got a red Mercedes pulling out of a townhouse down the street!"

"What the—" Commander John Jefferies looked at the screen. "All units! Red Mercedes approaching at point-blank range! Repeat! Red Mercedes approaching at point-blank range! Victoria! Hit the deck!"

• • •

SPECIAL AGENT MARK ROMANOV'S CAR
NEAR LIEUTENANT COMMANDER CAROLINE MCCORMICK'S TOWNHOUSE
NEAR THE INTERSECTION OF HUNTSMAN AND SYDENSTRICKER ROADS
OXFORD HUNT
6:38 A.M.

"What the heck!" Mark watched the Mercedes drive by his car just as Drone Command announced it. He cranked his car and hit the accelerator.

Just ahead, a hand and gun emerged from the Mercedes, taking aim at Victoria.

"Shots fired! Victoria's down!" Mark yelled, then cursed. He pulled out his 9-millimeter and fired at the taillights of the Mercedes.

Like a fighter pilot hitting the afterburners, the driver of the red Mercedes gunned his accelerator, opening the distance between the Mercedes and Mark's car.

"I'm in pursuit. All units follow that Mercedes. Drone Control! Call an ambulance for Victoria!"

"Drone Control. Roger that."

Mark ramped up his speed. "I've lost him! Where'd he go?"

"Task Force Leader. Drone Control. He's turned northwest onto Sydenstricker, sir."

"Roger that. I'm turning onto Sydenstricker in pursuit. What's going on with Lieutenant Fladager?"

"Task Force Leader. We've lost communication with Lieutenant Fladager. Her transmitter is off. Do you want me to break the drone off the target vehicle and circle the drone back around to check on her?"

Mark slammed his fist against the center console and swung the Taurus onto Sydenstricker Road. "That's a negative. Stay on that Mercedes. But call an ambulance for the lieutenant."

"Roger that. Already done. We'll keep the bird over the Mercedes. Be careful down there, Agent Romanov." Static. "Okay, update. The Mercedes is turning right on Huntsman."

"Copy that. Turning right on Huntsman," Mark said. "All units, report."

"Task Force One. Copy, sir. I'm just ahead of you. Turning right on Huntsman."

"Task Force Two. Following One onto Huntsman."

"Task Force Three. Right behind you, sir."

"Task Force Leader. Drone Control. He's turning right onto Old Keene Mill Road."

Mark cursed again. "Probably headed to 95."

"Task Force One. I'm on him, boss. Turning onto Old Keene Mill."

"Stay on his tail. I'm right behind you."

• • •

THE PENTAGON
SOUTH PARKING LOT
6:48 A.M.

The morning sun had already started to blanket the Pentagon parking lot as Captain Paul Kriete pulled into his reserved parking space. He had gotten no sleep all night. His mind had been consumed with the risky operation he had authorized using one of Drone Command's experimental drones and, frankly, with the safety of Caroline McCormick.

Paul reached down and turned up the volume on the closed-frequency military radio receiver. He didn't have two-way radio capability so as to avoid interfering with the NCIS radio traffic, and to avoid any charges that he was working in the law enforcement action. But as commander of Navy Drone Command, he wanted to keep track of the radio traffic, given that one of his drones was providing crucial air cover for the operation. So he had taken a receiver unit to monitor the radio traffic.

"Drone Control to all units! He's turning onto I-495 East!"

"All units. Drone Control. He's merging from 495 to I-395. He's in the HOV lane! Looks like he's headed toward the District!"

"Drone Control. Task Force Leader. I still don't see him. I'm a couple of minutes behind. Stay on him."

"Task Force Leader. Roger that."

Paul turned down the volume and calculated his position. If the Mercedes remained north on I-395, it would be passing the Pentagon in approximately three minutes.

He checked his watch, then glanced back over his shoulder at the Washington Monument, its marble and granite visage reflecting the orange glow of the morning sun.

Next he looked in his phone for the number for Commander Charlie Wong, his XO working under him at the Pentagon, then hit the speed dial.

"Navy Drone Command. Pentagon headquarters. Commander Wong speaking."

"Charlie. Captain Kriete."

"Morning, sir. How may I be of assistance to you?"

"Listen, Charlie. I need to be working on a project with Pax River today. If the admiral needs me, I'll be available by phone. Otherwise, don't expect me in."

"Roger that, sir. We'll hold down the fort for you."

"Thanks, Charlie."

Paul reached into the glove compartment and pulled out his service weapon, a 9-millimeter Beretta pistol that many Navy and Marine Corps officers elected to use.

He popped open the empty magazine and reached for a brick of bullets, also in the console, and began loading bullets into the magazine.

One.

Two.

Three.

• • •

I-395 NORTHBOUND
APPROACHING SHIRLINGTON ROAD EXIT
6:57 A.M.

Mark cursed just as he approached the Leesburg Pike exit. So far, by driving illegally in the HOV lanes at speeds of sixty to sixty-five miles per hour, he had been able to avoid much of the bumper-to-bumper crawl of the Washington rush hour.

But now intermittent brake lights had started to flash, even in the HOV lane.

The red Mercedes was nowhere in sight. In fact, neither Mark nor any of the other special agents in pursuit had seen it at all. They were totally dependent on their eye in the sky, the U.S. Navy drone.

"Drone Control. Task Force Leader. I've lost him. What've you got?"

"Task Force Leader. Drone Control. He's coming up on the South Glebe Road exit."

"Drone Control. Roger that." Mark cursed again. The Mercedes had opened distance on him.

That was part of the problem with working for a lower-level federal agency like NCIS. A Ford Taurus was hardly the vehicle suited for a high-speed chase into the District of Columbia.

The DOJ boys? Different animal. Those guys could drive anything they needed and match the bad guys horsepower for horsepower.

"Carraway. Frymier. Naylor. Report your positions."

"Task Force One." The voice of Special Agent Ralph Carraway. "We're behind you, sir. I'm at the Braddock Road intersection. Naylor and Frymier are behind me, around Seminary Road."

"Roger that. Stay on it."

"Task Force Leader. Drone Control. Subject vehicle is now approaching Arlington Cemetery and Pentagon exits. Stand by to see if he exits."

"Roger that, Drone Control. Let me know what he does."

Still dealing with slowing traffic, Mark looked down and punched up the live GPS depiction of the interstate half a mile or so ahead of him.

Where was this guy headed? Was he headed to the Pentagon parking lot? Possibly to open fire? Just like when he shot Caroline McCormick?

Or was he headed across the river into the District? Thank goodness the Virginia state police hadn't gotten involved in the chase, at least not yet. The last thing he needed was local interference.

"Task Force Leader! Drone Control. He's breaking off the right. Definitely headed across the bridge into the District."

"Drone Control. Roger that. Keep an eye on him." Mark tapped down on his brakes and blew the horn at the slower-moving car in front of him.

"Move, lady!"

• • •

THE PENTAGON
SOUTH PARKING LOT
7:04 A.M.

"That does it," Paul said to himself upon learning that the red Mercedes was now only a few hundred yards away from him and was about to break across the I-305 bridge into the District of Columbia.

He popped the loaded magazine of ammunition into his pistol, closed the gun up in his glove compartment, and wheeled out of his Pentagon parking space.

The driver of that Mercedes was probably the same guy who tried to kill Caroline. And for Paul, that made it personal.

DC had some of the strictest handgun laws in the country, so hopefully he wouldn't get pulled over once he crossed the bridge. But then again, those ridiculous laws clearly violated the Second Amendment, and DC handgun laws or not, Paul wasn't about to let Caroline's attempted killer get away.

He wheeled out of the parking lot and onto the on-ramp for I-395 North.

Now there was no turning back.

He would do this for his fellow naval officers who had been murdered.

He would do this for Caroline.

He would do this for his country.

• • •

SOUTHEAST WASHINGTON
I-695
NEAR WASHINGTON NATIONALS PARK
7:25 A.M.

"Drone Control. All units. He's pulled off I-695 and he's headed down First toward Potomac Southeast. Looks like he's headed down toward the Anacostia River waterfront across from Nationals Park."

Paul wheeled into the exit for Nationals Stadium as the radio traffic continued between Drone Control and the four NCIS cars behind him.

As Paul's Suburban reached the bottom of the exit ramp onto South Capitol Street Southwest, Mark Romanov's voice broke the airways in response to John Jefferies at Drone Control.

"Drone Control. Task Force Leader. I'm just pulling onto 695 now, so I'm a few minutes behind. The other three units are behind me. Just stay on top of him."

"Roger that. Still watching him."

"Task Force Leader. Will do."

Paul slowed down when he reached Capitol Street Southwest, awaiting further directional instructions from Pax River.

"Task Force Leader. Drone Control. He's headed south on South Capitol Street Southwest. He's slowing down. He's passing the stadium on his left. He's . . . he's swinging around the stadium and turning a hard left on Potomac Avenue. Driving real slow, like he's looking for something."

Paul punched Nationals Stadium into the Suburban's GPS.

"Okay. He's making a hard left from Potomac to First. He's slowing down, turning into a warehouse on the right, near the intersection of Potomac Avenue and First Street Southeast. Stand by for the address."

"That does it," Paul said to himself. "I'm headed there."

"All units. Drone Control. Okay, that address is 1448 First Street Southeast. Right across from Nationals Stadium and down by the river. Stand by. Suspect is getting out of the car."

Paul cruised down South Capitol Street, hanging on to every word being spoken by his second in command, Commander John Jefferies, back at Pax River.

The red light at M Street forced him to bring the Suburban to a stop. He looked up into the skies, just over the Nationals Stadium in the direction of his front left bumper, and for the first time caught a glimpse of the blue Blue Jay drone that was allowing the good guys to track down this killer.

In a strange way, he felt a sense of pride that his command, his brand-new command that had caused so much internal controversy, that had in fact not even been born yet, was playing a role in something so good, so essential to justice and protection of the Navy.

At the same time, a sick feeling permeated his stomach over Victoria Fladager. The last report received from Drone Command was that she was down and all communication with her had been lost. Paul prayed silently in that moment that she had survived the shooting.

But something told him in his gut to expect the worst.

He also prayed that they would nail the animal who had rained murder and destruction on Code 13, the JAG Corps, and the Navy.

Apparently, now that animal had caged himself in a warehouse in a crime-infested area of Southeast Washington.

Who knew what they would find at the warehouse, now less than a mile away? Part of him wished the NCIS agents were out in front of him. They were the professionals, and he certainly wasn't going to lead the assault of that warehouse. But if this sucker tried getting away again, Paul was prepared to stop him.

"All units. Drone Control. Suspect has parked behind the warehouse. Three other cars are present. Car is not visible from the road. Suspect is now emerging from the vehicle. Suspect is a white male wearing a blue denim jacket, looks like brown and gray hair. Stand by . . ." A pause. "Suspect is walking toward back of warehouse. Okay, suspect has entered warehouse and has disappeared from our cameras. Will maintain coverage until NCIS units arrive. Over."

Slowly, Paul drove past Nationals Stadium on his left. Then a moment later made a hard turn back onto Potomac Avenue Southeast, with the Anacostia River now just a few yards off to his right.

The short section of Potomac Avenue ended at the outer perimeter of Nationals Stadium and then cut back to the left, going up First Street Southeast.

There.

On the right, just past the turn.

1448 First Street Southeast.

The warehouse had a plain brick front, stretching maybe fifty yards from left to right. A concrete driveway stretched from the street to the right of the warehouse, appearing to lead around back.

No sign of the red Mercedes. At least not from out front.

He thought about parking in front of the warehouse and waiting.

But if he was spotted, that might blow cover for the NCIS agents on the way.

He decided to drive down the street a couple of blocks and do a U-turn.

"Task Force Leader to all units. I'm turning onto Potomac. Stand by."

Thank God.

"Task Force Leader to all units. I'm turning on First. I've got the warehouse in sight. I'm pulling up now. Stagger in threes and draw weapons upon arrival."

"Unit one. Acknowledge instructions, sir."

"Unit two. Acknowledge instructions."

"Unit three. Roger that."

Paul executed a U-turn and headed back toward the warehouse just as the first government Ford Taurus pulled up on the curb in front of the warehouse. A second later, as two other Tauruses rounded the corner from Potomac to First, Mark Romanov jumped out of his car and pulled out his pistol, then ran over and knelt down on one knee, pointing his pistol straight across the hood of his car toward the warehouse.

With a bullhorn attached to his belt on his left hip, Romanov had stashed another gun, a silver revolver stuck in the back of his pants.

Paul pulled the Suburban up across the street from the warehouse and stopped. He reached into the glove compartment and pulled out the 9-millimeter.

Three more NCIS agents pulled up in their cars, got out, pointed their guns toward the warehouse, and crouched down low behind their cars. Guns still pointed, they mimicked the posture of Mark Romanov.

Paul recognized two of the men as Special Agents Carraway and Frymier, the two agents who were in the Pentagon parking lot the same morning the animal inside the warehouse shot Caroline.

He didn't recognize the third agent.

He decided at that moment, with Nationals Park behind him, that he would play the role of the center fielder in this operation, hanging back with his gun, and would intervene if the red Mercedes or its driver emerged from that warehouse.

Still crouched down, Romanov moved forward, away from his car, into the side driveway, and motioned the other agents to follow.

They disappeared behind the corner, and suddenly Paul remained out front alone.

He picked up the gun, worked the action, and waited.

• • •

WAREHOUSE
1448 FIRST STREET SE
WASHINGTON, DC (NEAR NATIONALS STADIUM)
7:45 A.M.

They moved single-file up the driveway beside the warehouse, hugging the brick wall to his left. Mark took the point, followed by Special Agents Carraway, Frymier, and Naylor.

His heart pounding in the morning sun, with the breeze from the river in his face, Mark felt electricity flowing in his arms and legs.

Moments like this separated the men from the boys. Great lawmen like Jelly Bryce lived for these moments.

He had entered that zone. At a time when he and his men were on the blood trail, closing in on a cold-blooded killer, knowing their lives were on the line, Mark was stone-cold fearless.

What he felt, instead, was a killer instinct. In fact, this killer instinct saturated him. Nothing compared to it. Not drugs. Not sex. When the instinct kicked in, only killing could saturate it.

He knew his destiny was greatness. For only a rare man could stare death in the face without blinking. Jelly Bryce was such a rare man, and Mark Romanov would follow in Bryce's footsteps.

In his gut, he hoped the animal would not surrender, that this would end in a gunfight.

Mark wanted to kill this guy—and to kill whatever other vermin were in the rat's nest. Not only for trying to kill Caroline, but also for embarrassing him personally by slipping by the NCIS detail.

Nobody would embarrass him like that and get away with it. And if he got even a sliver of opportunity, that's exactly what he would do to them—put an end to this once and for all.

Now was the time for leadership. And leadership he would show.

Motioning his three subordinate agents to stay down and behind him in single file, Romanov crouched to the corner edge of the brick wall.

Staying low, his head just a few inches off the concrete, he peered around the edge of the building, looking to his left. The red Mercedes sported a New York license plate and was parked between three black Mercedes, all with District of Columbia plates.

A cloud blocked the sun, and a shadow, along with a gust of wind, swept across the back parking area. The empty loading dock showed no signs of life. But a large open bay led into the back of the warehouse.

The assassin obviously had huddled inside the warehouse.

Now was the time to execute.

Mark unholstered his megaphone and held it up to his lips.

"Attention inside the warehouse. You are surrounded by federal agents. Come out of the warehouse with your hands up, and you will not be harmed."

No response.

Mark motioned Agents Carraway and Naylor to fan out along the driveway, in a position out parallel to him but still not in open view of the back of the warehouse.

He again brought the megaphone to his lips. "You! Inside the warehouse! Federal agents! We know you're in there! I'm giving you one more chance! Now come out with your hands up! This is your final warning!"

Mark checked his watch. He would wait thirty seconds, and that would be it. Fifteen seconds passed.

Twenty seconds.

Now twenty-five.

That was it.

"Okay! Move out!" Mark turned and pointed at Carraway, crouched off to his right about thirty feet. "Carraway, establish position behind that Mercedes."

Carraway responded with a thumbs-up, then took off running at a diagonal angle, across the parking area, toward the black Mercedes.

• • •

The sharp, single shot rang across the concrete, the sound filling the air.

His heart racing, Paul thought about jumping out and running up the driveway to provide additional cover for the NCIS agents. But that wasn't the smart approach, he decided. The one shot could have been fired by Mark Romanov or one of the NCIS agents.

Perhaps they had already nabbed the assassin.

Or maybe the shot had been fired against the good guys.

Either way, no one was escaping. Not on his watch.

He cranked the Suburban and pulled forward, parking it in front of the driveway, blocking any car that might try to escape from around the corner.

If someone charged out the driveway, the driver's seat would be the most vulnerable and dangerous position to be in, in the line of fire of any gunshots. He got out of the Suburban, gun in hand, and crouched behind the vehicle, his pistol aimed across the hood and at the warehouse.

• • •

Special Agent Carraway lay in the middle of the parking area, his face kissing the concrete, his stomach bleeding in a puddle. He squirmed in pain, moaning in agony.

Mark held the wrist-radio transmitter to his mouth.

"Gentlemen, I'm going after Carraway. I'm going to open fire into the warehouse as I approach him. I need you to move out and pour fire inside as I make my move. Got it?"

"Got it, sir."

"Roger that."

Mark put down the bullhorn and, with his gun aimed in front of him, cut diagonally in front of the open bay door, firing multiple shots into the warehouse as he approached Carraway.

Naylor and Frymier stepped out into the open, unloading seven shots into the warehouse as Mark grabbed Carraway under the arms and started dragging him back to the side of the warehouse.

Return fire from the warehouse!

The first bullet whizzed by Mark's head, which made him want to drop Carraway and kill the sucker who fired it.

A second shot rang out.

"Aaah!" Naylor yelled out. "It's okay. My upper arm. I'm okay."

Mark dragged Carraway over to the side of the building, out of the direct line of fire.

Carraway was conscious, but the bleeding had increased. He needed an ambulance, and fast.

Therein lay the predicament.

Calling an ambulance would mean the DC police would soon show up. Once that happened, they would want to take control. He would resist relinquishing control, and a jurisdictional tug-of-war would follow over who was in charge of this operation. It would be the same thing the Alexandria cops tried after the Ross Simmons shooting.

NCIS arrived on the scene first, investigating the shooting of a U.S. Naval officer, and then the local-yokel cops would show up like they owned the place.

The inevitable "Who's in charge here?" argument would compromise the mission and undermine everything Mark was trying to accomplish.

Of course, because some of the thugs inside weren't using silencers, the DC police would soon be responding to calls about the sound of gunfire anyway.

He needed to act fast, to finish this job while he still had total control.

"How can I help?"

Mark looked up. Captain Paul Kriete, wearing his summer white U.S. Navy uniform, stood there holding a pistol.

"Captain! What are you doing here?"

"Couldn't resist. How can I help?"

"Pull this man down toward the street and call an ambulance."

"Will do," Paul said.

"I've got to get back in the fight," Mark said.

"Roger that."

How to get these clowns out?

An idea struck him. He held up his wrist and again spoke into it. "Naylor. Frymier. Any sign of movement?"

"Negative."

"That's a negative, sir. It's dark in that warehouse."

"Okay, I'm going to get something out of the car. If you see any signs of movement coming out of there, take 'em out."

"Yes, sir."

"Yes, sir."

Mark sprinted down the driveway to the Taurus and popped open the trunk, barely noticing Paul Kriete kneeling over Agent Carraway at the end of the driveway.

He picked up a tear-gas canister and a gas mask, then sprinted back up the driveway and spoke into his wrist transmitter.

"Okay, guys. I'm gonna drop a gas canister in there. That should stir things up. Shoot if you get resistance. Acknowledge."

"Acknowledge, boss. Roger that."

"Okay. Here we go. Three . . . two . . . one." Mark pulled the pin on the gas canister and reached around and tossed it into the open bay area. A shot ricocheted near his hand.

He held the wrist transmitter to his mouth. "Stand by, gentlemen. Stay covered."

"Hey, boss. We got somebody coming out with his hands up."

Mark looked up to see a white male, perhaps in his late fifties, stagger out of a cloud of smoke. He was coughing and holding his hands over his head.

"Don't shoot!" the man pleaded.

"You!" Mark screamed, pointing his gun at the man's head. "Over here. Facedown on the concrete! Now!"

Still coughing, the man stumbled toward Mark.

"On your knees, now, or I'll blow out your brains!"

"I'm not armed!" The man dropped to his knees.

"Naylor!" Mark screamed, his gun barrel jammed into the man's forehead. "Get over here! Secure this scumbag!"

"Yes, sir."

Naylor, who had been ducked down behind one of the black Mercedes alongside Frymier, made a low dash back across the concrete, exposing himself to potential gunfire. He arrived and stood beside Mark, looking at the pathetic man kneeling on the concrete.

"Cuff his hands and tie his feet."

"Yes, sir."

"Romanov! Heads-up!"

Shots rang out.

Another man sprinted out of the warehouse, running down the driveway toward Captain Kriete, guns blazing, firing in every direction as he ran.

Another shot rang out.

The man fell face-first onto the concrete, his loose pistol bouncing on the driveway beside him. And when he fell, Kriete stood on the other side of him, locked in a classic shooter's stance, gun pointed straight out, aimed into the space the man had occupied half a second earlier.

"Good shooting, Captain!" Mark blurted, but he was instantly jealous that Paul Kriete, who was not even a federal agent, had scored the first kill in this operation.

In fact, maybe the operation was over.

Jets of anger flushed his body. Even if he had headed the operation, this wasn't the way he wanted it to end.

But then, glancing first at the man Kriete had just gunned down, then at the man cuffed on his knees, he had another thought.

"The shooter's still inside."

"What do you mean, boss?"

"Remember the pictures from the drone?"

"What about it?"

"The shooter has gray hair. The guy the captain took out is bald. This guy we just captured has black hair. That means the shooter is still unaccounted for."

"Good point." Frymier pointed his gun at the man in captivity, still on his knees, hands cuffed behind his back, his feet shackled by chains.

Mark stepped over the man and jammed his pistol barrel into his right temple. "Who else is in there?"

The scumbag coughed. "I ain't sayin' nothin' till I talk to my lawyer."

"You want to talk to a lawyer, do you?" Mark put his shoe on the man's head and kicked him over. The back of his head hit the concrete and he screamed in pain.

Mark kneeled down, put his knee on the man's skull, grinding it into the concrete, and jammed his gun into the man's ear.

"Look, scumbag. Here's the way this is going down. You charged me with your gun, and I had to put a bullet through your head in self-defense. It's gonna be hard to talk to your lawyer with a bullet in your head. Now, how many people are left in there, and where are they located?"

No response.

"Want to be that way, do you?" Mark stepped down onto the man's head, riveting the pressure on his skull.

"Okay! Okay!"

"How many, scumbag? And where are they located?"

"Okay. One left. He's probably in the office."

"What's his name?"

No response.

Mark stepped on the man's head again. "I said, *what's his name?*"

"Mr. T.! We call him Mr. T.!"

"Where's the office?"

"Go through the garage. Through the door on the right. Down the hallway. Third door on the left. You'll find him there."

"Anybody else in there?"

"No! Just him."

"You'd better not be lying to me. Because if you're lying, your brains are scrambled eggs!" He jammed the gun barrel into the man's mouth. "Got it?"

"I ain't lying!"

"Watch him, Frymier. I'm going after that guy. If this one gives you any trouble, take him out."

"With pleasure, boss."

Mark strapped a gas mask over his face and moved toward the open bay of the warehouse.

Gun drawn, he stepped inside.

The tear gas was dissipating but not totally gone. Through the lenses of the gas mask, he could see boxes, wooden crates actually, stacked up against all four walls. The crates had "New York Concrete & Seafood Company" painted on them in red.

He realized he had stepped into a refrigerated warehouse, which seemed odd, considering that the bay door was wide open, allowing refrigerated air to escape into the warm morning sunshine outside.

Perhaps leaving the door open was a trap.

Or perhaps they just hadn't gotten around to closing it yet.

Or perhaps they were expecting a shipment of whatever they were storing.

The boxes said "seafood." But all boxes that contained illegal drugs were labeled with something else.

In Mark's gut, he knew he had just stumbled upon a huge drug bust. This would explain why they weren't too worried about refrigeration.

Cocaine didn't need to be refrigerated.

A new surge of adrenaline shot through his body. Not only would he get credit for leading the operation against the terrorist assassin of naval officers, which in and of itself would make him a national hero, but he'd also be credited with a mammoth drug bust.

His expertise would be sought after on national news and talk shows, much like Mark Fuhrman and other cops who became national celebrities as a result of high-profile cases.

But he could only let that thought sink in for half a second.

First, he had a job to finish.

Off to his right, a single steel door, almost like a refrigerator door, led into the rest of the warehouse. It was closed.

Mark remembered the instructions from the man in captivity. *"Through the door on the right. Down the hallway. Third door on the left. You'll find him there."*

Aiming his gun in his right hand, Mark put his left hand on the knob and opened the door.

Fluorescent lighting lit a long, wide hallway with a concrete floor. The hallway looked to be about fifty feet in length from the doorway. Seeing no one, Mark stepped inside and closed the door behind him.

He removed the gas mask and set it on the floor.

Thoughts flooded his mind.

What if the scumbag had lied about the number of thugs left in the building?

Could this be an ambush?

Perhaps he should wait for reinforcements.

He hesitated for a second.

No point in worrying about that now.

Besides, delays or reinforcements would guarantee a battle for control of this operation. The risk was worth it. The greater the risk, the greater the reward.

And in this case, the potential reward was off the charts.

Softly, he stepped forward. Past the first door. Past the second door.

His back against the wall, he stopped just before he reached the third door. Careful not to expose his body in front of the doorframe, he reached over and rapped on the door three times, then pulled back.

"Federal agent! I know you're in there. Come out with your hands up!"

Four shots rang out in rapid succession, with bullets flying through the door and into the opposite wall.

"Aaaaahhh!" Mark cried out, feigning being hit.

Another shot fired through the center of the door, and then a sixth shot down at the foot.

This cat was crazy.

Mark had to act. Now.

Holding his gun out, he stepped in front of the door, kicked it open, and with lightning speed unloaded six shots at the man behind the desk.

The man slumped forward. Blood gushed from his head and chest.

Mark stepped forward, pulled the .357 from his back belt, and laid it on the dead man's desk.

Mission accomplished.

CHAPTER 38

...

Phillip D'Agostino slammed down the telephone. The family kept lawyers retained all over the country and fed money to the topflight criminal defense lawyers in New York, Washington, Miami, Chicago, and LA, whether or not they had active cases going, just in case.

Still, Phil hated calls from lawyers. Calls from lawyers usually meant something bad was happening. The call he'd just gotten from the family's lead attorney in Washington, DC, Dickie DeMarco, was no exception.

And now Phil had to make another call.

"Hey, Vivian!"

"Yes, sir?"

"Get Big Sal on the phone for me, will ya?"

"Yes, sir."

Phil sat back and lit up a cigarette. The nicotine filled his lungs, bringing instant relief. After calling Big Sal, he would have to call Maria. She would survive the loss, which was a silver lining in the cloud as far as Phil was concerned.

"Big Sal is on the phone, sir."

Phil took another drag from the cigarette and picked up the phone.

"Sorry to call you with bad news, Sal. We just got a call from Dickie DeMarco in Washington. The feds raided our warehouse on the Anacostia River. Vinnie's dead. No . . . no, I haven't told Maria yet. No big loss as far as I'm concerned. The big problem is that they grabbed lots of stash, mostly cocaine.

"Now that the feds have raided our Washington facility, we'll need to leave the country for a while. I'm sending the jet to pick you up. Be ready to fly in thirty minutes. We need to get out of Dodge. It's just a matter of time before the feds will be crawling all over the place . . . Where are we going? First to Cuba, then Venezuela. We'll all be enjoying a little Caribbean sunshine while our lawyers get this all straightened out. Yes . . . yes . . . Dickie DeMarco says with the right money we can make Vinnie the scapegoat and the ringleader, and the press will report him as being the godfather, and we can be back in business in a few months. Meantime, Dickie says just enjoy the sunshine and he'll take care of the rest . . . Right . . . right . . . See you in a few."

Phil hung up the phone. "Vivian, I've got to take a little trip. Hold down the fort while I'm gone."

"Yes, sir."

. . .

WALTER REED NATIONAL MEDICAL CENTER
BETHESDA, MARYLAND
WEDNESDAY, 2:45 P.M.

"Commander," the nurse said, "Dr. Berman will be right in."

Caroline sat up in bed, frustrated that she was still stuck in this godforsaken place and ready to give Commander Lawrence Berman, Medical Corps USN, a piece of her Irish-Scottish mind if he didn't release her.

A moment later, Berman stepped in with a huge grin on his face, which didn't necessarily mean anything. He always had a grin on his face.

"Good news!"

"I hope 'good news' means you're letting me out of this place."

"Yes, it does, as a matter of fact. If you can just give us a couple of hours to process the paperwork, we should have you out of here by 1700 hours."

"You serious?"

"Dead serious. And not only that, I've got other good news."

"What's that?"

"You've got visitors. Top-brass visitors. Want them now?"

"Absolutely!"

Berman stepped into the hallway. "Gentlemen, she's ready for you."

Paul Kriete entered the room first, looking stunningly handsome, which made her feel guilty for noticing. Paul was followed by Admiral Brewer. They both smiled at her, though not as widely as Berman had grinned.

"How's the world's greatest JAG officer?" Paul asked.

"He's standing right there." Caroline nodded at Brewer. "Why don't you ask him?"

Brewer chuckled.

"I see you haven't lost that quick wit of yours," Paul said.

"Maybe my quick wit is back because the doc just told me I'm finally getting out of this place."

"Really?" Paul quipped, flashing a sly smile. "The doc told me he'd let you out only if you promised to celebrate with your favorite Navy captain."

"But—"

"And besides, the admiral tells me he's got some more good news you might be interested in."

"Really?" She looked over at Brewer, who nodded his head. "I can return to duty tomorrow morning?"

Brewer grinned. "Yes, I know Captain Guy will love to have you back, and I think you'll be happy to know no one at Code 13 is a target anymore."

"Sir?"

"We got the guy who killed P.J. and Ross Simmons. He's dead."

"Really?" Caroline felt her eyes widen. "What happened?"

"Let me put it this way. NCIS arranged a stakeout. Your friend Special Agent Romanov took charge of the operation. They wound up in a warehouse over in DC.

"Turns out the bad guys were part of an organized criminal syndicate that opposed the drone contract. It also appears that they were smuggling in cocaine by boats and bringing it into warehouses here in the U.S. That's why they didn't want the drones. They're afraid our drones would be bad for their business.

"Anyway, a gunfight broke out between three NCIS agents and three mobsters. And let me put it this way. Special Agent Mark Romanov took out the guy who's been shooting JAG officers."

"Really?"

"Yes, ma'am."

"He didn't try to shoot any more JAG officers, did he?"

Brewer and Paul looked at one another. Something was wrong.

"What?"

Paul nodded toward the admiral. "Would you like to handle that one, sir?"

Brewer looked at Caroline. "You're going to find out sooner or later anyway. But yes, the guy took a shot at Victoria Fladager."

"What? Is she okay?"

"Yes. She hit the deck before he got a shot off. The lady's got great reflexes."

"How did that happen? Where?"

Again the men exchanged glances, as if silently asking each other, *Should we tell her the details of what happened?*

"How about if we talk about all that later?" Brewer said.

Caroline hesitated. Admiral Brewer didn't want to share details about Victoria, for whatever reason. She changed the subject. "How do they know they got the right guy?"

"Because ballistics has already confirmed a match on the 9-millimeter the guy had. It's the same gun used to kill Ross Simmons and to take shots at you. Plus, they found the .357 at the scene that was used to kill P.J."

The reality of the admiral's words seemed difficult to comprehend. In a way, she felt relieved that it was over. In another way, she felt disappointed that she wasn't involved in killing the worthless dog who murdered P.J.

"I don't know what to say."

Paul spoke up. "Here's what you can say. Victoria, Mark, and I want you to join us for dinner tomorrow night. We'll meet at Mark's and drive over to the Sequoia Restaurant in Georgetown. It will give us a chance to sort of process it all, and hopefully start to bring about some closure."

Why should she still feel torn about having dinner with Paul? After all, P.J. was gone, and he wasn't coming back. On the other hand, going out with these three, as Paul said, "to bring about some closure," seemed like the right thing to do.

"Okay. Fine." She felt herself smile. "Let me know when you want to pick me up, and I'll be ready."

"It's a date." Paul grinned from ear to ear.

"And it sounds like we need to get out of here so Commander McCormick can get ready to check out," Brewer said.

"Aye, sir." Paul looked at Caroline. "I'll be back here at 1700 to pick you up and take you home. That a deal?"

"Deal." She smiled. "I look forward to it."

With that, the captain and the admiral walked out of the room, leaving her alone with her thoughts, memories, and a burgeoning flood of emotions.

• • •

SPECIAL AGENT MARK ROMANOV'S TOWNHOUSE
ALEXANDRIA, VIRGINIA
THURSDAY, 4:45 P.M.

He had invited her over for an early drink, just the two of them, in anticipation.

His suggestion had seemed harmless enough.

"Why don't you meet me about five? We can have a glass of

wine and chat, and then when Paul and Caroline arrive, we can all go together over to Georgetown."

She knew him well.

Well, she knew him well enough, anyway.

He would like to pour a couple of drinks, have a quick make-out session, and set the mood for the rest of the evening.

Of course, she had accepted Mark's invitation with mixed emotions. It's true. She had become interested in P.J. and would have kicked Mark Romanov to the curb in a skinny heartbeat had the opportunity presented itself to be with P.J.

But life was filled with unexpected and undesired twists and turns, and sometimes those twists and turns could lead one to destinations previously unplanned.

And indeed, although she had dated Mark while they were in Norfolk, and although he would have married her in a flash had she shown interest, she had hoped to embark on adventures yet unseen.

Now she had seen heartbreak and felt the heartbreak even more than she had seen it. And now Mark was back. He had earned the mantle, perhaps in his own eyes, of superhero. And indeed, his bravery had impressed her. It was a side of him she had never before seen. By bravely stopping P.J.'s killer in cold blood, how could his stock not have risen? But had it risen enough for Victoria to start thinking of him in the light he obviously desired?

Maybe so.

She looked at her watch.

She *was* here fifteen minutes early. Maybe subliminally Mark's heroism—he'd probably saved her life—had triggered just enough curiosity that she was willing to start her wine-sipping with him a few minutes early, just to see what happened.

Then again, she had given Caroline McCormick a heads-up, and also asked her to show up early, with Paul Kriete in tow, just in case.

Why did she feel suddenly confused, caught in a tug-of-war between the old and the new, dulled by the past but feeling an exciting electrical current about the future, even if the newfound electricity was slight at this point?

The modest-looking townhouse was what she would expect of Mark. This was the first time she'd seen it, since he had just moved in.

She stepped onto the porch and knocked on the door.

No answer.

Three more knocks on the door.

Still no answer.

She opened the door. The gushing sound of running water came from upstairs. "Anybody here? Mark?"

"In the shower!" She heard his voice. "Come on in. Be right there."

"Okay. Take your time!"

The townhouse was two stories and maybe fifteen hundred square feet. Based on the sound from the shower, Mark's bedroom was upstairs.

The foyer area had hardwood flooring and separated two rooms of about equal size. To the left was a living room with a sofa, two love seats, and a coffee table. On the coffee table was a bottle of red wine, opened, surrounded by two wineglasses and a silver tray with olives, cheeses, crackers, and nuts.

A stereo system played light jazz music, imparting a romantic ambience.

Mark obviously had plans.

Over to the right, across the foyer from the living room, Mark had set up his office. A desktop computer sat on a dark wooden desk, with a screensaver showing the USS *Theodore Roosevelt* plowing through the waters of the Mediterranean.

Mark had been an NCIS officer assigned to the USS *Theodore Roosevelt* before his transfer to Norfolk, a fact he had reminded her of a thousand times.

"Hey, feel free to pour a couple of glasses of wine. Be right there," he called down.

"Okay."

She stepped into the living room and read the label on the bottle: "Castle Rock Pinot Noir."

He remembered her favorite red of choice. How sweet. Mark was such a romantic. At least he was trying. Give him credit for that. And the vase of roses was another nice touch. She picked up the bottle and started to pour a glass.

The last time she had enjoyed Castle Rock was the night she had been with P.J. at the Grape + Bean. Even the smallest things triggered memories of what might have been.

"Shake it off, Victoria," she said to herself, bringing the wineglass to her lips.

She wandered out of the living room back into the foyer and looked over into the office.

Something about a man's office, especially a masculine office, was a turn-on to her. She wandered into the space, sipping her wine, and caressed her hand over the back of Mark's black leather chair.

With light jazz music still cascading from across the way, and the alluring sound of the shower still running upstairs, she caught a whiff of Mark's cologne on the back of the chair.

She took another sip and then sat down in it.

Ah. A swivel chair. Nice. She twirled around, her back to the computer, and looked across the way into the living room.

Nah. She could never see herself here.

But under the circumstances, the respite, the notion of going out with friends for the evening, seemed like a welcome way to wrap up the end of this shooting nightmare and turn over a new leaf.

Speaking of the evening, she realized she had forgotten to check the weather. No problem. She would pull it up on the internet.

She swirled back around to the computer and tapped the space bar.

The screensaver morphed into a Microsoft Word file. She was about to close out of the file and open Mark's Google browser when, emboldened by a few sips of red wine, her nosiness got the best of her.

She clicked the Recent Documents subfile.

Let's see what Mr. Supercop has been up to. Another sip.

Hmm. FBI Academy application. At least he's ambitious. Let's see . . . Pittsburgh Penguins . . . Pittsburgh Pirates . . . Yuck. She took another sip. What good came out of Pittsburgh? P.J. had been a southern gentleman. Another advantage he had over Mark's Yankee-fied ways.

But she could work with a Yankee if she had to.

What's this? she asked herself. *P.J. MacDonald? Wonder what that's about.*

She clicked the P.J. MacDonald subfile. Up came subfiles titled "Photos" and "Surveillance Photos."

What?

She clicked the Surveillance Photos subfile, and the first photo sent her heart into a race.

The picture showed her and P.J. the night of their date, sitting together at the Grape + Bean, smiling at one another, P.J.'s hand lightly touching hers.

She clicked to the next picture. How could he?

The photo showed the long, intimate kiss she had shared with P.J. out on Walnut Street in front of her Volvo, basking in the glow of the moonlight.

Swallowing the rest of her wine all at once, she clicked on a third photograph.

"Dear Jesus, no!"

P.J.'s body was lying on the Mall, bleeding from the head. Caroline was kneeling beside him, wailing.

Wait a minute.

How did he have this photo?

"You just had to get a bit nosy, didn't you?"

The sound of his voice startled her. She turned around, shaking, and saw him standing at the entrance of the foyer in a yellow bathrobe with a Pittsburgh Steelers logo on the left chest. "Couldn't leave well enough alone?"

"How did you . . . ? How could you . . . ?" she managed to say.

"I was never enough for you, was I?"

"What are you talking about?"

His eyes blazed at her with a piercing, ferocious anger that she had never seen him display. His face morphed into a smoldering contortion, and his voice turned ice cold. "It was always about your precious P.J., wasn't it?"

"I don't know what you're talking about."

"Of course you know what I'm talking about!" he screamed, and then his outburst subsided into a near-whisper. "I was never good enough for you. You always wanted some swashbuckling JAG officer."

"No. I never—"

"Don't lie to me! I saw it with my own eyes!"

Silence. Her heart pummeled her chest.

Just keep him talking, a voice from inside told her.

"So you invaded my privacy, spied on me."

He took a step closer to her. "What was I supposed to do? I wanted to know the truth. I deserved to know the truth! Did you think you could fool me?"

"Nobody was trying to fool you."

"Liar!"

"I'm not lying. We were done. We agreed to that when I left Norfolk. Who I was seeing or who I see is none of your business."

"Ah. I see." He sneered, pacing a few steps to his right but keeping his eyes drilled into her. "You thought you could just blow me off with one of those we-should-see-other-people talks, and then come up here and find yourself a handsome JAG officer and set your sights on him instead of me? You thought you could pull that over my eyes like I didn't know what was going on?"

"So rather than let things play out, you just took matters into your own hands, didn't you?"

His eyes shifted back and forth. "What did you expect? I always take matters into my own hands. And I have to say, the last week has been the most thrilling of my life. I took care of the animal who had his hands all over you that night. Then I took care of the animal who tried to kill you. You should be grateful."

"P.J. was not an animal."

"Shut up!" he screamed. "If I say he was an animal, he was an animal! Besides, any man who puts his hands all over you like that is worse than the lowest of all female dogs!" His eyes bulged. His face reddened. Veins surfaced in his forehead. "Now he's a very dead animal!"

She paused, then lowered her voice.

"So was it worth it all? Killing an innocent man to prove your masculinity? To prove something to me?"

"P.J. MacDonald was never innocent! He violated you and enjoyed every minute of it!"

"He did not violate—"

"Shut up! You talk when I say you talk."

Stay calm, Victoria. She lowered her voice. "Was it worth risking losing everything? Risking prison for the rest of your life?"

"I'll never go to prison. I'm too smart for that. Only I know what happened to P.J.! They've already pinned it on Vinnie Torrenzano."

"Wrong, Mark. You aren't the only one who knows. Now I know."

He stared at her, glaring angrily. Then, slowly, he reached his hand into the pocket of his bathrobe and pulled out a 9-millimeter pistol. "This is the gun that killed the guy who tried to kill you. He was a dumb guy, that Vinnie Torrenzano. The idiot took care of Ross Simmons and then took shots at you and Caroline McCormick. Made it real easy to pin P.J.'s death on him. Real easy. But like I say, I'm the only one who knows what happened to P.J., and it's gonna stay that way." He reached over and worked the action, chambering a bullet into firing position.

"Mark, you need help. You aren't well. Why don't you put the gun down? I'll help you."

"Shut up!" He pointed the gun straight at her head. "Hands up! In the other room! Now!" He nodded over to the living room.

"Okay. I'm moving."

"Get your hands up!"

"Okay." She complied. "You know you won't get away with this." She stepped around him and thought about going after his gun. But that would be utter stupidity. "There's no point in making matters worse for yourself, Mark. You've got a history of distinguished service. All that will be in your favor. You just need some help, that's all."

"If I wanted legal advice, I'd ask for it. And if I do need legal advice, it won't be from you."

"Okay, okay," she said. "I wasn't trying to upset you."

"Sit down on the sofa!"

"Okay. Fine." She sat.

"No. Move over to the center of the sofa."

"Okay." She scooted over to the center of the sofa as he ordered.

He started walking toward her, his gun held out straight at her head, walking closer, closer.

"Don't move," he said. "Just be still." His voice diminished to a whisper. "Perhaps your last minutes on earth may be more enjoyable than you think."

The steel gun barrel touched the middle of her head, igniting a cold rush that started in her neck and ran down her spine. He brought his left index finger to his lips and gave her a hideous shushing, about to deliver the coup de grâce.

She prayed silently that somehow God would stop him in his tracks, but that if he pulled the trigger, God would take her to heaven with Jesus.

"Now, if you'll just cooperate, you will enjoy immense pleasure before your death."

"What are you doing?"

"Something I've always wanted to do. Something you wanted to do with your P.J. But P.J. can't compete with me. And he never could."

"Mark, no. Just go ahead and shoot me. Please."

"Shut up!" He pushed her down onto the sofa and forced his mouth onto hers.

"No!" She tried to scream, but he stuffed his hand over her mouth.

She managed to free her hand and scratch him hard across the face. He pulled his hand away in reaction. Then as she belted out a loud scream, he slapped her across the face.

"You will cooperate!" he demanded.

"Never! Just kill me now!"

"Not until I get what I want!"

She tried scratching him again, and this time he punched her in the mouth. The room spun and a galaxy of stars rushed across her eyes. Somehow she wound up on the floor, although she wasn't sure if she fell or if he pushed her. She looked up.

He again brought his face close to hers—so close she could smell his breath—and tried to kiss her. Struggling against him, she freed her hand and poked him in the eyes.

"Aaaahh!" He slapped her again and blurted an obscenity, then a string of obscenities. "So you won't do this the easy way? Well, we can do this the hard way! No reason you have to be alive during all this." He reached up and grabbed a pillow off the sofa and shoved it down over her face and nose.

"I can't breathe! I can't breathe!" she screamed as a claustrophobic feeling of panic and suffocation blanketed her body and lungs.

"What are you doing?" She heard another man's voice. The pillow dropped off her nose as Paul Kriete yanked Mark back by the collar. Caroline rushed over to her.

Mark turned and threw a punch. Paul punched back.

"Get out of the room," Caroline said to Victoria. "I'm calling 911."

In a blur, like two Tasmanian devils in a dust cloud, the men rolled on the floor, angrily punching each other, each trying to gain superior leverage over the other.

"Yes, I need police here! Right now!" Victoria heard Caroline screaming into her cell phone as Paul pushed Mark down, shoulder blades first, like a wrestler about to pin his opponent.

Paul appeared to have subdued him. But then Mark, with his shoulders pinned, slipped his hand into the pocket of his bathrobe.

"He's got a gun!" Victoria screamed. As Mark pulled the pistol from his pocket, Paul lunged for it.

A shot rang out.

In a moment of eerie silence, except for jazz music playing low in the background, the fighting was over.

Both men lay on the floor, motionless.

EPILOGUE

...

Under the midafternoon sky, alone in thought, Caroline sat in her car in the parking lot with her sunroof open and windows down. She was glad she opened the windows, for the sparrows, cardinals, and purple martins sang melodically, making a joyful noise to the Lord that was just as beautiful, if not more so, as the finest anthem of the Mormon Tabernacle Choir.

The birds' chorus brought with it a single gust of cool breeze, carrying the smell of flowers into the car like a sweet, light perfume. Perhaps gardenias, but she wasn't sure, and it didn't really matter.

P.J. was here. At least his body was here. And she could sit here forever. Right now this was the most beautiful place on earth.

She had thought about inviting Victoria to join her. What an amazing friend Victoria had turned out to be, going from a vicious competitor for P.J.'s romantic affections to a friend who almost laid down her life in a brave scheme to attract P.J.'s murderer. Caroline had misjudged her at first.

But at the end of the day, she decided she wanted to be alone. Alone with P.J.

And now there was but one more matter she needed to check on. She looked at her watch. 1500 hours.

The vote should be complete by now.

She flipped on her satellite radio.

"This is Tom Miller from our Fox News studios in New York with breaking news from Washington.

"The United States Congress has narrowly approved a line-item appropriation for the largest military or civilian drone contract in history. Under the name Operation Blue Jay, the U.S. Navy will operate fifty thousand drones off the coastal waters of the United States and along the internal borders between the United States and Mexico, for the purpose of maintaining the stability of the borders and to ensure the United States is protected from invasion by sea or along its inland borders.

"The project as approved was scaled back from the original proposal, which called for some one hundred thousand drones to be shared jointly by the Navy and the Department of Homeland Security. But that idea was shelved when the Judge Advocate General of the Navy expressed concern in a legal opinion that the proposed joint use might violate the time-honored legal doctrine of *posse comitatus*, which prevents military assets from being used in domestic law-enforcement operations.

"The JAG opinion, co-drafted by two Navy JAG officers, the late Lieutenant Commander P.J. MacDonald and Lieutenant Commander Caroline McCormick, also expressed concern that domestic use of the drones inside the borders of the United States could raise Fourth Amendment concerns and violate citizens' rights to privacy without the issuance of search warrants, even when operated by the Department of Homeland Security.

"The scaled-down contract was awarded to defense contractor AirFlite out of Savannah, Georgia, and the first Navy Drone Command will be headed by Rear Admiral Select Paul Madison Kriete, who was today nominated by President Surber, with his final promotion to rear admiral to be confirmed by the senate.

"And speaking of Rear Admiral Select Kriete, he was personally involved in solving one of the most horrifying murder conspiracies against naval officers in history, having stopped the aggression of two different men, one being a rogue NCIS officer, who were involved in attacks on JAG officers.

"That JAG murder mystery was addressed at the Pentagon earlier today by Vice Admiral Zack Brewer, the Judge Advocate General of the Navy. Here is some of what Admiral Brewer had to say."

Caroline felt her heart leap. Just the sound of Zack Brewer's name and the soothing sound of his voice brought comfort to every member of the JAG Corps.

"Good afternoon," Brewer said. "Thank you for coming. It's been a tough couple of weeks for the Navy, and especially the JAG Corps. But our duty in service to our country goes on, and I am pleased to report two things. First, the JAG Corps has done its duty in providing legal advice to the Secretary of the Navy on the proposed drone contract for Operation Blue Jay, and we're expecting congressional approval today. Indeed, by the time you hear my voice, Congress may have already approved that project.

"Second, I've just received a call from the director at NCIS at Quantico, with information on the identity of shooters launching attacks on several JAG officers at Code 13.

"Ballistics and forensics show that the Glock 9-millimeter pistol used in the killing of Lieutenant Ross Simmons and the attempted murder of Lieutenant Victoria Fladager was owned by a Vinnie Torrenzano of New York, who was shot dead in a shoot-out with NCIS agents in Washington. Mr. Torrenzano's fingerprints were all over that weapon, as well as shell casings found in the gun. This was the same gun used in the attempted murder of Lieutenant Commander Caroline McCormick. Additionally, Mr. Torrenzano's car, a red Mercedes, was spotted at the Simmons shooting and at the shooting of Commander McCormick at the Pentagon. Forensics also suggests that Mr. Torrenzano was involved in the murder of a young family—a father, a mother, and a little girl in the Oxford Hunt section of West Springfield, Virginia—and that murder was connected with his plan to kill JAG officers. Mr. Torrenzano's motivation appears to be that he wanted to block the legal opinion written by these JAG officers, which authorized, partially, the drone contract. That's all I have on Mr. Torrenzano at this time.

"Moving on to Lieutenant Commander P.J. MacDonald's killer, I regret that this appears to have been the work of a rogue NCIS agent, Special Agent Mark Romanov, who was killed in his home in a struggle over his gun as he tried to murder yet another JAG officer who had blown his cover. Special Agent Romanov, who is the agent who shot and killed Vinnie Torrenzano, is tied to Commander MacDonald's murder through a gun, a .357 revolver he planted on Mr. Torrenzano's desk to try to pin the MacDonald murder on Torrenzano.

"He is also tied to the MacDonald murder through photographic evidence found on his computer, and by a confession he made to one of our JAG officers. I can't go into any more details at this time and will defer further questions on these cases to NCIS and local law enforcement.

"But suffice it to say, we do not consider any of our officers still under any threat, and to all military and civilian personnel who have brought this horrendous nightmare to a close, I would like to thank you on behalf of the U.S. Navy and the U.S. Navy JAG Corps."

Caroline flipped off the radio.

She should be ecstatic. After all, how many lawyers could say they drafted a legal opinion that led to passage of a bill by the U.S. Congress based on that recommendation?

But she could feel nothing other than satisfaction in the fulfillment of her duties.

She got out of the car and started walking toward P.J.'s grave.

As she strolled across the lush green grass under clear Carolina-blue skies, words came to her that she had memorized in Raleigh, back when she was a student at Ravenscroft School, and then again as an American history major at UNC.

"We cannot dedicate, we cannot consecrate, we cannot hallow this ground. The brave men living and dead who struggled here have consecrated it far above our poor power to add or detract."

These were the words of President Abraham Lincoln, spoken over 157 years ago at another national cemetery, in Gettysburg, after one of the bloodiest battles in American history.

Almost miraculously, she remembered the next lines of the speech, walking across the graves of the dead through a sea of green grass punctuated by small white flags.

It was almost as if she had learned them yesterday.

"The world will little note nor long remember what we say here, but it can never forget what they did here. It is for us the living, rather, to be dedicated here to the unfinished work which they who fought here have thus far so nobly advanced."

The Lord did work in mysterious ways, she decided, allowing the words spoken by a president two centuries before to assuage her grief as she set out to complete this, her last devotion to the duty she had begun when she arrived in Washington.

This time she spoke the words aloud.

"'It is rather for us to be here dedicated to the great task remaining before us—that from these honored dead we take increased devotion to that cause for which they gave the last full measure of devotion—that we here highly resolve that these dead shall not have died in vain, that this nation under God shall have a new birth of freedom, and that government of the people, by the people, for the people shall not perish from the earth.'"

And when she had finished speaking, with goose bumps on her arms and tears in her eyes, she looked down at the white gravestone of the only man she had ever loved.

A simple cross was carved into the top, front center, and under that was the inscription:

Peter Jefferson ("P.J.") MacDonald
Lieutenant Commander
Judge Advocate General's Corps
United States Navy
"Code 13"

A small American flag planted in the ground beside the grave flapped in the breeze, like the thousands of others dotting the massive cemetery.

Off in the distance, perhaps a half mile away, the U.S. Air Force conducted a burial of one of its own. But no one else was around, at least not in the immediate vicinity.

She was here, alone with P.J., just like she wanted it.

She brought her hand to her cover, saluting the grave, then dropped the salute. And then she dropped down to her knees, as if to have a more intimate conversation.

"P.J., I'm sure you're in a better place. And I don't know if you can hear me or not, but I pray to God that somehow he'll open the portals of heaven and let you hear me one last time."

She wiped a tear from her cheek, and as she did, a cardinal landed on the tombstone.

That brought a smile to her face. God was good.

The cardinal flew away, disappearing into the blue sky.

"I finished the job you started, and today Congress approved the contract. I wrote it just like I think you wanted it. In a way to strengthen us against enemy invasion but also to protect the Constitution. You were such a patriot."

She fell silent, allowing herself to absorb the beauty of the moment.

"I'm leaving Washington, P.J. I know I just got here, but I asked Admiral Brewer to approve orders to send me back to the fleet. I'm leaving for San Diego in the morning, where I'll take over as senior JAG on the USS *George Washington*." She wiped another tear. "I always wanted to go to an aircraft carrier. Now I'll get my wish."

Another cool gust descended across the cemetery.

"Anyway, Paul Kriete is a nice guy, and he's a great officer. Just got picked up for admiral, and it's well deserved. But he's not you." She paused again. "You're the only man I've ever loved, and you're the only man I will ever love."

She stood up, her eyes locked on the grave marker just for a few more moments.

"And so now I will take my capacity to love and love that which you loved. My dedication and my service will be to the U.S. Navy, and memories of your smiling face will burn in my heart forever."

She bent down, kissed the grave marker, then stood and gave him a final salute.

"With fair winds and following seas, my love. Until we meet again—in heaven."

She turned and walked away.

ACKNOWLEDGMENTS

• • •

With special acknowledgment and gratitude to my "West Coast Editor," U.S. Army Veteran Jack Miller of La Mesa, California, who along with his lovely wife Linda, have generously supported the San Diego Zoo, the Lambs Players Theater of Coronado and San Diego, and the San Diego Wild Animal Park.

With special acknowledgment and gratitude to the following churches and their pastors, all of whom have had a positive influence upon the author:

- The First Christian Church of Plymouth, North Carolina— Rev. Tom Banks, Pastor
- The First Baptist Church of Lemon Grove, California—Rev. Jeffrey Lettow, Pastor
- Calvary Church—Charlotte, North Carolina—Dr. John Munro, Senior Pastor
- Forest Hill Church—Charlotte, North Carolina—Dr. David Chadwick, Senior Pastor

DISCUSSION QUESTIONS

• • •

1. Are you concerned about drones over the United States? Why or why not?
2. Lieutenant Commander P.J. MacDonald struggles over which way he should slant his opinion letter to the Secretary of the Navy, and penned two different letters, one concluding one way, and one concluding another. What was Lieutenant Commander MacDonald struggling over, and can you relate to his struggle? How would you have written your recommendation to the Secretary of the Navy?
3. Lieutenant Commander MacDonald, in his original memo to the Secretary of the Navy, mentions a geographic zone "within 100 miles of the seacoast of all the United States," which he calls a "Fourth Amendment – Free Zone," otherwise known as the "Constitution-Free Zone," where stops can be made without search warrants. Did you know there was such a zone? Does this concern you? Why do you think most Americans don't know about this sort of thing?
4. Are you willing to sacrifice personal freedoms under the Constitution for national security? Why or why not?
5. Are there passages in the novel suggesting that Senator Bobby Talmadge is a believer in Christ? Do you believe that he was a believer? Why or why not?

6. Would you have advised Senator Talmadge to act differently once he was exposed? If so, how?

7. This novel features two principal female characters, U.S. Navy JAG Officers Caroline McCormick and Victoria Fladager. What are the strengths and weaknesses of each character?

8. Which of the two lead women, Caroline McCormick or Victoria Fladager, do you feel is the stronger character? Discuss your reasons.

9. How does the relationship between Caroline and Victoria evolve, and what can be learned by it?

10. Who is your favorite major character, and who is your least favorite character and why?

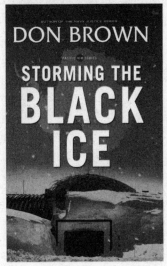 

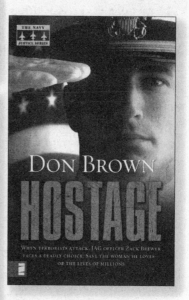

ABOUT THE AUTHOR

• • •

 Don Brown is the author of *The Malacca Conspiracy*, *The Black Sea Affair*, the Navy Justice Series, the Pacific Rim Series, and a submarine thriller that predicted the 2008 shooting war between Russia and Georgia. Don served five years in the U.S. Navy as an officer in the Judge Advocate General's (JAG) Corps, which gave him an exceptional vantage point into both the Navy and the inner workings "inside the Beltway" as an action officer assigned to the Pentagon. He left active duty in 1992 to pursue private practice, but remained on inactive status through 1999, rising to the rank of lieutenant commander. He and his family live in North Carolina, where he pursues his passion for penning novels about the Navy.

Visit his website at www.donbrownbooks.com

Facebook: Don-Brown